Sidetracked

Other Kurt Wallander mysteries by Henning Mankell:

Faceless Killers

The White Lioness

Sidetracked

Henning Mankell A KURT WALLANDER MYSTERY

Translated from the Swedish by STEVEN T. MURRAY

THE NEW PRESS NEW YORK

Library of Congress Cataloging-in-Publication Data
Mankell, Henning, 1948–
    [Villospår. English]
    Sidetracked: a mystery / Henning Mankell;
    translated from the Swedish by Steven T. Murray.
        p.   cm.
    ISBN 1-56594-507-2
    I. Murray, Steven T. II. Title.
PT9876.23.A49V5513   1999
839.73'74—dc21
98-43980

                                        CIP

Originally published as *Villospår* in Sweden by Ordfront Förlag, Stockholm
Published in the United States by The New Press, New York
Distributed by W. W. Norton & Company, Inc., New York

The New Press was established in 1990 as a not-for-profit alternative to the large,
commercial publishing houses currently dominating the book publishing industry.
The New Press operates in the public interest rather than for private gain,
and is committed to publishing, in innovative ways, works of educational, cultural,
and community value that are often deemed insufficiently profitable.

Book design by BAD

www.thenewpress.com

Printed in the United States of America

9 8 7 6 5 4 3 2 I

Sidetracked

Shall I bend, in vain, shall I shake
the old, hard, immovable bars?
—they will not stretch, they will not break
for the bars are riveted and forged inside myself,
and the bars will not shatter until I shatter too

From "A Ghasel" by GUSTAF FRÖDING

Skåne 21–24 June 1994

Chapter One

Before dawn he started his transformation.

He had planned everything meticulously so that nothing could go wrong. It would take him all day, and he didn't want to risk running out of time. He grasped the first paintbrush and held it in front of him. From the cassette player on the floor he could hear the tape of drum music that he had prepared. He looked at his face in the mirror. Then he drew the first black lines across his forehead. He noticed that his hand was steady. So he wasn't nervous, at least. Even though this was the first time he had actually put on his war paint. Until this moment it had been merely an escape, his way of defending himself against all the injustices he was continually subjected to. He now went through the great transformation in earnest. With each stroke he painted on his face, he seemed to be leaving his old life behind. There was no more turning back. On this very evening the game would be over for good, and he would go out into the war, where people would actually have to die.

The light in the room was very bright. He set up the mirrors in front of him precisely, so that the light didn't glare in his eyes. When he had come into the room and locked the door behind him, he started by checking one last time that he hadn't forgotten anything. But everything was where it was supposed to be. The well-cleaned brushes, the little porcelain cups of paint, the towels and water. Next to the little lathe, his weapons lay in rows on a black cloth: the three axes, the knives of various lengths, and the spray cans. This was the only decision he still hadn't made. Before sundown he would have to choose which of these weapons to take with him. He couldn't take them all. But he knew that the decision would resolve itself once he had begun his transformation.

Before he sat down on the bench and started to paint his face, he touched the edges of his axes and knives with his fingertips. They couldn't have been sharper. He couldn't resist the temptation to press a little harder on one of the knives with his fingertip. At once he started to bleed. He wiped his finger and the knife edge with a towel. Then he sat down in front of the mirrors.

The first strokes on his forehead had to be black. It was as if he were slicing two deep cuts, opening his brain, and emptying out all the memories and thoughts that had followed him all his life, tormenting him and humiliating him. Afterwards he would continue with the red and white stripes, the circles, the squares, and at last the snakelike designs on his cheeks. Not a bit of his white skin should be visible. And then the transformation would be complete. What was inside him would be gone. He would be resurrected in the guise of an animal, and he would never speak like a human being again. He would even cut out his own tongue if he had to.

The transformation took him all day. Just after six in the evening he was done. By then he had also decided to take along the largest of the three axes. He stuck the shaft into the thick leather belt he had fastened around his waist. The two knives were already there in their sheaths. He looked around the room. He had forgotten nothing. He stuffed the spray cans into the inside pockets of his jacket.

One last time he looked at his face in the mirror. He shuddered. Then he carefully pulled his motorcycle helmet over his head, turned off the light, and left the room barefoot, just as he had come in.

A t five minutes past nine Gustaf Wetterstedt turned down the sound on his TV and phoned his mother. It was a ritual he always followed. Ever since he had retired as the minister of justice more than twenty-five years earlier and left behind all his political dealings, he had watched the news on TV with repugnance and distaste. He couldn't come to terms with the fact that he was no longer involved. During his many years as minister, a man in the absolute center of the public eye, he had appeared on TV at least once a week. He had seen to it that each appearance was meticulously copied from film to video by a secretary. Now the tapes stood in his study, and they covered a whole wall. Once in a while he watched them again. For him it was a source of continual satisfaction to see that never once in all those years as minister of justice had he lost his composure in the face of an unexpected or trick question from a malicious reporter. With a feeling of unbounded contempt he could still recall how many of his colleagues had lived in fear of TV reporters. Far too often they would start stammering and get entangled in contradictions that they never could manage to straighten out. But that had never happened to him. He was a man no one could trap. The reporters had never managed to beat him. Nor had they ever discovered his secret.

He turned on his TV at nine to see the top stories. Then he turned down the sound. He pulled over the telephone and called his mother. She had given birth to him when she was still very young. Now she was ninety-four years old, with a clear mind and full of untapped energy. She lived alone in a big apartment in Stockholm's Old Town. Each time he lifted the receiver and dialed the number he hoped she wouldn't answer. Since he was over seventy years old himself he had begun to fear that she would outlive him. There was nothing he wanted more than for her to die. Then he'd be left alone. He wouldn't have to call her anymore, and soon he'd forget what she even looked like.

The telephone rang on the other end. He watched the silent anchorman. After the fourth ring he began to hope that she had finally died. Then he heard her voice. He softened his voice when he talked to her. He asked how she was feeling, how her day had been. Now that he had to accept that she was still alive, he wanted to make the conversation as brief as possible.

He hung up the phone and sat with his hand resting on the receiver. She's never going to die, he thought. She'll never die unless I kill her.

He remained sitting in the silent room. All he could hear was the roar of the sea and a lone moped driving past nearby. He got up from the sofa and walked over to the big balcony window facing the sea. The twilight was beautiful and rather moving. The beach below his huge estate was deserted. Everyone's sitting in front of their TVs, he thought. Once they sat there and watched me throttle the news reporters. I was minister of justice back then. I should have been made foreign minister. But I never was.

He shut the heavy curtains and checked carefully to see that there were no gaps. Even though he tried to live as anonymously as possible in this house located just east of Ystad, sometimes curiosity-seekers spied on him. Although it had been twenty-five years since he left office, he had not yet been entirely forgotten. He went out to the kitchen and poured a cup of coffee from a thermos he had bought during an official visit to Italy in the late sixties. He vaguely recalled that he had been there to discuss increased efforts to prevent the spread of terrorism in Europe. All over his house there were reminders of the life he had once lived. He often thought he should throw them all away. But finally the mere effort seemed meaningless to him.

He went back to the sofa with his coffee cup. With the remote he clicked off the TV. He sat in the dark and thought about the day that had passed. In the morning he'd had a visit from a journalist from one of the big monthly magazines. She was working on a series about famous people and their lives in retirement. Why she had decided to visit him he never quite managed to figure out. She brought a photographer with her and they took pictures on the beach and inside the house. He had decided in advance that he would present the image of an elderly man marked by kindness and reconciliation. He described his present life as very happy. He lived in great seclusion so that he could meditate, and he let drop with feigned embarrassment that he was considering whether he ought to write his memoirs. The journalist, who was in her forties, had been impressed and full of humble respect. Afterwards he escorted her and the photographer to their car and waved as they drove off.

With satisfaction he thought that he had avoided saying a single thing that was true during the entire interview. This was one of the few things that still held any interest for him. To deceive without being discovered. To spread pretense and illusion. After all his years as a politician he realized all that was left was the lie. The truth disguised as a lie or the lie veiled as truth.

He slowly drank the rest of his coffee. His feeling of well-being grew. The evenings and nights were his best time. That's when his thoughts sank beneath the surface, his thoughts about all that once had been and all that had been lost. But no one could rob him of the most important thing. The utmost secret, the one no one knew about but himself.

Sometimes he imagined himself as an image in a mirror that was both concave and convex at the same time. As a person he had the same ambiguity. No one had ever seen anything but the surface, the capable jurist, the respected minister of justice, the kind retiree strolling along the beach in Skåne. No one would have guessed that he was his own double. He had greeted kings and presidents, he had bowed with a smile, but in his head he was thinking, *if you only knew who I really am and what I think of you*. When he stood in front of the TV cameras he always held that thought—*if you only knew who I really am and what I think of you*—foremost in his mind. But no one had ever understood it. His secret: that he hated and despised the party he represented, the opinions he defended, and most of the people he met. His secret would stay hidden until he died. He had seen through the world, identified all its frailties, observed the meaninglessness of existence. But no one knew about his insight, and that's the way it would stay. He had never felt any need to share what he had seen and understood.

He felt a growing pleasure about what was to come. The next evening his friends would come to the house just after nine in the black Mercedes with the tinted windows. They would drive straight into his garage and he would wait for their visit in the living room with the curtains drawn, just as they were now. He could feel his anticipation rise at once when he started to fantasize about what the girl they were delivering to him this time would look like. He had told them there had been far too many blondes lately. Some of them had also been much too old, over twenty. This time he wanted a younger one, preferably of mixed race. His friends would wait in the basement where he had installed a TV; he would take the girl with him to his bedroom. Before dawn they would be gone, and he would already be fantasizing about the girl they would bring the following week.

The thought of the next day made him so excited that he got up from the sofa and went into his study. Before he turned on the light he drew the curtains. For a brief moment he thought he glimpsed the shadow of someone down on the beach. He took off his glasses and squinted. Sometimes late-night strollers would stop just below his property. In some cases it had even been necessary to call the police in Ystad and complain about the young people lighting bonfires on the beach and making noise.

He had a good relationship with the Ystad police. They always came right away and drove off anyone who was disturbing him. He often thought that he never would have imagined the knowledge and contacts he would gain by being minister of justice. Not only had he learned to understand the special mentality that prevails inside the Swedish police corps, but he had methodically acquired friends at strategic points in the Swedish machinery of justice. Just as important were all the contacts he had made in the criminal world. There were intelligent criminals, individuals who worked alone as well as leaders of great crime syndicates, whom he had made his friends. Even though much had changed in the twenty-five years since he left office, he still enjoyed his old contacts. Especially the friends who saw to it that each week he had a visit from a girl of a suitable age.

The shadow on the beach had been just his imagination. He straightened the curtains and unlocked one of the cabinets in the desk he had inherited from his father, an imposing professor of jurisprudence. He took out an expensive and beautifully decorated portfolio and opened it before him on the desk. Slowly, reverently, he paged through his collection of pornographic pictures from the earliest days of the art of photography. His oldest picture was a rarity, a daguerreotype from 1855 that he had bought in Paris. The picture showed a naked woman embracing a dog. His collection was renowned in the exclusive circle of men, unknown to the outside world, who shared his interest. His collection of pictures from the 1890s by Lecadre was surpassed only by the collection owned by an elderly steel magnate in the Ruhr. Slowly he leafed through the plastic-encased pages of the album. He lingered longest over the pages where the models were very young and one could see by their eyes that they were under the influence of drugs. He had often regretted that he himself had not begun to devote himself to photography earlier. Had he done so, he would today be in the possession of a unique collection.

After he had gone through the album he locked it in the desk again. From his friends he had extracted a promise that upon his death they would offer the pictures to an antiquities dealer in Paris who specialized in the sale of such items. The money would be donated to a scholarship fund for young law students he had already established, one which would not be announced until after his death.

He switched off the desk lamp and remained sitting in the dark room. The sound of the surf was very faint. Once again he thought he heard a moped passing nearby. He still had a hard time imagining his own death, even though he was already over seventy years old. On two occasions, during trips to the United States, he had managed to be present anonymously at executions, the first by electric chair, the second in the gas chamber, which was already rather rare back then. It had been a curiously pleasurable experience to watch people being killed. But his own death he could not imagine. He left the study and poured a little glass of liqueur from the bar cabinet in the living room. The hour was already approaching midnight. A short walk down to the sea was all that remained before he went to bed. He put on a jacket in the entryway, slipped his feet into a pair of worn clogs, and left the house.

Outside it was dead calm. His house was so isolated that he could not see the lights from any of his neighbors' homes. The cars on the road to Kåseberga roared by in the distance. He followed the path that led through the garden and down to the locked gate that let him out onto the beach. To his annoyance he discovered that the lamp that sat on a pole next to the gate was burned out. The beach awaited him. He fished out his keys and unlocked the gate. He walked the short distance to the beach and stopped at the water line. The sea was still. Far out on the horizon he saw the lights of a vessel heading west. He unbuttoned his fly and pissed in the water as he continued to fantasize about the visit he would have the next day.

Although he heard nothing, he suddenly knew that someone was standing behind him. He stiffened, and terror seized hold of him. Then he spun around.

The man standing there looked like an animal. Apart from a pair of shorts he was naked. With an instantaneous, hysterical dread the old man looked into the other man's face. He couldn't tell if it was deformed or hidden behind a mask. In one hand the man held an axe. In his confusion he thought that the hand around the shaft of the axe was very small, that the man reminded him of a dwarf.

He screamed and started to run, back up toward the garden gate.

He died the instant the edge of the axe severed his spine, right below the shoulders. And he never felt how the man who was perhaps an animal knelt down and slit an opening in his forehead and then with one violent wrench ripped most of the hair and skin from the top of his skull.

The time was just past midnight.

It was Tuesday, the 21st of June.

A lone moped started up somewhere nearby. A moment later the sound of the motor died away.

Everything was once again very still.

Chapter Two

Around noon on the 21st of June, Kurt Wallander walked out of the police station in Ystad. So that no one would notice his departure, he walked out through the garage entrance, got into his car, and drove down to the harbor. Since the day was warm he had left his sport coat hanging on his desk chair. Anyone looking for him in the next few hours would assume he must be somewhere in the building. Wallander parked by the theater. Then he walked out on the inner pier and sat down on the bench next to the red-painted hut of the Sea Rescue Service. He had taken along one of his notebooks. When he was ready to start writing he discovered that he hadn't brought a pen. Annoyed, his first impulse was to throw the pad into the harbor and forget the whole thing. But he realized this was impossible. His colleagues would never forgive him.

They were the ones who, despite his protests, had appointed him to make a speech on behalf of all of them at three o'clock when they were going to thank Björk, who that same day was leaving his post as Ystad chief of police.

Wallander had never made a speech in his life. The closest he had come were the innumerable press conferences he had been obligated to hold during various criminal investigations.

But how did you thank an outgoing chief of police? What did you actually thank him for? Did they have anything at all to be thankful for? Wallander would have preferred to talk about his uneasiness and anxiety about the vast, seemingly unplanned reorganizations and cutbacks to which the police force was increasingly subjected.

He had left the police station so he could think through in peace what he was going to say. He'd sat at his kitchen table until late the night before without getting anywhere. But now he was actually forced to do it. In less than three hours they would gather and present their farewell gift to Björk, who would start work the next day in Malmö as head of the county board of immigrant affairs. He stood up from the bench and walked along the pier to the harbor café. The fishing boats rocked slowly in their moorings. Wallander absentmindedly recalled that once, seven years ago, he had been involved in fishing a body out of the harbor. But he pushed away the image. The speech he had to make to Björk was more important right now. One of the waitresses loaned him a pen. He sat down at a table outside with a cup of coffee and forced himself to write a few words to Björk. By one o'clock he had put together half a page. He looked at it gloomily, and he knew it was the best he could do. He motioned the waitress over, who came and refilled his cup.

"Summer seems to be taking its time getting here," said Wallander.

"Maybe it won't show up at all," replied the waitress.

Aside from the impossible speech for Björk, Wallander was in a good mood. In a few weeks he would be going on vacation. He had a lot to be happy about. It had been a long, tiresome winter. He knew that he was in great need of a rest.

At three o'clock they gathered in the lunchroom of the police station and Wallander made his speech to Björk. Svedberg gave him a casting rod as a present, and Ann-Britt Höglund gave him flowers. Wallander managed to embellish his scanty speech on the spur of the moment by recounting a few of his escapades with Björk. There was great amusement when he recalled the time when they had both tumbled into a pool of liquid manure after a scaffold collapsed. Then everyone drank coffee and ate cake. In his thank-you speech, Björk wished his successor, a woman named Lisa Holgersson, good luck. She had just come from one of the bigger police districts in Småland and would take over at the end of the summer. For the time being Hansson would be the acting chief of police in Ystad. When the ceremony was over and Wallander had returned to his office, Martinsson knocked on his half-open door.

"That was a great speech," he said. "I didn't know you could do that sort of thing."

"I can't," said Wallander. "It was a lousy speech. You know it as well as I do."

Martinsson sat down carefully in Wallander's broken-down visitor's chair.

"I wonder how it'll go with a woman chief," he said.

"Why shouldn't it go well?" replied Wallander. "You should worry instead about what's going to happen with all these cutbacks."

"That's exactly why I came," said Martinsson. "There's a rumor going around that the Ystad staff is going to be cut back on Saturday and Sunday nights."

Wallander looked at Martinsson skeptically.

"That won't work, of course," he said. "Who's going to guard the suspects we might be holding?"

"Rumor has it that they're going to take bids for that job from private security companies."

Wallander gave Martinsson a quizzical look.

"Security companies?"

"That's what I heard."

Wallander shook his head. Martinsson got up.

"I thought you ought to know about it," he said. "Do you have any idea what's going to happen to the police force?"

"No," said Wallander. "And you should take that as the complete truth."

Martinsson lingered in the office.

"Was there something else?"

Martinsson took a piece of paper out of his pocket.

"As you know, the World Cup has started. 2–2 in the game against Cameroon. You bet 5–0 in favor of Cameroon. With this score, you came in last."

"How could I come in last? Either I bet right or wrong, didn't I?"

"We run statistics that show where we are in relation to everyone else."

"Good Lord! What's the point of that?"

"A patrol officer was the only one who picked 2–2," said Martinsson, ignoring Wallander's question. "Now for the next match. Sweden against Russia."

Wallander was totally uninterested in soccer. On the other hand, he had occasionally gone to see Ystad's handball team play, which had several times been ranked one of the best in Sweden. Lately, though, he couldn't avoid noticing how the entire country seemed to be directing all its attention toward a single thing. The World Cup. He couldn't turn on the TV or open a newspaper without being deluged by endless speculations about how it was going to go for the Swedish team. At the same time he knew that he couldn't really avoid taking part in the soccer pool. They would think he was arrogant. He took his wallet out of his back pocket.

"How much?"

"A hundred kronor. Same as last time."

He handed the bill to Martinsson, who checked him off on his list.

"Don't I have to guess the score?"

"Sweden against Russia. What do you think?"

"4–4," said Wallander.

"It's pretty rare to make that many goals in soccer," Martinsson said, surprised. "That sounds more like an ice hockey score."

"All right, let's say 3–1 for Russia," said Wallander. "Is that all right?"

Martinsson wrote it down.

"Maybe we can take the Brazil match while we're at it," Martinsson continued.

"3–0 for Brazil," said Wallander quickly.

"You don't have very high expectations for Sweden," said Martinsson.

"Not when it comes to soccer, anyway," replied Wallander, handing him another hundred.

After Martinsson left, Wallander thought about what he had been told. But then he dismissed the idea in annoyance. He would find out soon enough what was true and what wasn't. It was already four-thirty. Wallander pulled over a folder of investigative material about an organized crime ring exporting stolen cars to the former Eastern-bloc countries. He had been working on the

investigation for several months. So far the police had only succeeded in tracking down parts of the extensive operation. He knew that it would haunt him
for many months to come. During his leave, Svedberg would take over. He had
a strong suspicion that very little would happen while he was gone.

Ann-Britt Höglund knocked on the door and walked in. She had a black
baseball cap on her head.

"How do I look?" she asked.

"Like a tourist," replied Wallander.

"This is what the new police uniform caps are going to look like," she said.
"Imagine the word POLICE above the bill. I've seen pictures of it."

"They'll never get one of those on my head," said Wallander. "I guess I
should be glad I'm not a cop in uniform anymore."

"Someday we might discover that Björk was a really good chief," she said.
"I think what you said in there was great."

"I know the speech wasn't any good," said Wallander, starting to feel annoyed.
"But all of you are responsible for having the bad judgment to pick me."

Höglund stood up and looked out the window. She had managed to live up
to the reputation that preceded her when she came to Ystad the year before.
At the police academy she had revealed a great aptitude for police work, which
had been developed even more. She had been able to fill part of the void left
by Rydberg's death a few years back. Rydberg was the detective who had taught
Wallander most of what he knew, and sometimes Wallander thought it was his
responsibility to guide Höglund in the same way.

"How's it going with the cars?" she asked.

"They keep getting stolen," said Wallander. "This organization seems to
have an incredible number of branches."

"Can we manage to punch a hole in it?" she asked.

"We'll crack it," replied Wallander. "Sooner or later. There'll be a lull for a
few months. Then it'll start up again."

"But it'll never end?"

"Right, it'll never end. Because Ystad is located where it is. Two hundred
kilometers from here, across the Baltic, there's an endless number of people
who want what we've got. The only problem is they don't have any money to
pay for it."

"I wonder how much stolen property is shipped out with every single ferry,"
she mused.

"You don't want to know," said Wallander.

Together they went and got some coffee. Höglund was supposed to start
her vacation that week. Wallander had understood that she was going to spend
it in Ystad, since her husband, a traveling machinery installer with the whole
world as his workplace, was in Saudi Arabia.

"What are you going to do?" she asked when they started talking about their
upcoming leaves.

"I'm going to Denmark, to Skagen," said Wallander.

"With the woman from Riga?" Höglund wondered with a smile.

Wallander raised his eyebrows in surprise.

"How do you know about her?"

"Oh, everybody does," she replied. "Didn't you know? You might call it the result of an ongoing internal investigation, among us cops."

Wallander was truly astonished. He had never told anyone about Baiba, whom he had met during a criminal investigation some years before. She was the widow of a murdered Latvian policeman. She had been in Ystad over Christmas almost six months ago. During the Easter holiday Wallander had visited her in Riga. But he had never spoken about her or introduced her to any of his colleagues. Now he suddenly wondered why he hadn't. Even though their relationship was fragile, she had dragged him out of the melancholy that had marked his life since his divorce from Mona.

"All right," he said. "Yes, we're going to Denmark together. Then I'm going to spend the rest of the summer with my father."

"And Linda?"

"She called a week ago and said she was taking a theater class in Visby."

"I thought she was going to be a furniture upholsterer?"

"I did too. But now she's gotten the idea that she's going to do some kind of theater performance with a girlfriend of hers."

"That sounds exciting, don't you think?"

Wallander nodded dubiously.

"I hope she comes here in July," he said. "I haven't seen her in a long time."

They parted outside Wallander's door.

"Drop by and say hello this summer," she said. "With or without the woman from Riga. With or without your daughter."

"Her name is Baiba," said Wallander.

He promised he'd come by and visit.

After the conversation with Ann-Britt he sat for a good hour bent over the papers on his desk. Twice he called the police in Göteborg in vain, looking for a detective who was working on the same investigation from a different angle. At quarter to six he closed the folders and stood up. He had decided to go out to eat. He pinched his stomach and noticed that he was still losing weight. Baiba had complained that he was too fat. After that he hadn't had any problem eating less. On several occasions he had also squeezed into a sweatsuit and gone jogging, even though he found it boring.

He put on his jacket and decided to write a letter to Baiba that evening. Just as he was about to leave the office, the telephone rang. For a moment he couldn't decide whether to let it ring or not. Then he went back to his desk and picked up the receiver.

It was Martinsson.

"Nice speech you made," said Martinsson. "Björk seemed genuinely moved."

"You already said that," said Wallander. "What do you want? I'm on my way home."

"I just got a phone call that was a little strange," said Martinsson. "I thought I ought to confer with you."

Wallander waited impatiently for him to go on.

"It was a farmer calling from a farm out near Marsvinsholm. He claimed that there was a woman acting strange out in his rapeseed field."

"Is that all?"

"Yes."

"A woman acting strange out in a rapeseed field? What was she doing?"

"If I understood him correctly, she wasn't doing anything. The peculiar thing was that she was out in the rapeseed in the first place."

Wallander had to think a moment before he replied.

"Send out a squad car. It sounds like something for them."

"The problem is that all the units seem to be busy right now. There were two auto accidents almost simultaneously. One by the road into Svarte, the other outside the Hotel Continental."

"Serious?"

"No major injuries. But there seems to be quite a mess."

"They can drive out to Marsvinsholm when they have time, can't they?"

"That farmer seemed pretty upset. I don't know any better way to explain it. If I didn't have to pick up my kids I'd go out there myself."

"All right, I can do it," said Wallander. "I'll meet you in the hall and get the name and directions."

A few minutes later Wallander drove off from the police station. He turned left and took the road toward Malmö at the roundabout. Next to him on the seat was the note Martinsson had written for him. The farmer's name was Salomonsson, and Wallander knew the road to take. When he got out onto E65 he rolled down the window. The yellow rapeseed fields billowed on both sides of the road. He couldn't remember the last time he had felt as good as he did now. He stuck in a cassette of *The Marriage of Figaro* with Barbara Hendricks singing Susanna, and he thought about meeting Baiba in Copenhagen. When he reached the side road to Marsvinsholm he turned left, past the castle and the castle church, and turned left again. He glanced at Martinsson's directions and swung onto a narrow road that led straight across the fields. In the distance he caught a glimpse of the sea.

Salomonsson's house was an old, well-preserved Skåne farmhouse. Wallander got out of the car and looked around. Everywhere he looked were yellow rapeseed fields. The door of the house opened. The man standing on the steps was very old. He had a pair of binoculars in his hand. Wallander thought that he must have been imagining the whole thing. All too often, lonely old folks out in the country were deluded into calling the police by their own imaginations. He walked over to the steps and nodded.

"Kurt Wallander from the Ystad police," he introduced himself.

The man on the steps was unshaven and his feet were stuck into a pair of beat-up clogs.

"Edvin Salomonsson," said the man, stretching out his skinny hand.

"Tell me what happened," said Wallander.

The man pointed out at the rapeseed field that lay to the right of the house.

"I discovered her this morning," he began. "I get up early. She was already there at five. At first I thought it was a deer. Then I looked through the binoculars and saw that it was a woman."

"What was she doing?" asked Wallander.

"She was standing there."

"That's all?"

"She was standing and staring."

"Staring at what?"

"How should I know?"

Wallander sighed to himself. Probably the old man *had* seen a deer. Then his imagination had taken over.

"You don't know who she is?" he asked.

"I've never seen her before," replied the man. "If I knew who she was, why would I call the police?"

Wallander nodded.

"You saw her the first time early this morning," he went on. "But you didn't call the police until late this afternoon?"

"I wouldn't want to put you out for no reason," the man answered simply. "I assume the police have plenty to do."

"You saw her in your binoculars," said Wallander. "She was out in the rapeseed field and you had never seen her before. Then what did you do?"

"I got dressed and went out to tell her to leave. She was trampling down the rapeseed."

"Then what happened?"

"She ran."

"Ran?"

"She hid in the field. Hunkered down so I couldn't see her. First I thought she was gone. Then I discovered her again in the binoculars. It happened over and over. Finally I got tired of it and called you."

"When did you see her last?"

"Just before I called."

"What was she doing then?"

"Standing there staring."

Wallander glanced out at the field. All he could see was the billowing rapeseed.

"The officer you spoke with said that you seemed uneasy," said Wallander.

"Well, what's somebody doing standing in a rapeseed field? There's got to be something odd about that."

Wallander thought that he ought to end the conversation as quickly as possible. It was clear to him now that the old man had imagined the whole thing. He decided to contact Social Services the next day.

"There's not really much I can do," said Wallander. "She's probably gone by now. And in that case, there's nothing to worry about."

"She's not gone at all," said Salomonsson. "I can see her right now."

Wallander spun around. He followed Salomonsson's pointing finger.

The woman was about fifty meters out in the rapeseed field. Wallander could see that her hair was very dark. It stood out sharply against the yellow field.

"I'll go talk to her," said Wallander. "Wait here."

He took a pair of boots out of the trunk of his car. Then he walked toward the rapeseed field with a feeling of unreality about the whole situation. The woman was standing completely still, watching him. When he got closer he saw that not only did she have long black hair, but her skin was dark too. He stopped when he reached the edge of the field. He raised one hand and tried to wave her over. She continued to stand utterly motionless. Even though she was still quite far from him and the billowing rapeseed hid her face every so often, he had the impression that she was quite beautiful. He shouted to her to come toward him. When she still didn't move he took a step into the field. At once she was gone. It happened so fast that she looked like a spooked animal. At the same time he could feel himself getting angry. He kept walking out into the field, looking in every direction. When he caught sight of her again she had moved into the eastern corner of the field. So that she wouldn't get away, he started running. She moved very quickly and he could feel himself getting out of breath. When he came as close as twenty meters or so, they were out in the middle of the rapeseed field. He shouted at her to stop.

"Police!" he yelled. "Freeze!"

He started walking toward her. Then he stopped short. And everything happened very fast. She raised a plastic jug over her head and started pouring a colorless liquid over her hair, her face, and her body. He had a fleeting thought that she must have been carrying it the whole time. And now he could tell that she was terrified. Her eyes were wide open and she was staring straight at him.

"Police!" he shouted again. "I just want to talk to you."

At the same moment a smell of gasoline wafted toward him. Suddenly she had a flickering cigarette lighter in one hand, which she touched to her hair. Wallander cried out as she burst into flame like a torch. Paralyzed, he watched her lurch around the field as the fire sizzled and blazed over her body. Wallander could hear himself screaming. But the woman on fire was silent. Afterwards he couldn't remember hearing her scream at all.

When he tried to run up to her the entire field exploded in flames. He was suddenly surrounded by smoke and fire. He held his hands in front of his face and ran, without knowing which direction he was heading. When he reached the edge of the field he tripped and tumbled into the ditch. He turned around and saw her one last time before she fell over and vanished from his sight. She was holding her arms up as if appealing for mercy.

The rapeseed field was burning.

Somewhere behind him he could hear Salomonsson wailing.

Wallander got to his feet. His legs were shaking.

Then he turned away and threw up.

Chapter Three

A fterward Wallander would remember the burning girl in the rapeseed field the way you remember, with the greatest reluctance, a distant nightmare you'd rather forget. Even though he seemed to maintain at least an outward sense of calm for the entire evening and far into the night, later he could recall nothing but irrelevant details. Martinsson, Hansson, and especially Ann-Britt Höglund had been astonished by his impassiveness. But they couldn't see through the shield he had set up to protect himself. Inside him there was devastation like a house that had collapsed.

He got back to his apartment just after two in the morning. Only then, when he sat down on his couch, still wearing his dirty clothes and muddy boots, did the shield crumble. He poured himself a glass of whisky; the doors of his balcony stood open and let in the summer night, and he started to cry like a baby.

The girl who had burned herself to death had been a child. She reminded him of his own daughter Linda.

During all his years as a policeman he had learned to be prepared for whatever might await him when he arrived at a place where a person had met a violent and sudden death. He had seen people who had hanged themselves, stuck shotgun barrels in their mouths, or blown themselves to bits. Somehow he had learned to endure what he saw and then push it aside. But it never worked when there were children or young people involved. Then he was just as defenseless as when he had first started working as a cop. He knew that most cops reacted the same way. When children or young people died violently, for no reason, the defenses erected out of habit collapsed. And that's how it would be as long as he continued working as a police officer.

But by the time the shield crumbled he had put behind him the introductory phase of the investigation, which had been conducted in an exemplary manner. With traces of vomit clinging to his mouth he had run up to Salomonsson, who was incredulously watching his rapeseed field burn, and asked where the telephone was. Since Salomonsson didn't seem to understand the question, or maybe didn't even hear it, he shoved the old man aside and dashed into the house. There he encountered the acrid smell of a life lived by an unwashed old man, and in the hallway he found the telephone. He dialed 90-000, and the operator who took the call later claimed that he had sounded quite calm when he described what had happened and called for a full team.

The flames from the burning field were shining through the windows like floodlights lighting up the summer evening. He called Martinsson at home, talking first with his daughter and then his wife before Martinsson was called in from the back yard, where he had been mowing the lawn. As succinctly as possible he described what had happened and asked Martinsson to call Hansson and Höglund too. Then he went out in the kitchen and washed his face under the faucet. When he came back out to the courtyard, Salomonsson was still rooted to the same spot as before, as if mesmerized by the incomprehensible spectacle before him. A car came driving up with some of his closest neighbors in it. But Wallander shouted to them to stay back. He didn't even allow them to approach Salomonsson. In the distance he heard sirens from the fire trucks, which almost always arrived first. Soon afterwards, two patrol cars of uniformed officers and an ambulance arrived. It was Peter Edler who was directing the firefighting, a man in whom Wallander had the greatest confidence.

"What's going on?" he asked.

"I'll explain later," said Wallander. "But don't stomp around out in the field. There's a dead body out there."

"The house isn't threatened," said Edler. "We'll work on getting the fire contained."

Then he turned to Salomonsson and asked him how wide the tractor paths and the ditches between the fields were. Meanwhile, one of the ambulance crew came over. Wallander had met him before but couldn't remember his name.

"Is anyone hurt?" he asked.

Wallander shook his head.

"One person dead," he replied. "She's lying out in the field."

"Then we'll need a hearse," said the ambulance driver. "What happened?"

Wallander didn't feel like answering. Instead he turned to Norén, who was the patrol officer he knew best.

"There's a dead woman out in the field," he said. "Until the fire is put out we can't do anything but block it off."

Norén nodded.

"Was it an accident?" he asked.

"More like a suicide," said Wallander.

A few minutes later, about the same time Martinsson arrived, Norén handed him a paper cup of coffee. He stared at his hand and wondered why he wasn't shaking. Just then Hansson and Ann-Britt Höglund arrived in Hansson's car, and he told his colleagues what had happened.

Again and again he used the same phrase: *She burned like a torch.*

"This is just terrible," said Höglund.

"It was worse than you can imagine," said Wallander. "Not to be able to do anything. I hope none of you ever has to experience anything like this."

Silently they watched the firefighters work to contain the fire. A large group of bystanders had already gathered, but the policemen kept them back.

"What did she look like?" asked Martinsson. "Did you see her up close?"

Wallander nodded.

"Someone ought to talk to the old man," he said. "His name is Salomonsson."

Hansson took Salomonsson into his kitchen. Höglund went over and talked to Peter Edler. The fire had already begun to die down. When she came back she said it would be all over in a little while.

"Rapeseed burns fast," she said. "Besides, the field is wet. It rained yesterday."

"She was young," said Wallander, "with black hair and dark skin. She was dressed in a yellow windbreaker. I think she had jeans on. I don't know about her feet. And she was scared."

"What was she scared of?" asked Martinsson.

Wallander thought a moment before he replied.

"She was scared of me," he said. "I'm not completely sure, but I think she was even more frightened when I shouted at her that I was a policeman and told her to stop. What she was afraid of beyond that, I have no idea."

"She understood everything you said?"

"She understood the word *police* at least. I'm sure of that."

A thick pall of smoke was all that remained of the fire.

"There was no one else out there in the field?" asked Höglund. "You're sure she was alone?"

"No," said Wallander. "I'm not sure at all. But I didn't see anyone but her."

They stood in silence and thought about what he had said.

Who was she? thought Wallander. Where did she come from? Why did she set herself on fire? If she wanted to die, why did she choose to torture herself?

Hansson came back from the house, where he had been talking with Salomonsson.

"We should do like they do in the States," he said. "We should have menthol to smear under our noses. Damn, the smell in there. Old men shouldn't be allowed to outlive their wives."

"Get one of the ambulance crew to ask him how he's feeling," said Wallander. "He must have had a shock."

Martinsson went to deliver the message. Peter Edler took off his helmet and stood next to Wallander.

"It'll be over soon," he said. "But I'll leave a truck here tonight."

"When can we go out in the field?" asked Wallander.

"Within an hour. The smoke will hang around for a while yet. But the field has already started to cool off."

Wallander took Peter Edler aside.

"What am I going to see?" he asked. "She poured a five-liter jug of gasoline over herself. And the way everything exploded around her, she must have already poured more gasoline on the ground."

"It won't be pretty," Edler replied candidly. "There won't be a lot left."

Wallander said nothing more. Then he turned to Hansson.

"No matter how we look at it, we know that it was suicide," said Hansson. "We have the best witness we can get: a policeman."

"What did Salomonsson say?"

"He'd never seen her before she showed up out there at five o'clock this morning. There's no reason to think he's not telling the truth."

"In other words, we don't know who she is," said Wallander. "And we don't know what she was running from either."

Hansson looked at him in surprise.

"Why should she be running from something?" he asked.

"She was scared," said Wallander. "She was hiding in a rapeseed field. And when a policeman arrived she decided to set herself on fire."

"We don't have any idea about what she was thinking," said Hansson. "You may have been imagining that she was frightened."

"No," said Wallander. "I've seen enough fear in my life to know what it looks like."

One of the ambulance crew came walking toward them.

"We're taking the old man with us to the hospital," he said. "He seems to be in pretty bad shape."

Wallander nodded.

Soon the forensic technicians came driving up. Wallander tried to point out where in the smoke the body might be located.

"Maybe you ought to go home," said Höglund. "You've seen enough this evening."

"No," said Wallander. "I'll stay."

It was half past eight before the smoke had cleared and Peter Edler said they could go out in the field and start their examination. Even though the summer evening was still light, Wallander had ordered floodlights brought in.

"There might be something out there besides a dead body," said Wallander. "Watch your step. Everyone who doesn't absolutely have some business out there should stay back."

Then he thought that he really didn't want to do what he had to do. He would have preferred to drive away and leave the responsibility to the others.

He walked out into the field alone. The others stayed behind and watched. He was afraid of what he would see and he was afraid the knot he had in his stomach would burst.

He walked straight toward her. Her arms had stiffened in the upstretched motion he had seen her make before she died, surrounded by the raging flames.

Her hair and face, along with her clothes, were burned off. All that was left was a blackened body that still radiated terror and desolation. Wallander turned around and walked back across the blackened earth. For a brief moment he was afraid he was going to faint.

The forensic techs started to work in the harsh glare of the floodlights, where the moths were already swarming. Hansson had opened Salomonsson's kitchen window to air out the locked-in stink of the old man. They pulled out the chairs and sat around the kitchen table. At Höglund's suggestion they allowed themselves to make coffee on Salomonsson's ancient stove.

"All he has is ground coffee," she said after searching through the drawers and cupboards. "Is that all right?"

"That's fine," said Wallander. "Just so it's strong."

Beside the old cupboards with the sliding doors there was an old-fashioned clock hanging on the wall. Wallander suddenly noticed that it had stopped. He remembered that he had seen a clock like that once before, at Baiba's apartment in Riga, and that it too had a pair of immobile hands. Something stops, he thought. As though the hands were trying to ward off events that had not yet happened by stopping time. Baiba's husband was killed execution-style on a cold night in Riga's harbor. A lone girl appears as if shipwrecked in a sea of rapeseed and takes leave of her life by inflicting on herself the worst pain imaginable.

He thought she had set herself on fire as if she were her own enemy. It wasn't him, the policeman with the waving arms, she had wanted to escape.

It was herself.

He was jolted out of his reverie by the silence around the table. They were looking at him and waiting for him to take the initiative. Through the window he could see the technicians creeping around the dead body in the glare of the floodlights. A camera flash went off, then another.

"Did somebody call for the hearse?" asked Hansson suddenly.

For Wallander it was as if someone had struck his eardrums with a sledge-hammer. The simple, matter-of-fact question from Hansson brought him back to the reality he had wanted most of all to avoid.

The images flickered past inside his head, through the most vulnerable parts of his brain. He imagined himself driving through the beautiful Swedish summertime. Barbara Hendricks's voice is strong and clear. Then a girl skitters away like a frightened animal in the tall field of rapeseed. The catastrophe comes out of nowhere. Something happens that should not happen.

A hearse is on its way to carry off the summer itself.

"Prytz knows what to do," said Martinsson, and Wallander recognized the ambulance driver's name, the one he couldn't remember before.

He knew he had to say something.

"What do we know?" he began tentatively, as if each word were offering resistance. "An elderly farmer, living alone, rises early and discovers a strange woman in his rapeseed field. He tries calling to her, to get her to leave, since he doesn't want his field trampled down. She hides and then reappears, over and over. He calls us late in the afternoon. I drive out here, since our regular patrols are busy with traffic accidents. To be honest, I have a hard time taking him seriously. I decide to leave and contact Social Services, since Salomonsson gives the impression of being confused. Then the woman suddenly pops up among the rapeseed again. I try to make contact with her. But she moves away. Then she lifts a plastic jug over her head, drenches herself in gasoline, and sets fire to herself with a cigarette lighter. The rest you know. She was alone, she had a jug of gasoline, and she took her own life."

He broke off abruptly, as if he no longer knew what to say. A moment later he went on.

"We don't know who she is," he said. "We don't know why she killed herself. I can give a fairly good description of her. But that's all."

Ann-Britt Höglund got some cracked coffee cups out of a cupboard. Martinsson went out in the yard and took a piss. When he returned, Wallander continued his tentative attempt to sum up what he knew and decide what they ought to do.

"We have to find out who she was," he went on. "That's the most important thing. It's actually the only thing that's required of us. We'll have to search through missing persons. I'll write down her description. Since I had a sense she was dark-skinned, we can start by putting a little extra focus on checking on refugees and the refugee camps. Then we'll have to wait for what the techs come up with."

"At any rate, we know there was no crime committed," said Hansson. "So our task is to determine who she was."

"She must have come from somewhere," said Höglund. "Did she walk here? Did she ride a bike? Did she drive? Where did she get the gasoline? There are plenty of questions."

"And why here, of all places?" said Martinsson. "Why Salomonsson's rapeseed field? This farm is quite a ways off the main roads."

The questions remained hanging in the air. Norén came into the kitchen and said that some reporters had arrived who wanted to know what happened. Wallander, who knew that he had to get moving, stood up.

"I'll talk to them," he said.

"Tell them the honest truth," said Hansson.

"What else would I say?" Wallander replied in surprise.

He went out in the courtyard and recognized the two newspaper reporters. One was a young woman who worked for *Ystad's Allehanda,* the other an elderly man from *Arbetet.*

"It looks like a film shoot," said the woman, pointing at the floodlights in the burned-out field.

"It's not," said Wallander.

He told them what had happened. A woman had died in a fire. There was no suspicion of criminal activity. Since they still didn't know who she was, he didn't want to say anything more at this time.

"Can we take some pictures?" asked the man from *Arbetet*.

"You can take as many pictures as you like," replied Wallander. "But you'll have to take them from here. No one is allowed out in the field."

The reporters acquiesced and drove off in their cars. Wallander was just about to return to the kitchen when he saw that one of the technicians working out in the field was waving at him. Wallander went over to him. He tried to avoid looking at the remains of the woman with the upstretched arms. It was Sven Nyberg, their surly but brilliant head of forensics, coming toward him. They stopped at the edge of the area covered by the floodlights. A slight breeze came wafting from the sea across the burned rapeseed field.

"I think we've found something," said Nyberg.

In his hand he had a little plastic bag. He handed it to Wallander, who moved a few steps closer to one of the floodlights. In the plastic bag was a gold necklace with a tiny pendant.

"It has an inscription," said Nyberg. "The letters *D.M.S.* It's a picture of the Madonna."

"Why didn't it melt?" asked Wallander.

"A fire in a field doesn't generate enough heat to melt jewelry," Nyberg replied. Wallander could hear he was tired.

"This is exactly what we needed," said Wallander. "We don't know who she is, but now at least we've got some initials."

"We'll be ready to take her away soon," said Nyberg, nodding toward the black hearse waiting at the edge of the field.

"How does it look?" Wallander asked cautiously.

Nyberg shrugged.

"The teeth might give us something. The pathologists are excellent. They can find out how old she was. With the new DNA technology they can also tell you whether she was born in this country of Swedish parents or if she came from somewhere else."

"There's coffee in the kitchen," said Wallander.

"No thanks," said Nyberg. "I'll be done here pretty soon. In the morning we'll go over the entire field. Since there was no crime it can wait until then."

Wallander went back to the kitchen. He laid the plastic bag containing the necklace on the table.

"Now we have something to go on," he said. "A pendant in the form of a Madonna. With the inscribed initials *D.M.S.* I suggest you all go home now. I'll stay here a while longer."

"Nine o'clock tomorrow morning," said Hansson, getting up.

"I wonder who she was," said Martinsson. "The Swedish summertime is too beautiful and too short for something like this to have to happen."

They parted in the courtyard. Höglund lingered behind.

"I'm thankful I didn't have to see it," she said. "I think I understand what you're going through."

Wallander didn't answer.

"I'll see you tomorrow," he said.

When the cars had gone he sat down on the steps of the house. The floodlights shone as if over a desolate stage on which a play was being performed, and he was the only spectator.

The wind had started to blow. They were still waiting for the warmth of summer. The air was cold. Wallander noticed that he was freezing sitting there on the steps. He realized how intensely he longed for heat. He hoped it would come soon.

After a while he got up and went in the house and washed the coffee cups they had used.

Chapter Four

Wallander gave a start in his sleep. It felt like someone was trying to tear off one of his feet. When he opened his eyes he saw that his foot was stuck in the broken bed frame. He had to turn over on his side to free it. Then he lay completely still. The light of dawn filtered in through the crookedly drawn shade. He looked at the clock on the night stand. Half past four. He had slept only a few hours and he was very tired. He found himself back out in the rapeseed field again. He thought he could see the girl much more clearly now. It wasn't me she was afraid of, he thought. She wasn't hiding from me or Salomonsson. It was someone else.

He got up and shuffled out to the kitchen. While he waited for the coffee to brew he went into his messy living room and checked the answering machine. The red light was flashing. He pushed the replay button. First was his sister Kristina. "I want you to call me. Preferably within a couple of days." Wallander immediately thought it must be something to do with their elderly father. Even though he had married his home-care worker and no longer lived alone, he was still moody and unpredictable.

There was a scratchy, faint message from *Skånska Dagbladet,* asking if he was interested in a subscription. He was just heading back to the kitchen when he heard another message. "This is Baiba. I'm going to Tallinn for a few days. I'll be back on Saturday."

All at once he had an attack of violent jealousy that he was unable to control. Why was she going to Tallinn? She hadn't said anything about it the last time they spoke. He went out to the kitchen, poured a cup of coffee, and then called her number in Riga, even though he knew she was probably still asleep. But there was no answer. He dialed again with the same result. His feeling of unease was growing. She could hardly have left for Tallinn at five in the morning. Why wasn't she home? Or if she was home, why didn't she answer?

He picked up his coffee cup, opened the balcony door facing Mariagatan, and sat down on the only chair. Once again he saw the girl running through the rapeseed field. For an instant he thought she looked like Baiba. He forced himself to believe that his jealousy was unwarranted. He didn't even have a right to it, since they had both agreed not to encumber their fragile relationship with unnecessary vows of fidelity. He remembered the way they had sat up until far into the night on Christmas Eve and talked about what they actually wanted from each other. Most of all, Wallander wanted them to get married. But when Baiba spoke of her need for freedom, he had agreed with her at once. In order not to lose her, he was prepared to agree with her about everything.

Although it was still early in the morning, the air was already warm. The sky was clear blue. He drank his coffee in slow sips and tried to keep from thinking of the girl who had burned herself to death among the yellow rapeseed. When the coffee was gone he went back into the bedroom and had to search the wardrobe for a long time before he found a clean shirt. Before he went in the bathroom he gathered all the dirty clothes strewn around the apartment. He made a big pile in the middle of the living room floor. He would have to sign up for laundry time today.

It was quarter to six when he left the apartment and went down to the street. He got into his car and remembered that it was due for an inspection by the end of June. He drove off down Regementsgatan and then out along Österleden. Without having decided in advance, he turned onto the road heading out of town and stopped at the New Cemetery at Kronoholmsvägen. He left the car and strolled slowly along the rows of low gravestones. Now and then he would glimpse a name he vaguely recognized. When he discovered a birth year the same as his own he averted his eyes. Some youths in blue overalls were busy unloading a power mower from a platform moped. When he reached the memorial grove, he sat down on one of the benches. He hadn't been here since that windy autumn day four years ago when they had scattered Rydberg's ashes. Björk had been there on that occasion, along with some of Rydberg's distant and anonymous relatives. Wallander had often thought he ought to come back here. But he had never gotten around to it until now.

A gravestone would have been simpler, he thought. With Rydberg's name engraved on it. That would have served as a focal point for my memories of him. In this grove with the invisible spirits of the dead wafting all around I can't find a trace of him.

He discovered that he had a hard time remembering what Rydberg looked like. He's in the process of dying away even inside me, he thought. Soon even his memory will be gone.

He stood up suddenly, feeling distressed. The burning girl kept running through his mind. He drove straight back to the police station, went into his office, and closed the door. At seven thirty he forced himself to prepare the summary for the car theft investigation he had to turn over to Svedberg. He moved the folders onto the floor so that his desk would be completely clear.

He lifted up his desk blotter to see whether there were any reminders he had forgotten. Instead he found a scratch-off lottery ticket he had bought several months before. He rubbed it with a ruler until the numbers appeared, and saw that he had won 25 kronor. From the hall he could hear Martinsson's voice, then Ann-Britt Höglund's. He leaned back in his chair, put his feet up on the desk, and closed his eyes. When he woke up he had a cramp in one of his calf muscles. He had been asleep no more than ten minutes. At the same moment the telephone rang. When he picked up the receiver he heard that it was Per Åkeson from the prosecutor's office. They greeted each other and exchanged some words about the weather. Over the many years they had worked together, they had slowly developed a rapport that neither of them mentioned but that both of them knew was friendship. They often disagreed about whether an arrest was justified or whether remanding into custody was reasonable. But there was something else too, a trust that went deeper, even though they almost never socialized.

"I read in the morning paper about the girl who burned to death out in a field by Marsvinsholm," said Åkeson. "Is that something for me?"

"It was suicide," replied Wallander. "Other than an old farmer named Salomonsson, I was the only witness to the whole thing."

"What in heaven's name were you doing there?"

"Salomonsson had called. Normally a patrol would have been sent out. But they were busy."

"The girl must not have been a pretty sight."

"It was even worse than you'd think. We have to find out who she was. I assume the switchboard has already started ringing. People worried about their missing relatives."

"But you don't suspect any foul play?"

Without understanding why, he suddenly hesitated before answering.

"No," he said then. "I can't think of a more blatant way to take your own life."

"You don't sound entirely convinced."

"I had a bad night. It was like you said: a horrible experience."

They were both silent. Wallander knew that Åkeson had something else he wanted to talk about.

"There's another reason why I'm calling," he said. "But keep it between the two of us."

"I usually know how to keep my mouth shut."

"Do you remember I told you a few years ago that I was thinking about doing something else? Before it's too late, before I get too old?"

Wallander tried to remember.

"I remember you talked about refugees and the UN. Was it the Sudan?"

"Uganda. And I've actually gotten an offer. Which I've decided to accept. Starting in September I'm going to take a sabbatical for a year."

"What does your wife say?"

"That's just why I'm calling. For some moral support. I haven't talked to her about it yet."

"Is she supposed to go along?"

"No."

"Then I suspect she'll probably be surprised."

"Have you got any good ideas about how I should break it to her?"

"Unfortunately I don't. But I think you're doing the right thing. There's got to be more to life than putting people in jail."

"I'll let you know how it goes."

They were just about to hang up when Wallander remembered that he had a question.

"Does this mean that Anette Brolin is coming back as your replacement?"

"She's changed sides; she's working as a defense attorney in Stockholm now," said Åkeson. "Weren't you a little in love with her, by the way?"

"No," Wallander said, "I was just wondering."

He hung up. An unexpected feeling of jealousy hit him full force. He would have liked to travel to Uganda himself, to do something completely different. Nothing could be worse than seeing a young person commit suicide as a gasoline-soaked torch. He envied Per Åkeson, who wasn't going to let his desire to leave stop at mere words.

The joy he had felt the day before was gone. He stood by the window and looked out at the street. The grass by the old water tower was quite green. Wallander thought about the year before, when he had been on sick leave for a long time after he killed a man. Now he wondered whether he actually had ever recovered from that depression. I ought to do something like Per Åkeson, he thought. There must be a Uganda for me somewhere. For Baiba and me.

He stood by the window for a long time. Then he went back to his desk and tried to get hold of his sister Kristina. He tried several times but kept getting a busy signal. He took a notebook out of a desk drawer and spent the next half hour writing up a report of the events of the night before. Then he called Pathology in Malmö but couldn't get hold of a doctor who could tell him anything about the burned corpse.

At five to nine he got a cup of coffee and went into one of the conference rooms. Höglund was on the phone, and Martinsson was leafing through a catalog of gardening equipment. Svedberg was in his usual spot, scratching the back of his neck with a pencil. One of the windows was open. Wallander stopped just inside the door with a strong feeling of déjà vu. Martinsson looked up from his catalog and nodded, Svedberg grunted something unintelligible, and Höglund was preoccupied patiently explaining something to one of her kids. Hansson came into the room. He had a coffee cup in one hand and a plastic bag with the necklace the techs had found in the field in the other.

"Don't you ever sleep?" asked Hansson.

Wallander felt himself bristle at the question.

"Why do you ask?"

"Have you taken a look in the mirror lately?"

"It went late yesterday. I sleep as much as I need to."

"It's those soccer matches," said Hansson. "They're on in the middle of the night."

"I don't watch them," said Wallander.

Hansson gave him a surprised look.

"Aren't you interested? I thought everyone stayed up to watch."

"I'm not that interested," Wallander admitted. "I know it's a little unusual. But as far as I know, the chief of the National Police hasn't sent out any memo that it's a dereliction of duty not to watch the games."

"This might be the last time we'll have a chance to see it," Hansson said somberly.

"See what?"

"Sweden playing in the World Cup. I just hope it doesn't go completely to hell. I'm worried about our defense."

"I see," Wallander said politely. Höglund was still talking on the phone.

"Ravelli," Hansson went on, referring to Sweden's goalie.

Wallander waited for him to continue, but he didn't.

"What about him?"

"I'm worried about him."

"Why? Is he sick?"

"I think he's erratic. He didn't play well against Cameroon. Kicking the ball out at strange times, odd behavior in the goal area."

"Cops can also be erratic," said Wallander.

"You can't really compare them," said Hansson. "At least we don't have to make lightning-fast decisions about whether to rush out or stay back at the goal line."

"Hell, who knows?" said Wallander. "Maybe there's a similarity between the police who rush to a crime scene and the goalie who rushes out on the field."

Hansson gave him a baffled look but didn't say a word.

The conversation died out. They sat around the table and waited for Höglund to finish her phone call. Svedberg, who had a hard time accepting female police officers, drummed his pencil on the table in annoyance to let her know they were waiting for her. Wallander thought that soon he would have to tell Svedberg to stop his meaningless protests. Höglund was a good cop, in many ways much more talented than Svedberg.

A fly buzzed around his coffee cup. They waited.

Höglund finished her conversation and sat down at the table.

"A bike chain," she said. "Kids have a hard time understanding that their mothers might have something more important to do than come straight home and fix it."

"Go ahead," said Wallander suddenly. "We can do this run-through without you."

She shook her head.

"I can't let them get used to something that's not right," she said.

Hansson placed the plastic bag with the necklace on the table in front of him.

"An unknown woman commits suicide," he said. "No crime has been committed. We just have to figure out who she was."

Wallander got the feeling that Hansson was suddenly starting to act like Björk. He was about to burst out laughing but managed to control himself. He caught Ann-Britt's eye. She seemed to be thinking the same way.

"The phones have started ringing," said Martinsson. "I put a man on it; he's taking all the calls coming in."

"I'll give him a description," said Wallander. "Otherwise we have to concentrate on people who've been reported missing. She might be one of them. If she's not on that list, someone is going to miss her sooner or later."

"I'll take care of it," said Martinsson.

"The necklace," said Hansson, opening the plastic bag. "A Madonna medallion and the letters *D.M.S.* I think it's solid gold."

"There's a database of abbreviations and acronyms," said Martinsson, who knew the most about computers. "We can put in the combination and see if we get a match."

Wallander reached for the necklace. There were still soot marks on the medallion and chain.

"It's beautiful," he said. "But most people in Sweden wear a cross as a religious symbol, don't they? Madonnas are more common in Catholic countries."

"It sounds like you're talking about a refugee or immigrant," said Hansson.

"All I'm talking about is what the medallion represents," replied Wallander. "In any case, it's important that it be included in the description. The person taking the calls has to know what it looks like."

"Shall we release a description?" Hansson asked.

Wallander shook his head.

"Not yet. I don't want anyone shocked unnecessarily."

He thought about the events of the night before. The lone girl in the rapeseed field. He knew he wouldn't give up until he knew what it was that had made her burn herself to death. I'm living in a world where young people take their own lives because they can't stand it anymore, he thought. I have to understand why, if I'm going to keep on being a cop.

He gave a start. Hansson had said something he didn't catch.

"Do we have anything more to discuss right now?" Hansson asked again.

"I'll take care of the pathologist in Malmö," Wallander said. "Has anyone been in touch with Sven Nyberg? If not, I'll run over and talk to both of them."

The meeting was over. Wallander went to his office and got his jacket. He hesitated a moment, wondering whether he ought to make another attempt to get hold of his sister. Or Baiba in Riga. But he decided to forget it.

He drove out to Salomonsson's farm near Marsvinsholm. Some policemen were busy taking down the floodlight stands and rolling up the cables. The house looked locked up. He reminded himself that sometime today he had to check and see how Salomonsson was doing. Maybe he had remembered something else.

He walked out into the field. The blackened ground stood out sharply against the surrounding yellow rapeseed. Nyberg was kneeling in the mud. From a distance he glimpsed two other technicians who seemed to be searching along the edges of the burned area. Nyberg nodded curtly to Wallander. The sweat was running down his face.

"How's it going?" asked Wallander. "Have you found anything?"

"She must have had a lot of gasoline with her," said Nyberg, getting up. "We found remains of five half-melted jugs. They were apparently empty when the fire broke out. If you draw a line through the spots where we found them, you can see that she had actually surrounded herself."

"What do you mean?" Wallander asked.

Nyberg threw out one arm in a sweeping gesture.

"I mean that she built a fortress around herself. She poured gasoline in a wide circle. It was her moat, and there was no entrance to the fortress. And she was standing right in the middle, with the last jug, which she had saved for herself. Maybe she was hysterical and despondent. Maybe she was crazy or seriously ill. I don't know. But that's what she did. She knew full well what she was going to do."

Wallander nodded thoughtfully.

"Can you tell me anything about how she got here?"

"I've sent for a canine unit," said Nyberg. "But they probably won't be able to pick up her trail. The smell of gasoline has permeated the ground. The dog will just be confused. We haven't found a bicycle. The tractor paths that lead down toward E65 didn't have anything either. As far as I can tell, she landed in this field by parachute."

Nyberg took a roll of toilet paper out of one of his bags of equipment and wiped the sweat from his face.

"What do the doctors say?" he asked.

"Nothing yet," said Wallander. "I think they've got a difficult job ahead of them."

Nyberg suddenly turned more serious.

"Why would anyone do something like this to herself?" he said. "Could someone really have such strong reasons for not living that she'd end it all by torturing herself as much as she possibly could?"

"I've asked myself the same question," said Wallander.

Nyberg shook his head.

"What's going on around here?" he asked.

Wallander didn't reply. He had absolutely nothing to say.

He went back to the car and called in to the police station. Ebba answered. To avoid her motherly concerns, he pretended to be in a hurry.

"I'm driving out to talk to the farmer who had his field burned down," he said. "I'll be in this afternoon."

He drove back to Ystad. In the cafeteria at the hospital he had some coffee and a sandwich. Then he looked for the ward where Salomonsson was supposed to be admitted for observation. He stopped a nurse, introduced himself, and stated his business. She gave him a quizzical look.

"Edvin Salomonsson?"

"I don't remember whether his name was Edvin," Wallander said. "Did he come in last night in conjunction with the fire outside Marsvinsholm?"

The nurse nodded.

"I'd like to speak with him," said Wallander. "If he's not too sick, that is."

"He's not sick," replied the nurse. "He's dead."

Wallander gave her an astonished look.

"Dead?"

"He died this morning. Apparently it was a heart attack. He died in his sleep. It would probably be best if you spoke with one of the doctors."

"That's not necessary," said Wallander. "I just came by to see how he was doing. Now I have my answer."

Wallander left the hospital and walked out into the bright sunshine.

Suddenly he had no idea what to do.

Chapter Five

W allander drove home feeling that he had to get some sleep if he was ever going to be able to think clearly again. Neither he nor anyone else could be blamed for the old farmer's death. The person who might have been held responsible, the one who had set fire to the rapeseed field and had upset Salomonsson so much that he died, was already dead herself. It was the events themselves, the fact that they happened in the first place, that made him feel uneasy and out of sorts. He unplugged the phone and then lay down on the couch in the living room with a hand towel over his eyes. But sleep wouldn't come. After half an hour he gave up. He plugged in the telephone, lifted the receiver, and dialed Linda's number in Stockholm. On a piece of paper by the phone he had a whole list of numbers crossed out. Linda moved often, and her phone number was always changing. It rang a long time, but no one answered. Then he dialed his sister's number. She answered almost at once. They didn't talk to each other very often, and hardly ever about anything but their father. Sometimes Wallander thought that their contact would cease altogether the day their father passed away.

They exchanged the usual polite phrases without actually being interested in the answers.

"You called," Wallander said.

"I'm worried about Pappa," she said.

"Has something happened? Is he sick?"

"I don't know. When did you visit him last?"

Wallander tried to remember.

"It was about a week ago," he said, feeling a pang of guilt.

"Don't you really have a chance to see him more often?"

Wallander felt a need to defend himself.

"I'm working almost around the clock. The department is hopelessly understaffed. I visit him as often as I can."

Her silence told him that she didn't believe what he said for a minute.

"I talked to Gertrud yesterday," she went on, without commenting on what Wallander had said. "I thought she gave an evasive answer when I asked how Pappa was doing."

"Why would she do that?" Wallander wondered, surprised.

"I don't know. That's why I'm calling."

"A week ago he was the same as always," Wallander said. "He was mad that I was in a hurry and couldn't stay longer. But the whole time I was there he sat painting his pictures and acted like he didn't have time to talk to me. Gertrud was happy, as usual. But I have to admit I don't understand how she puts up with him."

"Gertrud likes him," she said. "It's a question of love. Then you can put up with a lot."

Wallander felt the need to end the conversation as quickly as possible. His sister reminded him more and more of their mother, the older she got. Wallander had never had a very happy relationship with his mother. When he was growing up it had been his sister and his mother against him and his father. The family was invisibly divided into two camps. Back then Wallander had been very close to his father. It wasn't until near the end of his teens, when he decided to become a policeman, that the rift between them developed. His father had never been able to accept Wallander's decision. But he couldn't explain to his son why he was so opposed to the profession he had chosen, or what he should do instead. After Wallander finished his training and started as a cop on the beat in Malmö, the rift had widened to a chasm. Some years later his mother was stricken with cancer. It progressed quickly. She was diagnosed at New Year's and was dead by May. His sister Kristina left the house the same summer and moved to Stockholm, where she got a job at a company then known as L. M. Ericsson. She got married, got a divorce, and married again. Wallander had met her first husband once, but he had no idea what her present husband looked like. He knew that Linda had visited their home in Kärrtorp on a few occasions, but from her comments he got the impression that the visits were never very successful. Wallander could imagine that the rift from their childhood and teenage years was still there. The day their father died it would widen for good.

"I'm going over to visit him tonight," said Wallander, thinking about the pile of dirty laundry on his floor.

"I'd appreciate it if you called me," she said.

Wallander promised he would.

Then he called Riga. When the phone was picked up he thought it was Baiba at first. Then he realized that it was her housekeeper, who spoke nothing but Latvian. He hung up quickly. At the same moment his phone rang and he jumped.

He picked up the phone and heard Martinsson's voice.

"I hope I'm not bothering you," said Martinsson.

"I just stopped by to change my shirt," said Wallander, wondering why he always felt it necessary to excuse himself for being at home. "Has something happened?"

"A few phone calls have come in about missing persons," said Martinsson. "Ann-Britt is busy going through them."

"I was thinking more of what you came up with on your computer screens."

"The mainframe has been down all morning," Martinsson replied glumly. "I called Stockholm a while ago. Somebody there thought it would be up and running again in an hour. But he didn't sound totally convinced."

"We're not chasing any crooks," Wallander said. "We can wait."

"A doctor called from Malmö," Martinsson continued. "A woman. Her name was Malmström. I promised her you'd call."

"Why couldn't she talk to you?"

"She wanted to talk to *you*. I suppose it's because you were the last one to see the woman alive, not me."

Wallander grabbed a pen and wrote down the number.

"I was out there today," he said. "Nyberg was on his knees in the mud, sweating. He was waiting for a police dog."

"He's like a dog himself," said Martinsson, without trying to hide his personal dislike for Nyberg.

"He can be grumpy," Wallander protested. "But he knows his stuff."

He was just about to hang up when he remembered Salomonsson.

"The farmer died," he said.

"Who?"

"The man whose kitchen we were drinking coffee in yesterday. He had a heart attack and died."

After he hung up, Wallander went in the kitchen and drank some water. For a long time he sat at the kitchen table doing nothing. It was two o'clock by the time he called Malmö. He had to wait while the doctor named Malmström was called to the phone. From her voice he could hear that she was very young. Wallander introduced himself and apologized for the delay in returning her call.

"Has any new information come out to indicate that a crime was committed?" she asked.

"No."

"In that case we won't have to do an autopsy," she replied. "That will make it easier. She burned herself to death using gasoline—leaded."

Wallander felt that he was about to be sick. He imagined her blackened body, as if it were lying right next to the woman he was speaking with.

"We don't know who she was," he said. "We need to know as much as possible about her in order to give a clear description."

"It's always hard with a burned body," she said, unmoved. "All the skin is burned away. The dental examination isn't ready yet. But she had good teeth. No fillings. She was 163 centimeters tall. She had never broken a bone in her body."

"I need her age," said Wallander. "That's almost the most important thing."

"That'll take a few more days. We can base it on her teeth."

"What if you take a guess?"

"I'd rather not."

"I saw her from twenty meters away," said Wallander. "I think she was about seventeen. Am I wrong?"

The female doctor thought a moment before she replied.

"I still don't like guessing," she said at last. "But I think she was younger."

"Why's that?"

"I'll tell you when I know. But I wouldn't be surprised if it turned out she was only fifteen."

"Can a fifteen-year-old really set fire to herself of her own free will?" Wallander said. "I have a hard time believing that."

"Last week I put together the pieces of a seven-year-old girl who blew herself up," replied the doctor. "She had planned it very carefully. She made certain that no one else would be hurt. Since she could barely write, she left behind a drawing as her farewell letter. And I heard about a four-year-old who tried to poke his own eyes out because he was afraid of his father."

"That isn't possible," said Wallander. "Not here in Sweden."

"It was here, all right," she said. "In Sweden. In the center of the universe. In the middle of summer."

Wallander could feel himself getting tears in his eyes.

"If you don't know who she was, we'll keep her here," she went on.

"I have a question," said Wallander. "It must be incredibly painful to burn to death, isn't it?"

"People have known that through the ages," she replied. "That's why they used fire as one of the worst punishments or tortures that someone could be subjected to. They burned Joan of Arc, they burned witches. In every era people have been tortured by fire. The pain is worse than you can possibly imagine. Besides, you don't lose consciousness as quickly as you would hope. There's an instinct to run from the flames that's stronger than the desire to escape the pain. That's why your mind forces you not to pass out. Then you reach a limit. For a while the burned nerves become numbed. There are examples of people with ninety percent of their body burned who for a brief time felt uninjured. But when the numbness wears off..."

She didn't finish her sentence.

"She burned like a torch," said Wallander.

"The best thing you can do is stop thinking about it," she said. "Death can actually be a liberator. No matter how reluctant we are to accept that."

When the conversation was over, Wallander got up, grabbed his jacket, and left the apartment. The wind had started blowing outside. Cloud cover had moved in from the north. On the way to the police station he pulled in to the vehicle testing station and made an appointment to have his car inspected. When he got to the police station it was a few minutes past three. He stopped at the reception desk. Ebba had recently fallen in her bathroom and broken her hand. He asked how she was feeling.

"It reminds me that I'm getting old," she said.

"You'll never get old," said Wallander.

"That's a nice thing to say," she said. "But it's not true."

On the way to his office Wallander stopped by to see Martinsson, who was sitting in front of his computer terminal.

"They got it up and running twenty minutes ago," he said. "I'm just checking the description to see whether there are any missing persons who would fit."

"Add that she was 163 centimeters tall," said Wallander. "And that she was between fifteen and seventeen years old."

Martinsson gave him a baffled look.

"Only fifteen? That can't be possible, can it?"

"I wish it weren't true," said Wallander. "But for now we have to consider it a possibility. How's it going with the letter combinations?"

"I haven't gotten that far yet," said Martinsson. "But I was planning to stay late this evening."

"We're trying to make an ID," said Wallander. "We're not searching for a fugitive."

"There's no one at home tonight anyway," said Martinsson. "I don't like going home to an empty house."

Wallander left Martinsson and looked in on Höglund's room, where the door stood open. It was empty. He went back down the hall to the police operations center, where all the emergency alerts and phone calls were received. Höglund was sitting at a table with a senior officer, going through a pile of papers.

"Any leads?" he asked.

"We've got a couple of tips we have to look into more closely," she said. "One is a girl from Tomelilla Folk College who's been missing for two days."

"Our girl was 163 centimeters tall," said Wallander. "She had perfect teeth. She was between fifteen and seventeen years old."

"That young?" she asked in amazement.

"Yep," said Wallander. "That young."

"Then it's not the girl from Tomelilla, anyway," said Höglund, putting down the paper in her hand. "She's twenty-three and very tall."

She searched through the stack of papers for a moment.

"Here's another one," she said. "A sixteen-year-old girl named Mari Lippmansson. She lives here in Ystad and works in a bakery. She's been missing from her job for three days. It was the baker who called. He was mad. Her parents evidently don't care about her at all."

"Look at her a little more closely," Wallander said encouragingly.

But he knew she wasn't the one.

He got a cup of coffee and went to his room. The stack of papers about the car thefts was lying on the floor. He thought he'd better turn them over to Svedberg now. At the same time he hoped no serious crimes would be committed before he started his vacation.

At four o'clock they met in the conference room. Nyberg had come in from the burned field, where he had finished his search. It was a short meeting. Hansson had excused himself because he had to read through a rush memo from national headquarters.

"We'll make it short," Wallander said. "Tomorrow we'll go over all the cases that can't wait."

He turned to Nyberg, sitting at the end of the table.

"How'd it go with the dog?" he asked.

"He didn't find a thing," Nyberg replied. "If there was ever anything to give him a scent, it was covered up by the residual gasoline odor."

Wallander thought for a moment.

"You found five or six melted gasoline jugs," he said. "That means that she must have come to Salomonsson's rapeseed field in some sort of vehicle. She couldn't have carried all that gasoline by herself. Unless she walked there several times. There's one more possibility, of course. That she didn't come alone. But that doesn't seem reasonable, to say the least. Who would help a young girl commit suicide?"

"We could try to trace the gasoline jugs," said Nyberg dubiously. "But is it really necessary?"

"As long as we don't know who she was, we have to try to trace her by any leads we have," Wallander replied. "She must have come from somewhere, somehow."

"Did anyone look in Salomonsson's barn?" asked Höglund. "Maybe the gasoline jugs came from there."

Wallander nodded.

"Someone will have to drive out there and check," he said.

Höglund volunteered.

"We'll have to wait for Martinsson's results," Wallander said, winding up the meeting. "And the pathologist's work in Malmö. They're going to give us her exact age tomorrow."

"And the gold medallion?" asked Svedberg.

"We'll wait on that until we have some idea of what the letters on it might mean," said Wallander.

He suddenly realized something he had completely overlooked earlier. Behind the dead girl there were other people. Who would mourn her. Who would forever see her running like a living torch in their heads, in a totally different way than he would.

In their minds the fire would leave its scars. For him it would gradually fade away like a bad dream.

They broke up the meeting and went their separate ways. Svedberg went with Wallander to get the investigative material on the car thefts. Wallander gave him a brief rundown. When they were done, Svedberg didn't get up. Wallander could tell there was something he wanted to talk about.

"We ought to get together sometime and talk," said Svedberg hesitantly. "About what's going on with the force."

"You're thinking about the cutbacks? And the guard services taking over the custody of suspects?"

Svedberg nodded glumly.

"What good does it do to have new uniforms if we can't do our jobs?" he went on.

"I don't really think it'll help to talk about it," Wallander said evasively. "We have a union that's paid to take care of these matters."

"We ought to protest, at least," said Svedberg. "We ought to talk to people on the street about what's going to happen."

"I think everybody's got enough of their own troubles," replied Wallander, and at the same time he thought that Svedberg was quite right. It was also his own experience that the public was prepared to bend over backwards to save and protect their police stations.

Svedberg stood up.

"That's about it," he said.

"Set up a meeting," Wallander said. "I promise I'll come. But wait until summer's over."

"I'll think about it," said Svedberg and left the room with the car thefts under his arm.

It was quarter to five. Through the window Wallander could see that it was about to rain.

He decided to have a pizza before he drove out to see his father in Löderup. For once he wanted to show up without calling ahead of time.

On the way out of the station he stopped at the doorway to the room where Martinsson was sitting in front of his computer screens.

"Don't sit there too long," he said.

"I still haven't found anything," said Martinsson.

"I'll see you tomorrow."

Wallander went out to his car. The first raindrops were already spattering it.

He was just about to pull out of his parking space when he saw Martinsson come running out waving his arms. We've got her, he thought suddenly. And the thought settled like a knot in his stomach. He rolled down the window.

"Did you find her?" he asked.

"No," said Martinsson.

Then Wallander saw by the look on Martinsson's face that something serious had happened. He got out of the car.

"What is it?" he asked.

"There was a phone call," said Martinsson. "They've found a body on the beach out past Sandskogen."

Damn, thought Wallander. Not that. Not now.

"It looks like a homicide," Martinsson went on. "It was a man that called. He seemed unusually lucid, even though I think he was in shock."

"We'll have to drive out there," said Wallander. "Get your jacket. It's raining."

Martinsson didn't move.

"The man who called seemed to know who the victim was."

Wallander could tell by Martinsson's face that he ought to dread what would come next.

"He said it was Wetterstedt. The former minister of justice."

Wallander stared at Martinsson.

"One more time?"

"He claimed it was Gustaf Wetterstedt. The justice minister. And he said something else. He said it looked like he'd been scalped."

They stared at each other, thoroughly baffled.

It was two minutes to five on Wednesday, the 22nd of June.

Chapter Six

B y the time they got to the beach it was raining harder. Wallander had waited while Martinsson ran in to get his jacket. During the ride in the car they spoke very little. Martinsson gave directions. They turned off on a little road past the tennis courts. Wallander wondered what awaited them. What he wanted least of all had finally happened. If the man who called the police station turned out to be right, his vacation was in danger; Wallander knew that. Hansson would appeal to him to postpone it, and eventually he would give in. What he had been hoping—that his desk would be cleared of pressing matters through the end of June—was not going to happen.

They saw the sand dunes ahead of them and stopped. A man came forward to meet them. Wallander was surprised that he didn't seem to be any older than thirty. If it was Wetterstedt who had died, this man couldn't have been more than ten years old when the minister of justice retired and vanished from public view. Wallander himself had been a young police detective at the time. In the car he had tried to picture Wetterstedt's face. His hair was cropped short and he wore glasses without frames. Wallander vaguely remembered his voice: blaring, always self-confident, never ready to admit a mistake. This is how he remembered him.

The man who met them introduced himself as Göran Lindgren. He was dressed in shorts and a thin sweater. He seemed very agitated. They followed him down to the beach, completely deserted now that it had started to rain. Göran Lindgren led them over to a big rowboat turned upside down. On the far side there was a wide opening between the sand and the boat's gunwale.

"He's in there," said Lindgren in an unsteady voice.

Wallander and Martinsson looked at each other as if they still hoped it was all the man's imagination. They knelt down and peered in under the boat. The light was dim. But they could plainly see a body lying there.

"We'll have to turn the boat over," said Martinsson in a low voice, as if afraid the dead man would hear him.

"No," said Wallander, "we're not turning anything over." Then he got up quickly and turned to Göran Lindgren.

"I assume you have a flashlight," he said. "Otherwise you couldn't have made out any details."

The man nodded in surprise and pulled a flashlight out of a plastic bag near the boat. Wallander bent down again and shone the light inside.

"Holy shit," said Martinsson at his side.

The dead man's face was covered with blood. But they could still see that the skin from the forehead up over his skull was torn off, and Lindgren had been right. It was Wetterstedt lying in there under the boat. They stood up. Wallander handed back the flashlight.

"How did you know it was Wetterstedt?" he asked.

"He lives here," said Lindgren, pointing up toward a villa just to the left of the boat. "Besides, everyone knows him. You remember a politician who was on TV all the time."

Wallander nodded dubiously.

"We'll have to get a full team out here," he said to Martinsson. "Go call in. I'll wait here."

Martinsson hurried off. It was raining harder now.

"When did you discover him?" asked Wallander.

"I don't have a watch on me," said Lindgren. "But it couldn't have been more than half an hour ago."

"Where did you call from?"

Lindgren pointed to the plastic bag.

"I have a cell phone with me."

Wallander regarded him with interest.

"He's lying under an overturned boat," he said. "He's invisible from outside. You must have bent down to be able to see him?"

"It's my boat," said Lindgren simply. "Or my father's, to be exact. I usually take a walk here on the beach when I finish work for the day. Since it was starting to rain I thought I'd put my bag under the boat. When I felt it bump into something I bent down. At first I thought it was a plank that had fallen down. Then I saw what it was."

"It's really none of my business," said Wallander, "but I wonder why you had a flashlight with you anyway."

"We have a summer cottage in the woods at Sandskogen," replied Lindgren. "Over by Myrgången. There isn't any light there since we're in the process of rewiring it. We're electricians, both my father and I."

Wallander nodded.

"You'll have to wait here," he said. "We'll have to ask you all these questions again in a while. Have you touched anything?"

Lindgren shook his head.

"Has anyone else seen him besides yourself?"

"No."

"When did you or your father last turn over this boat?"

Göran Lindgren thought for a moment.

"It was over a week ago," he said.

Wallander had no more questions. He just stood there thinking. He left the boat and walked in a wide arc up toward the villa where Wetterstedt lived. He tried the gate to the yard. Locked. Then he waved over Göran Lindgren.

"Do you live nearby?" he asked.

"No," he said. "I live in Åkesholm. My car is parked up on the road."

"And you still knew that Wetterstedt lived in this house?"

"He used to walk along the beach here. Sometimes he stopped to watch while we were working on the boat, Pappa and I. But he never said anything. He was a little stuck-up, I think."

"Was he married?"

"Pappa said he was divorced. He read that in a magazine."

Wallander nodded.

"That's fine," he said. "Don't you have some rain gear in that plastic bag?"

"I've got it up in the car."

"Go ahead and get it," Wallander said. "Did you call anyone besides the police and tell them about this?"

"I think I ought to call Pappa. It's his boat, after all."

"Hold off for the time being," said Wallander. "Leave the phone here, go get your rain things, and come back."

Göran Lindgren did as he was told. Wallander went back to the boat. He stood looking at it and tried to imagine what had happened. He knew that the first impression of a crime scene was often crucial. Afterwards, during an investigation that was often long and troublesome, he would always return to that first impression.

Some things he was already sure of. It was out of the question that Wetterstedt had been murdered underneath the boat. Someone had put him there. Someone had hidden him. Since Wetterstedt's villa was right nearby, there was a good chance he was killed there. Besides, Wallander had a hunch that the killer couldn't have acted alone. They must have lifted the boat to get the body inside. And the boat was the old-fashioned kind, a clinker-built wooden boat. It was heavy.

Then Wallander thought about the torn-off scalp. What was it that Martinsson had said? Göran Lindgren had told him on the phone that the man had been "scalped." Wallander tried to imagine that there might very well be other reasons for the wound to the head. They still didn't know how Wetterstedt had died. It wasn't natural to think that someone would intentionally have torn off his hair.

Still, there was something in the picture that didn't fit. Wallander felt uneasy. There was something about the torn-off skin that disturbed him.

Just then the police cars started to arrive. Martinsson had been smart enough to tell them not to turn on their sirens and blue lights. Wallander walked away from the boat about ten meters so that the others wouldn't trample the sand unnecessarily.

"There's a dead man underneath the boat," said Wallander when the police had gathered around him. "Apparently it's Gustaf Wetterstedt, who was once upon a time our top boss. Anyone as old as I am, at least, will remember the days when he was minister of justice. He was living here in retirement. And now he's dead. We have to assume that he was murdered. So we'll start by sealing off the area."

"It's a good thing the game isn't on tonight," said Martinsson.

"The person who did this is probably a soccer fan too," said Wallander.

He felt himself getting annoyed at the constant references to the World Cup tournament. But he stopped himself from showing his irritation to Martinsson.

"Nyberg is on the way," said Martinsson.

"We're going to have to work on this all night," said Wallander. "We might as well get started."

Svedberg and Ann-Britt Höglund were in one of the first cars to arrive. Hansson showed up right after they did. Göran Lindgren came back dressed in a yellow rain slicker. He had to repeat how he had discovered the dead man while Svedberg took notes. Since it was raining hard now, they gathered under a tree at the top of one of the sand dunes. Afterwards, Wallander asked Lindgren to wait. Since he still didn't want to turn the boat over, the doctor had to dig out some sand to get far enough in under the boat to confirm that Wetterstedt was indeed dead.

"He seems to have been divorced," said Wallander. "But we'll have to get confirmation on that. Some of you will have to stay here. Ann-Britt and I will go up to his house."

"Keys," said Svedberg.

Martinsson went down to the boat, lay down on his stomach, and reached in his hand. After a minute or so he managed to find a key ring in Wetterstedt's jacket pocket. Martinsson was covered with wet sand when he handed Wallander the keys.

"We've got to put up a canopy," said Wallander testily. "Why hasn't Nyberg shown up yet? Why's everything moving so slowly?"

"He's on his way," said Svedberg. "Today is Wednesday, the day he takes a sauna."

Together with Höglund they headed up toward Wetterstedt's villa.

"I remember him from the police academy," she said suddenly. "Somebody put up a photo of him on the wall and used it as a dart board."

"He was never popular with the police," Wallander said. "It was during his administration that we noticed something new was on the way. A change that came sneaking up on us. I remember it felt like someone had pulled a hood over our heads. It was almost shameful to be a policeman back then. It was a time when people seemed to worry more about how the prisoners were doing than the fact that crime was steadily on the rise."

"There's a lot I don't remember," said Höglund. "But wasn't he mixed up in some sort of scandal?"

"There were a lot of rumors," said Wallander. "About one thing and another. But nothing was ever proven. I've heard about a number of police officers in Stockholm who were quite upset back then."

"Maybe time caught up with him," she said.

Wallander looked at her in surprise. But he didn't say a word.

They had reached the gate in the wall dividing the beach from Wetterstedt's yard.

"You know, I've been here before," she said suddenly. "He used to call the police and complain about young people sitting on the beach and singing on summer nights. One of those young people wrote a letter to the editor of *Ystad's Allehanda* to complain. Björk asked me to drive out here and check it out."

"Check out what?"

"I have no idea," she said. "But Björk was very sensitive to criticism, as you recall."

"That was one of his best traits," said Wallander. "He defended us, at any rate. That doesn't happen all the time."

They found the key and unlocked the gate. Wallander noticed that the lamp was burnt out. The yard they stepped into was well tended. There were no fallen leaves on the lawn. There was a little fountain with two nude plaster children squirting water at each other from their mouths. A garden swing was hanging in the arbor. On a flagstone patio there was a table with a marble top and a group of chairs.

"Well tended and expensive," said Höglund. "What do you think a marble table like that costs?"

Wallander didn't answer, since he had no idea. They continued up toward the villa. He guessed that it had been built around the turn of the century. They followed the flagstone walk and came around to the front of the house. Wallander rang the bell. He waited for over a minute before he rang again. Then he looked for the key and unlocked the door. They stepped into an entryway where the light was on. Wallander called out into the silence. But there was no one there.

"Wetterstedt wasn't killed underneath the boat," said Wallander. "Of course he could have been attacked on the beach. But I still think it happened in here."

"Why's that?" she asked.

"I don't know," he said. "Just a hunch."

They went through the house slowly, from the basement to the attic, without touching anything but the light switches. It was a superficial examination. Yet for Wallander it was important. They didn't know what they were looking for, since they weren't looking for anything in particular. But until a few days before, the man who now lay dead on the beach had lived in this house. The best they could do was to search for traces of how this sudden emptiness had come about. Nowhere did they see the slightest sign of disorder. Wallander looked around for a possible crime scene. Even at the front door he had been looking for marks to indicate a break-in. When they were standing in the entryway listening to the silence, Wallander had told Höglund to take off her shoes. Now they padded soundlessly through the big villa, which seemed to grow larger with each step they took. Wallander could feel his companion looking as much at him as at the objects in the rooms they passed through. He remembered how he had done the same thing with Rydberg, back when he was still a young, inexperienced detective. Instead of considering it flattering, a sign that she respected his knowledge and experience, he noticed that it depressed him. The changing of the guard was already under way, he thought. Despite the fact that they were in the same house, she was the one on the way in, while he already felt that he was on the way out.

He thought about the day almost two years ago when they had first met. He thought she was a pale and far from attractive young woman who had graduated from the police academy with the highest marks. But the first thing she said to him was that she thought he'd be able to teach her everything that the insulated school environment could never tell her about the unpredictability of real life. It ought to be the other way around, he thought quickly, as he looked at an indistinct lithograph. Imperceptibly the transition had already taken place. I'm learning more from the way she looks at me than she can extract from my withering policeman's brain.

They stopped by a window on the upper floor where they had a view of the beach. The floodlights were already in place; Nyberg, who had finally arrived, was gesticulating angrily and supervising the setup of a plastic canopy slanting over the rowboat. The outer cordon was being guarded by policemen in long coats. It was raining very hard now, and there were only a few people outside the cordon.

"I'm beginning to feel like I was wrong," Wallander said as he watched the plastic canopy finally settle into place. "There aren't any signs here that Wetterstedt was killed indoors."

"The killer might have cleaned up," Höglund suggested.

"We'll find that out after Nyberg goes through the house with a fine-tooth comb," said Wallander. "Now I think it happened outside the house."

In silence they went back downstairs.

"There wasn't any mail on the floor inside the front door," she said. "The house is fenced off. There must be a mailbox somewhere."

"We'll take that up later," said Wallander.

He went into the large living room and stood in the middle of it. She waited in the doorway and watched him as though she expected him to give an extemporaneous lecture.

"I make a habit of asking myself what I'm missing," Wallander said. "But

everything here seems so obvious. A man living alone in a house where everything is in its place, no bills unpaid, and where loneliness lingers in the walls
like old cigar smoke. The only thing that breaks the pattern is that the man in
question is now lying dead underneath Göran Lindgren's rowboat down on
the beach."

Then he corrected himself.

"No, there's one thing that breaks the pattern," he said. "The fact that the
lamp by the garden gate wasn't working."

"It may have just burned out," she said, surprised.

"Right," said Wallander, "but it still breaks the pattern."

There was a knock on the door. When Wallander opened it, Hansson was
standing there in the rain with water streaming down his face.

"Neither Nyberg nor the doctor is going to get anywhere if we don't get that
boat turned over," he said.

"Turn it over," said Wallander. "I'll be right there."

Hansson disappeared into the rain.

"We have to start looking for his relatives," Wallander said. "He must have
an address book somewhere."

"There's one thing that's weird," she said. "There are souvenirs everywhere
from a long life with lots of traveling and countless meetings with various people. But there aren't any family photographs."

They had gone back to the living room, and Wallander looked around and
saw that she was right. It bothered him that he hadn't thought of it himself.

"Maybe he didn't want to be reminded that he was old," Wallander said
without conviction.

"A woman would have never been able to live in a house with no pictures
of her family," she said. "That's probably why I thought of it."

There was a telephone on a table next to the sofa.

"There's a phone in his study too," he said, pointing. "You look in there, and
I'll start here."

Wallander squatted by the low telephone stand. Next to the phone was the
remote control for the TV. Wetterstedt could talk on the phone and watch TV
at the same time, he thought. Just like me. We live in a world where people can
hardly stand it if they can't change the channel and talk on the phone at the
same time. He riffled through the phone books without finding any private
notes. Then he carefully pulled out two drawers in a bureau behind the telephone stand. In one there was a stamp album, in the other some tubes of glue
and a box of napkin rings.

As he was walking toward the study, the phone rang. He stopped. Höglund
appeared at once in the doorway to the study. Wallander sat down carefully on
the corner of the sofa and picked up the receiver.

"Hello," said a woman's voice. "Gustaf? Why haven't you called me?"

"Who's speaking, please?" asked Wallander.

The woman's voice suddenly turned formal.

"This is Gustaf Wetterstedt's mother calling," she said. "With whom am I speaking?"

"My name is Kurt Wallander. I'm a police officer here in Ystad."

He could hear the woman breathing. He had a sudden thought that she must be very old if she was Gustaf Wetterstedt's mother. He made a face at Höglund, who was standing looking at him.

"Has something happened?" asked the woman.

Wallander didn't know how to react. It went against all written and unwritten procedures to inform the next of kin of a sudden death over the telephone. But he had already told her his name, and that he was a police officer.

"Hello?" said the woman. "Are you still there?"

Wallander didn't answer. He stared helplessly at Höglund.

Then he did something which later he could never decide was justified or not. He hung up the phone.

"Who was that?" she asked.

Wallander shook his head and didn't answer.

Then he picked up the phone and called the headquarters of the Stockholm police on Kungsholm.

Chapter Seven

Just after nine o'clock in the evening, Gustaf Wetterstedt's telephone rang again. By that time Wallander had managed to get word of his death to Wetterstedt's mother by way of his colleagues in Stockholm. It was an inspector who introduced himself as Hans Vikander calling Wallander from the Östermalm police. In a few days, on July first, the old name would disappear and be replaced by "City Police."

"She's been informed," Vikander said. "Because she was so old I took a clergyman along with me. I must say she took it calmly, even though she's ninety-four years old."

"Maybe that's why," said Wallander.

"We're trying to track down Wetterstedt's two children," Vikander went on. "The oldest, a son, works at the UN in New York. The daughter lives in Uppsala. We hope to get hold of them sometime this evening."

"What about his ex-wife?" asked Wallander.

"Which one?" Vikander asked. "He was married three times."

"All three of them," said Wallander. "We'll have to contact them ourselves later."

"I've got something that might interest you," Vikander went on. "When we spoke with the mother she said that her son called her every night, at precisely nine o'clock."

Wallander looked at his watch. It was three minutes past nine. At once he understood the significance of what Vikander had said.

"He didn't call yesterday," Vikander continued. "She waited until nine-thirty. Then she tried to call him. No one answered, although she claimed she let it ring at least fifteen times."

"And the night before?"

"She couldn't remember too well. She's ninety-four, after all. She said that her short-term memory was pretty bad."

"Did she say anything else?"

"It was a little hard to know what to ask."

"We'll have to talk to her again," Wallander said. "Since she's already met you, it would be good if you could take it on."

"I'm going on vacation the second week in July," said Vikander. "Until then, no problem."

Wallander hung up. Höglund came into the entryway. She had been checking the mailbox.

"Newspapers from today and yesterday," she said. "A phone bill. No personal letters. He must not have been under that boat for very long."

Wallander got up from the sofa.

"Go through the house one more time," he said. "See if you can find any sign that anything is missing. I'll go down and take a look at him."

It was raining even harder now. As Wallander hurried through the back yard he remembered that he was supposed to be visiting his father tonight. With a grimace he went back to the house.

"Do me a favor," he asked Höglund when he came in the front door. "Call my father and tell him I'm tied up with an urgent investigation. If he asks who you are, tell him you're the new chief of police."

She nodded and smiled. Wallander gave her the number. Then he went back out into the rain.

The crime scene was a ghostly sight, lit up by the powerful floodlights. With a strong feeling of discomfort, Wallander walked in under the temporary canopy. Gustaf Wetterstedt's body lay stretched out on a sheet of plastic. The doctor was busy shining a flashlight down Wetterstedt's throat. He stopped when he noticed that Wallander had arrived.

"How are you?" asked the doctor.

Wallander hadn't recognized him until that moment. It was the same doctor who had attended to him in the emergency room a few years before when he thought he was having a heart attack.

"Apart from this business, I'm doing fine," said Wallander. "I never had a recurrence."

"Did you take my advice?" asked the doctor.

"Of course not," Wallander muttered evasively.

He looked at the dead man and thought that he gave the same impression in death as he once had on the TV screen. There was something obstinate and unsympathetic about his face, despite the fact that it was covered with dried blood. Wallander leaned forward and looked at the wound on his forehead, which extended up toward the top of his head, where the skin and hair had been ripped away.

"How did he die?" asked Wallander.

"From a powerful axe blow to the spine," replied the doctor. "It must have killed him instantly. The spine is severed just below the shoulder blades. He was probably dead before he hit the ground."

"Are you sure it happened outdoors?" Wallander asked.

"I think so. The blow to the spine must have come from someone standing behind him. It's most likely that the force of the blow made him fall forward. He has grains of sand in his mouth and eyes. It probably happened right nearby."

"There must be traces of blood somewhere," said Wallander.

"The rain makes it difficult," said the doctor. "But with a little luck maybe you can scrape through the surface layer and find some blood that penetrated deep enough so that the rain won't wash it away."

Wallander pointed at Wetterstedt's butchered head.

"How do you explain this?" he asked.

The doctor shrugged.

"The incision in the forehead was made with a sharp knife," he said. "Or maybe a straight razor. The skin and hair seem to have been torn off. I can't tell yet if it was done before or after he received the blow to the spine. That will be a job for the pathologist in Malmö."

"Malmström will have a lot to do," said Wallander.

"Who?"

"Yesterday we sent in the remains of a girl who burned herself to death. And now we're sending over a man who's been scalped. The pathologist I talked to was named Malmström. A woman."

"There's more than one," said the doctor. "I don't know her."

Wallander squatted next to the corpse.

"Give me your interpretation," he said to the doctor. "What do you think happened?"

"Whoever struck him in the back knew what he was doing," said the doctor. "A sharpshooter couldn't have done it any better. But to scalp him! That's the work of a madman."

"Or an Indian," said Wallander pensively.

He got up and felt a twinge in his knees. The days when he could squat without pain were long gone.

"I'm finished here," said the doctor. "I've already told Malmö that we're bringing him in."

Wallander didn't reply. He had discovered a detail in Wetterstedt's clothing that caught his interest. His fly was open.

"Did you touch his clothes?" he asked.

"Just on the back, around the wound to his spine," said the doctor.

Wallander nodded. He could feel the nausea rising.

"Could I ask you one thing?" he said. "Could you check inside Wetterstedt's fly and see if he's still got what's supposed to be in there?"

The doctor gave Wallander a questioning look.

"If someone cut off half his scalp, they might cut off other things too," Wallander explained.

The doctor nodded and pulled on a pair of latex gloves. Then he cautiously stuck his hand in and felt around.

"Everything that's supposed to be there seems to be there," he said when he pulled out his hand.

Wallander nodded.

Wetterstedt's corpse was taken away. Wallander turned to Nyberg, who was kneeling next to the boat, which had been turned right side up.

"How's it going?" asked Wallander.

"I don't know," said Nyberg. "With this rain, everything is washing away."

"We'll still have to dig tomorrow," said Wallander and told him what the doctor said. Nyberg nodded.

"If there's any blood, we'll find it. Any special place you want us to start looking?"

"Around the boat," said Wallander. "Then in the area from the garden gate down to the water."

Nyberg pointed at a case with the lid open. There were plastic bags inside.

"All I found was a box of matches in his pockets," said Nyberg. "You've got the bunch of keys. But the clothes are expensive. Except for the clogs."

"The house seems to be untouched," Wallander said. "But I'd appreciate it if you could take a look at it tonight."

"I can't be in two places at once," Nyberg grumbled. "If we're going to secure any evidence out here, we'll have to do it before it's all washed away by the rain."

Wallander was just about to return to Wetterstedt's house when he noticed that Göran Lindgren was still there. He went over to him. He could see that Lindgren was freezing.

"You can go home now," Wallander said.

"Can I phone my father and tell him about it?"

"Go right ahead."

"So what happened?" Lindgren asked.

"We don't know yet," said Wallander.

There was still a group of onlookers outside the cordon, watching the police work. Some senior citizens, a younger man with a dog, a boy on a moped. With dread Wallander thought about the days that lay ahead. A former minister of justice who had had his spine chopped in half and was scalped too was the sort of juicy tidbit that the newspapers, radio, and television begged for every day. The only positive thing about the situation that he could imagine was that the girl who burned herself to death in Salomonsson's rapeseed field would not wind up on the front page after all.

He had to take a piss. He went down to the water and unbuttoned his fly. Maybe it's that simple, he thought. Gustaf Wetterstedt's fly was open because he was standing taking a piss when he was attacked.

He started to walk back up toward the house, then stopped. He was overlooking something. He went back over to Nyberg.

"Do you know where Svedberg is?" he asked.

"I think he's trying to find some more plastic sheeting and a couple of big tarps. We've got to cover up the sand here so everything doesn't wash away."

"I'll talk to him when he gets back," said Wallander. "Where are Martinsson and Hansson?"

"I think Martinsson went to get something to eat," said Nyberg sourly. "Who the hell has time for food?"

"We can send out to get you something," said Wallander. "Where's Hansson?"

"He was going to inform some of the prosecutors. And I don't want anything."

Wallander walked back to the house. After he hung up his soaked jacket and pulled off his boots he realized he was hungry. Höglund was sitting in Wetterstedt's study going through his desk. Wallander went out to the kitchen and turned on the light. He thought about how they had sat in Salomonsson's kitchen drinking coffee. Now Salomonsson was dead. Compared with the old farmer's kitchen, Wallander now found himself in another world. Shiny copper pans hung on the walls. In the middle of the kitchen was an open grill with a smoke hood attached to an old oven chimney. He opened the refrigerator and took out a piece of cheese and a beer. He found some crisp-bread in one of the stylish cupboards along the walls. He sat down at the kitchen table and ate without thinking about a thing. By the time Svedberg came in the front door he had just finished his meal.

"Nyberg said you wanted to talk to me?"

"How'd it go with the tarps?"

"We're still trying to cover it up as best we can. Martinsson called the weather bureau and asked how long the rain was going to last. It's supposed to keep raining all night. Then we'll have a few hours' break before the next storm arrives. That one's supposed to blow up a real summer gale."

A puddle had formed on the kitchen floor around Svedberg's boots. But Wallander didn't feel like asking him to take them off. They were unlikely to find the secret of Gustaf Wetterstedt's death in his kitchen.

Svedberg sat down and dried off his hair with a handkerchief.

"I vaguely remember that you once told me you were interested in the history of the Indians," Wallander began. "Or am I wrong?"

Svedberg gave him a puzzled look.

"That's right," he said. "I've read a lot about Indians. I never liked watching movies that didn't tell the truth about them. I corresponded with an expert on Indians named Uncas. He won a prize on a TV show once. I think that was before I was born. But he taught me a lot."

"I assume you're wondering why I ask," Wallander went on.

"Actually, no," said Svedberg. "Wetterstedt was scalped, after all."

Wallander looked at him intently.

"Was he?"

"If scalping is an art, then in this case it was done almost perfectly. A cut with a sharp knife across the forehead. Then some cuts up by the temples. To get a firm grip."

"He died from a blow to the spine," Wallander continued. "Just below the shoulders."

Svedberg shrugged.

"Indian warriors struck at the head," he said. "It's hard to hit the spine. You have to hold the axe at an angle. It's particularly hard, of course, if the person you're trying to kill is in motion."

"What if he's standing still?"

"In any case, it's not very Indian-like," said Svedberg. "In fact, it's not at all Indian-like to murder people from the rear. Or to murder anyone at all, for that matter."

Wallander leaned his forehead in one hand.

"Why are you asking about this?" said Svedberg. "It could hardly be an Indian who murdered Wetterstedt."

"Who takes scalps?" said Wallander.

"A madman," said Svedberg. "Anyone who does something like this must be nuts. We'll have to catch him as fast as possible."

"I know," said Wallander.

Svedberg stood up and left. Wallander got a mop and cleaned the floor. Then he went in to see Höglund. It was almost ten-thirty.

"Your father didn't sound too happy," she said when he stood behind her at the desk. "But I think the main thing that was bothering him was that you hadn't called earlier."

"He's right about that," said Wallander. "What have you found?"

"Surprisingly little," she said. "On the surface nothing seems to have been stolen. No cabinets are broken open. I think he must have had a housekeeper to keep this big house clean."

"Why do you say that?"

"Two reasons. First, you can see the difference in the way a man and a woman clean. Don't ask me how. That's just the way it is."

"And the second reason?"

"I found a diary with a note that says 'charwoman' and then a time. The note comes up twice a month."

"Did he really write 'charwoman'?"

"A fine old contemptuous word."

"Can you tell when she was here last?"

"Last Thursday."

"That explains why everything seems so neat and clean."

Wallander sank down into a chair in front of the desk.

"How'd it look down there?" she asked.

"An axe blow through the spine. Dead instantly. The killer cut off his scalp and disappeared."

"Earlier you said you thought there had to be at least two of them."

"I know. But right now all I know is that I don't like this one bit. Why would someone murder an old man who's been living in isolation for twenty years? And why would someone take his scalp?"

They sat in silence. Wallander thought about the burning girl. About the man who had his hair torn off. And about the rain that kept falling. He tried to fend off the disagreeable thoughts by imagining how he and Baiba had once crept down in the hollow behind a dune at Skagen in Denmark. But the girl kept running with her hair on fire. And Wetterstedt lay on a stretcher on the way to Malmö.

He forced the thoughts out of his mind and looked at Höglund.

"Give me a rundown," he said. "What do you think? What happened here? Describe it for me. Don't hold anything back."

"He went out," she said. "A walk down to the beach. To meet someone. Or just to get some exercise. But he was only going for a short walk."

"Why?"

"The clogs. Old and worn out. Uncomfortable. But good enough if you're just going to be out for a short time."

"And then?"

"It happened at night. What did the doctor say about the time?"

"He's not sure yet. Keep going. Why at night?"

"The risk of being seen is too great in the daytime. At this time of year, the beach is never deserted."

"What else?"

"There's no obvious motive. But I think you can tell that the killer had a plan."

"Why?"

"He took time to hide the body."

"Why did he do that?"

"To delay its discovery. So he'd have time to get away."

"But nobody saw him, right? And why do you think it's a man?"

"A woman would never sever someone's spine. A desperate woman might strike her husband in the head with an axe. But she wouldn't scalp him. It's a man."

"What do we know about the killer?"

"Nothing. Unless you know something I don't."

Wallander shook his head.

"You've covered just about all we know," he said. "I think it's time for us to leave the house to Nyberg and his people."

"There's going to be a big commotion about this," she said.

"I know," said Wallander. "It'll start tomorrow. You can be glad you've got your vacation coming up."

"Hansson has already asked me whether I could postpone it," she said. "I said yes."

"You should go home now," Wallander said. "I think I'll tell the others that we'll meet at seven tomorrow morning to plan the investigation."

When Wallander was alone, he went through the house one more time. He knew that they had to form a picture as soon as possible of who Gustaf Wetterstedt was. They knew one of his habits, that every evening at the same time he called his mother. But what about all the habits they didn't know about? Wallander went back to the kitchen and searched for some paper in one of the drawers. Then he made himself a list of things to remember for tomorrow morning's introductory meeting. A few minutes later Nyberg came in. He took off his wet rain gear.

"What do you want us to look for?" he asked.

"A crime scene," Wallander answered. "Which doesn't exist. I want to be able to rule out that he was killed indoors. I want you to go over the house in your usual way."

Nyberg nodded and left the kitchen. Then Wallander heard him reprimanding one of his crew. Wallander thought he ought to drive home and sleep for a few hours. Then he decided to go through the house one more time. He started with the basement. An hour later he was on the top floor. He went into Wetterstedt's large bedroom and opened his wardrobe. He pulled the suits back and searched on the floor. From downstairs he could hear Nyberg's annoyed voice. He was just about to close the doors to the wardrobe when he caught sight of a little case in one corner. He bent down and took it out. He sat down on the edge of the bed and opened it. There was a camera inside. Wallander guessed that it wasn't particularly expensive. He could see that it was more or less the same type as the camera Linda had bought last year and that there was film in it. Seven pictures out of thirty-six were exposed. He put it back in the bag. Then he went downstairs to Nyberg.

"There's a camera in this bag," he said. "I want you to get the photos developed as fast as you can."

It was almost midnight when he left Wetterstedt's villa. It was still pouring outside.

He drove straight home.

When he got to his apartment he sat down at the kitchen table. He wondered what was in those pictures.

The rain pounded against his windows.

All at once he noticed a feeling of dread sneaking up on him.

Something had happened. But now he had a hunch that it was only the beginning of something much bigger.

Chapter Eight

On Thursday morning, the 23rd of June, there was no Midsummer Eve mood in the Ystad police station. Wallander had already been awakened at three in the morning by a reporter from *Dagens Nyheter* in Stockholm who had gotten the tip about Gustaf Wetterstedt's death from the Östermalm police. By the time Wallander finally managed to get back to sleep, *Expressen* called. Hansson had also been awakened during the night. When they gathered in the conference room just after seven, everyone looked haggard and tired. Nyberg also showed up, even though he had been busy going over Wetterstedt's house until five in the morning. On the way into the room Hansson took Wallander aside and told him that he would have to run the whole thing.

"I think Björk knew this would happen," said Hansson. "That's why he retired."

"He didn't retire," said Wallander. "He was promoted. Besides, seeing into the future was definitely not one of his talents. He worried enough about what was happening around him from day to day."

But Wallander knew that the responsibility for organizing the hunt for Wetterstedt's killer would fall to him. Their first big difficulty was the fact that they would be understaffed all summer. He was grateful that Ann-Britt Höglund had been willing to postpone her vacation. But what was going to happen with his own? He had planned to be on the way to Skagen with Baiba in two weeks.

He sat down at the table and looked at the exhausted faces around him. It was still raining outside, though it was starting to clear up. In front of him on the table he had a pile of phone messages that he had picked up at the reception desk. He pushed them aside and tapped on the table with a pencil.

"We have to get started now," he said. "The worst thing that could have happened has happened. We've had a homicide during vacation time. We'll have to organize ourselves as best we can. We also have a Midsummer holiday coming up that will tie up the patrol officers. But something always seems to happen that creates problems for the criminal division. We'll have to plan our search with this in mind."

No one said a word. Wallander turned to Nyberg and asked how the technical investigation was going.

"If only it would stop raining for a few hours," said Nyberg. "If we're going to find the murder site we'll have to dig through the surface layer of the sand. That's almost impossible to do until it's dry. Otherwise we'll just end up with clumps."

"I called the meteorologist at Sturup Airport a while ago," said Martinsson. "He's predicting the rain will stop here in Ystad just after eight. But a new storm will be blowing in this afternoon. And then we'll get more rain. After that it'll clear up."

"It's always something," said Wallander. "Usually it's easier on us if there's bad weather on Midsummer Eve."

"This time it looks like the soccer game will help us out," said Nyberg. "I don't think people will drink as much. They'll be glued to their TVs."

"What'll happen if Sweden loses to Russia?" asked Wallander.

"They won't," Nyberg proclaimed. "We're going to win."

Wallander hadn't realized that Nyberg was a soccer fan.

"I hope you're right," he said.

"Anyway, we haven't found anything of interest near the boat," Nyberg continued. "We also went over the part of the beach between Wetterstedt's yard, the boat, and down to the water. We picked up a number of items. But nothing that would be of any interest to us. With one possible exception."

Nyberg took out one of his plastic bags and placed it on the table.

"One of the officers reeling out the cordon tape found this. It's a spray can. The kind that women are advised to carry in their purses to defend themselves with if they're attacked."

"Aren't those illegal in Sweden?" asked Höglund.

"Yes, they are," said Nyberg. "But there it was, lying there. In the sand just outside the cordon. We're going to check it for prints. Maybe it'll turn up something."

Nyberg put the plastic bag back in his case.

"Can one man turn that boat over by himself?" asked Wallander.

"Not unless he's incredibly strong," said Nyberg.

"That means there were two of them," said Wallander.

"The murderer could have dug out the sand under the boat," said Nyberg hesitantly. "And then pushed it back in after he shoved Wetterstedt underneath."

"There is that possibility, of course," said Wallander. "But does it sound plausible?"

No one at the table said anything.

"There's nothing to indicate that the murder was committed inside the house," Nyberg continued. "We found no traces of blood or other signs of a crime. No one broke into the house either. We can't say whether anything was stolen. But it doesn't seem likely."

"Did you find anything else that seemed extraordinary?" asked Wallander.

"I think the entire house is extraordinary," said Nyberg. "Wetterstedt must have had plenty of money."

They thought for a moment about what Nyberg had said. Wallander saw that it was time for him to sum up.

"The most important thing is to find out when Wetterstedt was murdered," he began. "The doctor who examined the body thought that it probably happened on the beach. He found grains of sand in the mouth and eyes. But we'll have to wait for what the medical examiners have to say. Since we don't have any clues to go on or any obvious motive, we'll have to proceed on a broad front. We have to find out what kind of man Wetterstedt was. Who did he associate with? What sort of habits did he have? We have to draw a map of his character and find out what his life was like. We also can't ignore the fact that twenty years ago he was very famous. He was the minister of justice. He was very popular with some people, and he was hated by others. He was continually surrounded by rumors of various scandals. Could revenge be part of the picture? He was struck down with an axe and had his hair ripped off. He was scalped. Has anything like this happened before? Can we find any similarities with previous murders? Martinsson will have to get his computers going. And Wetterstedt had a housekeeper we'll have to talk to, today."

"What about his political party?" asked Höglund.

Wallander nodded.

"I was just getting to that. Did he have any unresolved political agendas? Did he associate with old party friends? We have to clear this up too. Is there anything in his background that might point to a conceivable motive?"

"Since the news broke, two people have already called in to confess to the murder," said Svedberg. "One of them called from a phone booth in Malmö. He was so drunk it was hard to understand what he said. We asked our colleagues in Malmö to question him. The other one who called was a prisoner at Österåker. His last leave was in February. So it's quite clear that Gustaf Wetterstedt still arouses strong feelings."

"Those of us who have been around for a while know that the police hold a grudge too," said Wallander. "During his tenure as minister of justice, a lot of things happened that none of us can forget. Of all the justice ministers and national police chiefs who have come and gone, Wetterstedt was probably the one who did the least for us."

They went over the various assignments and divided them up. Wallander himself was going to question Wetterstedt's housekeeper. They agreed to meet again at four o'clock.

"We have three items left," said Wallander. "First, we're going to be invaded by photographers and reporters. This is the sort of thing the media love.

We're going to be seeing headlines like 'The Scalp Murderer' and 'The Scalping Murder.' So we might as well hold a news conference today. I would prefer not to have to run it."

"You have to," said Svedberg. "You have to take charge. Even if you don't want to, you're the one who does it best."

"All right, but I don't want to do it alone," said Wallander. "I want Hansson with me. And Ann-Britt. Shall we say one o'clock?"

They were just about to end the meeting when Wallander asked them to wait.

"We can't shut down the investigation of the girl who burned herself to death in the rapeseed field either," he said.

"You think there's some connection?" Hansson asked in astonishment.

"Of course not," said Wallander. "It's just that we still have to try and find out who she was while we're busy working on Wetterstedt."

"We haven't gotten any positive hits on our database search," said Martinsson. "Not even on the combination of letters. But I promise to keep working on it."

"Someone must miss her," said Wallander. "A young girl. I think this is very odd."

"It's summer," said Svedberg. "A lot of young people are on the road. It might take a couple of weeks before someone is missed."

"You're right, of course," Wallander admitted. "We'll have to be patient."

At quarter to eight they broke up. Wallander had run the meeting at a brisk pace since they all had a lot of work ahead of them. When he got to his office he went quickly through his phone messages. There was nothing that seemed urgent. He took a notebook out of a drawer and wrote Gustaf Wetterstedt's name at the top of the page.

Then he leaned back in his chair and closed his eyes. *What does his death tell me? Who would strike him down with an axe and scalp him?*

Wallander leaned over his desk again.

He wrote: *Nothing indicates that Gustaf Wetterstedt was murdered by a burglar, but of course that can't be excluded yet. It wasn't a murder of convenience either, unless it was committed by someone insane. The killer took the time to hide the body. So the revenge motive remains. Who would want to take revenge on Gustaf Wetterstedt and see him dead?*

Wallander put down his pen and read through what he had written, with increasing dissatisfaction.

It's too soon, he thought. I'm drawing impossible conclusions. I have to know more.

He got up and left the room. When he walked out of the police station it had stopped raining. The meteorologist at Sturup Airport was right. Wallander drove straight to Wetterstedt's villa.

The barricades on the beach were still there. Nyberg was already at work. Along with his crew he was busy removing the tarps covering a section of the beach. There were a lot of spectators standing outside the cordon this morning.

Wallander unlocked the front door with Wetterstedt's bunch of keys and then went straight to the study. Methodically he continued the search that Höglund had begun the night before. It took him almost half an hour to find the name of the woman Wetterstedt had called the "charwoman." Her name was Sara Björklund. She lived on Styrbordsgången, which Wallander knew lay just past the big warehouses at the west end of town. He picked up the telephone on the desk and dialed the number. After eight rings someone answered. Wallander heard a harsh male voice.

"I'm looking for Sara Björklund," said Wallander.

"She's not home," said the man.

"Where can I get in touch with her?"

"Who's asking?" said the man evasively.

"Kurt Wallander with the Ystad police."

There was a long silence on the other end.

"Are you still there?" said Wallander, who didn't bother to conceal his impatience.

"Does this have something to do with Wetterstedt?" asked the man. "Sara Björklund is my wife."

"I have to speak with her."

"She's in Malmö. She won't be back till this afternoon."

"When can I get hold of her? What time? Try to be exact!"

"I'm sure she'll be home by five."

"Then I'll come by your house at five," said Wallander and hung up.

He left the house and went down to Nyberg on the beach. There was a crowd packed in behind the cordon.

"Find anything?" he asked.

Nyberg was standing with a bucket of sand in one hand.

"Nothing," he said. "But if he was killed here and fell into the sand, there has to be some blood. Maybe not from his back. But from his head. It must have spurted blood. There are some big veins in the scalp."

Wallander nodded.

"Where did you find the spray can?" he asked.

Nyberg pointed to a spot beyond the cordon.

"I doubt it has anything to do with this," said Wallander.

"Me too," said Nyberg.

Wallander was just about to go back to his car when he remembered that he had one more question for Nyberg.

"The lamp by the gate to the yard is burnt out," he said. "Can you take a look at it?"

"What do you want me to do?" Nyberg wondered. "Should I change the bulb?"

"I just want to know why it's not working," said Wallander. "That's all."

He drove back to the police station. The sky was gray. But it wasn't raining.

"Reporters are calling constantly," said Ebba as he passed the reception desk.

"They're welcome to come to the press conference at one o'clock," said Wallander. "Where's Ann-Britt?"

"She left a while ago. She didn't say where she was going."

"What about Hansson?"

"I think he's in Per Åkeson's office. Should I find him for you?"

"We have to get ready for the press conference. Have someone bring more chairs into the conference room. There are going to be lots of people."

Wallander went to his office and started to prepare what he was going to tell the press. After about half an hour Höglund knocked on the door.

"I drove out to Salomonsson's farm," she said. "I think I figured out where that girl got all the gasoline from."

"Salomonsson had a gasoline supply in his barn?"

She nodded.

"Well, that's solved," said Wallander. "That means that she actually could have walked to that rapeseed field. She wouldn't have had to come by car or bicycle. She could have walked there."

"Could Salomonsson have known her?" she asked.

Wallander thought for a moment before he answered.

"No," he said then. "Salomonsson wasn't lying. He'd never seen her before."

"So the girl walks to the farm from somewhere. She goes into Salomonsson's barn and finds a number of jugs of gasoline. She takes five of them with her out into the rapeseed. Then she sets herself on fire."

"That's about it," said Wallander. "Even if we manage to find out who she was, we'll probably never know the whole story."

They got coffee and discussed what they were going to say at the press conference. It was almost eleven when Hansson joined them.

"I talked to Per Åkeson," he said. "He told me he would contact the national prosecutor."

Wallander looked up from his papers in surprise.

"Why?"

"Gustaf Wetterstedt was an important person. Ten years ago the prime minister of this country was murdered. Now we find a justice minister killed. I assume that he wants to know whether the investigation of this murder should be handled in any special way."

"If he were still justice minister today I could understand it," said Wallander.

"But he was an old retiree who had left his public duties behind a long time ago."

"You'll have to talk to Åkeson yourself," said Hansson. "I'm just telling you what he said."

At one o'clock they took their seats on the little dais at one end of the conference room. They had agreed to keep the meeting with the press as brief as possible. The most important thing was to head off too many wild, unfounded speculations. So they decided to be purposely vague when it came to answering the question of how Wetterstedt had actually been killed. They wouldn't say anything at all about his scalp being sliced off.

The room was full to the bursting point with reporters. Just as Wallander had imagined, the national newspapers had decided instantly that Gustaf Wetterstedt's murder was a major event. Wallander counted cameras from three different TV stations when he looked out over the crowd.

Afterwards, when it was all over and the last reporter had left, Wallander thought the whole thing had gone unusually well. They were as terse as possible with their answers, always citing investigative reasons for limiting greater candor or wealth of detail. Finally the reporters realized they weren't going to break through the invisible wall that Wallander had erected around himself and his colleagues. When the reporters had left the room, he allowed himself to be interviewed by the local radio station while Höglund stood in front of one of the TV cameras. He looked at her and felt glad that for once he didn't have to be the one on camera.

At the end of the press conference Per Åkeson had slipped into the room unnoticed and stood at the back of the room. Now he stood waiting for Wallander to emerge.

"I heard you were going to call up the national prosecutor," said Wallander. "Did he give you any directives?"

"He wants to be kept informed," replied Åkeson. "The same way you keep me informed."

"You'll get a summary every day," said Wallander. "And whenever we make any breakthroughs in the case."

"You don't have anything conclusive yet?"

"Not a thing."

The investigative group had a quick meeting at four o'clock. Wallander knew that this was the time for work, not reports. He went once around the table before he asked everyone to go back to what they were doing. They decided to meet again at eight o'clock the next morning if nothing happened that dramatically affected the investigative work.

Just before five o'clock Wallander left the police station and drove out to Styrbordsgången, where Sara Björklund lived. It was a part of town that Wallander almost never visited. He parked the car and went in through the garden gate. The door was opened before he reached the house. The woman standing there was younger than he had imagined. He guessed her age to be around thirty. And to Gustaf Wetterstedt she had been a charwoman. He wondered fleetingly whether she knew what Wetterstedt had called her.

"Good afternoon," said Wallander. "I called earlier today. Are you Sara Björklund?"

"I recognize you," she said, nodding.

She invited him in. In the living room she had set out a tray of buns and coffee in a thermos. Wallander could hear a man upstairs scolding some children for making a racket. Wallander sat down in a chair and looked around. It was as if he expected one of his father's paintings to be hanging on the wall. That's all that's missing, he thought. Here's the old fisherman, the gypsy woman, and the crying child. My father's landscape is the only thing missing. With or without the grouse.

"Would you like coffee, sir?" she asked.

"No need to call me sir," said Wallander. "Yes, please."

"You had to be formal with Gustaf Wetterstedt," she said suddenly. "You had to call him Mr. Wetterstedt. He gave strict instructions about that when I started working there."

Wallander was thankful to be able to start talking right away about what was important. He took a little note pad and a pen out of his pocket.

"So you know that Gustaf Wetterstedt has been murdered," he began.

"It's just terrible," she said. "Who could have done it?"

"We're wondering the same thing," said Wallander.

"Was he really lying on the beach? Under that ugly boat? The one you could see from the top floor?"

"Yes, he was," said Wallander. "But let's begin at the beginning. You cleaned house for Gustaf Wetterstedt?"

"Yes."

"How long have you been with him?"

"Almost three years. I was unemployed. This house costs money. I was forced to start doing cleaning work. I found the job in a classified ad in the paper."

"How often did you go to his house?"

"Twice a month. Every other Thursday."

Wallander made a note.

"Always on Thursdays?"

"Always."

"Did you have your own keys?"

"No. He never would have given them to me."

"Why do you say that?"

"When I was in his house he watched every step I took. It was incredibly nerve-wracking. But he paid well."

"You never noticed anything special?"

"What would that be?"

"There was never anyone else there?"

"No, never."

"He didn't have any guests to dinner?"

"Not that I know of. There were never any dishes waiting for me when I came."

Wallander thought for a moment before he continued.

"How would you describe him as a person?"

Her reply was swift and firm.

"He was the type you'd call stuck-up."

"What do you mean by that?"

"He patronized me. To him I was nothing more than an insignificant clean-ing woman. Despite the fact that he once belonged to the party that suppos-edly represented our cause. The cleaning women's cause."

"Did you know that he called you a charwoman in his diary?"

"That doesn't surprise me in the least."

"But you stayed on with him?"

"I already told you, he paid well."

"Try to remember your last visit. You were there last week?"

"Everything was the same as usual. I've tried to remember. But he was just the way he always was."

"Over the past three years, then, nothing out of the ordinary happened?"

He noticed at once that she hesitated before she answered. He was imme-diately on the alert.

"There was one time last year," she began tentatively. "In November. I don't know why, but I forgot what day it was. I went there on a Friday morning instead of Thursday. Just then a big black car pulled out of the garage. The kind with windows you can't see through. Then I rang the bell at the front door as I always do. It took a long time before he came to open the door. When he laid eyes on me he was furious. He slammed the door. I thought I was going to get the sack. But when I came back the next time he didn't say a thing. He completely ignored what had happened."

Wallander waited for her to go on.

"Was that all?"

"Yes."

"A big black car leaving his house?"

"That's right."

Wallander knew that he wouldn't get any farther. He quickly finished his coffee and stood up.

"If you remember anything else, I'd appreciate it if you'd call me," he said as he left.

He drove back toward town.

A big black car visiting Wetterstedt's house, he thought. Who was in the car?

It was six o'clock. A strong wind had started blowing.

At the same time it began to rain again.

Chapter Nine

By the time Wallander returned to Wetterstedt's house, Nyberg and his crew had moved indoors. They had carted off tons of sand without finding the crime site they were looking for. When it started raining again, Nyberg immediately decided to lay out the tarps. They would be forced to wait until the weather improved. Wallander returned to the house feeling that what Sara Björklund had said about showing up on the wrong day and the big black car meant they had knocked a small hole in Wetterstedt's impenetrable shell. She had seen something that no one was supposed to see. Wallander couldn't interpret Wetterstedt's rage in any other way, or the fact that he didn't fire her afterwards and never even mentioned the incident. The anger and the silence were two sides of the same temperament.

Nyberg was sitting on a chair in Wetterstedt's living room drinking coffee. Wallander thought Nyberg's thermos looked very old. It reminded him of the fifties. Nyberg was sitting on a newspaper to protect the chair cushion.

"We haven't found the murder site yet," said Nyberg. "And now there's no point in looking because of the rain."

"I hope you've secured the tarps," Wallander said. "It's blowing harder all the time."

"They're not going anywhere," said Nyberg.

"I thought I'd finish going through his desk," said Wallander.

"Hansson called. He spoke with Wetterstedt's children."

"It took him this long?" said Wallander. "I thought he'd done that a while ago."

"I don't know anything about it," said Nyberg. "I'm just telling you what he said."

Wallander went into the study and sat down at the desk. He adjusted the lamp so that it cast its light in as big a circle as possible. Then he pulled out one of the drawers in the left-hand cabinet. There lay a copy of this year's tax return. Wallander picked it up and placed it before him on the desk. He could see that

Wetterstedt had declared an income of almost one million kronor. When he went through the return he saw that the income came primarily from Wetterstedt's own private pension plan and stock dividends. In a summary from the Securities Register Center, Wallander could see that Wetterstedt held shares in traditional Swedish heavy industry. He had invested in Ericsson, Asea Brown Boveri, Volvo, and Rottneros. Apart from this income, Wetterstedt had reported an honorarium from the foreign ministry and royalties from Tidens publishing company. Under the entry "Net Worth" he had declared five million kronor. Wallander memorized this figure.

He put the tax return back and pulled out the next drawer. It contained something that looked like a photo album. Here come the family pictures Ann-Britt was missing, he thought. He placed the album on the desk and opened it. With growing astonishment he leafed through the pages. The album was full of old-fashioned pornographic pictures. Some of them were quite sophisticated. Wallander noticed that some of the pages fell open more easily than others. Wetterstedt had a preference for the pages with young models. Suddenly he heard the front door close. Martinsson walked in. Wallander nodded and pointed to the open album.

"Some people collect stamps," said Martinsson, "others evidently collect pictures like this."

Wallander closed the album and put it back in the desk drawer.

"A lawyer named Sjögren called from Malmö," said Martinsson. "He said he had Gustaf Wetterstedt's will. There are rather large assets in the estate. I asked him whether there were any unexpected beneficiaries. But everything goes to the direct heirs. Wetterstedt had also set up a foundation to distribute scholarships to young law students. But he put the money into it long ago and paid tax on it."

"So, we know that much," said Wallander. "Gustaf Wetterstedt was a wealthy man. But wasn't he born the son of a poor longshoreman?"

"Svedberg is working on his history," said Martinsson. "I heard he located an old party secretary with a good memory who had a lot to say about Wetterstedt. But I came here to talk about the girl who committed suicide in Salomonsson's field."

"Did you find out who she was?"

"No. But through the computer I've found more than two thousand possibilities for what the letter combination might mean. It was a pretty long printout."

Wallander thought for a moment. What should they do now?

"We'll have to put it out on Interpol," he said. "And what's the new one called? Europol?"

"That's right."

"Send out a query with her description. Tomorrow we'll have to take a photo of the necklace. The Madonna medallion. Even if everything else is getting pushed aside in the wake of Wetterstedt's death, we have to try and get that picture in the papers."

"I had a jeweler look at the medallion," said Martinsson. "He said it was solid gold."

"Somebody must be missing her," said Wallander. "It's pretty rare for someone to have no relatives at all."

Martinsson yawned and asked whether Wallander needed any help.

"Not tonight," he said.

Martinsson left the house. Wallander continued going through the desk for another hour. Then he turned off the lamp and sat there in the dark. Who was Gustaf Wetterstedt? he thought. The picture I have of him is still pretty vague.

An idea came to him. He went out to the living room and looked up a name in the telephone book. It was not yet nine o'clock. He dialed the number and got an answer almost at once. He identified himself and asked whether he could drop by. Then he hung up. He found Nyberg upstairs and told him he'd be back later that evening.

The wind was blowing hard and the rain pelted him in the face when he left the house. He ran to his car so he wouldn't get completely soaked. Then he drove into town and stopped outside an apartment house near Österport School.

He rang the bell and the door was opened. When he reached the third floor Lars Magnusson was standing there waiting for him in his stocking feet. He could hear beautiful piano music coming from the apartment.

"Long time no see," said Lars Magnusson as he shook hands with Wallander.

"You're right," said Wallander. "It must be more than five years ago we saw each other last."

A long time ago Lars Magnusson had been a journalist. After a number of years at *Expressen* he had gotten tired of the big city and returned to Ystad where he was born. He and Wallander met when their wives became friends. The two men discovered that they shared an interest in opera. It wasn't until many years later, after he and Mona had divorced, that Wallander found out Lars Magnusson was a confirmed alcoholic. But when the truth finally did come out, it came with a vengeance. By chance, Wallander had been at the police station late one night when a patrol dragged in Lars Magnusson. He was so drunk he couldn't stand up straight. He had been driving his car in that condition, and he lost control and went straight through the plate-glass window of a bank. He was later sentenced to six months in jail.

When he returned to Ystad he didn't go back to the newspaper. By that time his wife had also given up on their childless marriage. He continued drinking but managed not to step too far over the line after that. After he gave up his career in journalism, he made a living thinking up chess problems for various newspapers. The only reason he hadn't drunk himself to death yet was that every day he forced himself to hold off on that first drink until he had created at least one chess problem. Now that he had a fax machine, he didn't even have to go to the post office anymore. He could send his problems straight from home.

Wallander walked into his simple apartment. He could tell by the smell that Magnusson had been drinking. On the coffee table stood a bottle of vodka. But Wallander didn't see a glass.

Lars Magnusson was a good many years older than Wallander. He had a mane of gray hair falling over his dirty shirt collar. His face was red and swollen. But Wallander saw that his eyes were curiously clear. No one had ever had reason to doubt Magnusson's intelligence. Rumor had it that he'd once had a book of poetry accepted by Bonniers, but that he had withdrawn it at the last minute and repaid the small advance he had managed to obtain.

"This is an unexpected visit," said Magnusson. "Have a seat. What can I get you?"

"Nothing, thanks," said Wallander and made himself comfortable on a sofa after moving a pile of newspapers.

Magnusson casually took a swig from the bottle of vodka and sat down across from Wallander. He had turned down the piano music.

"It's been a long time," said Wallander. "I'm trying to remember when it was."

"At the state liquor store," Magnusson replied quickly. "Almost exactly five years ago. You were buying wine and I was buying everything else."

Wallander nodded. He remembered now.

"There's nothing wrong with your memory," he said.

"I haven't drunk *that* to death yet," said Magnusson. "I'm saving it for last."

"Have you ever considered quitting?"

"Every day. But I assume you didn't come here to convince me to go on the wagon."

"You've probably read in the papers that Gustaf Wetterstedt was murdered, haven't you?"

"I saw it on the tube."

"I seem to remember vaguely that you once told me something about him. About the scandals surrounding him that were always hushed up."

"And that was the biggest scandal of them all," Magnusson interrupted him.

"I'm trying to get a handle on who he was," Wallander went on. "I thought you might be able to help me."

"The question is whether you want to hear the unconfirmed rumors or whether you want to know the truth," said Magnusson. "I'm not sure I can tell them apart."

"Rumors don't usually get started for no reason," said Wallander.

Lars Magnusson pushed away the vodka bottle as though he suddenly decided it was too close to him.

"I started as a fifteen-year-old intern at one of the Stockholm newspapers," he said. "That was in the spring of 1955. There was an old night editor there named Ture Svanberg. He was almost as big a drunk as I am now. But he paid meticulous attention to his work. And he was a genius at writing headlines that sold papers. He wouldn't stand for anything sloppily written. I can still recall how one time he flew into such a rage over a slipshod story that he tore up the manuscript and ate the pieces. He chewed up the paper and swallowed it. Then he said: 'This isn't worth coming out as anything but shit.' It was Ture Svanberg who taught me to be a journalist. He used to say that there were two kinds of newspaper reporters. 'The first kind digs in the ground for the truth. He stands down in the hole shoveling out dirt. But up on top there's another guy, shoveling the dirt back in. He's the second kind. There's always a duel going on between these two. The fourth estate's test of strength for dominance, which never ends. You've got some journalists who want to expose and reveal things. You've got other journalists who run errands for those in power and help conceal what's really happening.' And that's how it really was. I learned it fast, even though I was only fifteen years old. Men in power always ally themselves with sym bolic cleaning companies and funeral parlors. There are plenty of journalists who won't hesitate to sell their souls to run errands for them. To shovel the dirt back into the hole. Cover up the scandals. Pile on the semblance of truth, guarantee the illusion of the squeaky-clean society."

With a grimace he grabbed the bottle again and took a swig. Wallander noticed that he was putting on weight around the middle.

"Gustaf Wetterstedt," he said. "So what was it that actually happened?"

Magnusson fished a crumpled pack of cigarettes out of his shirt pocket. He lit a cigarette and blew out a cloud of smoke.

"Whores and art," he said. "For years it was common knowledge that the good Gustaf had a girl delivered to the apartment building in Vasastan every week, where he kept a small apartment his wife didn't know about. He had a personal officer who took care of the whole thing. I heard rumors back then that this man was hooked on morphine, supplied by Wetterstedt. He had a lot of doctor friends. The fact that he went to bed with whores was nothing the newspapers cared to bother with. He was neither the first nor the last Swedish minister to do that. An interesting question would be whether we're talking about the rule or the exception. Sometimes I wonder. But one day it went too far. One of the hookers got her courage up and reported him to the police for assault."

"When was that?" Wallander interrupted.

"In the mid-sixties. Her complaint said he'd beaten her with a leather belt and cut the soles of her feet with a razor. It was probably the part about the razor and her feet that made all hell break loose. The perversion had suddenly started to get interesting and newsworthy. The only problem now was that the police had lodged a complaint against the highest defender of Swedish law and order, next to the king. So the whole thing was hushed up. The police report disappeared."

"Disappeared?"

"It literally went up in smoke."

"But the girl who reported him? What happened to her?"

"She suddenly became the proprietor of a lucrative boutique in Västerås."
Wallander shook his head.

"How do you know all this?"

"I knew a journalist back then named Sten Lundberg. He decided to dig around in the whole mess. But when rumors started going around that he was about to snoop his way to the truth, he was frozen out, blacklisted."

"And he accepted it?"

"He had no choice. Unfortunately he had a weakness that couldn't be covered up. He gambled. Had huge debts. There was a rumor that those gambling debts suddenly went poof. The same way the hooker's assault report did. So everything was back to square one. And Gustaf Wetterstedt continued sending his morphine addict out after girls."

"You said there was one more thing," Wallander said.

"There was a rumor that he was mixed up in some of those art thefts perpetrated in Sweden during his term as justice minister. Paintings that were never found again, and which now hang on the walls of collectors who have no intention of showing them to the public. The police arrested a fence once, a middleman. By mistake, unfortunately. And he swore that Wetterstedt was involved. But of course it could never be proven. It was buried. There were more people filling up the hole than there were people standing down in it and tossing the dirt out."

"You don't paint a pretty picture," said Wallander.

"Remember what I asked you? Do you want the truth or the rumors? Because the rumor about Gustaf Wetterstedt was that he was a talented politician, a loyal party member, an amiable human being. Educated and competent. That's how his obituary will read. As long as none of the girls he whipped decide to start yelling about what they know."

"What happened when he left office?" asked Wallander.

"I don't think he got along so well with some of the younger ministers. Especially the female ones. There was a big change of generations in those days. I think he realized that his time was over. Mine was too. I quit being a journalist. After he came to Ystad I never wasted a thought on him. Until now."

"Can you think of anyone who would be prepared to kill him, so many years later?"

Lars Magnusson shrugged his shoulders.

"That's impossible to answer."

Wallander had just one question left.

"Can you recall whether you've ever heard of a murder in this country where the victim was scalped?"

Magnusson's eyes narrowed. He looked at Wallander with a sudden, alert interest.

"Was he scalped? They didn't say that on TV. They would have, if they knew about it."

"Just between the two of us," Wallander said, looking at Magnusson, who nodded assent.

"We didn't want to release it just yet," he went on. "We can always say we can't reveal it for so-called 'investigative reasons.' The all-inclusive excuse the police have for presenting half-truths. But this time it's actually true."

"I believe you," said Magnusson. "Or I don't believe you. It doesn't really matter, since I'm no longer a journalist. But I can't recall any murderer who scalped people. That would have made a great headline. Ture Svanberg would have loved it. Can you manage to avoid leaks?"

"I don't know," Wallander answered frankly. "Unfortunately I've had a number of bad experiences."

"I won't sell the story," said Magnusson.

Then he accompanied Wallander to the door.

"How the hell can you stand being a cop?" he asked after Wallander had already stepped out the door.

"I don't know," he said. "I'll let you know when I figure it out."

The storm had grown stronger. The wind gusts were up to gale force. Wallander drove back to Wetterstedt's house. Some of Nyberg's men were busy taking fingerprints upstairs. Looking out the balcony window, Wallander discovered Nyberg up on a wobbly ladder leaning on the light pole by the garden gate. He had to hold on tight to the pole so that the wind wouldn't blow the ladder over. Wallander decided to go and help him when he saw that Nyberg was ready to climb down. He met him coming in the entryway.

"That could have waited," said Wallander. "You could have been blown off the ladder."

"If I fell off I might have hurt myself," Nyberg said sullenly. "And of course checking the lamp could have waited. It might have been forgotten and never done. But since you were the one who wondered about it, and I have a certain respect for your ability to do your job, I decided to look at the lamp. But I can promise you it was only because you were the one who asked me."

Wallander was surprised by Nyberg's admission. But he tried not to show it.

"What did you find?" he asked instead.

"The bulb wasn't burnt out," said Nyberg. "It was unscrewed."

Wallander swiftly thought about what this might mean. Then he made a quick decision.

"Hold on a minute," he said, and went into the living room to call Sara Björklund. She picked up the phone herself.

"Excuse me for disturbing you so late at night," he began. "But I have an urgent question. Who changed the light bulbs in Wetterstedt's house?"

"He did it himself."

"Outdoors too?"

"I think so. He took care of the garden himself. I was probably the only one who set foot inside his house."

Except for the ones in the black car, thought Wallander.

"There's a lamp by the garden gate," he continued. "Was it usually turned on?"

"In the winter, when it was dark, he always kept it lit."

"That's all I wanted to know," said Wallander. "Thanks for your help."

"Can you manage to climb up the ladder one more time?" he asked Nyberg when he came back to the entryway. "I'd like you to screw in a new bulb."

"The spare bulbs are in the room inside the garage," said Nyberg and started to pull on his boots.

They went back out into the storm. Wallander held the ladder while Nyberg climbed up and screwed in the bulb. It went on at once. Nyberg put on the outer fixture and climbed back down the ladder. They walked out onto the beach.

"There's a big difference," said Wallander. "It's light all the way down to the water."

"Tell me what you're thinking," said Nyberg.

"I think the place where he was murdered is somewhere within the circle of light from the lamp," said Wallander. "If we're lucky maybe we can get fingerprints from the inside of the globe."

"So you think the murderer planned the whole thing? Unscrewed the bulb because it was too bright?"

"Yes," said Wallander, "that's pretty much what I'm thinking."

Nyberg went back into the garden with the ladder. Wallander stayed behind and felt the rain whipping against his face.

The cordons were still there. A police car was parked just above the outermost sand dunes. Except for a man on a moped there were no onlookers left.

Wallander turned around and went back inside the house.

Chapter Ten

He stepped into the basement just after seven in the morning. The floor was cool under his bare feet. He stood still and listened. Then he closed the door behind him and locked it. He squatted to inspect the thin layer of flour he had strewn over the floor the last time he was here. But no one had intruded into his world. There were no footprints in the dust on the floor. Then he checked the rat traps. He had been lucky. He had a catch in all four cages. One of the cages held the biggest rat he had ever seen.

Once, toward the end of his life, Geronimo told the story of the Pawnee warrior he had vanquished in his youth. His name was Bear with Six Claws, since he had six fingers on his left hand. That had been his first enemy. Geronimo came close to dying that time, even though he was very young. He cut off his enemy's sixth finger and left it in the sun to dry. Then he carried it in a little leather pouch on his belt for many years.

He decided to try out one of his axes on the big rat. On the small ones he would test what effect the can of Mace actually had.

But that would be much later. First he had to undergo the big transformation. He sat down before the mirrors, adjusted the light so that there was no glare, and then gazed at his face. On his left cheek he had made a small cut. The wound had already healed. It was the first step in his final transformation.

The blow had been perfect. It had been like chopping down a tree when he cut into the spine of the first monster. Within himself he had heard jubilation from the spirit world. He had flopped the monster over on his back and cut off his scalp, without hesitation. Now it lay where it belonged, buried in the earth, with one tuft of hair sticking up from the ground.

Soon another scalp would join it.

He looked at his face and considered whether he ought to make the second cut next to the first one. Or should he let the knife consecrate the other cheek? It really made no difference. When he was finished, his whole face would be full of cuts.

Scrupulously he started to prepare himself. From his knapsack he pulled out his weapons, paints, and brushes. Last of all he took out the red book in which the Revelations and the Mission were written. He placed it carefully on the table between himself and the mirrors.

It was last night when he buried the first scalp. There was a guard by the hospital grounds. But he knew about the place where the fence had fallen over. The locked-ward building, where there were bars on the windows and doors, was located by itself on the outskirts of the large, parklike grounds. When he had visited his sister he had figured out which window was hers. It was dark. A faint light from the corridor was all that escaped from the ponderous, menacing building. He had buried the scalp and whispered to his sister that he had taken the first step. He would destroy the monsters, one by one. Then she would be able to come out into the world again.

He pulled off his shirt. Even though it was summer, he shivered in the cold that lingered in the basement. He opened the red book and turned past what was written about the man named Wetterstedt, who no longer existed. It was on page seven that the second scalp was described. He read what his sister had written and thought that this time he would use the smallest axe.

He closed the book and looked at his face in the mirror. His face was the same shape as his mother's. But he had inherited his father's eyes. They were set deep, like two retracted cannon muzzles. Because of these eyes, he might have felt sorry that his father would have to be sacrificed too. But that was the only reason, and it was a hint of doubt that he could easily conquer. Those eyes were his first childhood memory. They had stared at him, they had threatened him, and ever since then he couldn't see his father as anything but a pair of enormous eyes with arms and legs and a bellowing voice.

He wiped off his face with a towel. Then he dipped one of the wide brushes into the black paint and drew the first line across his brow, precisely where the knife had cut open the skin on Wetterstedt's forehead.

He had spent many hours outside the police cordon. It was exciting to see all these policemen expending their energy trying to figure out what happened and who had killed the man lying underneath the rowboat. On several occasions he had felt a compulsion to call out that he was the one.

It was a weakness that he still hadn't completely mastered. What he was doing, the mission he had undertaken from his sister's book of revelations, was for her sake alone, not his. He had to conquer this weakness.

He drew the second line across his face. Even though the transformation had barely begun, he could already feel large parts of his outer identity starting to leave him.

He didn't know why he had been named Stefan. On one occasion, when his mother had been more or less sober, he had asked her. Why Stefan? Why that name and not something else? Her reply had been very vague. It's a fine name, she said. He remembered that. A fine name. A name that was popular. He would be spared from having a name that was different. He still remembered how upset he had been. He left her lying there on the sofa in their living room and stomped out of the house. Then he rode his bike down to the sea.

He walked along the beach and chose a different name for himself. He chose Hoover. For the head of the FBI. He had read a book about him. It was rumored that he had a drop of Indian blood in his veins. He wondered whether there had been Indians in his own bloodline too. His grandfather had told him that many of their relatives emigrated to America a long time ago. Maybe one of them had taken up with an Indian. Even if the blood didn't run through his own veins, it might be in the family.

It wasn't until his sister had been locked up in the hospital that he decided to merge Geronimo and Hoover. He reminded himself how his grandfather once showed him how to melt pewter and pour it into plaster molds to make miniature soldiers. He had found the molds and the pewter ladle when his grandfather died. They were in a cardboard box in the basement. He took them out and changed the mold so that the molten pewter would make a figure that was both a policeman and an Indian. Late one evening when everyone was asleep and his father was in jail, so he couldn't come storming into their apartment at any time of the day or night, he locked himself in the kitchen and carried out the great ceremony. By melting Hoover and Geronimo together he created his own new identity. He was a feared policeman with the courage of an Indian warrior. He would be invulnerable. Nothing would prevent him from wreaking the required vengeance.

He continued drawing the curved black lines above his eyes. They made his eyes sink even deeper into their sockets. They lurked there like beasts of prey. Two predators, watching. He carefully went over what awaited him. It was Midsummer Eve. The fact that it was rainy and windy would make the task more difficult. But it wouldn't stop him. He thought he would have to dress warmly before the trip to Bjäresjö. The question he couldn't answer was whether the party he was going to visit had been moved indoors because of the weather. But he convinced himself that he had to trust his ability to wait. This was a virtue Hoover had always preached to his recruits. Just like Geronimo. There would always be a moment when the enemy's alertness began to flag. That's when he had to strike. The same would be true if the party was moved indoors. Sooner or later the man he had come to visit would have to leave the house. Then it would be time.

He had been there the day before. He left his moped in a grove of trees and made his way to the top of a hill where he could watch undisturbed. Arne Carlman's house lay all alone, just like Wetterstedt's. There were no neighbors anywhere nearby. An avenue of sheared willows led up to the old whitewashed Scanian farm.

Preparations for the Midsummer festivities had already begun. He saw people unloading bunches of folding tables and stackable chairs from a flatbed truck. In one corner of the yard they were busy putting up a serving tent.

Arne Carlman was there too. In his binoculars he could see the man he would visit the next day walking around in the yard and directing the work.

He was dressed in a jogging suit. He had a beret pulled over his head.

He couldn't help thinking of his sister being with this man, and nausea overwhelmed him at once. Then he didn't need to see any more. He knew what his plan would be.

When he was finished painting his forehead and the shadows around his eyes, he drew two heavy white lines down each side of his nose. He could already feel Geronimo's heart pounding in his chest. He bent down and started the tape player on the basement floor. The drums were very loud. The spirits started talking inside him.

He didn't finish until late afternoon. He selected the weapons he would take with him. Then he released the four rats into a large box. In vain they tried to scramble up the walls. He aimed the axe he wanted to try at the biggest of the fat rats. The blow split the rat in two. It was so fast that the rat didn't even have time to squeak. The other rats started scratching at the walls to escape. He went to the hook on the wall where his leather jacket was hanging. He put one hand in the inside pocket to take out the spray can. But it was gone. He felt in the other pockets. He couldn't find it anywhere. For a moment he stood frozen. Had someone been here after all? He decided that was impossible.

To collect his thoughts, he sat down in front of the mirrors again. The spray can must have fallen out of his jacket pocket. Slowly and methodically he went over the days that had passed since he had visited Gustaf Wetterstedt. Then he understood how it had happened. He must have dropped the can when he was watching the police from outside the cordon. At one point he took off his jacket so he could put on a sweater. That's how it must have happened. He decided that it presented no danger. Anyone could have dropped a spray can. Even if his fingerprints were on it, the police didn't have them on file. FBI chief Hoover would have been helpless if he tried to trace that spray can.

He got up from his place in front of the mirrors and returned to the rats in the box. When they caught sight of him they began rushing back and forth between the walls. With three blows of his axe he killed them all. Then he dumped the bloody rat bodies into a plastic bag, tied it carefully, and put it inside yet another plastic bag. He wiped off the edge of the axe and then felt it with his fingertips.

By a little past six in the evening he was ready. He had stuffed the weapons and the bag of rat corpses into his knapsack. Since it was raining and windy outside, he put on socks and running shoes. Earlier he had filed off the pattern on the bottom of the shoes. He turned off the light and left the basement. Before he went out on the street he pulled his helmet over his head.

Just past the turnoff to Sturup he turned into a parking lot and stuffed the plastic bag of rat bodies into a garbage can. Then he continued on toward Bjäresjö. The wind had died down. There had been a sudden change in the weather. The evening would be warm.

Midsummer Eve was one of art dealer Arne Carlman's biggest occasions of the year. For more than fifteen years it had been a tradition for him to invite his friends to a party he held at the Scanian farm where he lived in the summertime. In a certain circle of artists and gallery owners it was important to be invited to Carlman's summer party. He had a decisive influence on everyone who bought and sold art in Sweden. He could grant fame and fortune to any artist he decided to promote. He could topple others who didn't follow his advice or do as he said. More than thirty years ago he had traveled all over the country in an old car as an art peddler. Those were lean years. But it taught him what kind of pictures he could sell to specific types of customers. He had learned the business, and once and for all divested himself of the notion that art was something elevated above the reality controlled by money. He had saved up enough to open a combined frame shop and gallery on Österlånggatan in Stockholm. With a ruthless mixture of flattery, alcohol, and crisp banknotes he bought up paintings from young artists and then built up their reputations. He bribed, threatened, and lied his way to the top. In ten years he owned thirty galleries all over Sweden. He had also started selling art by mail order. By the mid-seventies he was a wealthy man. He bought the farm in Skåne and began holding his summer parties a few years later. They were events that had become famous far and wide for their boundless extravagance. Each guest could expect a present that cost no less than five thousand kronor. This year he had had a limited number of fountain pens made specially by an Italian designer.

When Arne Carlman woke up beside his wife early on the morning of Midsummer Eve, he went to the window and gazed out over a landscape weighed down by rain and wind. A cloud of vexed irritation passed quickly across his face. But he had learned to accept the inevitable. He had no power over the weather. Five years before he had had a special collection of rainwear designed, which was available to guests when they arrived. Those who wanted to be out in the garden could do so, and those who preferred to be inside could stay in the old barn, which he had converted into a huge open space many years before.

The guests began arriving around eight o'clock in the evening. The persistent rain had stopped. What had promised to be a wet, nasty Midsummer Eve had been suddenly transformed into a beautiful summer evening. Arne Carlman showed up in a tuxedo, and one of his sons followed him holding an umbrella. He always invited one hundred people, of which half had to be first-time guests. Just after ten o'clock he clinked on his glass and gave his traditional summer speech. He did so in the knowledge that at least half of those present hated or despised him. But now, at the age of sixty-six, he had stopped worrying about what people thought. His solid empire could speak for itself. Two of his sons were prepared to take over the business when he could no longer run it. But he wasn't ready to retire yet. This is what he said in his speech, which was devoted solely to himself. They couldn't count him out yet. They could still look forward to a number of Midsummer parties at which the weather, he hoped, would be better than this year. His words were met with halfhearted applause. Then an orchestra started playing inside the barn. Most of the guests made their way indoors. Arne Carlman led off the dancing with his wife.

"What did you think of my little speech?" he asked her as they danced.

"You've never been more spiteful than you were this year," she replied.

"Let them hate me," he said. "What do I care? What do *we* care? I still have a lot of things to do."

Just before midnight, Arne Carlman strolled with a young woman artist from Göteborg to an isolated arbor at the edge of the huge garden. One of the talent scouts on his payroll had advised him to invite her to his summer party. He had seen a number of color slides of her paintings and realized at once that she had something original. It was a new type of idyllic painting. Cold suburbs, stone deserts, lonely people, surrounded by Elysian fields of flowers. He already knew he was going to promote the woman as the leading exponent of a new school of painting, which could be called New Illusionism. She was very young, he thought as they walked toward the arbor. But she was neither beautiful nor mysterious. Arne Carlman had learned that just as important as the painting was the image presented by the artist. He wondered what he was going to do with this skinny, pale young woman.

The grass was still wet. It was a magnificent evening. The dance was still in full swing. But many of the guests had started gathering around the television sets at Carlman's farm. The broadcast of Sweden's soccer match against Russia would be starting in about half an hour. He wanted to finish his conversation with her so that he could watch the match too. He had a contract in his pocket.

It would provide her with a large cash sum in exchange for giving him the exclusive right to sell her work for three years. On the surface it seemed a very advantageous contract. The fine print, however, which was impossible to read in the pale light of the summer night, granted him a large number of other rights to her future paintings. When they entered the arbor he wiped off two chairs with a handkerchief and asked her to have a seat. It took him less than half an hour to convince her to sign the contract. Then he handed her one of the pens designed by the Italian and she signed.

She left the arbor and went back to the barn. Later she would claim with absolute certainty that it had been exactly three minutes to midnight. For some reason she had glanced at her watch as she walked along the gravel path up toward the house. With equal conviction she swore that Arne Carlman had been the same as always when she left him. He had given no impression that he was uneasy. Nor that he was waiting for anyone. He had merely said that he was going to sit there for a few minutes and enjoy the fresh air after the rain.

She never turned around. But she was still positive that there was no one else in the garden. And she hadn't seen anyone heading toward the arbor either.

Hoover had been hiding on top of the hill all evening long. The dampness from the ground made him feel cold even though it had stopped raining. Now and then he got up to shake some life into his frozen limbs. Just after eleven he had seen in his binoculars that the moment was approaching. There were fewer and fewer people out in the garden. He took out his weapons and stuck them in his belt. He also took off his shoes and socks and put them in his knapsack. Then, crouching, he carefully slipped down the hill and ran along a tractor path in the cover of a rapeseed field. He had reached the back end of the property, where he sank onto the wet ground. Through the hedge he had a view of the garden.

Scarcely an hour later his wait was over. Arne Carlman came walking straight toward him. He was accompanied by a young woman. They sat down in the arbor. Hoover had a hard time hearing what they were talking about. After about half an hour the woman got up, but Arne Carlman remained seated. The garden was deserted. No more music was coming from the barn; instead he could hear the sound of several loud television sets. Hoover got up, drew his axe, and squeezed through the hedge right behind the arbor. One last time he hastily checked to see that no one was in the garden. Then all doubt vanished, and his sister's revelations exhorted him to carry out his task. He rushed into the arbor and buried the axe deep in Arne Carlman's face. The powerful blow split his skull all the way to his upper jaw. He was still sitting on the bench, with the two halves of his face pointing in opposite directions. Hoover pulled out his knife and cut off the hair on the part of Carlman's head that was closest. Then he vanished as quickly as he had come. He went back up the hill, picked up his knapsack, and then ran down to the little gravel road where he had leaned his moped against one of the road administration's huts.

Two hours later he buried the scalp next to the other one beneath his sister's window.

The wind had subsided. There was no longer a cloud in the sky.

Midsummer Day would be both fair and warm.

Summer had arrived. More quickly than anyone could have imagined.

Skåne 25–28 June 1994

Chapter Eleven

The emergency call came in to the Ystad police station after two in the morning.

At the same moment Thomas Brolin scored a goal for Sweden in the match against Russia. He rammed in a penalty kick. A cheer rose in the Swedish summer night. It had been an unusually calm Midsummer Eve. The officer who received the call did so standing, since he had jumped up from his chair and yelled when Brolin scored. Despite his joy he realized at once that the phone call was serious. The woman shrieking in his ear seemed sober. Her hysteria stemmed from a shocking experience that was quite real. The officer called Hansson, who felt his temporary appointment as police chief to be so burdensome that he hadn't even dared leave the police station on Midsummer Eve. He kept trying to ascertain how his limited personnel resources could best be used in each individual case. At eleven o'clock, two fights had broken out simultaneously at two different private parties. In the one instance it was a matter of jealousy. But in the other the Swedish goalie Thomas Ravelli was the cause of the tumult that erupted. In a report later drafted by Svedberg, he stated that it was Ravelli's action when Cameroon scored their second goal that triggered the violent argument, which ended with three people landing in the hospital to have their injuries patched up. But by the time he heard about the call from Bjäresjö, one of the patrol cars had already returned. Normally, bad weather was the best guarantee of a calm Midsummer Eve. But this year history had refused to repeat itself.

Hansson went out to the operations center and spoke with the officer who had taken the call.

"Did she really say that a man had his head split in half?"

The officer nodded. Hansson pondered this.

"We'll have to ask Svedberg to drive out there," he said.

"But isn't he busy with that domestic violence thing in Svarte?"

"Right, I forgot," said Hansson. "Then you'd better call Wallander."

For the first time in over a week Wallander had managed to get to sleep before midnight. In a moment of weakness he considered joining the rest of the country in watching the broadcast of the soccer match against Russia. But he fell asleep while he was waiting for the players to take the field. The telephone yanked him to the surface of consciousness, and at first he didn't know where he was. He fumbled for the telephone next to the bed. Only a few months ago, after many years of procrastination, he had gotten around to having another jack installed so he wouldn't have to get out of bed to answer the phone.

"Did I wake you up?" asked Hansson.

"Yes," replied Wallander. "What is it?"

Wallander was surprised to have told the truth. He usually claimed that he was awake when someone called, no matter what time it was.

Hansson told him briefly about the call that had just come in. Later Wallander would brood endlessly about why he didn't immediately figure out that what had happened in Bjäresjö reminded him of what happened to Gustaf Wetterstedt. Was it because he didn't want to believe that they had a serial killer on their hands? Or was he simply incapable of imagining that a murder like Wetterstedt's could be anything but an isolated event? The only thing he did now, with the clock at twenty past two, was to ask Hansson to dispatch a regular patrol to the scene, and then he would go out there as soon as he got dressed.

At five to three he pulled up outside the farm in Bjäresjö to which he had been directed. On the car radio he heard that Martin Dahlin had scored his second goal against Russia. He realized that Sweden was going to win and that he had lost yet another hundred kronor.

When he caught sight of Norén running over to him, he knew at once that something serious had happened. But it wasn't until he went into the garden and passed a number of people who were either hysterical or dumbstruck that he understood what had really happened. The man who had been sitting on the bench in the arbor had actually had his head split in half. On the left half of his head, someone had also sliced off a large piece of skin with the hair attached.

Wallander stood there completely motionless for more than a minute. Norén said something, but it didn't register. He stared at the dead man and thought that it had to be the same killer who had axed Wetterstedt to death several days before. Then for a brief moment he felt an indescribable sorrow inside.

Later, talking to Baiba, he tried to explain the unexpected and very un-police-like feeling that had struck him. It was as though the last dam inside him had burst. And that dam had been an illusion. Now he knew that there were no longer any invisible dividing lines in this country. The violence that previously was concentrated in the large cities had also reached his own police district once and for all. The world had both shrunk and expanded at the same time.

Then horror replaced his feeling of sorrow. He turned to Norén, who was very pale.

"It looks like the same perp," said Norén.

Wallander nodded.

"Who's the victim?" he asked.

"His name is Arne Carlman. He's the one who owns this farm. There was a Midsummer party going on."

"See to it that no one leaves. Find out if anyone saw anything."

Wallander took out his phone, punched in the number of the police, and asked to talk to Hansson.

"It looks bad," he said when Hansson came on the line.

"How bad?"

"I'm having a hard time thinking of anything worse. There's no doubt it's the same murderer who killed Wetterstedt. This one was scalped too."

Wallander could hear Hansson's breathing.

"You'll have to mobilize everything we've got," Wallander went on. "And I want Per Åkeson to come out here."

Wallander hung up before Hansson could ask any more questions. What'll I do now? he thought. Who am I looking for? A psychopath? A perpetrator who acts in a careful and calculated way?

But deep inside he knew what he had to do. There had to be a connection between Gustaf Wetterstedt and the man named Arne Carlman. That was the first thing he had to look for.

After twenty minutes the emergency vehicles started arriving. When Wallander caught sight of Nyberg, he ushered him straight to the arbor.

"Not a pretty sight," was Nyberg's first comment.

"This has got to be the same guy who killed Gustaf Wetterstedt," said Wallander. "He struck again."

"It doesn't look like we have to wonder about the scene of the crime this time," said Nyberg, pointing at the blood sprayed all over the hedge and the little serving table.

"He had his hair sliced off too," said Wallander.

Nyberg summoned his crew and set to work. Norén had assembled all the partygoers in the barn. The garden was strangely deserted. Norén came over to Wallander and pointed up toward the residence.

"He's got a wife and three kids in there. They're in shock, of course."

"Maybe we ought to call a doctor."

"She called one herself."

"I'll go talk to them," said Wallander. "When Martinsson and Ann-Britt and the others get here, tell them to talk to anyone who might have seen something. The rest can go home. But write down their names. And don't forget to ask for ID. There weren't any eyewitnesses?"

"Nobody has come forward."

"Have you got a timetable?"

Norén took a note pad out of his pocket.

"At eleven-thirty Carlman was definitely seen alive. At two he was found dead. So the murder took place sometime in between."

"It must be possible to shorten the time span," said Wallander. "Try and find out who was the last one to see him alive. And of course who found him."

Wallander went into the house. The residential wing of the old Scanian farm had been lovingly restored. Wallander stepped into a large room that served as living room, kitchen, and dining area. Oil paintings covered all the walls. In one corner of the room, the dead man's family sat on a sofa upholstered in black leather. A woman in her fifties stood up and came over to him.

"Mrs. Carlman?" asked Wallander.

"Yes."

Wallander could see that she had been crying. He looked for signs of whether she was about to break down. But she gave the impression of being surprisingly calm.

"I'm sorry about what happened," said Wallander.

"It's just terrible."

Wallander perceived something a little mechanical in her answer. He thought for a moment before he asked his first question.

"Do you have any idea who might have done this?"

"No."

Wallander thought at once that the answer came too quickly. She had been prepared for that question. In other words, there are plenty of people who might have considered killing him, he told himself.

"May I ask what your husband did?"

"He was an art dealer."

Wallander stiffened. She misconstrued his intense gaze and repeated her answer.

"I heard you," said Wallander. "Excuse me for a moment."

Wallander went back out to the courtyard. With all his senses on edge he thought about what the woman inside had said. He put it together with what Lars Magnusson had told him about the rumors that had once surrounded Gustaf Wetterstedt. It was a matter of stolen art. And now an art dealer was dead, murdered by the same hand that took Wetterstedt's life. With a feeling of relief and gratitude he realized that there was already a possible connection between the two at this early stage. He was just about to go back inside when Ann-Britt Höglund came around the corner of the house. She was paler than usual. And very tense. Wallander remembered his early years as a detective, when he took every violent crime personally. From the start, Rydberg had taught him that a policeman could never permit himself to befriend a victim of violence. That had taken Wallander a long time to learn.

"Another one?" she asked.

"Same perp," said Wallander. "Or perps. The pattern is repeating itself."

"Was he scalped too?"

"Yes."

He saw her flinch involuntarily.

"I think I've already found something that ties these two men together," Wallander went on, and explained. In the meantime Svedberg and Martinsson arrived. Wallander quickly repeated what he had told Höglund.

"You'll have to interview the guests," said Wallander. "If I understood Norén correctly, there are at least a hundred. And they all have to show some ID before they leave."

Wallander went back inside the house. He pulled up a wooden chair and sat down near the sofa where the family was gathered. Besides Carlman's widow there were two boys in their twenties and a girl a couple of years older. All of them seemed unexpectedly calm.

"I promise that I'll only ask questions that we absolutely have to have answered as quickly as possible," he said. "The rest we can return to later."

It was silent in the room. None of them said a word.

"Do you know who the murderer is?" Wallander asked. "Was it one of the guests?"

"Who else could it be?" replied one of the sons. He had short-cropped blond hair. Wallander had an uneasy feeling that he could discern a resemblance to the deformed face he had just been forced to examine out in the arbor.

"Is there anyone in particular that comes to mind?" Wallander continued.

The boy shook his head.

"It doesn't seem very likely that an outsider would have chosen to come here when a big party was going on," said Mrs. Carlman.

Someone cold-blooded enough wouldn't have hesitated, thought Wallander. Or someone crazy enough. Someone who might not even care whether he gets caught or not.

"Your husband was an art dealer," Wallander went on. "Can you describe for me what that involves?"

"My husband has over thirty galleries around the country," she said. "He also has galleries in the other Nordic countries. He sells paintings by mail order. He rents paintings to companies. He's responsible for a large number of art auctions each year. And much more."

"Did he have any enemies?"

"A successful man is always looked down on by those who have the same ambitions but lack the talent."

"Did your husband ever say he felt threatened?"

"No."

Wallander looked at the children sitting on the sofa. They shook their heads almost simultaneously.

"When did you see him last?" he continued.

"I danced with him at around ten thirty," she said. "Then I saw him a few more times. It might have been around eleven when I saw him last."

None of the children had seen him any later than that. Wallander knew that all the other questions could wait. He put his note pad back in his pocket and stood up. He wanted to offer some words of sympathy. But he couldn't think of anything. He just nodded curtly and left the house.

Sweden had won the soccer game 3 to 1. Ravelli, the goalie, had been brilliant; Cameroon was forgotten, and Martin Dahlin was a genius with his header shot. Wallander picked up fragments of conversations going on around him. Pieced them together and added them up. Apparently Höglund and two other police officers had guessed the right score. Wallander sensed that he had strengthened his position as the biggest loser. He couldn't decide whether this annoyed or pleased him.

They worked hard and efficiently for the next few hours. Wallander set up temporary headquarters in a storeroom attached to the barn. Just after four in the morning Höglund came in with a young woman who spoke a distinct Göteborg dialect.

"She was the last one to see him alive," said Höglund. "She was with Carlman in the arbor just before midnight."

Wallander asked her to sit down. She told him her name was Madelaine Rhedin and she was an artist.

"What were you doing in the arbor?" asked Wallander.

"Arne wanted me to sign a contract."

"What sort of contract?"

"To sell my paintings."

"And you signed it?"

"Yes."

"Then what happened?"

"Nothing."

"Nothing?"

"I got up and left. I looked at my watch. It was three minutes to twelve."

"Why did you look at your watch?"

"I usually do when something important happens."

"The contract was important?"

"I was supposed to get two hundred thousand kronor on Monday. For a poor artist that's a big deal."

"Was there anyone in the vicinity when you were sitting in the arbor?"

"Not that I could see."

"And when you left?"

"It was deserted."

"What did Carlman do when you left?"

"He stayed there."

"How do you know? Did you turn around?"

"He told me he was going to enjoy the fresh air. I didn't hear him get up."

"Did he seem uneasy?"

"No, he was in a good mood."

Wallander concluded the interview.

"Try to think it over," he said. "Maybe tomorrow you'll remember something else. Anything you remember might be important. I want you to keep in touch."

When she left the room, Per Åkeson came in from the other direction. He was totally white in the face. He sat down heavily on the chair Madelaine Rhedin had just vacated.

"That's the most disgusting thing I've ever seen," he said.

"You didn't have to look at him," said Wallander. "That's not why I wanted you to come."

"I don't know how you stand it," said Åkeson.

"Me neither," said Wallander.

Suddenly Åkeson was all business.

"Is it the same man who killed Wetterstedt?" he asked.

"Without a doubt."

They looked at each other and knew that they were thinking the same thought.

"In other words, he may strike again?"

Wallander nodded. Åkeson grimaced.

"If there was ever a time to give priority to an investigation, this is it," he said. "I assume you need more personnel, don't you? I can pull some strings if necessary."

"Not yet," said Wallander. "A large number of police might facilitate the capture of a person if we knew his name and what he looked like. But we're not that far yet."

Then he told him what Lars Magnusson had said, and that Arne Carlman was an art dealer.

"There's a connection," he concluded. "And that will make the work easier."

Åkeson was doubtful.

"I hope you aren't putting all your eggs in one basket too early," he said.

"I'm not closing any doors," said Wallander. "But I have to lean on any wall I find."

Åkeson stayed for another hour before he drove back to Ystad. By five in the morning reporters had begun to show up at the farm. Wallander angrily made a call to Ystad and demanded that Hansson deal with the reporters. He already knew that they wouldn't be able to conceal the fact that Arne Carlman had been scalped. Hansson held an improvised and exceedingly chaotic press conference on the road outside the farm. Meanwhile Martinsson, Svedberg, and Höglund herded out the guests, who all had to undergo a short interrogation. Wallander himself had a long conversation with the extremely drunk sculptor who had discovered Carlman's body.

"Why did you go out in the garden?" asked Wallander.

"To throw up."

"And did you?"

"Yes."

"Where did you throw up?"

"Behind one of the apple trees."

"Then what happened?"

"I thought I'd sit down in the arbor to clear my head."

"Then what happened?"

"I found him."

With that reply Wallander had been forced to break off the interview since the sculptor started feeling sick again. He got up and went down to the arbor. The sky was completely clear, and the sun was already high. Wallander thought that Midsummer Day would be both warm and beautiful. When he reached the arbor he saw to his relief that Nyberg had covered Carlman's head with an opaque plastic sheet. Nyberg was on his knees next to the hedge that separated the garden from the adjacent rapeseed field.

"How's it going?" asked Wallander encouragingly.

"There's a slight trace of blood on the hedge here," he said. "It couldn't have sprayed this far from the arbor."

"What does that mean?" asked Wallander.

"It's your job to answer that," replied Nyberg.

He pointed at the hedge.

"Right here it's quite sparse," he said. "It would have been possible for someone with a slight build to slip in and out of the garden this way. We'll have to see what we find on the other side. But I suggest you get a dog out here. ASAP."

Wallander nodded.

The canine officer arrived with his German shepherd at five-thirty. The last of the guests were leaving the garden. Wallander nodded to the canine officer, whose name was Eskilsson. The police dog was old and had been in service for a long time. His name was Shot.

The dog picked up a scent in the arbor at once and started toward the hedge. He wanted to push through the hedge just at the spot where Nyberg had found the traces of blood. Eskilsson and Wallander found another spot where the hedge was thin and emerged onto the tractor path that divided Carlman's property from the field. The dog found the scent again and headed alongside the field toward a dirt road that led away from the farm. At Wallander's suggestion Eskilsson released the dog and told him to seek. Wallander felt a sudden excitement. The dog sniffed along the dirt road and came to the end of the rapeseed field. Here he seemed to lose his bearings for a moment. Then he found the scent and kept following it toward a hill that lay near a pond half full of water. The trail ended on the hill. Eskilsson searched in various directions, but the dog couldn't find the scent again.

Wallander looked around. A lone tree bent by the wind stood on top of the hill. Remnants of an old bicycle frame lay half buried in the ground. Wallander stood next to the tree and looked at the farm in the distance. He noticed that the view of the garden was excellent. With binoculars it would have been possible to see who was outside the house at any given time.

Suddenly Wallander shuddered. A feeling that someone else, someone unknown to him, had stood on the same spot earlier that night gave him the willies. He went back to the garden. Hansson and Svedberg were sitting on the steps of the farmhouse. Their faces were gray with fatigue.

"Where's Ann-Britt?" asked Wallander.

"She's getting rid of the last guest," said Svedberg.

"Martinsson? What's he doing?"

"He's on the phone."

Wallander sat down next to the others on the steps. The sun was already starting to feel hot.

"We've got to keep at it a little longer," he said. "When Ann-Britt is done we'll drive back to Ystad. We have to sum up what we know and decide what to do next."

No one spoke. No comment was necessary. Höglund emerged from the barn. She hunkered down in front of the others.

"To think that so many people can see so little," she said in a weary voice. "It's beyond me."

Eskilsson passed by with his dog. They heard Nyberg's grumpy voice near the arbor.

Martinsson came striding around the corner of the house. He had a telephone in his hand.

"This may be beside the point right now," he said. "But we've received a message from Interpol. They have a positive ID on the girl who burned herself to death. They think they know who she is."

Wallander looked at him quizzically.

"The girl in Salomonsson's rapeseed field?"

"Yes."

Wallander got up.

"Who is she?"

"I don't know. But there's a message waiting for you at the station."

They left Bjäresjö at once and headed back to Ystad.

Chapter Twelve

Dolores María Santana.

It was quarter to six on the morning of Midsummer Day when Martinsson read aloud the message from Interpol identifying the girl who burned herself to death.

"Where's she from?" asked Höglund.

"The message is from the Dominican Republic," replied Martinsson. "It came via Madrid."

Puzzled, he looked around the room.

Höglund knew the answer.

"The Dominican Republic is on the other half of the island where Haiti is located," she said. "In the West Indies. Isn't it called Hispaniola?"

"How in the hell did she wind up here, in Salomonsson's rapeseed field?" asked Wallander. "Who is she? What else did Interpol say?"

"I haven't had time to go through the message in detail," said Martinsson. "But if I understand it correctly, her father has been looking for her, and she was reported missing in late November last year. The report was originally filed in a city called Santiago."

"Isn't that in Chile?" Wallander interrupted, surprised.

"This city is called Santiago de los Treinta Caballeros," said Martinsson. "Don't we have a map of the world somewhere?"

"I'll get one," said Svedberg and left the room.

A few minutes later he returned, shaking his head.

"It must have been Björk's private map," he said. "I couldn't find it."

"Call the bookseller and wake him up," said Wallander. "I want a map here now."

"Are you aware that it's not even six in the morning on Midsummer Day?" Svedberg wondered.

"It can't be helped. Call him. And send a car over to pick up the map."

Wallander took a hundred-krona bill out of his wallet and gave it to Svedberg.

A few minutes later he had roused the dazed bookseller and the car was on its way to pick up the map.

They got coffee and went into the conference room. Hansson told them that they wouldn't be disturbed by anyone except Nyberg for the next few hours. Wallander took a look around the table. He met the gazes of a group of gray and weary faces and wondered how he looked himself.

"We'll have to come back to the girl in the rapeseed field later," he began. "Right now we need to concentrate on what happened last night. And we might as well assume from the start that the same perpetrator who killed Gustaf Wetterstedt has struck again. The M.O. is the same, even though Carlman was struck in the head and Wetterstedt had his spine severed. Both of them were scalped, though."

"I've never seen anything like it," said Svedberg. "The guy who did this must be a complete animal."

Wallander held up his hand.

"Hold on a minute," he said. "There's something else we know too. That Arne Carlman was an art dealer. And now I'm going to tell you something I found out yesterday."

Wallander told them about his conversation with Lars Magnusson, about the rumors that once surrounded Gustaf Wetterstedt.

"In other words, we have a conceivable connection," he concluded. "The key word and the link is art: stolen art and fenced art. And somewhere, when we find the point that connects them, we'll find the perpetrator there too."

No one said a word. Everyone seemed to be pondering what Wallander had said.

"In other words, we know what we have to concentrate our investigative work on," Wallander continued. "Finding the link between Wetterstedt and Carlman. But this doesn't mean we don't have another problem."

He looked around the table and could see that they understood what he was getting at.

"This man could strike again," said Wallander. "We don't know why he killed Wetterstedt and Carlman. So we don't know whether he's after other people too. And we don't know who they might be. The only thing we can hope for is that the people who may be threatened are aware of it."

"There's one more thing we don't know," said Martinsson. "Is the man insane or isn't he? We don't know whether the motive is revenge or something else. We can't even be sure that the perpetrator hasn't invented a motive that has no basis in actual events. No one can predict what goes on inside a crazed mind."

"You're right, of course," replied Wallander. "We'll be dealing with a lot of uncertainties."

"Maybe we're just seeing the beginning of this," Hansson said grimly. "In a worst-case scenario, do you think we've got a serial killer on our hands?"

"It could be that bad," said Wallander firmly. "That's why I also think we should get some help from outside. Above all from the Criminal Psychiatric Division in Stockholm. This man's M.O. is so remarkable, especially because he takes scalps, that maybe they can do one of those psychiatric profiles on him."

"Has this perp killed before?" asked Svedberg. "Or is this the first time he's on the loose?"

"I don't know," said Wallander. "But he's cautious. I got a strong feeling that he plans what he does very carefully. When he finally strikes he does it without hesitation. There could be at least two reasons for this. First, he may simply not want to get caught. Second, in any case he doesn't want to be interrupted before he finishes what he set out to do."

At this remark a wave of revulsion and distaste passed through the room.

"This is where we have to start," he said in conclusion. "Where is the point of convergence between Wetterstedt and Carlman? Where do their paths cross? That's what we have to clarify. And we have to do it as quickly as humanly possible."

"Maybe we should also realize that we won't be working in peace any longer," said Hansson. "Reporters will be swarming around us. They know that Carlman was scalped. They've gotten the story they've been longing for. For some strange reason Swedes seem to love to read about crime when they're on vacation."

"That might not be such a bad thing," said Wallander. "At least it might send a warning to anyone who may have reason to fear that they're on the murderer's hit list."

"We ought to stress that we want tips from the public," said Höglund. "If we assume that you're right, that the murderer has a list he's following, and that certain people should be able to figure out they could also be at risk, then there might be a chance that some of them know, or at least have an idea about, who the perpetrator is."

"You're right," said Wallander, turning to Hansson. "Call a press conference as soon as possible. We'll tell everything we know. That we're looking for a single perpetrator. And that we need all the tips we can get."

Svedberg got up and opened a window. Martinsson yawned loudly.

"I know we're all tired," said Wallander. "But we have to carry on. Try to grab some sleep when you get a chance."

There was a knock on the door. A patrolman handed over a map. They spread it out on the table and looked for the Dominican Republic and the city of Santiago.

"We'll have to wait with this girl until later," said Wallander. "We can't worry about it now."

"In any case I'll send a reply," said Martinsson. "And we can always ask for in-depth information about her disappearance."

"I wonder how she wound up here," muttered Wallander.

"The message from Interpol gives her age as seventeen," said Martinsson.

"And her height as about 160 centimeters."

"Send them a description of the medallion," said Wallander. "If the father can identify it, the case is closed."

At ten minutes past seven they left the conference room. Martinsson went home to talk to his family and cancel their trip to the island of Bornholm. Svedberg went down to the basement and took a shower. Hansson vanished down the corridor to organize the meeting with the press. Wallander followed Höglund into her office.

"Do you think we'll catch him?" she asked gravely.

"I don't know," said Wallander. "We've got a lead that seems solid. We can write off any idea that this is a perp who simply kills anyone who gets in his way. He's after something. The scalps are his trophies."

She sat down in her chair as Wallander leaned against the door jamb.

"Why do people take trophies?" she asked.

"So they can brag about them."

"To themselves or to others?"

"Both."

Suddenly he realized why she had asked about the trophies.

"You're thinking that he took these scalps so he could show them to somebody?"

"It can't be ruled out," she said.

"No," said Wallander, "it can't be ruled out. Any more than anything else can."

He was just about to leave the room when he turned around.

"Will you call Stockholm?" he asked.

"It's Midsummer Day," she said. "I don't think they'll be on duty."

"You'll have to call someone at home," said Wallander. "Since we don't know whether he's going to strike again, we've got no time to lose."

Wallander went to his own office and sat down heavily in the visitor's chair. One of its legs creaked precariously. He leaned his head back and closed his eyes. Soon he was asleep.

He woke up with a start when someone entered the room. He glanced at his watch and saw that he'd been asleep for almost an hour. He still had a headache. But some of his weariness was gone.

It was Nyberg. His eyes were bloodshot and his hair was sticking up.

"I didn't mean to wake you," he said by way of apology.

"I was just dozing," said Wallander. "Have you got any news?"

Nyberg shook his head.

"Not much," he said. "All I can come up with is that the person who killed Carlman must have had his clothes drenched with blood. If I may anticipate the forensic examination, I think we can assume that the blow came from directly overhead. That would mean that the person holding the axe was standing quite close."

"Are you sure it was an axe?"

"I'm not sure about anything," said Nyberg. "Of course, it could have been a heavy saber. Or something else. But Carlman's head did seem to be split like a log."

Wallander instantly felt sick to his stomach.

"All right, then," he said. "So the killer got his clothes covered with blood. Someone might have seen him. And that lets out the guests at the party. Nobody there was soaked with blood."

"We looked along the hedge," said Nyberg. "We searched all the way along the rapeseed field and up toward that hill. The farmer who owns the fields around Carlman's farmhouse came and asked whether he could harvest the rapeseed. I told him yes."

"You made a wise decision," said Wallander. "Isn't it unusually late this year?"

"I think so," said Nyberg. "It's Midsummer already, after all."

"What about the hill?" asked Wallander.

"Someone had been there," said Nyberg. "The grass was trampled down. At one spot it looked as if someone had been sitting there. We took samples of the grass and the soil."

"Anything else?"

"I don't think that old bicycle is of any interest to us," said Nyberg.

"The police dog lost the scent," said Wallander. "Why?"

"You'll have to ask the canine officer about that," said Nyberg. "But it could be that a foreign substance is suddenly so strong that the dog loses the scent he was originally following. There are plenty of reasons why tracks suddenly stop."

Wallander pondered what Nyberg had said.

"Go home and get some sleep," he said then. "You look beat."

"I am," said Nyberg.

After Nyberg left, Wallander went into the lunch room and fixed himself a sandwich. A girl from the front desk came and gave him a stack of telephone messages. He leafed through them and saw that reporters were calling. He wondered whether he should go home and change clothes. Then he quickly decided to do something entirely different. He knocked on the door to Hansson's office and told him he was driving out to Carlman's farm.

"I said we'd talk to the press at one o'clock," said Hansson.

"I'll be back by then," replied Wallander. "But unless something urgent happens, I don't want anyone to look for me out there. I need to think."

"And everybody needs to get some sleep," said Hansson. "I never imagined we'd wind up in such a hellish situation."

"It always happens when you least expect it," said Wallander.

He drove out toward Bjäresjö in the beautiful summer morning with his windows rolled down. He thought he ought to visit his father today. And he had to call Linda too. Tomorrow Baiba would be back in Riga after her trip to

Tallinn. In less than two weeks his vacation would be starting.

He parked the car by the cordon surrounding Carlman's extensive farm. Small groups of curiosity-seekers had gathered on the road. Wallander nodded to the officer guarding the cordon. Then he walked around the large garden and followed the dirt road up toward the hill. He stood at the spot where the dog had lost the scent and looked around. *He had chosen the hill with care. From here he could see everything going on in the garden. He also must have been able to hear the music coming from inside the barn. Late in the evening the crowd in the garden thinned out. The partygoers agreed that everyone went indoors. At about eleven-thirty Carlman came walking toward the arbor with Madelaine Rhedin. Then what did you do?*

Wallander didn't answer the question he was thinking. Instead he turned around and looked at the back side of the hill. At the bottom there were tractor tracks. He followed the grassy slope until he reached the road. In one direction the tractor tracks led into a wood lot, and in the other down toward a side road heading for the highway to Malmö and Ystad. Wallander followed the tracks toward the woods. He entered the shadow of a clump of tall beech trees. The sunshine shimmered through the foliage. The earth smelled pungent. The tractor tracks stopped at a tree-cutting site where some newly felled and stripped trees awaited transport.

Wallander searched in vain for a path that went further. He tried to visualize the road map. Anyone wanting to reach the highway from the woods would have to pass by two houses and several fields. He calculated the distance to the highway at two kilometers. Then he returned the way he had come and continued in the opposite direction. He counted his steps to almost a kilometer before he came to the place where the side road reached highway E65. The side road was full of car tracks.

By the side of the road was a road maintenance hut. He tried the door, which was locked. He stood there and looked around. Then he went around in back of the hut. There lay a folded tarp and a couple of iron pipes. He was just about to leave when he caught sight of something lying on the ground. He bent down and saw that it was a piece torn from a brown paper bag. It had some dark spots on it. He picked it up gingerly. He couldn't make out what kind of spots they were. He carefully placed the piece of paper back on the ground. For the next few minutes he made a meticulous search of the area behind the hut. But it wasn't until he looked underneath the hut, which was raised on four concrete blocks, that he discovered the rest of the paper bag. He reached in one arm and pulled it out. He saw at once that the piece had been torn from this bag. But there were no spots on the bag itself. He stood motionless, thinking. Then he put down the bag and called in to the police station. He got hold of Martinsson, who had just come back from his brief trip home.

"I need Eskilsson and his dog," said Wallander.

"Where are you? Did something happen?"

"I'm out by Carlman's farm," replied Wallander. "I just want to make sure of one thing."

Martinsson promised to get hold of Eskilsson. Wallander gave him a description of his location.

After half an hour Eskilsson arrived with his dog. Wallander explained what he wanted.

"Go over to the hill where the dog lost the scent," he said. "Then come back here."

Eskilsson left. After about ten minutes he returned. Wallander saw that the dog had stopped searching. But just as he reached the hut he reacted. Eskilsson gave Wallander a questioning look.

"Let him go," said Wallander.

The dog went straight for the piece of paper and halted. But when Eskilsson tried to get him to continue his search he quickly gave up. The scent had disappeared again.

"Is it blood?" asked Eskilsson, pointing at the piece of torn paper.

"I think so," said Wallander. "At any rate, we've found something associated with the man who was up on the hill."

Eskilsson left with his dog. Wallander was just about to call Nyberg when he discovered that he had a plastic bag in one pocket. He remembered that he had stuffed it in there when they were doing the technical examination of Wetterstedt's house. Carefully he deposited the piece of paper in it. *It couldn't have taken you more than a few minutes to get here from Carlman's farm. Presumably there was a bicycle here. You changed clothes since you had blood all over them. But you also wiped off some object. Maybe a knife or an axe. Then you took off, either toward Malmö or Ystad. You probably crossed the highway and chose one of the many little roads that criss-cross this area. I can follow you this far right now. But no further.*

Wallander walked back to Carlman's farm and got his car. He asked the officer guarding the cordon whether the family was still there.

"I haven't seen anybody," he said. "But no one has left the house."

Wallander nodded and walked to his car. There was a crowd of onlookers standing outside the cordon. Wallander glanced at them hastily and wondered what kind of people would give up a summer morning for the opportunity to smell some blood.

He didn't realize until he drove off that he had noticed something important without reacting to it. He slowed down and tried to remember what it was.

It had something to do with the people who were standing outside the cordon. What was it he had thought? Something about people sacrificing a summer morning in order to smell blood?

He braked and made a U-turn in the middle of the road. When he got back to Carlman's house the curiosity-seekers were still there outside the cordon. Wallander looked around without finding any explanation for his reaction. He asked the officer whether any of the onlookers had just left.

"Maybe. People come and go all the time."

"Nobody special that you recall?"

The patrolman thought for a moment.

"No."

Wallander went back to his car.

It was ten minutes past nine on the morning of Midsummer Day.

Chapter Thirteen

When Wallander got back to the police station just before nine-thirty, the girl at the front desk told him he had a visitor waiting in his office. For once Wallander completely lost his temper and started swearing and yelling at the girl, who was a summer intern. He shouted that no one, no matter who it was, was to be allowed into his office to wait. Then he stomped down the hall and threw open the door, only to find his father waiting in the visitor's chair looking at him.

"The way you tear open doors," said his father. "Somebody might think you were mad about something."

"All they told me was that someone was waiting in my office," said Wallander in amazement. "They didn't say it was you."

This was the first time Wallander's father had ever visited him at work. When he was a patrolman, his father had even refused to let him cross the threshold in uniform. But now here he was, wearing his best suit.

"I'm surprised," said Wallander. "Who drove you here?"

"My wife has both a driver's license and a car," replied his father. "She drove in to visit one of her relatives while I visited you. Did you see the game last night?"

"No. I was working."

"It was great. I remember the way it was back in '58, when the World Cup was held in Sweden."

"But you were never interested in soccer, were you?"

"I've always liked soccer."

Wallander gazed at him in surprise.

"I didn't know that."

"There's a lot of things you don't know. In 1958 Sweden had a back named Sven Axbom. He was having big problems with one of Brazil's wings, as I recall. Have you forgotten about that?"

"How old was I in 1958? I was just a baby back then."

"You never were much for playing ball. Maybe that's why you became a cop."

"I bet that Russia would win," said Wallander.

"That's not hard to believe," said his father. "I bet 2–0 myself. Gertrud, on the other hand, was cautious. She thought it would be 1–1."

The soccer conversation was over.

"Would you like some coffee?" asked Wallander.

"Yes, please."

In the hall Wallander ran into Hansson.

"Will you see to it that I'm not disturbed for the next half hour?" he said.

Hansson gave him a worried look.

"I absolutely must speak with you."

Hansson's stuffy way of speaking bothered Wallander.

"In half an hour," he repeated. "Then we'll talk as much as you like."

He went back to his room and closed the door. His father took the plastic cup in both hands. Wallander sat down behind the desk.

"I must say this is unexpected," he said. "I never thought I'd see you in the police station."

"It's unexpected for me too," said his father. "I wouldn't have come if I didn't have to."

Wallander set his plastic cup on the desk. He should have known right off that it would have to be something very important to make his father visit him at the station.

"Has something happened?" asked Wallander.

"Nothing except the fact that I'm sick," replied his father simply.

Wallander at once felt a knot in his stomach.

"What do you mean?" he asked.

"I'm starting to lose my mind," his father went on calmly. "It's a disease with a name I can't remember. It's like getting senile. But it can make you angry at everything. And it can progress very fast."

Wallander knew what his father was talking about. He remembered that Svedberg's mother was stricken with the same disease. But he couldn't remember the name either.

"How do you know?" he asked. "Have you been to the doctor? Why didn't you say something before now?"

"I've even been to a specialist, in Lund," said his father. "Gertrud drove me there."

His father fell silent and drank his coffee. Wallander didn't know what to say.

"Actually, I came here to ask you something," his father said, looking at him. "If it's not too much to ask."

At that moment the telephone rang. Wallander put the receiver on the desk.

"I've got time to wait," said his father.

"I told them I didn't want to be disturbed. So tell me what it is you want."

"I've always had a dream of going to Italy," his father said. "Before it's too late, I'd like to take a trip there. And I thought you could go with me. Gertrud doesn't have any interest in Italy. I don't think she wants to go. And I'll pay for the whole thing. I've got the money."

Wallander looked at his father. He seemed small and shrunken sitting there in the chair. At that moment he suddenly looked his real age. Almost eighty.

"Of course, let's go to Italy," said Wallander. "When did you have in mind?"

"It's probably best that we don't wait too long. I've heard it's not too hot in September. But maybe you don't have time then?"

"I can take a week off anytime. Or did you want to stay away longer than that?"

"A week would be fine."

His father leaned forward and put down the coffee cup. Then he stood up.

"Well, I won't bother you any longer," he said. "I'll wait for Gertrud outside."

"It would be better if you waited here," said Wallander.

His father waved his cane at him.

"You've got a lot to do," he said. "Whatever it is. I'll wait outside."

Wallander accompanied him out to the reception area, where his father sat down on a sofa.

"I don't want you to wait with me," said his father. "Gertrud will be here soon."

Wallander nodded.

"We'll go to Italy together, don't you worry about it," he said. "I'll come out and see you as soon as I can."

"The trip might be a lot of fun," said his father. "You never know."

Wallander left him and went over to the girl at the front desk.

"My apologies," he said. "It was quite all right that you let my father wait in my office."

He went back to his room. Suddenly he noticed that he had tears in his eyes. Even though his relationship with his father was strained and colored by a guilty conscience, he felt a great sorrow that his father was now in the process of leaving him. He stood by the window and looked out at the beautiful summer weather. *There was a time when we were so close that nothing could come between us. That was back when the Silk Knights used to come in their shiny American land yachts and buy your paintings. Even then you talked about going to Italy. Another time, only a few years ago, you actually started off for Italy. That's when I found you, dressed in pajamas, with a suitcase in your hand in the middle of a field. But now we have to make that trip. And I won't allow anything to come between us.*

Wallander returned to his desk and called his sister in Stockholm. An answering machine informed him that she wouldn't be back until that evening.

It took him a good hour to push aside his father's visit and concentrate on the investigation again. He felt restless and noticed that he was having a hard time collecting his thoughts. He still refused to acknowledge the import of what he had heard. He didn't want to accept the truth.

After talking with Hansson he made an extensive review and evaluation of the status of the investigation. Just before eleven he called Per Åkeson at home and gave him his opinion. When they finished talking he drove over to Mariagatan, took a shower, and changed his clothes. By noon he was back at the station. On the way to his room he stopped in to see Ann-Britt Höglund. He told her about the bloody paper he found behind the road maintenance hut.

"Did you get hold of the psychologists in Stockholm?" he asked.

"I found a man named Roland Möller," she said. "He was at his summer house outside Vaxholm. All we need is for Hansson to make a formal request as acting chief."

"Did you talk to him?"

"He's already done it."

"Good," said Wallander. "Now let's discuss something else. If I say that criminals return to the scene of the crime—what do you say to that?"

"That it's both a myth and the truth."

"In what sense is it a myth?"

"That it's supposed to be a general truth. Something that always happens."

"And what's the real truth?"

"That it actually does happen once in a while. The most classic example in our own legal history is probably from here in Skåne. The policeman who committed a series of murders in the early fifties and was later on the team investigating what happened."

"That's not a good example," Wallander objected. "He was forced to return. I'm talking about the ones who return voluntarily. Why do they do it?"

"To taunt the police. To puff up their egos. Or to find out how much the police actually know."

Wallander nodded pensively.

"Why are you asking me this?"

"I had a peculiar experience," said Wallander. "I got a feeling that I saw someone out by Carlman's farm that I'd seen down by the beach too. When we were investigating the murder of Wetterstedt."

"What would prevent it from being the same person?" she asked, surprised.

"Nothing, of course. But there was something special about this person. I just can't put my finger on what it was."

"I don't think I can help you."

"I know," said Wallander. "But in the future I want someone to photograph, as discreetly as possible, everyone standing outside the cordon."

"In the future?"

Wallander knew that he had said too much. He tapped on the desk three times with his index finger.

"Naturally I hope nothing else will happen," he said. "But if it does."

Wallander accompanied Höglund to her office. Then he continued out of the station. His father was no longer sitting on the sofa. He drove up to a grill kiosk near one of the roads out of town and ate a hamburger. On a thermometer he could see that it was 26 degrees Celsius. At a quarter to one he drove back to the station.

The press conference on that Midsummer Day at the Ystad police station was memorable because Wallander lost his temper and left the room before it was all over. Afterwards he refused to apologize. Most of his colleagues thought he did the right thing. The next day, however, Wallander got a phone call from the National Police Board, and a meddlesome officer in the position of director pointed out that it was highly unsuitable for the police to direct abusive comments at journalists. The relationship between the media and the police corps was strained enough as it was, and no additional aggravations could be tolerated.

It all happened toward the end of the press conference. A journalist from an evening paper stood up and started to pressure Wallander with detailed questions concerning the fact that the unknown perpetrator had taken the scalps of his victims. Wallander tried for as long as he could to keep it on a certain level and avoid going into the goriest details. He made do by saying that some the hair of both Wetterstedt and Carlman had been torn off. But the reporter refused to give up. He kept demanding details even though by that point Wallander had refused to say anything more with reference to the status of the technical investigation. By then Wallander had developed a splitting headache. When the reporter claimed that it was Wallander's intention from the start to invoke the status of the technical investigation to avoid giving more detailed information about the scalpings, and that now, toward the end of the press conference, it seemed like pure hypocrisy to withhold details, Wallander suddenly had had enough. He banged his fist on the table and stood up.

"I will not let police policy be dictated by a nosy journalist who doesn't know where to draw the line!" he shouted.

The flashbulbs went off in an explosion. Then he quickly ended the press conference and left the room. Afterwards, when he had calmed down, he asked Hansson to excuse his indiscretion.

"I hardly think that will change the way certain headlines will read tomorrow morning," Hansson replied.

"I had to draw the line somewhere," said Wallander.

"I'm on your side, of course," said Hansson. "But I suspect there are others who won't be."

"They can suspend me," said Wallander. "They can fire me. But they can't ever make me apologize to that reporter."

"That apology will probably be discreetly presented from the National Police Board to the editor-in-chief of the newspaper," said Hansson. "And we won't ever hear about it."

At four in the afternoon the investigative group shut themselves behind closed doors. Hansson had given strict orders that they were not to be disturbed. At Wallander's request a patrol car had gone to pick up Per Åkeson.

He knew that the decision they made this afternoon would be crucial. They would be forced to go in many directions at once. All doors had to be kept wide open. But at the same time Wallander knew that they had to concentrate on the primary lead.

After getting a couple of aspirin from Höglund, Wallander closed the door to his office for fifteen minutes and thought once more about what Lars Magnusson had said, and the fact that there was a common denominator between Wetterstedt and Carlman. Or was there something else he'd missed? He ransacked his tired brain without coming up with any solid reason to change his mind. From now on they would have to concentrate their investigation along the main track, which dealt with art sales and art thefts. They would be forced to dig deep into the rumors almost thirty years old surrounding Wetterstedt, and they would have to dig fast. Wallander had no illusions that they would get very much help along the way. Lars Magnusson had talked about the cover-up artists who cleaned up in the brightly lit meeting halls and dark alleyways haunted by the servants of power. They had to find a way to shine their lamps in there, and it would be very difficult.

The investigative meeting began on the dot at four o'clock and was one of the longest Wallander had ever attended. They sat for almost nine hours before Hansson blew the final whistle. By then everyone was gray with fatigue. Höglund's bottle of aspirin had made the rounds and was now empty. A heap of plastic coffee cups covered the table. Cartons of half-eaten pizza stood piled in a corner of the room.

But Wallander also thought that this long meeting of the investigative team had been one of the best he had ever experienced in the criminal police. Concentration had never flagged, everyone contributed their opinions, and the plans for the investigation developed as a result of the collective will to think logically.

After Svedberg went over the telephone conversations he had had with Gustaf Wetterstedt's two children and his third ex-wife, they still couldn't uncover any conceivable motive. Hansson had also managed to talk with the almost eighty-year-old man who was party secretary during Wetterstedt's tenure as justice minister without finding out anything remarkable. He had confirmed that Wetterstedt had been discussed within the party. But no one had ever been able to ignore his strong party loyalty.

Martinsson had had a lengthy conversation with Carlman's widow. She was still very controlled, even though Martinsson thought she must be under the influence of sedatives. Neither she nor any of the children could think of any obvious motive for the murder. Wallander reported on his talk with Sara Björklund, Wetterstedt's "charwoman." He also told them about the discovery that the light bulb on the pole by the back gate had been unscrewed. And concluding the first part of the meeting, he told them about the bloody piece of paper he found behind the road maintenance hut.

None of the participants could tell that he was also thinking about his father the whole time. Afterwards he found occasion to ask Höglund whether she had noticed how scattered he had been all evening. She told him it was news to her. He had seemed more dogged and focused than ever.

At nine o'clock they aired out the room and took a break. Martinsson and Höglund called home, while Wallander finally got hold of his sister. She started to cry when he told her about their father's visit and the fact that he had a terminal illness. Wallander tried to console her as best he could, but he was fighting a lump in his throat himself. At last they agreed that she should call and talk to Gertrud the next day and that she would come down to visit as soon as possible. Before they hung up she asked whether he really believed that their father would be able to handle a trip to Italy. Wallander told her the truth, that he didn't know. But he defended the idea of taking the trip and reminded her how their father had dreamed about getting a chance to go to Italy ever since they were kids.

During the break Wallander also tried to call Linda. After fifteen rings he gave up. Annoyed, he decided he would have to give her the money to buy an answering machine.

When they returned to the meeting room Wallander started by talking about the point of convergence. That was what they had to search for, without ruling out other possibilities.

"Carlman's widow was sure that her husband had never had anything to do with Wetterstedt," said Martinsson. "Her children said the same thing. They searched through all his address books without finding Wetterstedt's name."

"Arne Carlman wasn't in Wetterstedt's address book either," said Höglund.

"So the link is invisible," said Wallander. "Invisible or, more precisely, elusive. Somewhere we must be able to find a connection. If we do, we may also glimpse a conceivable perpetrator. Or at least a conceivable motive. We have to dig deep and fast."

"Before he strikes again," said Hansson. "None of us knows whether that will happen."

"We also don't know who to warn," said Wallander. "The only thing we know about the perpetrator, or perpetrators, is that they plan out what they do."

"Do we know that?" Per Åkeson interjected. "It seems to me you're jumping to that conclusion too soon."

"At any rate there's nothing to indicate that we're dealing with an impulse killer who also has a spontaneous desire to rip the hair off his victims," replied Wallander, feeling his temper rise.

"It's the conclusion that I'm objecting to," said Åkeson. "It's not the same thing as disavowing the evidence."

The mood in the room grew quite oppressive for a moment. No one could help but notice the tension between the two men. Under normal circumstances Wallander wouldn't hesitate to go into open battle with Åkeson. But this evening he chose to retreat, mainly because he was very tired and knew he would have to keep the meeting going for several hours yet.

"I agree," was all he said. "We'll strike that conclusion and settle for saying that presumably it was planned."

"A psychologist from Stockholm is coming down tomorrow," said Hansson. "I'm going to pick him up at Sturup Airport myself. Let's just hope he can help us."

Wallander nodded. Then he threw out a question that he hadn't really prepared. But now seemed a suitable time.

"The murderer," he said. "For the sake of argument let's think of him for the time being as a man who acts alone. What do you see? What do you think?"

"Strong," said Nyberg. "The axe blows were delivered with tremendous force."

"I'm afraid he's collecting trophies," said Martinsson. "Only a crazy person would do something like that."

"Or someone who purposely wants to throw us off the track with the scalps," said Wallander.

"I have no impression at all," said Höglund. "But it must be someone who's profoundly disturbed."

In the end the question of the perpetrator was left hanging. Wallander summed up everything in one last run-through, in which they planned the investigative work to be done and divided up the tasks among them. At about midnight Åkeson left, after saying that he would help out by getting reinforcements for the investigative team when they thought it was necessary. Although they were all exhausted, Wallander went over the coming investigative work one more time.

"None of us is going to get a lot of sleep the next few days," he said in closing. "And I realize that this will throw vacation plans into chaos. But we have to muster all our forces. There's no other option."

"We'll need reinforcements," said Hansson.

"Let's decide about that on Monday," said Wallander. "Let's wait until then."

They decided to meet early the following afternoon. Before then Wallander and Hansson would present an overview to the psychologist from Stockholm.

Then they broke up and went their separate ways.

Wallander stood by his car and looked up at the pale night sky.

He tried to think about his father.

But the whole time something else kept intruding.

The fear that the unknown perpetrator would strike again.

Chapter Fourteen

At seven o'clock on Sunday morning, the 26th of June, the doorbell rang at Wallander's apartment on Mariagatan in central Ystad. He was jerked out of a deep sleep and thought at first it was the telephone ringing. When the doorbell rang again he got out of bed quickly, found his bathrobe lying halfway under the bed, and went out to the entryway to open the door. Outside the door stood his daughter Linda with a girlfriend Wallander had never seen before. He hardly recognized his daughter either, since she had cut her long blonde hair to a stubble and then dyed it red. But mainly he felt relieved and happy to see her again.

He let them in and said hello to Linda's friend, who introduced herself as Kajsa. Wallander was full of questions. He wondered in particular how they came to be ringing his doorbell at seven o'clock on a Sunday morning. Were there really train connections this early? Linda explained that they had arrived the night before, but they spent the night at the house of a girl Linda had gone to school with, since her parents were away. They would be staying there for the whole week. They stopped by so early because after reading the paper the past few days before Midsummer, Linda knew it would be hard to get hold of her father.

Wallander made breakfast for them from leftovers he dug out of his refrigerator. While they sat at the kitchen table he found out that they would be spending a week rehearsing a play they had written. Then they were going to the island of Gotland to take part in a theater seminar. Wallander listened and tried to hide the fact that he was extremely unhappy that she was giving up on her old dream, to become a furniture upholsterer, settle down in Ystad, and open her own shop. He also felt a great need to talk with her about her grandfather. He knew that the two of them were very close. He was sure she'd visit him while she was in Ystad. He made an attempt to say something while Kajsa was in the bathroom.

"There's so much going on. I'd like to talk with you in peace and quiet. Just you and me."

"That's the best thing about you," she said. "You're always so glad to see me."

She wrote down her phone number and promised to come over when he called.

"I saw the papers," she said. "Is it really as bad as they make out?"

"It's worse," Wallander said. "I've got so much to do that I don't really know how I'm going to manage. It was pure luck you caught me at home."

They sat and talked until after eight. Then Hansson called and said he was at Sturup Airport with the psychologist from Stockholm. They agreed to meet at the police station at nine o'clock.

"I have to go now," he told Linda.

"We do, too," she said.

"Does this play you're putting on have a name?" Wallander wondered when they got out to the street.

"It's not a play," replied Linda. "It's a cabaret."

"I see," said Wallander, as he tried to decide what the difference was. "And does it have a name?"

"Not yet," said Kajsa.

"Can I see it?" Wallander asked tentatively.

"When we're ready," said Linda. "Not before."

Wallander asked whether he could drive them somewhere.

"I'm going to show her the town," said Linda.

"Where are you from?" he asked Kajsa.

"Sandviken, up north," she said. "I've never been to Skåne before."

"Then we're even," said Wallander. "I've never been to Sandviken."

He watched them disappear around the corner. The fine weather was holding. Wallander thought it would be even warmer today. He was in a good mood because of his daughter's unexpected visit, even though he never could get used to the drastic way she had been experimenting with her looks the past few years. When she stood in the doorway this morning he saw for the first time that what many people had told him before was actually true. Linda looked like him. He had suddenly discovered his own face in hers.

When he got to the police station he could feel that Linda's sudden appearance had given him renewed vigor. He strode down the corridor, thinking with some irony that he clumped along like an overweight elephant, and he threw off his jacket when he entered his room. He grabbed the telephone before he even sat down and asked the receptionist to get hold of Sven Nyberg. Just as he was falling asleep last night an idea came to him that he wanted to check out. It took five minutes before the girl at the front desk managed to locate Nyberg for the impatient Wallander.

"It's Wallander," he said. "Do you remember telling me about a can of some sort of tear-gas spray that you found outside the cordon on the beach?"

"Of course I remember," snapped Nyberg.

Wallander ignored the fact that Nyberg was obviously in a bad mood.

"I thought we ought to check it for fingerprints," he said. "And compare them to whatever you can find on that bloody piece of paper I picked up near Carlman's house."

"Will do," said Nyberg. "But we would have done it anyway even if you hadn't asked us to."

"I know," said Wallander. "But you know how it is."

"No, I don't," said Nyberg. "You'll have the results as soon as I've got something."

Wallander slammed down the receiver, confirming his newfound energy. He stood by the window and looked out at the old water tower while he planned what he wanted to get done that day. From experience he knew that something almost always came up to scrub the plan. If he managed to get half the things done he'd be doing well.

At nine o'clock he left his office, got some coffee, and went into one of the small meeting rooms, where Hansson was waiting with the psychologist from Stockholm. He was a man around sixty, who introduced himself as Mats Ekholm. His handshake was firm, and Wallander immediately had a favorable impression of him. Like many police officers, Wallander had previously felt quite dubious about what psychologists could actually contribute to an ongoing criminal investigation. But from conversations with Ann-Britt Höglund he had begun to realize that his negative attitude was unfounded and possibly also unfair. Now that he was sitting at the same table with Mats Ekholm he decided to give him a real chance to show them what he could do.

The investigative material lay before them on the table.

"I've read through it as best I could," said Ekholm. "I propose that we start by talking about what isn't in the paperwork."

"It's all there," said Hansson, surprised. "If there's one thing the police are forced to learn, it's how to write reports."

"I suppose you want to know what *we* think," interrupted Wallander. "Isn't that right?"

Ekholm nodded.

"There's a fundamental psychological rule that says that policemen are always searching for something specific," he said. "If they don't know what a perpetrator looks like they insert a proxy. A person that many policemen visualize only from the back. But it's often the case that the phantom image turns out to have similarities with the perpetrator who is finally apprehended."

Wallander recognized his own reactions in Ekholm's description. In his head there was always a projected image of a criminal for as long as an investigation lasted. He never searched in an absolute vacuum.

"Two murders have been committed," Ekholm continued. "The M.O. is the same, even though there are some interesting differences. Gustaf Wetterstedt was killed from behind.

"The murderer struck him in the back, not in the head. Which is also interesting. He chose the more difficult alternative. Or could it be that he wanted to avoid smashing Wetterstedt's head? We don't know. After the deed he cut off the scalp and took the time to hide the body. If we then look at what happened to Carlman, we can easily identify the similarities and differences. Carlman was also struck down with an axe. He too had a piece of his scalp torn off. But he was killed from directly in front. He must have seen the man who killed him. The perpetrator also chose a time when there were many people in the vicinity. The risk of discovery is thus relatively great. He makes no attempt to hide the body. He realizes that it would be virtually impossible. The first question we have to ask is: Which is more important? The similarities or the differences?"

"He's a killer," said Wallander. "He selected two people. He made plans. He must have visited the beach outside Wetterstedt's house on several occasions. He even took the time to unscrew a bulb to obscure the area between the back yard and the sea."

"Do we know whether Gustaf Wetterstedt was in the habit of taking an evening walk on the beach?" asked Ekholm.

"No," said Wallander. "We don't actually know that. But of course we ought to look into it."

"Keep going," said Ekholm.

"On the surface the pattern looks completely different when it comes to Carlman," said Wallander. "Surrounded by people at a Midsummer party. But maybe the killer didn't see it that way. Maybe he thought he could make use of the isolation that is also a built-in factor at a party. The fact that no one sees anything at all. Nothing is as hard as getting a detailed impression from people in a large group who have to try and remember."

"To answer that question we have to examine what alternatives he may have had," said Ekholm. "Arne Carlman was a businessman who moved around a lot. Always surrounded by people. Maybe the party was the right choice after all."

"The similarity or the difference," said Wallander. "Which one is crucial?"
Ekholm threw out his hands.

"It's too early to say, of course. What we can surmise is that he plans his deeds carefully and that he's extremely cold-blooded."

"He takes scalps," said Wallander. "He collects trophies. What does that mean?"

"He's exercising power," said Ekholm. "The trophies are the proof of his deeds. For him it's no more peculiar than a hunter putting up a pair of horns on his wall."

"But the decision to scalp," Wallander went on. "Where does that come from?"

"It's not that strange," said Ekholm. "I don't want to seem cynical. But what part of a human being is more suitable to be taken as a trophy? A human body rots. A piece of skin with hair on it is easier to preserve."

"I guess I still can't stop thinking of Indians," said Wallander.

"Naturally it can't be excluded that your perpetrator has a fixation on some Indian warrior," said Ekholm. "People who find themselves in a psychic borderland often choose to hide behind another person's identity. Or transform themselves into a mythological figure."

"Borderland?" said Wallander. "What does that involve?"

"Your perpetrator has already committed two murders. We can't rule out that he intends to continue, since we don't know his motive. This indicates he has probably passed a psychological boundary, which means he has freed himself from all normal inhibitions. A person can commit murder or manslaughter without premeditation. A killer who repeats his actions is following completely different psychological laws. He finds himself in a twilight zone where we can only partially follow him. All the boundaries that exist for him are ones he has drawn himself. On the surface he can live a completely normal life. He can go to a job every morning. He can have a family and devote his evenings to playing golf or cultivating his flower beds. He can sit on his sofa with his children around him and watch the news reports about the murders he himself has committed. Without showing the slightest emotion, he can decry the fact that such people are allowed to run around loose. He has two different identities which he controls utterly. He pulls his own strings. He is both marionette and puppet master simultaneously."

Wallander sat in silence and thought about what Ekholm had said.

"Who is he?" he finally asked. "What does he look like? How old is he? I can't search for a sick mind that looks completely normal on the surface. All I can do is search for a specific person."

"It's too early to answer that," said Ekholm. "I need time to get into the material before I can sketch a psychological profile of the perpetrator."

"I hope you're not considering this Sunday a day of rest," said Wallander wearily. "We'll need that profile as soon as humanly possible."

"I'll try to get something together by tomorrow," said Ekholm. "But you and your colleagues have to realize that the difficulties and the margins of error are both numerous and daunting."

"I realize that," said Wallander. "We still need all the help we can get."

When the conversation with Mats Ekholm was over Wallander left the station. He drove down to the harbor and walked out onto the pier, where he had sat a few days earlier while trying to formulate his going-away speech for Björk. He sat down on the bench and watched a fishing boat on its way out of the harbor. He unbuttoned his shirt and closed his eyes, facing the sun. Somewhere close by he heard some children laughing. He tried to empty his mind and just enjoy the heat. But after a few minutes he stood up and left the harbor.

Your perpetrator has already committed two murders. We can't rule out that he intends to continue, since we don't know his motive. Ekholm's words might have been his own. His uneasiness would not subside until they had caught the person who killed Gustaf Wetterstedt and Arne Carlman. Wallander knew himself. His strength was that he never gave up. And sometimes he even showed sudden flashes of insight. But his weakness was also easy to identify. He couldn't keep his professional responsibility from becoming a personal matter. *Your* perpetrator, Ekholm had said. There was no better description of his weakness. The man who killed Wetterstedt and Carlman was actually his own responsibility. Whether he liked it or not.

He sat in his car and decided to follow the plan he had devised for himself that morning. He drove out to Wetterstedt's villa. The cordons on the beach were gone. Göran Lindgren and an older man, who he assumed was Lindgren's father, were busy sanding the boat. He didn't feel like going over to say hello.

He still had Wetterstedt's keys, and he unlocked the front door. The silence was numbing. He sat down in one of the leather chairs in the living room. He could faintly hear distant sounds from the beach. He looked around the room. What did the objects tell him? Had the perpetrator ever been inside the house? He felt that he was having a hard time gathering his thoughts. He got up from the chair and went over to the big picture window facing the garden, the beach, and the sea. Gustaf Wetterstedt had undoubtedly stood here many times. He could see that the parquet floor was worn at this spot. He looked out the window. Someone had shut off the water to the fountain in the garden, he noticed. He let his gaze wander and came back to the train of thought he had been following earlier. *On the hill outside Carlman's house my perpetrator stood and observed the party under way. He may have been there many times. From there he could exercise the power of seeing without being seen. The question now is: Where is the hill from which you would have the same view of Gustaf Wetterstedt? From what point could you see him without being seen?*

He walked around in the house and stopped at all the windows. From the kitchen window he looked for a long time at a pair of trees growing just outside Wetterstedt's property. But they were young birches that wouldn't have held the weight of anyone climbing them.

Not until he came to the study and looked out the window did he realize that he had found an answer. From the projecting garage roof it was possible to see straight into the room. He left the house and went around the garage. He knew that a younger man in good physical condition could jump up and grab hold of the eaves and then pull himself up. Wallander went and got a stepladder he had seen on the other side of the house. He leaned it against the garage roof and climbed up. The roof was the old-fashioned tarpaper type. Since he wasn't sure how much weight it could hold, he crawled on all fours over to a spot where he could look straight into Wetterstedt's study. Then he searched methodically until he found the point farthest away from the window that still had a good view inside. On his hands and knees he inspected the tarpaper. Almost at once he discovered some cuts in it criss-crossing each other. He ran his fingertips across the tarpaper. Someone had slashed it with a knife. He looked around. It was impossible to be seen either from the beach or from the road above Wetterstedt's house.

Wallander climbed down and put the ladder back. Then he carefully inspected the ground next to the foundation of the garage. The only thing he found was some ragged pages torn out of a magazine that had blown onto the property. He went back inside the house. The silence was still oppressive. He went upstairs. Through the window in Wetterstedt's bedroom he could see Göran Lindgren and his father turning their boat right side up. He could see that it took two people to turn it over.

And yet he now knew that the perpetrator had been alone, both here and when he killed Arne Carlman. Even though the clues were few, all his intuition told him that it had been a lone person sitting on Wetterstedt's roof and Carlman's hill.

I'm dealing with a lone perpetrator, he thought. A lone man who leaves his borderland and chops people to death so he can then take their scalps as trophies.

It was eleven o'clock when he left Wetterstedt's house. When he emerged into the sunshine again it was a great relief. He drove over to the OK gas station and ate at their lunch counter. A young woman at a table nearby nodded to him and said hi. He greeted her but couldn't remember who she was. Not until he left did he recall that her name was Britta-Lena Bodén and that she was a bank cashier. Once her excellent memory had been of great use to him during a criminal investigation.

By twelve o'clock he was back at the police station.

Ann-Britt Höglund met him in the foyer.

"I saw you from my window," she said.

Wallander knew at once that something had happened. He waited tensely for her to continue.

"There *is* a point of contact," she said. "In the late sixties Arne Carlman did some time in prison. At Långholmen. Gustaf Wetterstedt was justice minister at the time."

"That link isn't enough," said Wallander.

"I'm not finished. Arne Carlman wrote a letter to Gustaf Wetterstedt. And when he got out of prison they met."

Wallander stood motionless.

"How do you know this?"

"Come to my office and I'll tell you."

Wallander knew what this meant.

If the link had been found, they had broken through the hard, outermost shell of the investigation.

Chapter Fifteen

I t started with the telephone ringing.

Ann-Britt Höglund had been on her way down the corridor to talk to Martinsson when she was paged over the loudspeaker system. She returned to her office and took the call. It was a man who spoke in such a low voice that at first she thought he was sick, or maybe injured. But she understood that he wanted to talk to Wallander. No one else would do, least of all a woman. She then explained that Wallander had gone out, no one knew where he was, and no one could say when he was coming back. But the man on the phone was extremely stubborn, although she didn't understand how a man who spoke so softly could give the impression of having such a strong will. For a moment she considered transferring the call to Martinsson and letting him play the role of Wallander. But she decided against it. Something in the way the man talked told her that he might know Wallander's voice.

Right from the start he said that he had important information. She asked him whether it had to do with Gustaf Wetterstedt's death. *Maybe*, he replied. Then she asked whether it was about Arne Carlman. *Maybe*, he said once again. She realized that somehow she had to keep him talking, although he had refused to give his name or phone number.

He was the one who finally resolved the impasse. By that time he had been quiet on the line for so long that Höglund thought he had hung up. But just at that moment he spoke again and asked for the police fax number. *Give it to Wallander*, the man said. *Not to anyone else.*

An hour later the fax arrived. And now it lay on her desk. She handed it to Wallander, who had sat down in her visitor's chair. He discovered to his astonishment that the fax was sent from Skoglund's Hardware in Stockholm.

"I looked up the number and called them," she said. "I also thought it was strange that a hardware store would be open on Sunday. From a message on their answering machine I got hold of the owner via his cellular phone. He had no idea either how someone could have sent a fax from his office. He was on his way to play golf but promised to look into the matter. Half an hour later he called and reported excitedly that someone had broken into his office."

"Weird story," said Wallander.

Then he read the fax. It was written by hand and hard to read in places. Once again he thought about getting reading glasses soon. The feeling that the letters were slipping away before his eyes could no longer be explained with the excuse that he was tired or overstressed. The fax switched back and forth from cursive writing to printed letters and seemed to have been written in great haste. Wallander read it silently to himself. Then he read it aloud to make sure he hadn't misunderstood anything.

"'Arne Carlman was serving time in Långholmen during the spring of 1969 for fraud and fencing stolen goods. At that time Gustaf Wetterstedt was justice minister. Carlman wrote letters to him. He bragged about it. When he got out he met with Wetterstedt. What did they talk about? What did they do? We don't know. But later things went well for Carlman. He never went to prison again. And now they're dead. Both of them.' Have I read this correctly?"

"I came up with the same thing," she said.

"No signature," said Wallander. "And what is he really getting at? Who is he? How does he know this stuff? Is any of it true?"

"I don't know," she said. "But I had a feeling that this man knew what he was talking about. Anyway, it's not hard to check whether Carlman was really at Långholmen in the spring of 1969. We already know that Wetterstedt was justice minister then."

"Wasn't Långholmen closed down by then?" Wallander wondered.

"That happened a few years later. In 1975, I think. I can check on exactly when it was, if you want."

Wallander waved it off.

"Why did he only want to talk to me?" he asked. "Did he give any explanation?"

"I got a feeling he'd heard about you."

"So he wasn't claiming that he knew me?"

"No."

Wallander thought for a moment.

"Let's hope what he wrote is true," he said. "Then we've already established a connection between them."

"It shouldn't be too hard to check it out," said Höglund. "Even if it is Sunday."

"I know," said Wallander. "I'll go out and talk to Carlman's widow right now. She must know whether her husband was ever in prison."

"Do you want me to come along?"

"That's not necessary."

Half an hour later Wallander parked his car outside the cordon in Bjäresjö. A bored-looking patrolman sat in a car reading the paper. He straightened up when he saw Wallander approaching.

"Is Nyberg still working here?" asked Wallander in surprise. "Isn't the crime scene inspection finished?"

"I haven't seen any techs around," said the officer.

"Call in to Ystad and ask them why the cordons haven't been removed," said Wallander. "Is the family home?"

"The widow is probably there," said the officer. "And the daughter. But the sons took off in a car a few hours ago."

Wallander entered the grounds of the farm. He discovered that the bench and the table in the arbor were gone. In the beautiful summer weather the events of a few days before seemed utterly unbelievable. He knocked on the door. Arne Carlman's widow opened it almost at once.

"I'm sorry to bother you," said Wallander. "But I have a few questions that I need answered as soon as possible."

He saw that she was still very pale. As he stepped inside he smelled a faint odor of alcohol. Somewhere inside, Carlman's daughter shouted, asking who was at the door. Wallander tried to remember the name of the woman leading the way. Had he ever heard her name? Then he remembered that it was Anita. He had heard Svedberg say it during the long investigative meeting on Midsummer Day. He sat down on the sofa facing her. She lit a cigarette and looked at him. She was wearing a light summer dress. A trace of disapproval flitted through Wallander's mind. Even if she didn't love her husband, he had been murdered. Didn't people care anymore about showing respect for the dead? Couldn't she have chosen more somber attire?

Then he thought that sometimes he had such conservative views he surprised himself. Sorrow and respect didn't follow any color scheme.

"Would the inspector like something to drink?" she asked.

"No thank you," said Wallander. "I'll be as brief as I can."

Suddenly he noticed that she shot a glance past his face. He turned around. Her daughter Erika had silently entered the room and was sitting on a chair in the background. She was smoking and gave the impression of being nervous.

"Do you mind if I listen?" she asked in a voice that Wallander perceived at once as belligerent.

"Not at all," he said. "You're welcome to join us."

"I'm fine over here," she said.

Her mother shook her head almost imperceptibly. To Wallander this seemed to indicate a sense of resignation about her daughter.

"Actually I came here because today happens to be Sunday," Wallander began. "Which means that it's difficult to get information from various files and archives. And since we need to have an answer as soon as possible, I came here."

"You don't have to excuse yourself because it's Sunday," said the woman. "What is it you want to know?"

"Was your husband in prison in the spring of 1969?"

Her reply was swift and resolute.

"He was in Långholmen between the 9th of February and the 19th of June. I drove him there and I picked him up. He had been convicted of fraud and fencing stolen goods."

Her frankness made Wallander lose his train of thought for a moment. What had he expected, anyway? That she would deny it?

"Was this the first time he was sentenced to a prison term?"

"The first and the last."

"He'd been convicted of fraud and fencing stolen property?"

"That's right."

"Can you tell me any more about it?"

"He was convicted, even though he denied it. He had neither received stolen paintings nor forged any checks. It was other people who did it and used his name."

"So you think he was innocent?"

"It's not a matter of what I think. He *was* innocent."

Wallander decided to change his tactics.

"Information has surfaced which indicates your husband knew Gustaf Wetterstedt. Despite the fact that both you and your children claimed earlier that this was not the case."

"If he knew Gustaf Wetterstedt then I would have known about it."

"Could he have had contact with him without your knowledge?"

She thought for a moment before she replied.

"I have a very hard time believing that," she said.

Wallander knew at once that she wasn't telling the truth. But he couldn't figure out what the lie involved. Since he had no more questions he got to his feet.

"Perhaps you can find your own way out," said the woman on the sofa. She suddenly seemed very tired.

Wallander walked toward the door. As he approached the daughter sitting on the chair who followed his every move, she stood up and blocked his way. She was holding her cigarette in her left hand.

Out of nowhere came a slap that struck Wallander hard on his left cheek. He was so surprised that he took a step back, tripped, and fell to the floor.

"Why did you let it happen?" she shrieked.

Then she started pounding on Wallander, who with great difficulty managed to fend her off as he tried to get up. The woman on the sofa had stood up and come to his rescue. She did the same thing to her daughter as Erika had just done to Wallander. She slapped her hard in the face. When the daughter calmed down, her mother led her over to the sofa. Then she returned to Wallander, who was standing there with his burning cheek, alternating between rage and astonishment.

"Erika's been so depressed about what happened," said Anita Carlman. "She's lost control of herself. The inspector must forgive her."

"Maybe she should see a doctor," said Wallander, noticing that his voice was unsteady.

"She already has."

Wallander nodded and went out the door. He was still shocked at the violent slap. He tried to remember the last time he had been struck. It was more than ten years ago. He was interrogating a man suspected of burglary. Suddenly the man jumped up from the table and slugged him in the mouth. That time Wallander struck back. His rage was so fierce that he broke the man's nose. Afterwards the man tried to sue Wallander for police brutality and assault, but Wallander was found innocent, of course. The man later sent a complaint to the judiciary ombudsman about Wallander, but that too was dropped with no measures taken.

He had never been hit by a woman before. When his wife Mona got so worked up that she could no longer control herself, she used to throw things at him. But she had never tried to slap him. He often wondered anxiously what would have happened if she had tried. Would he have struck back? He knew there was a good chance he would.

He stood in the garden touching his cheek, which was stinging. It was as if all the energy he had felt that morning when Linda and her girlfriend stood outside his door had now vanished. He was so tired that he couldn't even manage to hold on to the unexpected surge of energy they gave him.

He walked back to his car. The patrolman was slowly rolling up the yellow crime scene tape.

He stuck *The Marriage of Figaro* in the cassette deck. He turned up the volume so high that it thundered inside the car. His cheek was still stinging. In the rearview mirror he could see that it was red. When he got to Ystad he turned into the big parking lot by the furniture store. Everything was closed, the parking lot deserted. He opened the car door and let the music flow. Barbara Hendricks made him forget about Wetterstedt and Carlman for a moment. But the girl in flames still ran through his consciousness. The rapeseed field seemed endless. She kept running and running. And burning and burning.

He turned down the music and started pacing back and forth in the parking lot. As always when he was thinking, he walked along staring at the ground. That's why Wallander never noticed the press photographer who discovered him by chance and took a picture of him through a telephoto lens as he paced around the parking grid, where there were no cars but his own on that summer day. A few weeks later, when Wallander to his astonishment discovered the photo of himself in the parking lot, he had forgotten that he had actually stopped there to try and take stock of himself and the complex criminal investigation.

The investigative team met very briefly that Sunday at two o'clock. Mats Ekholm joined them and summed up what he had discussed earlier with Hansson and Wallander. Höglund presented the contents of the anonymous fax that had arrived, and Wallander reported that Anita Carlman had confirmed the anonymous information. He said nothing about the slap in the face. When Hansson cautiously asked whether he would consider talking to the reporters who were camped out around the police station and always seemed to know when the investigative group was meeting, he said no.

"We have to teach these reporters that we're working on a legal matter," Wallander said, and could hear for himself how affected it sounded. "Ann-Britt can take care of them. I'm not interested."

"Is there anything I shouldn't say?" she asked.

"Don't say we have a suspect," said Wallander. "Because it's not true."

After the meeting Wallander exchanged a few words with Martinsson.

"Has anything more come out about the girl who burned herself to death?" he wondered.

"Not yet," said Martinsson.

"Let me know as soon as something happens."

Wallander went into his room. The telephone rang immediately. He jumped. Every time it rang he expected someone in the operations room to tell him that there was a new murder. But it was his sister. She told him that she had talked to Gertrud, the home-care worker who had married their father. There was no doubt that he had developed Alzheimer's disease. Wallander could hear that she was upset.

"He's almost eighty years old, after all," he consoled her. "Sooner or later something was bound to happen."

"But even so," she said.

Wallander knew quite well what she was talking about. He could have used the same words himself. All too often life was reduced to those powerless words of protest, *but even so.*

"He won't be able to handle a trip to Italy," she said.

"If he wants to, then he will," said Wallander. "Besides, I promised him."

"Maybe I should come with you."

"No. It's our trip."

He hung up, unsure whether she was offended that he didn't want to take her along to Italy. But he put aside those thoughts and decided that he really had to drive out and visit his father. He located the scrap of paper he had written Linda's phone number on and called her. Since he expected they would be outside on such a beautiful day, he was surprised when Kajsa answered at once. When Linda took the phone he asked whether she could get out of rehearsal and drive out with him to see her grandfather.

"Can Kajsa come along?" she asked.

"Normally I'd say yes," replied Wallander. "But today I'd prefer it if it was just you and me. There's something I need to talk to you about."

He picked her up half an hour later at Österport Square. On the way out to Löderup he told her about his father's visit to the police station, and that he was ill.

"No one knows how fast it will progress," said Wallander. "But he will be leaving us. Sort of like a ship sailing farther and farther out toward the horizon. We'll still be able to see him clearly, but for him we'll seem more and more like shapes in the fog. Our faces, our words, our common memories, everything will become indistinct and finally disappear altogether. He might act mean without even knowing it. He could turn into a totally different person."

Wallander could tell that she was getting worried.

"Can't anything be done?" she asked after sitting for a long time in silence.

"Only Gertrud can answer that," he said. "But I don't think there is any medicine for it."

He also told her about the trip that he and his father wanted to take to Italy.

"It'll be just him and me," said Wallander. "Maybe we can work out all the stuff that's come between us for so many years."

Gertrud met them on the steps when they pulled in to the courtyard. Linda ran inside to see her grandfather, who sat painting out in the studio he had fixed up in the old barn. Wallander sat down in the kitchen and talked to Gertrud. It was just as he thought. There was nothing to be done but try to live a normal life and wait.

"Will he be able to travel to Italy?" asked Wallander.

"That's all he talks about," she said. "And if he should die while he's there, it wouldn't be the worst thing that could happen."

She told him that his father had taken the news of his illness with great calm. This surprised Wallander, who had always seen his father fret about the slightest ailment.

"I think he's come to terms with his old age," said Gertrud. "He probably thinks that by and large he would have chosen to live the same life over again if he had another chance."

"But in that life he would no doubt have stopped me from becoming a cop," said Wallander.

"It's terrible, what I read in the papers," she said. "All the horrible things you have to deal with."

"Someone has to do it," said Wallander. "That's just the way it is."

They stayed and ate dinner in the garden. Wallander sensed that his father was in an unusually good mood the whole evening. He assumed that Linda was the main reason. It was already eleven by the time they drove home.

"Grownups can be so childish," she said suddenly. "Sometimes because they're showing off. Or trying to act young. But Grandpa can be childish in a way that seems completely genuine."

"Your grandpa is a very special person," said Wallander. "He always has been."

"Do you know you're starting to look like him?" she asked all of a sudden. "You two are becoming more alike every year."

"I know," said Wallander. "But I don't know if I like it."

He dropped her off at the same spot where he picked her up. They decided that she would call in a few days. He watched her disappear past Österport School and realized to his astonishment that he hadn't thought about the investigation even once the whole evening. He immediately felt guilty, then pushed the feeling away. He knew that he couldn't do any more than he had already done.

He drove up to the police station and stopped abruptly. None of the detectives were in. There weren't any messages important enough for him to answer that evening. He drove home, parked his car, and went up to his apartment.

Wallander stayed up for a long time that night. He had the windows open to the warm summer air. On his stereo he played some music by Puccini. He poured himself the last of the whisky. For the first time he thought he had rediscovered some of the happiness he had felt the afternoon he was driving out to Salomonsson's farm. That was before the catastrophe had struck. Now he was in the middle of an investigation that was marked by two basic assumptions. First, they had very little to go on when it came to identifying the perpetrator. Second, it was quite possible that he was busy carrying out his third murder at that very moment. Still, Wallander thought that he could push the investigation out of his mind at this late night hour. For a short while the girl in flames stopped running through his mind too. He had to admit that he couldn't single-handedly deal with all the violent crimes that befell Ystad's police district. He could only do his best. That's all anyone could do.

He lay down on the sofa and dozed off to the music and the summer night with the whisky glass within reach.

But something drew him back to the surface again. It was something that Linda had said in the car. Some words in a conversation that suddenly took on a whole new meaning. He sat up on the sofa with a furrowed brow. What was it she had said? *That grownups are often so childish.* There was something there that he couldn't get a fix on. *Grownups are often so childish.*

Then he realized what it was. At that moment he couldn't understand how he could have been so negligent and sloppy. He put on his shoes, found a flashlight in one of the kitchen drawers, and left the apartment. He drove out along Österleden, turned right, and stopped outside Wetterstedt's house, which lay in darkness. He opened the gate to the front yard. He gave a start when a cat vanished like a shadow among the grape bushes. Then he shone the flashlight along the foundation of the garage. He didn't have to search long before he found what he was looking for. He took the torn-out pages of the magazine between his thumb and forefinger and shone the light on them. They were from an issue of *The Phantom*. He searched in his pockets for a plastic bag and put the pages inside.

Then he drove home. He was still annoyed that he had been so sloppy. He should have known better.

Grownups are like children.

A grown man could very well have sat on the garage roof reading an issue of *The Phantom*.

Chapter Sixteen

When Wallander awoke just before five in the morning, a cloud bank had drifted in from the west and reached Ystad. It was Monday, the 27th of June. Still no rain. Wallander lay in bed and tried in vain to go back to sleep. Right before six he got up, took a shower, and made coffee. The fatigue, the lack of sleep, was like a dull pain in his body. He thought with regret about when he was ten or fifteen years younger and almost never felt tired in the morning, no matter how little sleep he got. But those days were gone and would never return.

At five to seven he walked through the doors to the police station. Ebba had already arrived, and she smiled at him as she handed him some phone message slips.

"I thought you were on vacation," said Wallander in surprise.

"Hansson asked me to stay a few extra days," said Ebba. "Now that there's so much happening."

"How's your hand doing?"

"Like I said. It's no fun getting old. Everything just starts to fall apart."

Wallander couldn't recall ever having heard Ebba make such a drastic statement. For a moment he wondered whether to tell her about his father and his illness, but decided not to. He got some coffee and sat down at his desk. After looking through the phone messages and stacking them on top of the pile from the night before, he picked up the phone and called Riga. At once he felt a pang of guilt because it was a personal call, and he was still old-fashioned enough not to want to burden his employer with an expense that was really his own. He thought about the situation a few years back, when Hansson had been consumed by a passion for playing the horses. He had spent half his workday calling around to various racetracks all over the country hunting for the latest stable tips. Everyone knew about it, but no one said anything. Wallander had been astonished that apparently he was the only one who thought somebody ought to have a talk with Hansson about it. But then one day all the racing forms and half-completed betting slips suddenly vanished from Hansson's desk. Through the grapevine Wallander heard that Hansson had simply decided to stop gambling before he wound up in debt.

Baiba picked up the phone after the third ring. Wallander was nervous. With every phone call he still had the feeling that this time she was going to tell him they shouldn't see each other anymore. He was as unsure of her feelings as he was sure of his own. But when he heard her voice she sounded happy. Her happiness was infectious. She told him that her decision to go to Tallinn had been made quite hastily. One of her women friends was going there and asked whether Baiba wanted to go along. She had no classes at the university that week. The translation job she was working on didn't have a pressing deadline, either. She told him briefly about the trip and then asked how things were in Ystad. Wallander decided for the time being not to mention that their upcoming trip to Skagen together might be jeopardized by the events of the past week. He just said that everything was fine. They agreed that he would call her that evening. Afterwards, Wallander sat with his hand resting on the phone. He immediately started to worry how she'd react if he was forced to postpone their vacation.

Wallander thought this was a bad character trait, which was growing stronger and more dominant the older he got. He worried about everything. He worried when she went to Tallinn, he worried that he was going to get sick, he worried that he might oversleep or that his car might break down. He wrapped himself in unnecessary clouds of anxiety. With a grimace he wondered whether Mats Ekholm might be able to do a psychological profile of him and suggest things he could do to free himself from all the problems he kept conjuring up in advance.

His thoughts were interrupted when Svedberg knocked on his half-open door and walked in. Wallander saw that he hadn't been careful in the sun the day before. The top of his head was completely sunburned, as were his forehead and nose.

"I'll never learn," Svedberg moped. "It hurts like hell."

Wallander thought about the burning sensation he felt after the slap he had received the day before. But he didn't mention it.

"I spent yesterday talking to the people who live in Wetterstedt's neighborhood," Svedberg said. "I found out that Wetterstedt was a man who went for walks quite often. Sometimes in the morning, sometimes in the evening. He was always polite and said hello to the people he met. But he didn't socialize with anyone in the neighborhood."

"Did he also have a habit of taking walks at night?"

Svedberg checked his notes.

"He used to go down to the beach."

"So this was a routine of his?"

"As far as I can tell, yes."

Wallander nodded.

"Just as I thought," he said.

"Something else came up that might be of interest," Svedberg continued. "A retired civil service director named Lantz said that a reporter from some newspaper had rung his doorbell on Monday the 20th of June. He asked directions to Wetterstedt's house. Lantz understood that the reporter and a photographer were on their way over there to do a story. In other words, that means someone was in his house on the last day he was alive."

"And that photographs exist," said Wallander. "Which newspaper was it?"

"Lantz didn't know."

"You'll have to get someone to start making some calls," said Wallander. "This could be important."

Svedberg nodded and left the room.

"And you ought to put some cream on that sunburn," Wallander shouted. "It doesn't look good."

After Svedberg left, Wallander called Nyberg. A few minutes later he came in and picked up the pages torn from *The Phantom*.

"I don't think your man came on a bicycle," said Nyberg. "We found some tracks behind the hut that indicate a moped or motorcycle may have stood there. We managed to find out that everyone on the road maintenance crew who uses the hut drives a car."

An image flashed through Wallander's mind, but he couldn't hold on to it. In his notebook he wrote down what Nyberg had said.

"What do you expect me to do with this?" asked Nyberg, holding up the bag with the comic book pages.

"Fingerprints," said Wallander. "Which may match other prints."

"I thought only kids read *The Phantom*," said Nyberg.

"No," replied Wallander. "There you're wrong."

When Nyberg had gone, Wallander hesitated for a moment over what he should do next. Rydberg had taught him that a cop always had to tackle whatever was most important at the moment. But what was it? They were in a phase of the investigation where everything was nebulous and no one thing could be assumed to be more important than anything else. Wallander knew that what mattered now was to trust his patience.

He went out in the corridor and knocked on the door of the office that had been assigned to Mats Ekholm. When he heard Ekholm's voice he opened the door. Ekholm was sitting with his feet on the desk, reading through some papers. He nodded toward the visitor's chair and tossed the papers on the desk.

"How's it going?" asked Wallander.

"Not so good," said Ekholm evenly. "It's hard to pin down this person. It's a shame we don't have a little more material to go on."

"In other words, he should have committed more murders?"

"To put it bluntly, that would have made the case easier," said Ekholm. "In many American investigations of serial killers conducted by the FBI, breakthroughs often come only after the third or fourth murder. By then you can sift out the things that are irrelevant in the individual case and start to filter out a consistent pattern. And a pattern is what we're looking for. A pattern we can use as a mirror so we can start to see the mind behind it all."

"What can you say about grownups who read comic books?" asked Wallander.

Ekholm raised his eyebrows.

"Does this have something to do with the case?"

"Maybe."

Wallander told him about his discovery the day before. Ekholm listened intently.

"Emotional immaturity or emotional abnormality is almost always present in individuals who commit repetitive acts," said Ekholm. "They lack the ability to acknowledge the value of other human beings. That's also why they don't react to the suffering they cause other people."

"But all grownups who read *The Phantom* aren't murderers," said Wallander.

"Just as there have been examples of serial killers who were experts on Dostoevsky," replied Ekholm. "You have to take a piece of the puzzle and see whether it fits anywhere. Or whether it might belong to a completely different puzzle."

Wallander was starting to get impatient. He didn't have time to get into a protracted discussion with Ekholm.

"Now that you've read through our material," he said, "what sort of conclusions have you come up with?"

"Just one, actually," said Ekholm. "That he will strike again."

Wallander waited for something more, an explanation, but it didn't come.

"Why?"

"Something about the total picture tells me so. And I can't say why except that it's based on experience. From other cases with trophy hunters."

"What kind of image do you see?" asked Wallander. "Tell me what you're thinking right now. Anything at all. And I promise I won't hold you to it later."

"A grown man," replied Ekholm. "Considering the age of the victims and the fact that he may have had something to do with them, I'd say he's at least thirty. But maybe older. The possible identification with a myth, perhaps an Indian, makes me think that he's in very good physical condition. He's both cautious and cunning. Which means that he's the calculating type. I think he lives a regular, orderly life. He hides his inner drama behind a surface of undramatic normality."

"And he's going to strike again?"

Ekholm threw out his hands.

"Let's hope I'm wrong. But you asked me to tell you what I'm thinking right now."

"Wetterstedt and Carlman were separated by three days," said Wallander. "If he keeps to the three-day interval, he's going to kill somebody else today."

"That's not necessarily inevitable," said Ekholm. "Since he's cunning, the time factor doesn't play a crucial role. He strikes when he's sure of success. Something might happen today, of course. But it could also take several weeks. Or years."

Wallander had no more questions. He asked Ekholm to attend the meeting with the investigative group an hour later. He went back to his room and felt a growing anxiety about what Ekholm had said. The man they were looking for, whom they knew nothing about, was going to strike again.

He pulled over the notebook in which he had written down what Nyberg told him, and he tried to recapture the fleeting images that had passed through his mind. Wallander had a feeling that this was important. He was sure it had something to do with the road maintenance hut. But he couldn't figure out what.

Then he got up and went to the conference room. Right now he missed Rydberg more than ever.

Wallander sat in his usual seat at one end of the table. He looked around. Everyone who was supposed to be there had come. He immediately sensed the special air of concentration that arose when everyone hoped they were going to make a breakthrough in an investigation. Wallander knew they'd be disappointed. But none of them would show it. The detectives gathered in this room were all pros.

"Let's start with a review of what's happened in the past twenty-four hours in the scalping case," he began.

He hadn't planned to say *the scalping case;* it just came out. But from that moment on the investigation was never called anything else by the team.

Unless circumstances demanded it, Wallander usually waited until last to give his report. The main reason for this was that everyone expected him to sum up and direct them further. It was natural for Höglund to be the first to speak. She passed around the table the fax that had come from Skoglund's Hardware. The information that had already been confirmed by Anita Carlman had been checked in the national prison register. But Höglund had just begun the most difficult task. To track down some corroboration and preferably copies of the letters that Carlman supposedly wrote to Wetterstedt.

"The problem is that it all happened so long ago," she concluded. "Although we live in a country in which files and archives are well organized, it takes a long time to track down events that occurred and documents that were written more than twenty-five years ago. In addition, we're dealing with a time before computers had completely taken over the handling of various files and archives."

"We still have to keep digging, though," said Wallander. "The link between Wetterstedt and Carlman is crucial to our ongoing progress."

"The man who called," said Svedberg, rubbing his sunburned nose. "Why wouldn't he say who he was? Who would break into a store just to send a fax?"

"I've thought about that," said Höglund. "Obviously he wanted to divert us onto a specific track. And there could be a lot of reasons why he wants to protect his identity. One of them might be that he's just plain scared."

The whole room fell silent.

Wallander could see that Höglund was on the right track. He nodded to her to continue.

"Naturally, it's pure guesswork. But let's say he feels threatened by the man who killed Wetterstedt and Carlman. He would be extremely eager for us to capture the perpetrator, obviously. Without revealing his own identity."

"In that case he should have been more specific," said Martinsson.

"Maybe he couldn't be," Höglund objected. "If my hunch is right, that he contacted us because he's scared, then he probably told us everything he knows."

Wallander lifted his hand.

"Let's take this even further," he said. "The man who sends the fax gives us information relating to Carlman. Not Wetterstedt. That's a crucial point. He claims that Carlman wrote letters to Wetterstedt and that they met after Carlman was released from prison. Who would have this kind of information?"

"Another inmate at the prison," said Höglund.

"That was exactly my thought," said Wallander. "But on the other hand we have your hypothesis that he's contacting us because he's afraid. Would that be true if his contact with Carlman was only that of some fellow prisoner?"

"There's more to it than that," said Höglund. "He knows that Carlman and Wetterstedt met after Carlman got out of prison. This indicates that the contact has continued."

"He could have been a witness to something," said Hansson, who until now had kept silent. "For some reason this has now become the cause of two murders twenty-five years later."

Wallander turned to Mats Ekholm, who was sitting by himself far down one side of the table.

"Twenty-five years is a long time," said Wallander.

"The incubation period for revenge can last forever," said Ekholm. "Psychological processes have no prescribed time limits. It's one of the oldest truths in criminology that an avenger can wait as long as he wants. If this *is* a matter of revenge, that is."

"What else could it be?" asked Wallander. "We can rule out crimes against property. In all probability when it comes to Gustaf Wetterstedt, and with complete certainty in Carlman's case."

"The fabric of a motive can have many components," said Ekholm. "Even a murder of pure passion can be based on a motive that's invisible at first glance. A serial killer may choose his victims for reasons that to us seem utterly inexplicable. Take the scalps, for instance; we might ask ourselves whether he's after a special kind of hair. In photographs I can see that Wetterstedt and Carlman had the same full head of gray hair. We can't exclude anything. But as a layman when it comes to police methods of directing investigations, I agree that right now the point of contact ought to be the most important thing to focus on."

"Is it possible that we're thinking along the wrong lines altogether?" asked Martinsson suddenly. "Maybe the perpetrator thinks there's a *symbolic* link between Wetterstedt and Carlman. While we search and dig for the facts, maybe he sees a symbolic connection that's invisible to us. Something that's completely inconceivable to our rational minds."

Wallander knew that at certain moments Martinsson had the ability to turn an investigation around on its axis and get it back on the right track.

"You're thinking of something," he said. "Keep going."

Martinsson shrugged his shoulders and already seemed about to back down from his suggestion.

"Wetterstedt and Carlman were wealthy men," he said. "They both belonged to the upper class. As symbolic representatives of political and economic power, both of them were well chosen."

"Are you suggesting a terrorist motive?" Wallander asked, surprised.

"I'm not suggesting anything," said Martinsson. "I'm listening to what you're saying and trying to think myself. I'm just as afraid as everyone else in this room that he's going to strike again."

Wallander looked at the people sitting around the table. Pale, serious faces. Except for Svedberg with his sunburn.

Only now did he realize that they were all as scared as he was.

He wasn't the only one who dreaded the next ring of the telephone.

The meeting broke up before ten o'clock. But Wallander asked Martinsson to stay behind.

"How's it going with the girl?" he asked. "Dolores María Santana?"

"I'm still waiting for Interpol to respond."

"Give them a nudge," said Wallander.

Martinsson gave him a puzzled look.

"Do we really have time for her right now?"

"No. But we can't just let it drop either."

Martinsson promised to send off another request for information about Dolores María Santana. Wallander went in his office and called Lars Magnusson. It took a long time before he answered. Wallander could hear from his voice that he was drunk.

"I need to continue our conversation," he said.

"You're calling too late," said Magnusson. "I don't conduct any conversations this time of day."

"Fix some coffee," said Wallander. "And put away the bottles. I'm coming over in half an hour."

He hung up amidst Magnusson's protests. Then he read through the two preliminary autopsy reports that someone had placed on his desk. Over the years Wallander had learned how to decipher the often impenetrable reports written by pathologists and forensic doctors. Many years ago he had also taken a course arranged by the National Police Board. That was in Uppsala, and Wallander could still remember how unpleasant it was to visit an autopsy room.

He didn't notice anything unexpected in the two reports. He put them aside and looked out the window.

He tried to visualize the perpetrator they were looking for. What did he look like? What was he doing right now?

He came up blank. Wallander saw nothing but darkness before him.

Depressed, he got up and left.

Chapter Seventeen

Wallander left Lars Magnusson's apartment after more than two hours of fruitlessly trying to conduct a coherent conversation. All he wanted was to go home and take a bath. The first time he'd been at Magnusson's he hadn't noticed the filth, but this time the decay was obvious. The front door was ajar when Wallander arrived. Magnusson was lying on his couch while a saucepan of coffee boiled over in the kitchen. He greeted Wallander by telling him to go to hell. Don't come around anymore, just get out and forget there's anyone called Lars Magnusson. But Wallander stood his ground. His interpretation of the coffee on the stove was that for a brief moment Magnusson had reconsidered whether he would talk to someone in the middle of the day after all. Wallander searched in vain for a couple of clean cups. In the sink were plates on which the food and grease had congealed into weird fossilized concretions. Finally he found two cups, which he washed and carried into the living room.

Magnusson wore only a pair of dirty shorts. He was unshaven and clutched a bottle of dessert wine in his hands like a crucifix. Wallander was repelled by his dissipation. What he found most disgusting was that Lars Magnusson was losing his teeth. Then Wallander grew annoyed and finally angry that the man on the sofa didn't seem to be listening. He yanked the bottle away from him and bluntly demanded answers to his questions. He had no idea what authority he was invoking. But Magnusson did as he was told. He even hauled himself up to a sitting position. Wallander tried to penetrate deeper into the bygone era when Gustaf Wetterstedt was a justice minister surrounded by veiled rumors of scandal. But Magnusson seemed to have forgotten everything. He could no longer remember what he'd said the last time Wallander came by. Not until Wallander gave him back the bottle and he took a few more slugs did some feeble memories begin to surface.

By the time Wallander left the apartment he had managed to eke out one lead. In an unexpected moment of clarity, Magnusson remembered that there was a cop on the Stockholm vice squad who had developed a particular interest in Gustaf Wetterstedt. Rumor had it that this man, who Magnusson with some difficulty recalled was named Hugo Sandin, had set up a private archive on Wetterstedt. As far as Magnusson knew, nothing had ever come of it. On the other hand, he heard that Hugo Sandin had moved south when he retired and now lived with his son, who had a pottery workshop outside Hässleholm.

"If he's still alive," Magnusson said, smiling his toothless smile, as though deep down he hoped that Hugo Sandin had passed on ahead of him.

Wallander drove back to the police station determined to locate Hugo Sandin. In the lobby he ran into Svedberg, whose sunburned face was still tormenting him.

"Wetterstedt was interviewed by a journalist from *MagaZenit*," said Svedberg. Wallander had never heard of the magazine.

"All the retirees get it," Svedberg told him. "The journalist's name was Anna-Lisa Blomgren. She had a photographer with her. Now that Wetterstedt is dead they aren't going to publish their material."

"Talk to her," said Wallander. "And ask the photographer for the pictures."

Wallander went to his office. He called the switchboard and asked them to find Nyberg, who called back fifteen minutes later.

"Do you remember I gave you a bag with the camera from Wetterstedt's house?" Wallander asked.

"Of course I remember," said Nyberg grumpily.

"I just wonder whether the film has been developed yet. I think there were seven pictures exposed."

"Didn't you get them?" Nyberg asked, surprised.

"No."

"They should have been sent over to you last Saturday."

"I never got them."

"Are you sure?"

"Maybe they're lying around somewhere."

"I'll have to check this out," said Nyberg. "I'll get back to you."

Wallander knew somebody would soon bear the brunt of Nyberg's wrath, and he was glad it wasn't him.

He found the number of the Hässleholm police and after some difficulty managed to get hold of an officer who knew Hugo Sandin's phone number. When Wallander asked about Sandin, he was told that he was about eighty-five years old but that his mind was still sharp.

"He usually stops by to visit a couple of times a year," said the officer, who introduced himself as Mörk.

Wallander wrote down the number and thanked him for his help. Then he called Malmö. He was immediately connected to the doctor who had done the autopsy on Wetterstedt.

"There's nothing here about the time of death," said Wallander. "That's a piece of important information for us."

The doctor asked him to wait a moment while he went to get his file. After about a minute he returned and said he was sorry.

"Unfortunately, it was left out of the report. Sometimes my Dictaphone acts up. But Wetterstedt died less than twenty-four hours before he was found. We're still waiting for some results from the lab that will enable us to reduce the time span even more."

"Then we'll wait for those results," said Wallander and thanked him.

He went in to see Svedberg, who was at his computer.

"Did you talk to that journalist?"

"That's just what I'm typing up."

"Did you get any times?"

Svedberg looked through his notes.

"They got to Wetterstedt's house at ten and stayed until one."

"After one o'clock, nobody else saw him alive?"

Svedberg thought for a moment.

"Not that I know of."

"So, we know that much," said Wallander and left the room.

He was just about to call Hugo Sandin, when Martinsson came in.

"Have you got a minute?" he asked.

"Always," said Wallander. "What's up?"

Martinsson waved a letter.

"This came in the mail today," he said. "It's from someone who claims he gave a girl a ride from Helsingborg to Tomelilla on Monday night, June 20th. From the descriptions in the papers of the girl who burned herself to death, he thinks it might have been her."

Martinsson handed the envelope to Wallander, who took out the letter and read it.

"No signature," he said.

"But the letterhead is interesting."

Wallander nodded.

"Smedstorp Congregation," he said. "Genuine State Church stationery."

"We'll probably have to check this out," said Martinsson.

"We certainly will," said Wallander. "If you take care of Interpol and all the other things you're busy with, I'll take care of this."

"I still don't see how we have time for this," said Martinsson.

"We'll make time," said Wallander.

After Martinsson left, Wallander realized that he had just been subtly criticized for not dropping everything that had to do with the dead girl for the time being. For a moment Wallander thought Martinsson might be right. There was no time right now for anything but Wetterstedt and Carlman. Then he decided the criticism was unjustified. There was no limit to what the police could get done. They just had to make time to handle everything.

As if to prove that his view was correct, Wallander left the station and drove out of town toward Tomelilla and Smedstorp. The drive also gave him time to think about Wetterstedt and Carlman. The summer landscape seemed a surreal frame for his thoughts. Two men are axed to death and scalped, he thought. A young girl walks into a rapeseed field and burns herself to death. And all around me it's summertime. Skåne couldn't get any more beautiful than this. There's a paradise hidden in every corner of this countryside. To find it, all you have to do is keep your eyes open. But you might also see the invisible hearses sneaking along the highways.

He knew where the parish pastor's office was in Smedstorp. After he passed Lunnarp he turned left. He also knew that the church offices kept very irregular hours. But when he reached the whitewashed building he saw some cars parked outside. A man was mowing the lawn nearby. Wallander tried the door. It was locked. He rang the bell as he read the brass plate, which said that the next time the pastor's office would be open was on Wednesday. He waited. Then he rang again and knocked on the door. A lawnmower chugged in the background. Wallander was just about to leave when a window on the floor above opened. A woman stuck her head out.

"We're open on Wednesdays and Fridays," she shouted.

"I know," said Wallander. "But this is urgent. I'm from the Ystad police."

Her head disappeared. Then the door opened. A blonde woman dressed in black stood before him, heavily made up and wearing high heels. But what surprised Wallander was the small white pastor's collar contrasting with all that black. He shook hands and introduced himself.

"Gunnel Nilsson," she replied. "I'm the pastor of this congregation."

Wallander followed her inside. If I were walking into a nightclub I could better understand it, he thought. Pastors nowadays don't look the way I imagined.

She opened the door to an office and asked him to have a seat. Wallander noticed that Gunnel Nilsson was a very attractive woman. But he couldn't decide whether the fact that she was a pastor contributed to the way he felt.

He saw a letter lying on her desk. He recognized the congregation's letterhead.

"The police received a letter on your letterhead. That's why I'm here."

He told her about the girl who had burned herself to death. He could see that the pastor seemed upset. When he asked her about this, she explained that she had been sick for a few days and hadn't read the papers.

Wallander showed her the letter.

"Do you have any idea who wrote it? Or who has access to your letterhead?"

She shook her head.

"A pastor's office isn't like a bank," she replied. "And only women work here."

"It's not clear whether a man or a woman wrote the letter," Wallander pointed out.

"I don't know who it could be," she said.

"Does anyone in the office live in Helsingborg? Or drive there often?"

She shook her head again. Wallander felt she was really trying to help him.

"How many people work here?" he asked.

"There are four of us. And then there's Andersson, who takes care of the garden. We also have a full-time watchman, Sture Rosell. But he mainly stays in the churchyards and in our churches. Either one of them could have taken some letterhead from here, of course. Plus anyone who visited the pastor's office on business."

"You don't recognize the handwriting?"

"No."

"It's not against the law to pick up hitchhikers," said Wallander. "Why would someone write an anonymous letter? Because they wanted to hide the fact that they had been in Helsingborg at all? To me this anonymity is puzzling."

"Naturally I could ask whether anyone here was in Helsingborg that day," she said. "And I can try to see whether the handwriting matches up with anyone's."

"I'd appreciate the help," said Wallander and stood up. "You can reach me at the Ystad police station."

He wrote his phone number on the slip of paper she handed him. She followed him out.

"I've never met a woman pastor before," he said.

"Many people are still surprised," she replied.

"In Ystad we have our first woman chief of police," he said. "Everything changes."

"For the better, I hope," she said and smiled.

Wallander looked at her and decided she was quite beautiful. He didn't see a ring on her finger. When he got back to the car he couldn't help thinking some forbidden thoughts. She really was very attractive.

The man cutting the grass was now sitting on a bench smoking. Later Wallander couldn't explain why he did it, but he sat down on the bench and started talking to the man, who was about sixty years old. He was dressed in an open blue work shirt and dirty corduroy pants. He had on a pair of ancient tennis shoes. Wallander noticed that he was smoking unfiltered Chesterfields. He remembered from his childhood that his father once smoked the same brand.

"She doesn't usually open the door when the office is supposed to be closed," the man said philosophically. "To be honest, this is the first time it's ever happened."

"The pastor is quite good-looking," said Wallander.

"She's nice too," said the man. "And she gives a good sermon. I don't know whether we've ever had such a good pastor. But of course there are plenty of people who would rather have a man."

"There are?" said Wallander absentmindedly.

"Quite a few people would never think of having anything but a male pastor. People in Skåne are conservative. For the most part."

The conversation died out. It was as if both men had run out of steam. Wallander listened to the birds. He could smell the new-mown grass. He thought he ought to get hold of his colleague in the Östermalm police, Hans Vikander, and find out whether anything had come of the interview he presumably had conducted with Gustaf Wetterstedt's old mother. He had a lot of things to do. He certainly didn't have time to sit on a bench outside the pastor's office in Smedstorp.

"Were you here to get a change of address certificate?" the man asked suddenly.

"I just had a few questions to ask," he said, getting up.

The man squinted at him.

"I recognize you," he said. "Are you from Tomelilla?"

"No," said Wallander. "I'm originally from Malmö. But I've lived in Ystad for many years."

He was about to say goodbye when he noticed the white T-shirt showing under his unbuttoned work shirt. It advertised the ferry line between Helsingborg and Helsingør, in Denmark. He knew it could be a coincidence, but quickly decided that it wasn't. He sat back down on the bench. The man stubbed out his cigarette in the grass, about to get up.

"Hang on for a minute," said Wallander. "There's something I'd like to ask you about."

The man heard the change in Wallander's voice. He gave him a wary look.

"I'm a police officer," said Wallander. "I didn't actually come here to talk to the pastor. I came to talk to you. I wonder why you didn't sign the letter you sent us. About the girl you gave a lift to from Helsingborg."

It was a reckless move, he knew. It went against everything he had been taught. It was a punch below the belt; a cop didn't have the right to lie to extract a truth. Especially when no crime had been committed.

But the trick worked. The man jumped, caught off guard. It startled him so badly that any reasonable objections he had seemed to have vanished. How could Wallander know he had written the letter? How could he know anything at all, for that matter?

Wallander saw him thinking all of this. Now that the blow had fallen, he could pick him up off the imaginary floor and reassure him.

"It's not against the law to write anonymous letters," he said. "Or to pick up hitchhikers. I just want to know why you did it. And what time you picked her up and where you let her off. The exact time. And whether she said anything in the car during the trip."

"Now I recognize you," muttered the man. "You're the cop who shot a man in the fog a few years ago. On the shooting range outside Ystad."

"You're right," said Wallander. "That was me. My name is Kurt Wallander."

"She was standing at the freeway entrance heading south," said the man suddenly. "It was seven o'clock in the evening. I had driven over to Helsingborg to buy a pair of shoes. My cousin has a shoe store there. He gives me a discount. I don't usually pick up hitchhikers. But she looked so forlorn."

"Then what happened?"

"Nothing happened. What do you mean?"

"When you stopped the car. What language did she speak?"

"I have no idea what language it was. It wasn't Swedish, that's for sure. And I don't speak English. I said I was going to Tomelilla. She nodded. She nodded at everything I said."

"Did she have any luggage?"

"Not a thing."

"Not even a purse?"

"Nothing."

"And then you drove off?"

"She sat in the back seat. She never said a word. I thought there was something funny about the whole thing. I was sorry I picked her up."

"Why's that?"

"Maybe she wasn't going to Tomelilla at all. Who the hell goes to Tomelilla?"

"So she didn't say anything?"

"Not a word."

"What did she do?"

"Do?"

"Did she sleep? Look out the window? What did she do?"

The man tried to remember.

"There was one thing I worried about afterwards. Every time a car passed us she would crouch down in the back seat. As if she didn't want to be seen."

"So she was scared?"

"She sure was."

"Then what happened?"

"I stopped at the traffic circle outside Tomelilla and let her out. To tell you the truth, I don't think she had any idea where she was."

"So she wasn't going to Tomelilla?"

"If you ask me, I think she just wanted to get out of Helsingborg. I drove off. But when I was almost home I thought, I can't just let her stand there. Then I drove back. But by that time she was gone."

"How long did it take you?"

"No more than ten minutes."

Wallander thought for a moment.

"When you picked her up outside Helsingborg, she was standing at the entrance to the freeway. Is it possible she got a lift to Helsingborg? Or was she coming from the city?"

The man thought about this.

"From the city," he said. "If she'd been left off farther north she wouldn't have been standing where she was."

"Then you never saw her again? You didn't drive after her?"

"Why would I do that?"

"What time was it when all this happened?"

"I let her off at eight o'clock. I remember that the news on the car radio started just as she was getting out of the car."

Wallander thought about what he had heard. He knew he was in luck.

"Why did you write to the police?" he asked. "Why did you write anonymously?"

"I read about the girl who burned herself to death," he said. "All at once I had a feeling it might have been her. But I preferred not to identify myself. I'm a married man. The fact that I picked up a female hitchhiker might have been misinterpreted."

Wallander could tell that the man next to him was telling the truth.

"This conversation is off the record," he said. "But I still have to ask you for your name and telephone number."

"My name is Sven Andersson," said the man. "I hope there won't be any trouble."

"Not if you told me the truth," said Wallander.

He wrote down the phone number.

"One more thing," he said. "Can you recall whether she was wearing a necklace?"

Sven Andersson thought about it. Then he shook his head. Wallander got up and shook his hand.

"You've been a great help," he said.

"Was it her?" Andersson asked.

"Possibly," said Wallander. "The question now is what she was doing in Helsingborg."

He left Sven Andersson and walked to his car.

Just as he opened the door his car phone rang.

His first thought was that the man who killed Wetterstedt and Carlman had struck again.

Chapter Eighteen

In the car on the way back to Ystad, Wallander decided to drive up to Hässleholm later that day to talk with retired detective Hugo Sandin. When Wallander picked up his phone and heard it was Nyberg telling him that the seven developed photos were waiting on his desk, not a message that the man who killed Wetterstedt and Carlman had struck again, he felt a great sense of relief. Later, when he had left Smedstorp behind, he thought he should learn to control his anxieties better. There was no guarantee that the man had more victims on his invisible list, but Wallander couldn't shake the disturbing thought. Like his colleagues, he had to continue his investigative work as if nothing more was going to happen. Otherwise they'd waste all their time in fruitless anticipation.

He went straight to his office and wrote up a report of his conversation with Sven Andersson. He tried unsuccessfully to get hold of Martinsson; all Ebba knew was that he had left the station without saying where he was going. When Wallander tried to reach him on his mobile phone, a message told him it was turned off. He was annoyed that Martinsson was often impossible to contact. At the next investigative group meeting, he would announce that everyone had to be reachable at all times. Then he remembered the photos Nyberg claimed were lying on his desk. Without noticing, he had put his notebook on top of the envelope. He took them out, turned on his desk lamp, and looked at them one by one. Although he didn't really know what he had expected, he was disappointed. The photos showed nothing more than the view from Wetterstedt's house. They were taken from the top floor. He could see Lindgren's overturned boat and the sea, which was calm. There were no people in the pictures. The beach was deserted. Two of the pictures were blurry. He wondered why Wetterstedt had taken them—if, indeed, he had taken them himself. He found a magnifying glass in a desk drawer, but still couldn't see anything of interest. He put them back in the envelope and thought he'd have to ask someone else on the team to take a look, just to confirm he hadn't missed anything.

He was just about to call Hässleholm when a secretary knocked on the door with a fax from Hans Vikander in Stockholm. It was a report, five single-spaced pages, of a conversation he had had with Wetterstedt's mother. He read through it quickly; it was accurately done but completely lacking in imagination. There was not one question that Wallander couldn't predict. In his experience, an interview or other type of conversation related to a criminal investigation had to contain just as many background inquiries as surprise questions. At the same time he thought he was probably being unfair to Hans Vikander. What was the chance that a ninety-four-year-old lady would say something unexpected about her son, whom she hardly ever saw and exchanged only brief phone calls with? Wallander could find nothing to further the investigation.

He got some coffee and thought idly about the female pastor in Smedstorp. When he got back to his room he called the number in Hässleholm. A young man answered. Wallander introduced himself and stated his business. It took several minutes before Hugo Sandin came to the phone. He had a clear, resolute voice. Sandin told Wallander that he was prepared to meet with him that same day. Wallander grabbed his notebook and wrote down the directions.

It was past three when he left the police station. On the way to Hässleholm he stopped to eat. It was after five when he turned off at the remodeled mill with a sign for the pottery workshop. An elderly man was walking around outside the house pulling up dandelions. When Wallander got out of the car the man wiped off his hands and came toward him. Wallander had a hard time believing that this vigorous man was over eighty, and that Hugo Sandin and his own father were almost the same age.

"I don't get many visitors," said Hugo Sandin. "All my friends are gone. I have one colleague from the old homicide squad who's still alive. But now he's in a home outside Stockholm and can't remember anything that happened after 1960. Getting old is really shit."

Sandin was expressing the same sentiments Wallander had heard from Ebba. That was one difference from his own father, at least, who almost never complained about his age.

In an old coach house that had been converted to a showroom for the products of the ceramics workshop there was a table with a thermos and cups set out. Wallander suspected that courtesy required him to spend a few minutes admiring the ceramics on display. Sandin sat down at the table and served coffee.

"You're the first cop I've met who's interested in ceramics," he said ironically.

Wallander sat down.

"Actually, I'm not," he admitted.

"Cops usually like to fish," said Sandin. "At lonely, isolated mountain lakes. Or deep in the forests of Småland."

"I didn't know that," said Wallander. "I never go fishing."

Sandin looked at him intently.

"What do you do when you're not working?"

"I guess I have a pretty hard time relaxing."

Sandin nodded in approval.

"Being a cop is a calling," he said. "Just like being a doctor. We're always on duty. Whether we're in uniform or not."

Wallander decided not to argue, even though he didn't agree with Sandin at all that a policeman's job was a calling. Once he may have believed that. But not anymore. At least he didn't think so.

"So tell me," Sandin prodded. "I read in the papers about what's going on in Ystad. Tell me what they left out."

Wallander recounted the circumstances surrounding the two murders. Now and then Sandin would interrupt with a question, always to the point.

"In other words, it's likely that he may kill again," he said when Wallander was done.

"We can't ignore that possibility."

Sandin shoved his chair back from the table so he could stretch out his legs.

"And now you want me to tell you about Gustaf Wetterstedt," he said. "I'll be happy to. May I first ask you how you found out that once, a long time ago, I took a special interest in him?"

"A journalist in Ystad told me. Lars Magnusson. Unfortunately, quite an alcoholic."

"I don't recognize the name."

"Anyway, he's the one who knew."

Hugo Sandin sat silently, stroking his lips with one finger. Wallander got a feeling that he was looking for the right place to begin.

"The truth about Gustaf Wetterstedt is very simple," said Sandin. "He was a crook. As minister of justice he may have been technically competent. But he was totally unsuitable."

"Why?"

"His political activities were marked more by attention to his own career than to the good of the country. That's the absolute worst testimonial you can give about a government minister."

"And yet he was under consideration to be leader of the party?"

Sandin shook his head vigorously.

"That's not true," he said. "It was the newspapers that were speculating about that. Within the party it was obvious that he could never be their leader. The question is whether he was even a member of the party."

"But he was justice minister for many years. He couldn't have been totally incompetent."

"You're too young to remember. But there was a dividing line sometime in the fifties. It was invisible, but it was there. Sweden was sailing along on unbelievably fair winds. There were unlimited means available to obliterate the last remnants of poverty. At the same time a hidden trend was emerging in political life. The politicians were turning into professionals. Career politicians. Before, idealism had been a dominant part of political life. Now this idealism began to be diluted. People like Gustaf Wetterstedt started their climb upwards. Political youth associations became the hatcheries for politicians who would be suitable in the future."

"Let's talk about the scandals that surrounded him," said Wallander, afraid that Sandin would get lost in agitated political reminiscences.

"He associated with prostitutes," said Sandin. "And he wasn't the only one, of course. But he had particular inclinations that he took out on the girls."

"I heard about one girl who filed a complaint," said Wallander.

"Her name was Karin Bengtsson," said Sandin. "She came from unhappy family circumstances in Eksjö. She ran away to Stockholm and appeared in the vice squad's records for the first time in 1954. A few years later she wound up with the group from which Wetterstedt picked his girls. In January 1957 she filed a complaint against him. He cut her feet with a razor blade. I met her myself at that time. She could hardly walk. Wetterstedt realized that this time he had gone too far. The complaint was dropped, and Karin Bengtsson was paid off. She received money to invest in a clothing boutique in Västerås. In 1959, enough money magically appeared in her bank account to buy a house. In 1960, she started vacationing in Mallorca every year."

"Who came up with the money?"

"Even back then there were slush funds. The Swedish royal family had established a precedent by paying off women who had been too intimate with the old king."

"Is Karin Bengtsson still alive?"

"She died in May of 1984. She never married. I never saw her after she moved to Västerås. But she called once in a while. Right up to the last year of her life. She was usually drunk when she called."

"Why did she call you?"

"As soon as the rumors started that there was a prostitute who wanted to file a complaint against Wetterstedt, I got in touch with her. I wanted to help her. Her life had been destroyed. Her self-esteem evidently wasn't very high."

"Why did you get involved?"

"I was upset. I was pretty radical in those days. Too many cops accepted the corruption. I didn't. No more than I do now."

"What happened afterwards, when Karin Bengtsson was out of the picture?"

"Wetterstedt continued as before. He sliced up lots of girls. But none of them filed any complaints. But two of the girls did disappear."

"What do you mean?"

Sandin looked at Wallander in surprise.

"I mean they were never heard from again. We searched for them, tried to trace them. But they were gone."

"What happened? What's your opinion?"

"I think they were killed, of course. Dissolved in lime, dumped in the sea. How do I know?"

Wallander had a hard time believing what he was hearing.

"Can this really be true?" he said doubtfully. "It sounds incredible, to say the least."

"What is it people say? Amazing but true?"

"So you think Wetterstedt committed murder?"

Sandin shook his head.

"I'm not saying he did it himself. Actually I'm convinced he didn't. Exactly what happened, I don't know. We'll probably never find out. But we can still draw conclusions, even if there's no evidence."

"I'm still having a hard time believing this," said Wallander.

"It's absolutely true, believe me," said Sandin firmly. "Wetterstedt had no conscience. But nothing could ever be proved, of course."

"There were a lot of rumors about him."

"They were all justified. Wetterstedt used his position and his power to satisfy his perverted sexual desires. But he was also mixed up in secret deals that made him rich."

"Art deals?"

"Art thefts, more likely. In my free time I tried to track down all the connections. I dreamed that someday I'd be able to slam down a report on the prosecutor's desk so airtight that Wetterstedt would not only be forced to resign, but would end up with a stiff prison sentence. Unfortunately I never got that far."

"You must have a great deal of material left from those days, don't you?"

"I burned it all a few years ago. In my son's pottery kiln. There were at least ten kilos of paper."

Wallander swore silently. He hadn't imagined that Hugo Sandin would get rid of the material he had so laboriously gathered.

"I still have a good memory," said Sandin. "I could probably remember everything in the stuff I burned."

"Arne Carlman," said Wallander. "Who was he?"

"A man who raised art peddling to a higher level," replied Sandin.

"In the spring of 1969 he was sitting in Långholmen prison," said Wallander. "We got an anonymous tip that he had contact with Wetterstedt. And that they met after Carlman got out of jail."

"Carlman popped up now and then in various reports. I think he wound up in Långholmen for something as simple as passing a bad check."

"Did you ever find any links between him and Wetterstedt?"

"There was information that they had met as early as the late fifties. Apparently they had a mutual interest in playing the horses. Their names came up in connection with a raid on Täby racetrack around 1962. Although

Wetterstedt's name was deleted, since it wasn't considered a good idea to tell the public that a justice minister had been frequenting a racetrack."

"What kind of dealings did they have with each other?"

"Nothing we could pin down. They circled like planets in separate orbits which happened to cross now and then."

"I need to find that point of connection," said Wallander. "I'm convinced we have to find that link so we can identify the person who killed them."

"You can usually find what you're looking for if you dig deep enough," said Sandin.

Wallander's mobile phone rang. He instantly felt an icy fear that something serious had happened.

But he was wrong again. It was Hansson.

"I just wanted to hear whether you'll be back today. Otherwise I'll set up a meeting for tomorrow."

"Has anything happened?"

"Nothing crucial. Everyone's immersed in their own assignments."

"Tomorrow morning at eight," said Wallander. "Nothing more tonight."

"Svedberg went to the hospital to get his sunburn looked at," said Hansson.

"He ought to be more careful," said Wallander. "This happens every year."

He said goodbye and put down the phone.

"You're in the papers a lot," said Hugo Sandin. "You seem to have gone your own way occasionally."

"Most of what they say isn't true," said Wallander evasively.

"I often ask myself what it's like to be a cop nowadays," said Sandin.

"So do I," said Wallander.

They got up and walked toward Wallander's car. It was a beautiful evening.

"Can you think of anyone who might have wanted to kill Wetterstedt?" asked Wallander.

"There are probably quite a few," said Sandin.

Wallander stopped short.

"Maybe we're thinking about this the wrong way," he said. "Maybe we should separate the investigations. Not look for a common denominator, but for two separate solutions. And find the link that way."

"The murders were committed by the same man," said Sandin, "so the investigations have to be intertwined. Otherwise I think you might end up on the wrong track."

Wallander nodded.

"Call me again sometime," said Sandin. "I have all the time in the world. Growing old means loneliness. A hopeless wait for the inevitable."

"Did you ever regret joining the police?" asked Wallander.

"Never," said Sandin. "Why would I?"

"Just wondering," said Wallander. "Thanks for taking the time to talk to me."

"You'll catch him," said Sandin encouragingly. "Even if it takes a while."

Wallander nodded and got into his car. As he drove off he could see Hugo Sandin in the rearview mirror, pulling dandelions from the lawn.

It was almost a quarter to eight by the time Wallander got back to Ystad. He parked the car outside his building and was just about to walk through the main door when he remembered that he didn't have any food in the house.

He also remembered that he had forgotten to have the car inspected again. He swore out loud.

Then he walked into town and ate dinner at the Chinese restaurant on the square. He was the only patron in the place. After dinner he strolled down to the harbor and walked out on the pier. As he watched the boats rocking gently at their moorings he thought about the two conversations he had had that day.

A girl by the name of Dolores María Santana had stood at the freeway entrance from Helsingborg one evening looking for a ride. She didn't speak Swedish and she was afraid of the cars that passed them. All they knew was that she was born in the Dominican Republic.

He stared at an old, well-kept wooden boat as he formulated the crucial questions.

Why and how did she come to Sweden? What was she running from? Why had she burned herself to death in Salomonsson's rapeseed field?

He walked farther out along the pier.

On a sailboat there was a party going on. Someone raised a glass and said *"Skål"* to Wallander. He nodded back and raised an invisible glass in his hand.

At the end of the pier he sat down on a bollard and went over the conversation he had had with Hugo Sandin. He still felt that everything was one big tangle. He couldn't see any openings, any clues that might lead to a breakthrough.

At the same time he still felt a sense of dread. He couldn't get away from the possibility that it might happen again.

It was almost nine o'clock. He tossed a fistful of gravel in the water and got up. The party on the sailboat was still in progress. He walked back through town. The heap of dirty clothes still lay in the middle of his floor. He wrote himself a note and put it on the kitchen table. *Car inspection, damn it!* Then he switched on the TV and lay down on the sofa.

At ten o'clock he phoned Baiba. Her voice sounded clear and close by.

"You sound tired," she said. "Have you got a lot to do?"

"It's not so bad," he said evasively. "But I miss you."

He heard her laugh.

"We'll see each other soon," she said.

"What were you doing in Tallinn, anyway?"

She laughed again.

"Meeting another man. What did you think?"

"Just that."

"You need to get some sleep," she said. "I can hear that all the way over here in Riga. I understand it's going well for Sweden in the World Cup."

"Are you interested in sports?" asked Wallander, surprised.

"Sometimes. Especially when Latvia is playing."

"People here are completely nuts about it."

"But not you?"

"I promise to improve. When Sweden plays Brazil I'll try to stay up and watch."

He heard her laugh again.

He wanted to say something more, but he couldn't think of anything. After he hung up he went back to the TV. For a while he tried to watch a movie. Then he turned it off and went to bed.

Before he fell asleep he thought about his father.

This fall they were going to take a trip to Italy.

Chapter Nineteen

T he glow-in-the-dark hands of the clock looked like two intertwined snakes. Right now they showed ten minutes past seven on Tuesday evening, the 28th of June. A few hours later Sweden would play Brazil. That too was part of his plan. Everybody would be focused on what was happening on TV. No one would think about what was happening outside in the summer night.

The basement floor was cool under his bare feet. He had been sitting in front of his mirrors since early that morning. He had already completed his great transformation several hours before. This time he made a change in the pattern on his right cheek. He painted the circular decoration with a blue paint that was almost black. Earlier he had used the blood-red paint. His whole face had deepened with a look that was even more frightening.

He put down the last brush and thought about the task awaiting him that night. It would be the greatest sacrifice yet that he could make for his sister, even though he had been forced to make a change in his plans. The situation that had come up was unexpected. For a brief moment he felt the evil forces surrounding him had gotten the upper hand. To plan his strategy, he had spent an entire night in the shadows below his sister's window. He sat between the two scalps he had buried earlier and waited for the power from the earth to enter him. In the beam of a flashlight he read from the holy book she had given him, and he realized that nothing prevented him from changing the order that he had drawn up.

The last victim should have been the evil man who was their father. Since the man who was supposed to meet his fate this evening had suddenly left the country, the sequence had to be changed.

He had listened to Geronimo's heart beating in his chest. The beats were like signals reaching him from the past. His heart drummed a message: the most important thing was not to shirk from his sacred task. The earth under his feet was already crying for the third retribution.

The third man would have to wait until he returned from abroad. Their father would have to take his place.

All day long, as he sat in front of the mirrors and underwent the great transformation, he looked forward to meeting his father with a special anticipation. The mission had demanded a number of special preparations. When he closed the doors to the basement room behind him early that morning, he began by preparing his tools. It had taken him more than two hours to attach the new blade to the toy axe he had once received from his father as a birthday present. He was seven at the time. He could still remember how even then he knew that one day he would use it against the man who had given it to him. Now the occasion had finally arrived. So that the plastic shaft with the poorly executed painted decoration wouldn't break when he struck his blow, he had reinforced it with special tape that ice hockey players use on the blades of their sticks. *You don't know what it's called. It's not a regular axe for chopping wood. It's a tomahawk.* He felt vehement contempt when he thought about how his father had presented the gift so long ago. It was a meaningless toy then, a plastic replica manufactured in some Asian country. Now, with the proper blade, he had transformed it into a real axe.

He waited until eight thirty that night. He went over the plan one last time. He looked at his hands and saw that he wasn't shaking. Everything was under control. The preparations he had made over the past two days guaranteed that everything would go well.

He packed up his weapons, the glass bottle wrapped in a handkerchief, and the rope in his backpack. Then he pulled on his helmet, turned off the light, and left the room. When he came out onto the street he looked up at the sky. It was cloudy. Maybe it would rain. He started up the moped he had stolen the day before and rode down to the center of Malmö. At the railroad station he went into a phone booth. He had selected one in advance that was off in a corner. On one side of the glass window he had pasted up a poster for a fictitious concert at a nonexistent youth club. There was no one around. He pulled off his helmet and stood with his face pressed against the poster. Then he stuck in his phone card and punched the number. With his left hand he held a rag in front of his mouth. The time was seven minutes to nine. He waited as the phone rang. He was totally calm, since he knew what he was going to say. His father picked up the phone and answered. Hoover could hear that he was irritated. That meant he had started drinking and didn't want to be disturbed.

He spoke into the rag, holding the receiver away from his mouth.

"This is Peter," he said. "I've got something that should interest you."

"What is it?" His father was still annoyed. But he believed it was Peter calling. The greatest problem was avoided.

"Stamps. Worth almost half a million."

His father hesitated.

"Are you sure?"

"At least half a million. Maybe more."

"Speak up a little, will you?"

"We must have a bad connection."

"Where are they coming from?"

"A house in Limhamn."

His father now sounded less irritated. His interest was sparked. Hoover had chosen stamps, since his father had once taken his own collection—which Hoover had worked on for a long time—and sold it.

"Can't it wait till tomorrow? The match with Brazil is starting soon."

"I'm leaving for Denmark tomorrow. Either you take them tonight, or some-one else will."

Hoover knew his father would never let such a large sum of money wind up in someone else's pocket. He waited, still completely calm.

"All right, I'll come," his father said. "Where are you?"

"At the boat club in Limhamn. The parking lot."

"Why aren't you in Malmö?"

"I told you it was a house in Limhamn. Didn't I say that?"

"I'll be there," said his father.

Hoover hung up and put on his helmet.

He left the telephone card sitting in the pay phone. He knew that he had plenty of time to ride out to Limhamn. His father always got undressed before he started drinking. And he never did anything in a hurry. His laziness was as great as his greed. He started up the moped and rode through the city until he came out on the road that led to Limhamn. There were only a few cars in the parking lot outside the boat club. He ditched the moped behind some bushes and threw away the keys. He pulled off his helmet and took out the axe. He stuffed the helmet into his backpack carefully so he wouldn't dam-age the glass bottle.

Then he waited. He knew that his father usually parked his van in one cor-ner of the parking lot when he was delivering stolen property. Hoover guessed that he would do so again. His father was a creature of habit. In addition, he was already drunk, his judgment muddled and his reactions dulled.

Twenty minutes later Hoover heard the van. The headlights swept across the trees before his father turned into the parking lot. Just as Hoover had pre-dicted, he stopped in the corner. In the shadows Hoover ran barefoot across the parking lot until he reached the van. When he heard his father open the door on the driver's side, he moved quickly around to the other side. As he had predicted, his father looked out toward the parking lot with his back turned to him. Hoover raised the axe and struck him with the blunt end on the back of the head. This was the most critical point. He didn't want to hit his father so hard that he'd die instantly. But hard enough that his father, who was big and very strong, would be knocked out.

His father fell without a sound to the pavement. Hoover waited a moment with the axe raised in case he came to, but he lay still. Hoover reached for the car keys and unlocked the side doors of the van. He lifted his father up and dragged him over to it. He was prepared for him to be a heavy burden. It took him several minutes to get his whole body inside. Then he got his backpack, climbed into the van, and shut the doors. He turned on the overhead light and saw that his father was still unconscious. He took out the rope and tied his hands behind his back. With a running noose he tied his legs to a seat stanchion. Then he taped his father's mouth shut and turned off the light. He climbed into the driver's seat and started the engine. He remembered how his father had taught him to drive a few years before. He had always had a van. Hoover knew the gear layout and where the instruments were located. He pulled out of the parking lot and headed toward the ring road that skirted Malmö. Since his face was painted he didn't want to drive where the streetlights might shine through the van's windows. He drove out onto E65 and continued east. It was a few minutes to ten. The game with Brazil was about to begin.

He had found the place by accident. He had been on his way back to Malmö after observing the police at work on the beach outside Ystad, where he had carried out the first in the series of sacred tasks assigned him by his sister. He was driving along the coast road when he discovered the dock, which was almost impossible to see from the road. He realized at once that he had found the right spot.

It was past eleven when he reached it and turned off the road with his headlights off. His father was still unconscious but had started to moan softly. He hurried to loosen the rope tied to the seat and then pulled him out of the van. His father groaned as Hoover dragged his body down to the dock. Then he turned him over on his back and tied his arms and legs to the iron rings on the dock. He thought his father looked like an animal skin stretched out to dry. He was dressed in a wrinkled suit. His shirt was unbuttoned down to his belly. Hoover pulled off his father's shoes and socks. Then he got the backpack from the van. There was a light breeze. A few cars drove past up on the highway. Their headlights never reached the dock.

When he came back with his backpack, his father had come to. His eyes were wide. He thrashed his head back and forth. He struggled with his arms and legs but couldn't get loose. Hoover couldn't resist stopping in the shadows to watch him. He no longer saw a human being before him. His father had undergone the transformation he had planned for him. He was an animal.

Hoover came out of the shadows and went out on the dock. His father stared at him with his eyes wide. Hoover realized he didn't recognize him. He thought about all the times he had felt an icy fear when his father stared at him. Now the tables were turned. Terror had changed its shape. He leaned in so close to his father's face that he could see through the paint and realize it was his own son. This would be the last thing he would see. This would be the image he would carry with him when he died.

Hoover had unscrewed the cap on the glass bottle. He was holding it behind his back. Then he quickly poured a few drops of hydrochloric acid into his father's left eye. Somewhere underneath the tape the man started screaming. He struggled with all his might against the ropes. Hoover pulled open his other eyelid and poured acid into that eye. Then he stood up and threw the bottle into the sea. What he saw before him was a beast thrashing back and forth in its death throes. Hoover looked down at his own hands again. His fingers were quivering a little. That was all. The beast lying on the dock in front of him was jerking spasmodically. Hoover took his knife out of his backpack and cut off the skin from the top of the animal's head. He raised the scalp to the night sky. Then he took his axe and smashed it straight through the beast's forehead with such force that the axe blade stuck in the dock underneath.

It was over. His sister was about to be brought back to life.

J ust before one in the morning he drove into Ystad. The town was deserted. For a long time he had wondered whether he was doing the right thing. But Geronimo's throbbing heart had convinced him. He had seen the police fumbling on the beach, he had watched them move as if in a fog outside the farm where he had visited a Midsummer party in progress. Geronimo had exhorted him to defy them.

He turned in at the railroad station. He had already picked out the spot. Work was under way to replace some old sewer lines. There was a tarp covering the excavation. He turned off the headlights and rolled down the window. From a distance he heard some drunken men yelling. He got out of the van and drew back part of the tarp. Then he listened again. Nobody was on the street; there were no cars. Quickly he opened the doors of the van, dragged his father's body out, and shoved him into the hole. After he replaced the tarp he started the engine and drove off. It was ten minutes to two when he parked the van in the open-air parking lot outside Sturup Airport. He checked carefully to see if he had forgotten anything. There was a lot of blood in the van. He had blood on his feet. He thought about all the confusion he was going to cause, which would make the police fumble even more.

That's when he got the idea. He had closed the doors of the van. Suddenly he stopped and stood motionless. *The man who had left the country might not return. That would mean he'd need a replacement. He thought about the policemen he had seen on the beach by the overturned boat. He thought about the ones he had seen outside the farmhouse where the Midsummer party was held. One of them. One of them could be sacrificed so that his sister could come back to life. He would choose one of them. He would find out their names and then toss stones onto a grid, just as Geronimo had done, and he would kill the one that chance selected for him.*

He pulled the helmet down over his head. Then he went over to his moped, which he had ridden there the day before and parked near one of the streetlights. He had locked it with a chain and then taken an airport bus back to Malmö. He started up the engine and rode off. It was already light when he buried his father's scalp underneath his sister's window.

At four thirty he carefully unlocked the door to the apartment in Rosengård. He stood still and listened. Then he peeked in the room where his brother lay sleeping. Everything was quiet. His mother's bed was empty. She was lying on the sofa in the living room, sleeping with her mouth open.

Next to her on the table stood a half-empty wine bottle. He carefully placed a blanket over her. Then he locked himself in the bathroom and wiped the paint off his face. He flushed the paper down the toilet.

It was almost six o'clock before he undressed and went to bed. He could hear a man coughing outside on the street.

His mind was completely blank.

He fell asleep at once.

Skåne 29 June – 4 July 1994

Chapter Twenty

The man who lifted the tarp screamed.

Then he fled.

One of the railroad ticket agents was standing outside the station smoking a cigarette. It was a few minutes to seven on the morning of June 29th. It was going to be a hot day. The ticket agent was jarred from his thoughts, which just then were focused less on selling tickets than on the trip to Greece he would be taking a few days later. He turned his head when he heard the scream. The man dropped the tarp and ran off toward the ferry terminal. The ticket agent flicked away his cigarette butt and walked over to the pit. He stared down at a bloody head. He dropped the tarp as if it had burned him and ran into the station, tripping over a couple of suitcases that an early traveler to Simrishamn had carelessly dropped in the middle of the floor, and then grabbed one of the telephones inside the dispatcher's office.

The call arrived at the Ystad police station on the 90-000 line at four minutes past seven. Svedberg, who was in unusually early that morning, was summoned to take the call. When he heard the distraught ticket agent talking about a bloody head he froze. His hand shook as he wrote down a single word, *railroad*, and hung up. Twice he dialed the wrong number and had to start over before managing to get hold of Wallander.

"I think it's happened again," said Svedberg.

For a few brief seconds Wallander didn't understand what Svedberg meant, even though every time the phone rang, whether at home or at the station, early in the morning or late at night, he feared that very thing. But now that it had happened he experienced a moment of shock, or perhaps a desperate attempt, doomed from the start, to deny the whole thing.

He knew he was experiencing something he would never forget. He thought fleetingly that it was like having a premonition of your own death, a moment when denial and escape were both impossible. *I think it's happened again.* He felt as if he were a wind-up toy. Svedberg's stammered words were like hands twisting the invisible police key sticking out of his back. He was wrenched out of his sleep and his bed, out of dreams he couldn't remember but which might have been pleasant. He got dressed in a desperate frenzy with buttons popping off, and his shoelaces flopped untied as he raced down the stairs and outside.

When he came screeching to a stop in his car, still in need of inspection, Svedberg was already there. Directed by Norén, some patrol officers were busy rolling out the striped crime scene tape. Svedberg stood awkwardly patting a weeping ticket agent on the shoulder, while some men in blue overalls stared at the pit they were supposed to climb into, now transformed into a nightmare. Wallander left his car door open and ran over to Svedberg. Why he ran he didn't really know. Maybe the internal police clockwork inside him had started to speed up. Or maybe he was so afraid of what he was going to see that he simply didn't dare approach it slowly.

Svedberg was white in the face. He nodded toward the pit. Wallander walked slowly over and took several deep breaths before looking into the hole.

It was worse than he could have imagined. He thought for a moment that he was looking straight into a dead man's brain. Ann-Britt Höglund came up next to Wallander. She flinched and turned away. Her reaction made him suddenly start thinking clearly.

"No doubt about it," he said to Höglund, turning back to the pit. "It's him again."

She was very pale. For a moment Wallander was afraid she was going to faint. He put his arm around her shoulders.

"How are you doing?" he asked.

She nodded without answering.

Martinsson arrived with Hansson. Wallander saw them both give a start when they looked in the hole. He was suddenly overcome with rage. The man who had done this had to be stopped at all costs.

"It must be the same perpetrator," said Hansson in an unsteady voice. "Isn't it ever going to end? I can't take responsibility for this anymore. Did Björk know about this when he left? I'm going to request reinforcements from the National Criminal Bureau."

"Do that," said Wallander. "But first let's get him out of there and see whether we can solve this ourselves."

Hansson stared in disbelief at Wallander, who realized that Hansson thought they were going to have to lift the dead man out of the pit themselves.

A large crowd had already gathered outside the cordon. Wallander remembered what he had sensed in connection with Carlman's murder. He took Norén aside and asked him to borrow a camera from Nyberg and take pictures, as discreetly as possible, of the people standing outside the cordon. In the meantime the emergency van from the fire department had arrived on the scene. Nyberg had already started directing his people around the pit. Wallander went over to him, at the same time trying to avoid looking at the corpse.

"One more time," said Nyberg. Wallander could hear that he was being neither cynical nor indifferent. Their eyes met.

"We've got to catch him," said Wallander.

"As soon as possible, I hope," said Nyberg. He lay down on his stomach so he could see deep enough into the hole to study the dead man's face. When he straightened up again he called to Wallander, who was just heading off to talk to Svedberg. He came back to the pit.

"Did you see his eyes?" asked Nyberg.

Wallander shook his head.

"What about them?"

Nyberg grimaced.

"Apparently the murderer wasn't content just taking a scalp this time," said Nyberg. "It looks like he poked his eyes out too."

"What do you mean?"

"I mean the guy he shoved into the pit doesn't have any eyes," said Nyberg. "There are two holes where they used to be."

It took them two hours to get the body out of the pit. In the meantime Wallander had a talk with the municipal worker who had lifted the tarp and the ticket agent who had been standing by the steps of the train station dreaming about Greece. He wrote down a timetable. He asked Nyberg to search the dead man's pockets so they could establish his identity, but they were empty.

"Nothing at all?" asked Wallander in surprise.

"Not a thing," said Nyberg. "But something may have fallen out. We'll look around down there."

They hauled him up in a sling. Wallander forced himself to look at his face. Nyberg was right. The man had no eyes. The torn-off hair gave Wallander the feeling that it was a dead animal, not a human being, lying on the plastic sheet at his feet.

Wallander sat down on the steps of the train station. He studied his timetable. He called Martinsson, who was talking to the doctor called to the scene.

"This time we know he hasn't been here long," he said. "I talked to the workmen replacing the sewer lines. They put the tarp down at four o'clock yesterday afternoon. So the body was put there after that, but sometime before seven o'clock this morning."

"There are a lot of people around here in the evening," said Martinsson. "People taking a walk, traffic to and from the station and the ferry terminal. It must have happened sometime during the night."

"How long has he been dead?" asked Wallander. "That's what I want to know. And who he is."

Nyberg hadn't found a wallet. They had nothing to help establish the dead man's identity. Höglund came over and sat down next to them.

"Hansson's talking about requesting reinforcements from the NCB," she said.

"I know," said Wallander. "But he won't do anything until I ask him to. What did the doctor say?"

She looked at her notes.

"About forty-five years old," she said. "Strong, well-built."

"That makes him the youngest one so far," said Wallander.

"Strange place to hide the body," said Martinsson. "Did he think that work stopped during the vacation month?"

"Maybe he just wanted to get rid of the body," said Höglund.

"Then why did he pick this pit?" asked Martinsson. "It must have been a lot of trouble to get him down there. Besides, there was the risk that someone might see him."

"Maybe he wanted the body to be found," Wallander said thoughtfully. "We can't rule out that possibility."

They looked at him in astonishment, waiting in vain for him to explain.

The body was taken away. Wallander told them to take it straight to Malmö. At quarter to ten they left the cordoned-off area and drove to the police station. Wallander saw that Norén had been taking pictures off and on of the large crowd milling around outside the crime scene.

Mats Ekholm showed up by nine o'clock. He stared at the corpse for a long time. Then Wallander went over to him.

"You got your wish," he said. "Another victim."

"I didn't wish for this," replied Ekholm, shaking his head.

Wallander regretted what he had said. He would have to explain what he actually meant to Ekholm.

Just after ten they closed the door to the conference room. Hansson gave strict orders not to put through any phone calls. But they had barely started the meeting when the phone rang. Hansson snatched the receiver and barked into it, completely red in the face. Then he sank slowly back in his chair. Wallander knew at once that someone very high up was calling. Hansson had inherited Björk's cringing obsequiousness. He made some brief comments, answered questions, but mostly listened. When the call was over he placed the receiver back in its cradle as if it were a fragile antique.

"Let me guess—the National Police Board," said Wallander. "Or the national prosecutor. Or a TV reporter."

"The Commissioner of the National Police," said Hansson. "He expressed as much displeasure as encouragement."

"That sounds like a pretty strange combination," Höglund said dryly.

"He's welcome to come down here and help out," said Svedberg.

"What does he know about police work?" Martinsson sputtered. "Absolutely nothing."

Wallander tapped his pen on the table. He knew that everyone was upset and uncertain how to proceed. Wallander knew they had very little time before they would be subjected to a barrage of criticism for alleged passivity and incompetence. They could never make themselves totally immune from outside pressure. They could only counteract it by focusing their attention inward, on shifting the center of the search, and by pretending that the success of the investigation was also the alpha and omega of their world. He tried to collect his thoughts even though he knew they didn't have a thing to go on.

"What do we know?" he began, and looked around the table. Wallander felt like a pastor who had lost his faith. Yet he had to say something that would lead them out again, as a unit, with at least a sense that they had understood something of what was happening around them.

"The man wound up in that pit with the sewer pipes sometime last night," he went on. "Let's assume that it took place in the wee hours. We can start with the fact that he wasn't murdered right next to the pit. There must have been plenty of blood evidence concentrated in one spot. Nyberg hadn't found a thing by the time we left the scene. This means he was transported there in some kind of vehicle. Maybe the people working at the hot dog stand next to the railroad crossing noticed something. According to the doctor, he was killed by a powerful blow from the front. It went all the way through his skull. In other words, this is the third variant we have of what a chopping implement can do."

Martinsson turned completely white. He got up and left the room without a word. Wallander decided to continue without him.

"He was scalped like the others. In addition, he had his eyes put out. The doctor wasn't sure what happened to them. There were some spots near the eyes that might indicate a corrosive agent. Maybe our specialist has some opinion on what this might mean."

Wallander turned to Ekholm.

"Not yet," said Ekholm. "It's too soon."

"We don't need a comprehensive analysis," said Wallander firmly. "At this stage we have to think out loud. Among all the nonsense, mistakes, and bad ideas we come up with, maybe some truth will sneak in. We don't believe in miracles. But we'll take them whenever they come along in spite of everything else."

"I do think the eyes being put out means something," said Ekholm. "We can assume that the same man is involved. This victim was younger than the other two. In addition, he suffered the loss of his sight. Presumably this occurred while he was still alive. It must have been terribly painful. Before, the murderer took scalps from those he killed. And he did so this time too. But he also blinded the man. Why did he do that? What kind of special revenge was he exacting this time?"

"The man must be a sadistic psychopath," said Hansson suddenly. "A serial killer like I thought existed only in the United States. But here? In Ystad? In Skåne?"

"There's still something controlled about him," said Ekholm. "He knows what he wants. He kills and scalps. He pokes out or dissolves the eyes. There's nothing to indicate uncontrolled rage. Psychopath, yes. But he still has control over his actions."

"Are there any examples of something like this happening before?" asked Höglund.

"Not that I can recall at the moment," replied Ekholm. "At least not here in Sweden. In the USA studies have been done on the role that eyes have played for various killers with grave mental disturbances. I'll read up on it today."

Wallander had been listening to the conversation between Ekholm and his colleagues with half an ear. A thought that he couldn't quite get a grasp on had popped into his head.

It was something about eyes.

Something somebody had said about eyes. What was it?

He returned to the reality of the meeting room. But the thought lingered like a vague, uneasy ache.

"Anything else?" he asked Ekholm.

"Not at the moment."

Martinsson came back into the room. He was still very pale.

"I've got an idea," said Wallander. "I don't know whether it means anything, but after hearing Mats Ekholm I'm even more convinced than before that the murder took place somewhere else. The man who had his eyes put out must have screamed. It definitely couldn't have been done outside the railroad station without someone seeing or hearing something. Naturally we'll have to check it out. But for the time being let's say I'm right. That leads me to the question of why he picked that hole as a hiding place. I talked to one of the men who worked there. Persson was his name, Erik Persson. He said that the excavation had been there since Monday afternoon. So less than two days. The person who chose the place could have stumbled on it by chance, of course. But that doesn't fit with the fact that everything gives the impression of being well planned. In other words, it means that the perpetrator had been outside the train station sometime after Monday afternoon. He must have looked into the pit to see if it was deep enough. So we have to interview all the men who work there. Did they notice anybody who showed unusual interest in their excavation? Did the railroad personnel notice anything?"

He could see that everyone around the table was listening more intently. This strengthened his belief that his ideas weren't completely off the track.

"I also think the question of whether it was meant as a hiding place or not is crucial," he went on. "He must have realized that the body would be found the next morning. So why did he choose the pit? So it would be discovered? Or is there some other explanation?"

Everyone in the room waited for him to continue.

"Is he taunting us?" said Wallander. "Does he want to help us in his own sick way? Or is he trying to fool us? Does he want to trick me into thinking exactly the way I'm thinking now? What would the alternative be?"

No one spoke.

"The time factor is also important," said Wallander. "This murder was very recent. That might help us."

"For that we need help," said Hansson. He'd been waiting for a suitable opportunity to bring up the matter of reinforcements.

"Not yet," said Wallander. "Let's decide later on today. Or maybe tomorrow. As far as I know, no one in this room is going on vacation anytime soon. Let's keep this group intact for a few more days. Then we can reinforce if necessary."

Hansson bowed to Wallander, who wondered fleetingly whether Björk used to do the same thing.

"What about the connection?" said Wallander in conclusion. "Now there's one more person to fit into the picture we're trying to piece together."

He looked around the table one more time.

"Of course we also have to realize that he could strike again," he said. "As long as we don't know what this is all about, we have to assume that he will."

The meeting was over. They all knew what they had to do. Wallander remained sitting at the table while the others filed out the door. He was trying to recapture that memory. Now he was convinced that it was something someone had said in conjunction with the investigation of the three murders. Somebody had talked about eyes. He went back in his mind to the day he first heard that Gustaf Wetterstedt had been found murdered. He searched in the deepest, darkest recesses of his memory, but found nothing. Annoyed, he tossed his pen aside and went out to the lunch room for a cup of coffee. When he got back to his office he set the coffee cup on his desk and was about to shut the door when he saw Svedberg coming down the hall.

Svedberg was walking fast. He only did that when something important had happened. Wallander instantly got a knot in his stomach. Not another one, he thought. We just can't handle it.

"We think we've found the murder scene," said Svedberg.

"Where?"

"Our colleagues at Sturup found a bloody delivery van in the airport parking lot."

A van. That fit. That could be right.

A few minutes later they left the police station. Wallander was in a hurry. He couldn't remember ever in his life feeling that he had so little time.

When they got outside of town he told Svedberg to turn on the blue dome light.

Out in the fields alongside the road a farmer was belatedly harvesting his rapeseed.

Chapter Twenty-one

T hey arrived at Sturup Airport just after eleven in the morning. The air felt stagnant in the oppressive heat.

It took them less than an hour to determine that the van was very likely the site of the murder.

And they also thought they knew who the dead man was.

The van was an old Ford from the late sixties, with sliding side doors. It was sloppily painted black with the original gray showing through in spots. The body was banged up and dented in many places. Parked in an isolated spot in the lot, it resembled an old prizefighter who had just been counted out, hanging on the ropes in his corner.

Wallander knew some of the officers at Sturup from the old days. He also knew that he wasn't particularly popular there after an incident that occurred the year before. He and Svedberg climbed out of the car. The side doors of the Ford were standing open. Some police techs were already going over the van. A police inspector named Waldemarsson came to meet them. Even though they had driven like madmen from Ystad, Wallander tried to give the impression of total nonchalance.

"It's not a pretty sight," said Waldemarsson as they shook hands.

Wallander and Svedberg went over to the Ford and looked in. Waldemarsson shone a flashlight inside. The floor of the van was literally covered with blood.

"We heard on the morning news that he had struck again," said Waldemarsson. "I called and talked to a female detective whose name I can't remember."

"Ann-Britt Höglund," said Svedberg.

"Whatever her name is, she said you were looking for a crime scene," Waldemarsson went on. "And a vehicle."

Wallander nodded.

"When did you find the van?" he asked.

"We check out the parking lot every day. We've had a good deal of problems with car thefts here. But you know all about that."

Wallander nodded again. During the pointless investigation into the organized export of stolen cars to Poland he had been in contact with the airport
police several times.

"We know the van wasn't here yesterday afternoon," said Waldemarsson.
"It couldn't have been here more than eighteen hours."

"Who's the owner?" asked Wallander.

Waldemarsson took a note pad out of his pocket.

"Björn Fredman," he said. "He lives in Malmö. We called his number but
didn't get an answer."

"Could he be the one we found in the pit?"

"We know a little about Björn Fredman," said Waldemarsson. "Malmö has
come up with some info for us. He was known as a fence and has done time on
several occasions."

"A fence," said Wallander, feeling a flash of excitement. "For works of art?"

"They didn't say. You'll have to talk with our colleagues yourself."

"Who should I ask for?" he asked, taking his cell phone out of his pocket.

"An inspector named Forsfält. Sten Forsfält."

Wallander had the number of the Malmö police on his speed-dial. After
about a minute he got hold of Forsfält. He explained who he was and that
he was at the airport. For a few seconds the conversation was drowned out by
the sound of a plane taking off. Wallander suddenly thought of the trip to
Italy he planned to take with his father.

"First of all, we have to identify the man in the pit," said Wallander when
the plane had disappeared in the direction of Stockholm.

"What did he look like?" asked Forsfält. "I met Fredman several times."

Wallander gave as accurate a description as he could.

"It might be him," said Forsfält. "He was big, at any rate."

Wallander thought for a moment.

"Can you drive to the hospital and identify him?" he asked. "We need a
positive ID as fast as possible."

"Sure, I can do that," said Forsfält.

"Prepare yourself, because it's not a pretty sight," said Wallander. "He had
his eyes poked out. Or eaten away."

Forsfält didn't reply.

"We're coming to Malmö," said Wallander. "We need some help getting
into his apartment. Did he have any family?"

"As far as I can recall he was divorced," said Forsfält. "I'm pretty sure the
last time he was in, it was for battery."

"I thought it was for fencing stolen property."

"That too. Björn Fredman had his fingers in a lot of pies in his day. But never
anything legal. At least he was consistent about that."

Wallander said goodbye and called Hansson to give him a brief rundown.

"Good," said Hansson. "Let me know as soon as you have more information.

By the way, do you know who called?"

"No. The national commissioner again?"

"Almost. Lisa Holgersson. Björk's successor. She wished us good luck. Said she just wanted to check on the situation."

"It's great that people are wishing us good luck," said Wallander, who couldn't understand why Hansson was telling him about the call in such an ironic tone of voice.

Wallander borrowed Waldemarsson's flashlight and shone it inside the van. At one spot he discovered a footprint in the blood. He shone the light on it and leaned forward.

"Someone was barefoot," he said, surprised. "That's no shoe print. It's a left foot."

"Barefoot?" said Svedberg.

"So he wades around barefoot in the blood of the people he kills?"

"We don't know that it's a he," said Wallander dubiously.

They said goodbye to Waldemarsson and his colleagues. Wallander waited in the car while Svedberg ran inside the airport café and bought some sandwiches.

"The prices are outrageous," he complained when he came back. Wallander didn't bother answering.

"Just drive," was all he said.

It was almost twelve-thirty when they stopped outside the police station in Malmö. Just as he stepped out of the car Wallander discovered Björk heading his way. Björk stopped short and stared at him, as if he had caught Wallander doing something he shouldn't.

"You, here?" he said.

"I thought I'd ask you to come back," said Wallander in a lame attempt at a joke. Then he quickly explained what had happened.

"It's terrible, the things that are going on," said Björk, and Wallander could hear that his worried tone was completely genuine. It hadn't struck him before that Björk might miss the people he worked with for so many years in Ystad.

"Nothing is quite the same," said Wallander.

"How's Hansson doing?"

"I don't think he's enjoying his role."

"He can always call me if he needs any help."

"I'll tell him."

Björk left and they went into the station. Forsfält still wasn't back from the hospital. They drank coffee in the lunch room while they waited.

"I wonder what it would be like to work here," said Svedberg, looking around at all the policemen eating lunch.

"One day we may all wind up here," said Wallander. "If they close down the district. One police station per county."

"That would never work."

"No, probably not. But it could happen. Whether it works or not. The

National Police Board and those political bureaucrats have one thing in common. They always try to do the impossible."

Out of nowhere, Forsfält appeared standing next to them. They stood up, shook hands, and followed him to his office. Wallander immediately got a positive impression of him. In some way he reminded him of Rydberg. Forsfält was at least sixty and had a friendly face. He had a slight limp. Forsfält brought in an extra chair. Wallander sat down and looked at some pictures of laughing children tacked up on the wall. He guessed that they were Forsfält's grandchildren.

"Björn Fredman," said Forsfält. "It's him, all right. It was appalling the way he looked. Who would do such a thing?"

"If we only knew," said Wallander. "Who was Björn Fredman?"

"A man of about forty-five who never had an honest job in his life," Forsfält began. "There are a lot of details I don't know. But I've asked the computer people to print out everything for us. He was a fence and he did time for battery. Quite violent attacks, as I recall."

"Could he have been involved with buying and selling works of art?"

"Not that I can remember."

"That's too bad," said Wallander. "Then we could have linked him to Wetterstedt and Carlman."

"I have a hard time imagining that Björn Fredman and Gustaf Wetterstedt could have had any use for each other," said Forsfält pensively.

"Why not?"

"Let me put it simply and bluntly," said Forsfält. "Björn Fredman was what used to be called a rough customer. He drank a lot and got into fights. His education was basically nonexistent, except that he could read, write, and do arithmetic tolerably well. His interests could hardly be called very sophisticated. And he was a brutal man. I interrogated him myself on several occasions. I can still remember that his vocabulary consisted almost exclusively of swear words."

Wallander listened attentively. When Forsfält stopped he looked at Svedberg.

"So we're back to square one again," Wallander said slowly. "If we find no connection between Fredman and the other two."

"Of course there could be something I don't know about," said Forsfält.

"I'm not drawing any conclusions," said Wallander. "I'm just thinking out loud."

"What about his family?" said Svedberg. "Do they live here in Malmö?"

"He's been divorced for a number of years," said Forsfält. "I definitely remember that."

He picked up the phone and made an in-house call. After a few minutes a secretary came in with a file on Fredman and handed it to Forsfält. He took a quick look and then put it down on the table.

"He got divorced in 1991. His wife stayed in the apartment with the children. It's located in Rosengård. There are three children; the youngest was just a baby when they split up. Björn Fredman moved back to an apartment on Stenbrottsgatan that he'd kept for many years. He used it mostly as an office and storeroom. I don't think his wife knew about it. That's where he also took his other women friends."

"We'll start with his apartment," said Wallander. "The family can wait. I assume you'll see to it that they're informed of his death?"

Forsfält nodded. Svedberg had gone out to the corridor to tell Ystad they had identified the dead man. Wallander stood by the window, trying to decide what was most important. He was worried that there seemed to be no link between the first two victims and Björn Fredman. For the first time he had a premonition that they were following a false lead. Had he missed the fact that there might be a completely different explanation for what had happened? He decided he'd have to go over all the investigative material that evening and examine it again with no preconceived ideas.

Svedberg came over and stood next to him.

"Hansson was relieved," he said.

Wallander nodded. But he didn't say a word.

"According to Martinsson an important message came in from Interpol about the girl in the rapeseed field," Svedberg went on.

Wallander hadn't been paying attention. He had to ask Svedberg to repeat what he had said. The girl he had seen running like a burning torch seemed to be part of something that had happened a long time ago. And yet he knew that sooner or later he'd have to take an interest in her again.

They stood in silence.

"I don't like it in Malmö," said Svedberg suddenly. "Actually I only feel good when I'm home in Ystad."

Wallander knew that Svedberg hated to leave the town where he was born. At the police station it had become a running joke whenever Svedberg wasn't around. At the same time Wallander wondered when he himself ever really felt good.

But he remembered the last time he had. When Linda was standing at his door at seven on a Sunday morning.

Forsfält had finished his business and came to tell them they could leave. They took the elevator down to the police garage and then drove out toward an industrial area north of the city. The wind had started to blow. The sky was still cloudless. Wallander sat next to Forsfält in the front seat.

"Did you know Rydberg?" he asked.

"Did I know Rydberg?" he replied slowly. "I certainly did. We knew each other quite well. He used to come in to Malmö once in a while and drop by."

Wallander was surprised at his answer. He had always thought that Rydberg was an old cop who had long ago written off anything to do with the job, including his friends.

"He was the one who taught me everything I know," said Wallander.

"It was tragic that he left us so soon," said Forsfält. "He should have had a chance to live a while longer. He always dreamed about going to Iceland someday."

"Iceland?"

Forsfält threw him a hasty glance and nodded.

"That was his big dream. To go to Iceland. But nothing ever came of it."

Wallander was struck by a vague feeling that Rydberg had kept something from him that he should have known about. He never would have guessed that Rydberg harbored a dream about a pilgrimage to Iceland. He never imagined that Rydberg had any dreams at all. Above all, he never would have imagined that Rydberg had any hidden secrets.

Forsfält pulled up outside a three-story apartment building. He pointed to a row of windows on the ground floor with the curtains drawn. The building was old and poorly maintained. The windowpane in the outside door was patched with a piece of Masonite. Wallander had a feeling that he was walking into a building that no longer existed. Isn't the existence of this building in direct contradiction to the Swedish constitution? he thought sarcastically. There was a smell of urine in the stairwell.

Forsfält unlocked the door. Wallander wondered where he'd gotten the key. They walked into an entryway and turned on the light. There was nothing but some junk mail lying on the floor. Since Wallander was in foreign territory, he let Forsfält lead the way. First they walked through the apartment as if checking that no one was there. It consisted of three rooms and a tiny, cramped kitchen that looked out on a warehouse full of oil drums. Apart from the bed, which seemed new, the apartment had an air of indifference. The furniture seemed to be strewn haphazardly around the rooms. On a fifties-style bookshelf stood some cheap, dusty porcelain figurines. In one corner there was a stack of magazines and some barbells. On the sofa was a CD that someone had spilled coffee on. To his great surprise Wallander saw from its label that it was Turkish folk music. The curtains were drawn.

Forsfält went around the apartment, systematically turning on all the lights. Wallander followed a few steps behind him, while Svedberg took a seat in a Windsor chair in the kitchen so he could call Hansson and tell him where they were. Wallander pushed open the door to the pantry with his foot. There were several unopened cartons of Grant's whisky inside. From a dirty freight bill he saw they had been shipped from the Scottish distillery to a wine merchant with an address in Ghent, Belgium. He wondered how they had wound up in Björn Fredman's apartment.

Forsfält came into the kitchen with a couple of photographs of the apartment's owner. Wallander nodded. There was no doubt that he was the one they found pushed into the pit next to Ystad's railroad station. He went back to the living room and tried to decide what he really hoped to find. Fredman's apartment was the exact opposite of Wetterstedt's house and the expensively renovated farmhouse owned by Arne Carlman. This is what Sweden looks like, he thought. The differences between people are just as great now as they were when some people lived in the manor house and others in hovels.

His gaze fell on a desk piled high with magazines about antiques. He assumed they were related to Fredman's activities as a fence. There was only one drawer in the desk. It was unlocked. In addition to a stack of receipts, broken pens, and a cigarette case, there was a framed photograph inside. It showed Fredman surrounded by his family. He was smiling broadly at the photographer. Next to him sat the woman who must have been his wife. She was holding a newborn baby in her arms. Behind the mother and off to one side stood a girl in her early teens. She was staring into the camera with a look of terror in her eyes. Next to her, directly in back of the mother, stood a boy who was a few years younger. He had a pinched face, as if he was determined to resist the photographer to the very end. Wallander took the photo over to the window and pulled back the curtain. He stared at it for a long time and tried to understand what he was looking at. An unhappy family? A family that hadn't yet discovered its unhappiness? A newborn child who had no idea what awaited him? There was something in the picture that disturbed him, almost depressed him, but he couldn't put his finger on it. He took the picture with him into the bedroom, where Forsfält was on his knees looking under the bed.

"You said that he did time for battery," said Wallander.

Forsfält got up and looked at the photo Wallander was holding.

"He beat his wife senseless," he said. "He beat her up when she was pregnant. He beat her when the child was a baby. But strangely enough, he never went to prison for it. Once he broke a cab driver's nose. He beat a former partner half to death when he suspected him of cheating."

They continued searching the apartment. Svedberg had finished talking to Hansson. He shook his head when Wallander asked him if anything important had happened. It took them two hours to search the apartment systematically. Wallander thought his own apartment was a cozy idyll compared to Björn Fredman's. They found nothing of interest except for a travel bag with antique candlesticks in it that Forsfält pulled out of the back of a wardrobe. Wallander was understanding more and more about what it meant that Fredman's language was peppered with an almost unbroken string of swear words. The apartment was just as empty and powerless as his vocabulary.

At three-thirty they left the apartment and went back out to the street. The wind had picked up. Forsfält called in to the station and got confirmation that Fredman's family had been informed of his death.

"I'd like to talk to them," said Wallander when they got into the car. "But I think it's probably better to wait until tomorrow."

He knew he wasn't being honest.

He should have told the truth, that he never liked the idea of bothering a family in which a relative had recently suffered a violent death. Above all, he couldn't stand the thought of talking to children who had just lost a parent. Waiting until the next day, of course, made no difference to them. But to Wallander it meant some breathing space.

They said goodbye outside the police station. Forsfält would get hold of Hansson to clear up a few formal details between the two police districts. He made an appointment to meet with Wallander at ten o'clock the next day.

Wallander and Svedberg got into their own car and drove back toward Ystad. Wallander's mind was swarming.

They didn't say a word to each other the whole trip.

Chapter Twenty-two

T he skyline of Copenhagen was dimly visible in the sunny haze across the Sound.

Wallander wondered whether he would really get to meet Baiba there in less than ten days, or whether the perpetrator they were looking for—about whom they now knew even less, if that was possible—would force him to postpone his vacation.

He stood thinking about this as he waited outside the hovercraft terminal in Malmö. It was the following morning, the 30th, the last day of June. The night before, Wallander had already decided to take Höglund with him instead of Svedberg when he returned to Malmö to talk with Björn Fredman's family. He called her at home, and she asked whether they could leave early enough for her to take care of an errand on the way, before they met with Forsfält at nine-thirty. Svedberg hadn't complained in the least when Wallander told him he didn't have to come along to Malmö. His relief over not having to leave Ystad two days in a row was unmistakable. While Höglund took care of her errand inside the terminal—Wallander hadn't asked what it was, of course—he walked along the pier and looked out across the Sound toward Copenhagen. A hydro-foil, the *Runner*, he thought it said on the bow, was on its way out of the harbor. It was hot. He took off his jacket and slung it over his shoulder. He yawned.

The night before, after they came back from Malmö, he'd had a hastily arranged meeting with the investigative team, since none of them had gone home yet. In the reception area he also held an improvised press conference with Hansson's help. Ekholm had attended the earlier meeting. He was still working on an in-depth psychological profile of the perpetrator in which he could include details of the gouged-out or obliterated eyes and assign them some conceivable explanation to provide the team with a real clue. But they had agreed that Wallander should now inform the press that they were definitely looking for a man who couldn't be considered dangerous to the general public, but who was certainly extremely dangerous to the victims he selected.

There had been differing opinions on whether it would be wise to take this action. But Wallander had adamantly maintained they couldn't ignore the fact that a possible victim might come forward and contact the police out of sheer self-preservation. The reporters had jumped all over his statement. Feeling more and more uncomfortable, he had been forced to acknowledge that they had given the newspapers the best possible news at this critical point, when the whole country was about to shut down and everyone would lock themselves inside the fortress of Sweden's collective summer vacation. Afterwards, when both the meeting and the press conference were over, he felt very tired.

But he still hadn't gone over the long telex from Interpol with Martinsson. They now knew that the burning girl in the rapeseed field had vanished from Santiago de los Treinta Caballeros sometime last December. Her father, Pedro Santana, apparently a farm worker, had reported her disappearance to the police on January 14th. Dolores María, who was then sixteen years old, but who had turned seventeen on February 18th—and this was a detail that made Wallander particularly depressed—had been in Santiago looking for work as a housekeeper. Before that she had lived with her father in a little village seventy kilometers outside the city. She had been living with a distant relative, a cousin of her father, when she suddenly disappeared. Judging by the scanty report, the Dominican police had not taken much interest in her disappearance. It was the persistent father who had hounded them to keep looking for her. He had managed to interest a journalist in her case, and finally the police determined that she had probably left the country to seek her fortune elsewhere.

The trail ended there. The investigation stopped and faded into oblivion. Interpol's comments were brief. There was no indication that Dolores María Santana had been seen later in any of the countries belonging to the worldwide police network. Not until now.

That was all.

"She disappears in a city called Santiago," said Wallander. "About six months later she pops up in farmer Salomonsson's rapeseed field, where she burns herself to death. What does that mean?"

Martinsson shook his head dejectedly.

Even though Wallander was so tired he could hardly think, he instantly roused himself. Martinsson's passivity made him mad.

"We know quite a bit," he said with determination. "We know that she didn't vanish from the face of the earth. We know that she had been in Helsingborg and got a lift from a man from Smedstorp. We know she seemed to be fleeing something. And we know she's dead. We should send a message back to Interpol telling them all this. And I want you to make a special request that the girl's father be properly informed of her death. When this other hellish situation is over, we'll have to find out who she was afraid of in Helsingborg. I suggest you make contact with our colleagues there first thing in the morning. They might have some idea what happened."

After this muted outburst of protest against Martinsson's passivity, Wallander drove home. He stopped at a stand and ordered a hamburger to go. There were newspaper placards posted everywhere, proclaiming the latest news from the World Cup. He suddenly had an urge to rip them all down and scream that enough was enough. But of course he didn't say a word. He waited patiently in line until it was his turn. He paid, picked up his burger, and went back to his car.

When he got home he sat down at the kitchen table and tore open the bag. He drank a glass of water with the hamburger. Then he made some strong coffee and cleaned off the kitchen table. Even though he should have gone to bed, he forced himself to go over all the investigative material again. The feeling that they were on the wrong track was still with him. Wallander was not the one who had dropped bread crumbs along the path they were following. But he *was* the one who was leading the work of the investigative group; in other words, he was the one who both set the course and decided when it was time to stop and change direction. He looked for the places along the way where they should have moved more slowly and paid more attention; where they should have asked themselves whether the links between Wetterstedt and Carlman were already clearly visible, but they simply hadn't noticed.

He carefully went over all the traces of the perpetrator's presence that they had gathered, sometimes with solid evidence, sometimes without. Beside him he had a notebook in which he wrote down all the unanswered questions. It bothered him that the results from many of the lab tests still weren't available. When it was already past midnight, his impatience tempted him to call up Nyberg and ask him whether the analysts and chemists in Linköping had closed for the summer. But he wisely refrained. He sat bent over his papers until his back started to hurt and the letters began blurring on the page.

He didn't give up until almost two-thirty. His exhausted mind had formulated a status report which was nevertheless a confirmation that they couldn't do much else but continue along the path they had chosen. There simply had to be a point of contact between the men who had been murdered and scalped. He also thought the fact that Björn Fredman seemed to fit so poorly might help them find the solution.

When he finally went to bed, the pile of dirty laundry was still on the floor, reminding him of the disarray inside his own head. Once again he had forgotten to get a car inspection appointment. He wondered whether he would have to request reinforcements from the NCB. He decided to talk to Hansson about it early in the morning, after a few hours' sleep.

But by the time he got up at six o'clock, he had changed his mind. He wanted to wait one more day. So he called Nyberg, who was a morning person, and complained that they still didn't have answers on some of the objects and blood samples that had been sent to Linköping. He expected Nyberg to have a fit. But to Wallander's great surprise he agreed that it was taking an unusually long time. He promised Wallander he would follow up on the delay. They talked for a while about Nyberg's examination of the pit where they found Björn Fredman. Blood traces indicated that the killer had parked his car right next to it. Nyberg had also managed to get out to Sturup Airport and look at Fredman's van himself. There was no doubt that it was used to transport the body. But Nyberg was dubious about the possibility that it was the actual site of the murder.

"Björn Fredman was big and strong," he said. "How anyone could have killed him inside the van is more than I can comprehend. I think the murder happened somewhere else."

"So the question is who drove the van," said Wallander, "and where did the murder occur."

Just after seven o'clock Wallander arrived at the police station. He called Ekholm at his hotel and found him in the breakfast room.

"I want you to concentrate on the eyes," he said. "I don't know why. But I'm convinced they're important. Maybe crucial. Why would he do that to Fredman and not to the others? That's what I want to know."

"The whole thing has to be viewed in its entirety," said Ekholm. "A psychopath almost always creates rational patterns, which he then follows as if they were written in a sacred book. The eyes have to be fit into that framework."

"Do whatever you want," Wallander said curtly. "But I want to know what it means that only Fredman had his eyes put out. Concept or no concept."

"It was probably acid," said Ekholm.

Wallander had forgotten to ask Nyberg about that particular detail.

"Can we assume that's what happened?" he asked.

"It seems so. Someone put acid in Fredman's eyes."

Wallander grimaced in disgust.

"We'll talk this afternoon," he said and hung up.

Just after eight o'clock he had left Ystad with Höglund. It was a relief to get out of the station. Reporters were calling all the time. And now the public had started calling too. The hunt for the perpetrator had moved beyond the confines of the local police district and had become a matter of concern for the whole country. Wallander knew that this was both good and necessary. But it required great effort on the part of the police to gather and check out all the tips that were starting to flood in.

Höglund emerged from the hovercraft terminal and caught up with him on the pier.

"I wonder what kind of summer it'll be this year," he said.

"My grandmother in Älmhult can predict the weather," said Höglund. "She says we're going to have a long, hot, dry summer."

"Is she usually right?"

"Almost always."

"I think it'll be the opposite. Rainy and cold and crappy."

"Can you predict the weather too?"

"No. But even so."

They walked back to the car. Wallander was curious about what she'd been doing inside the hovercraft terminal. But he didn't ask.

At nine-thirty they pulled up in front of the Malmö police station. Forsfält was already waiting on the sidewalk. He got into the back seat and gave Wallander directions, talking to Höglund about the weather at the same time. When they stopped outside the apartment building in Rosengård he gave them a rundown of what had happened the day before.

"When I told them that Björn Fredman was dead, she took it calmly. I didn't notice it myself, but my female colleague claimed there was alcohol on her breath. The place was a mess, quite a shabby apartment. The youngest boy is only four. He probably won't react much to the fact that the father he almost never saw is dead. But the older son seemed to understand what it was all about. His older daughter wasn't home."

"What's her name?" asked Wallander.

"The daughter?"

"The wife. The estranged wife."

"Anette Fredman."

"Does she have a job?"

"Not that I know of."

"How does she make a living?"

"No idea. But I doubt that Fredman was very generous to his family. He didn't seem to be the type."

Wallander had no more questions. They got out of the car and went inside, taking the elevator up to the fifth floor. Someone had smashed a bottle on the floor of the elevator. Wallander glanced at Höglund and shook his head. Forsfält rang the doorbell. It took almost a minute before the door opened. The woman standing in the doorway was very thin and pale. The impression was reinforced because she was dressed all in black. She looked with frightened eyes at the two unfamiliar faces. As they stood in the entryway hanging up their coats, Wallander saw someone peek out quickly through the doorway to the apartment and then disappear. He thought it must have been the older son or the daughter.

Forsfält introduced Wallander and Höglund. He spoke gently and with great kindness. There was nothing hurried about his demeanor. Wallander thought he might be able to learn from Forsfält as he once had from Rydberg. The woman asked them to come into the living room.

Considering the description Forsfält had given them in the car, it looked as if she must have done some cleaning. Wallander saw no trace of the shabbiness Forsfält had mentioned. The living room had a sofa group that looked almost unused. There was a phonograph, a VCR, and a TV from Bang & Olufsen, a Danish brand Wallander had always had his eye on but never thought he could afford. She had set out cups and saucers. Wallander listened for sounds.

There was supposed to be a four-year-old boy in the family. Children that age were seldom quiet. They sat down around the coffee table.

"Please allow me to apologize for the inconvenience," he said, trying to sound just as friendly as Forsfält.

"Thank you," she replied in a low, fragile-sounding voice, as if it might break at any moment.

"Unfortunately, I have to ask you a few questions," continued Wallander. "I wish they could wait until later."

She nodded but said nothing. At that moment a door opened to one of the rooms connected directly to the living room. A husky boy of fourteen came into the room. He had an open, friendly-looking face, although his eyes were wary.

"This is my son," she said. "His name is Stefan."

The boy was very well brought up, Wallander noticed. He came and shook hands with each of them. Then he sat down next to his mother on the sofa.

"I'd like him to hear this too," she said.

"I have no objections to that," said Wallander. "I just want to say that I'm sorry about what happened to your father."

"We didn't see each other very much," replied the boy. "But thank you all the same."

Wallander at once got a positive impression of him. He seemed unusually mature for his age. Wallander assumed it was because he had had to fill the void left by his absent father.

"If I understand correctly, there's another son in your family," Wallander went on.

"He's with a friend of mine, playing with her son," said Anette Fredman. "I thought it would be quieter here without him. His name is Jens."

Wallander nodded to Höglund, who was taking notes.

"And there's an older sister too?"

"Her name is Louise."

"But she's not home?"

"She's away for a few days, resting."

It was the boy who said she was away. He took over from his mother, as if he wanted to spare her a heavy burden. His answer had been calm and polite. Even so, Wallander had a feeling there was something about the sister that was not quite right. Maybe his answer had come a little too quickly. Or had he hesitated before replying? Wallander was immediately on the alert. His invisible antennas silently unfolded.

"I understand that what has happened must have been trying for her," he continued cautiously.

"She's very sensitive," replied her brother.

Something doesn't add up here, Wallander thought again. At the same time something told him that he shouldn't go any further right now. It would be better to come back to the girl later. He shot a quick glance at Höglund. She didn't seem to have noticed.

"I won't have to repeat the questions you've already answered," said Wallander, pouring himself a cup of coffee, as if to show that everything was normal. He noticed that the boy had his eyes fixed on him. There was a wariness in his eyes that reminded Wallander of a bird. He thought that the boy must have been forced too soon to take on a responsibility he wasn't ready for. The thought depressed him. There was nothing that bothered Wallander more than seeing children and young people fare badly. He thought that at least he had never forced Linda to take over the role of housekeeper after Mona moved out. Even though he might have been a pretty bad parent, he hadn't made her endure that.

"I know that none of you had seen Björn in several weeks," he went on. "Was that true of Louise too?"

This time it was the mother who answered.

"The last time he was home, Louise was out," she said. "It's probably been several months since she saw him last."

Wallander now gingerly approached the most difficult questions. Even though he knew that it wouldn't be possible to avoid painful memories, he tried to move as cautiously as he could.

"Someone killed him," he said. "Do either of you have any idea who might have done it?"

Anette Fredman looked at him with a surprised expression on her face. When she opened her mouth, her reply was shrill. Her previous reticence was gone.

"You ought to be asking who wouldn't have done it. I don't know how many times I wished I'd had the strength to kill him myself."

Her son put his arm around her.

"I don't think that's what the detective meant," he said soothingly.

She quickly pulled herself together after her brief outburst.

"I don't know who did it," she said. "And I don't want to know. But I don't have a guilty conscience for feeling a great relief that he won't be walking through this door again."

She stood up abruptly and went to the bathroom. Wallander saw that Höglund couldn't decide whether she should follow her. But she remained seated as the boy on the sofa started talking.

"Mamma is extremely upset," he said.

"We understand that," said Wallander, who was starting to have more sympathy for him. "But you seem to be quite calm; maybe you have some ideas yourself. Even though I know this must be unpleasant for you."

"I don't think it could be anybody except one of Pappa's friends. My pappa was a thief," he added. "He also used to beat people up. I'm not sure about it, but I think he was also what people call an enforcer. He collected debts, he threatened people."

"How do you know that?"

"I don't know."

"Are you thinking about somebody in particular?"

"No."

Wallander sat in silence and let him think.

"No," he repeated. "I don't know."

Anette Fredman returned from the bathroom.

"Can either of you recall whether he had any contact with a man named Gustaf Wetterstedt? He was the minister of justice at one time. Or an art dealer named Arne Carlman?"

After looking at each other for confirmation, they both shook their heads.

The interview floundered along. Wallander tried to help them remember. Now and then Forsfält would make some quiet remarks. Finally Wallander realized that they weren't going to get any further. He also decided not to ask anything more about the daughter. Instead he nodded to Höglund and Forsfält. He was finished. But when they said goodbye out in the entryway he said that he would undoubtedly have to call on them again, probably quite soon and maybe even the next day. He gave them his phone numbers at the station and at home.

When they got out onto the street he saw Anette Fredman standing in the window looking down at them.

"The daughter," said Wallander. "Louise Fredman. What do we know about her?"

"She wasn't here yesterday either," said Forsfält. "She may have left home, of course. She's seventeen, I know that."

Wallander stood for a moment in thought.

"I want to talk to her," he said.

The others didn't react. He knew that he was the only one who had noticed the rapid change from politeness to wariness when he asked about her.

He was also thinking about the boy, Stefan Fredman. About his watchful eyes. He felt sorry for him.

"That'll be all for now," said Wallander when they parted outside the Malmö police station. "But let's keep in touch."

They shook hands with Forsfält and said goodbye.

They drove back toward Ystad, through the summer countryside of Skåne during the most beautiful time of the year. Höglund leaned back in her seat and closed her eyes. Wallander heard her humming some improvised melody. He wished he could have shared her ability to take a break from the investigation, which filled him with so much anxiety. Rydberg had said many times that a police officer was never completely free from his responsibility. At a moment like this, Wallander wished that on this point Rydberg might have been wrong.

Just after they passed the exit to Skurup he noticed that Höglund had fallen asleep. He tried to drive as smoothly as possible so she wouldn't wake up.

She didn't open her eyes until he had to brake and then stop at the entrance to the traffic circle outside Ystad. At that moment the phone rang. He nodded to her to pick it up. He couldn't tell who she was talking to. But he saw at once that something serious had happened. She listened without asking any questions. They were almost to the driveway of the police station when she hung up.

"That was Svedberg," she said. "Carlman's daughter tried to commit suicide. She's on a respirator at the hospital."

Wallander didn't say a thing until he pulled the car into an empty parking place and shut off the engine.

Then he turned to her. He knew that she hadn't told him everything yet.

"What else did he say?"

"She's probably not going to make it."

Wallander stared out the windshield.

He thought about how she had slapped his face.

Then he got out of the car without saying a word.

Chapter Twenty-three

The heat wave continued.

Wallander realized that he was already in the middle of summer without having noticed it. He was sweating when he walked down the hill from the police station toward town and the hospital.

He hadn't even stopped by the front desk to see whether he had any messages when they came back from Malmö and got the call from Svedberg. He had stood completely motionless next to the car, as if he had suddenly lost all his bearings, and then slowly, almost drawling, he told Ann-Britt Höglund that she would have to make the report to their colleagues while he walked down to the hospital where Carlman's daughter lay dying. He hadn't waited for any answer from her; he just turned and left, and it was then, on the hill, after he had already started to sweat, that he knew he was enveloped by a summertime that might be long and hot and dry. He never noticed when Svedberg drove past him and waved.

He walked looking down at the pavement, a habit he had whenever he had a lot on his mind. This time he tried to make use of the short distance from the police station to the hospital entrance by working on an idea that was entirely new, and which he wasn't sure how to handle. The starting point was quite simple. In a brief period of time, less than ten days in fact, a girl had burned herself to death in a rapeseed field, another had tried to commit suicide after her father was murdered, and a third, whose father had also been murdered, had disappeared in some unspecified and rather mysterious manner. They were of different ages; Carlman's daughter was the oldest, but even so, all of them were young. Two of the girls had indirectly run afoul of the same perpetrator, while the third had killed herself. What distinguished them was that the girl in the field had nothing whatsoever to do with the other two. But in Wallander's mind it felt as if he once again had assumed personal responsibility for all these events on behalf of his own generation, and especially as the bad father he thought he had been to his own daughter Linda. Wallander had a tendency to criticize himself. Then he would grow gloomy and distant, filled with a melancholy that he could scarcely define. Often this led to a period of sleepless nights. But since he was now forced to function in spite of everything, as a cop in a far corner of the world, and as the leader of an investigative team, he tried to shake off his uneasiness and sort out his thoughts by taking a walk.

What kind of a world was he living in? A world in which young people burned themselves to death or tried to kill themselves some other way. He decided they were living in the midst of an era that could be called the Age of Failure. Something they had believed in and built up had turned out to be less tenable than expected. They had thought they were building a house, when in reality they were busy raising a monument to something already gone and half forgotten. Now all of Sweden raged around him, as if a gigantic political shelving system was about to tip over. No one knew which carpenters were waiting out in the entryway for their turn to put up new shelves. And no one knew what the new shelves would look like either. It was all extremely baffling, despite the fact that it was summertime and warm. Young people took their own lives, or at least tried. People lived so they could forget, not remember. Houses were hiding places rather than cozy homes. And the police stood by mutely, waiting for the moment when their jails would start to be guarded by men in other uniforms, men from private security companies.

Wallander wiped the sweat from his brow and thought that this had to be enough. He couldn't stand any more. He thought about the boy with the wary eyes sitting next to his mother on the sofa. He thought about Linda, and in the end he didn't know what he was thinking.

Just about then he reached the hospital. Svedberg was standing on the steps waiting for him. Suddenly Wallander staggered, as if about to fall over, struck by an unexpected fit of dizziness. Svedberg took a step toward him and reached out his hand. But Wallander waved him away and continued up the hospital steps. To protect himself from the sun, Svedberg had put on a funny but much too large cap. Wallander muttered something unintelligible but then dragged him along to the cafeteria, which lay to the right of the entrance. Pale people in wheelchairs or with mobile IVs in tow sat drinking coffee with supportive friends and relatives who wanted nothing more than to go back out in the sunshine and forget about anything to do with hospitals, death, and misery. Wallander bought coffee and a sandwich, while Svedberg settled for a glass of water. Wallander knew it was completely inappropriate to take time for this lunch break, since it was obvious that Carlman's daughter was dying. At the same time it was an incantation against everything that was happening around him. The coffee break was his very last defense.

"Carlman's widow phoned," said Svedberg. "She was totally hysterical."

"What did the girl do?" asked Wallander.

"She took pills."

"What happened?"

"Someone discovered her by chance. But by that time she was in a deep coma. Her pulse was almost gone. Her heart stopped just as they got to the hospital. She's in very bad shape. Don't expect to be able to talk to her."

Wallander nodded. He knew that his walk to the hospital had been more for his own sake.

"What did her mother say?" he asked. "Was there a letter? Any explanation?"

"No, apparently it was quite unexpected."

Wallander recalled again the slap in the face she had given him.

"She seemed totally unbalanced when I met her," he said. "She really didn't leave a note?"

"If she did, the mother didn't mention it."

Wallander thought for a moment.

"Do me a favor," he said. "Drive out there and find out if there was a note or not. If there *is* something, you'll have to check it out carefully."

They left the cafeteria. Wallander drove back to the police station with Svedberg. He thought he might as well get hold of a doctor by telephone to hear how the girl was doing.

"I put a few reports on your desk," said Svedberg. "I did a phone interview with the reporter and photographer who visited Wetterstedt the day he died."

"Anything new?"

"It just confirmed what we already know. That Wetterstedt was his usual self. There didn't seem to be anything threatening him. Nothing he was aware of, anyway."

"In other words, I don't need to read the report?"

Svedberg shrugged.

"It's always better to have four eyes look at something than two."

"I'm not so sure about that," said Wallander distractedly as he looked out the car window.

"Ekholm is busy putting the finishing touches on a psychological profile," said Svedberg.

Wallander muttered something in reply.

Svedberg dropped him off outside the police station and then drove out to talk to Carlman's widow. Wallander picked up a pile of messages at the front desk. A new girl was sitting there again. He asked about Ebba and was told that she was at the hospital having the cast taken off her wrist. I could have stopped in and said hello to her, thought Wallander. Since I was over there anyway. If it was possible to say hello to someone who was just having a cast removed.

He went to his office and opened the window wide. Without sitting down he shuffled through the reports Svedberg had mentioned. Suddenly he remembered that he had also asked to see the photographs. Where were they? Unable to control his anger, he found Svedberg's mobile number and called him.

"The photos," he asked. "Where are they?"

"Aren't they on your desk?" Svedberg replied, surprised.

"There's nothing here."

"Then they must be in my office. I must have forgotten them. They came in the mail today."

The pictures were in a brown envelope on Svedberg's organized desk. Wallander spread them out and sat in Svedberg's chair. Wetterstedt posing in his home, in the garden, and down on the beach. In one of the pictures the overturned rowboat could be seen in the background. Wetterstedt was smiling at the camera. The gray hair that would soon be torn from his head was ruffled by the wind. The photos exuded a harmonious equilibrium, showing a man who seemed to have made peace with his old age. Nothing in the pictures hinted at what was about to happen. Wallander thought that Wetterstedt had less than fifteen hours left to live when the pictures were taken. The photos lying before him showed how Wetterstedt had looked on the last day of his life. Wallander kept on studying the pictures for a few minutes before he stuffed them back in the envelope and left Svedberg's room. He started toward his own office but suddenly changed his mind and stopped outside Höglund's door, which was always open.

She was bent over some papers.

"Am I interrupting anything?" he asked.

"Not at all."

He went in and sat down in her visitor's chair. They exchanged a few words about Carlman's daughter.

"Svedberg is hunting for a suicide note," said Wallander. "If there is one."

"She must have been very close to her father," said Höglund.

Wallander didn't reply. He changed the subject.

"Did you notice anything strange when we were visiting the Fredman family?"

"Strange?"

"A cold wind that suddenly blew through the room?"

At once he regretted the way he expressed himself. Höglund wrinkled her brow as if he had said something inappropriate.

"I mean, the fact that they seemed evasive when I asked questions about Louise," he clarified.

"No, I didn't," she replied. "But I did notice that you acted different."

He explained the feeling he had had. She thought about it and tried to remember before she answered.

"You might be right," she said. "Now that you mention it, they did seem to be on their guard. That cold wind you were talking about."

"The question is whether it applied to both of them or just one," said Wallander gloomily.

"Is that right?"

"I'm not sure. I'm talking about a feeling I had."

"Didn't the boy start answering the questions you were actually asking his mother?"

Wallander nodded.

"That's just it," he said. "I wonder why."

"Still, you have to ask yourself whether it's really important," she said.

"Of course," he admitted. "Sometimes I have a tendency to get hung up on unimportant details. But I still want to have a talk with that girl."

This time she was the one who changed the subject.

"It gives me chills when I think about what Anette Fredman said. That she felt relief that her husband would never walk through their door again. I guess I have a hard time understanding what it means to live under conditions like that."

"He was abusing her," said Wallander. "Maybe he beat the children too. But none of them filed a complaint."

"The boy seemed quite normal," she said. "And well brought up, too."

"Children learn to survive," said Wallander, thinking for a moment of his own childhood and the childhood he had given Linda.

He stood up.

"I'm going to try and get hold of the girl," he said. "Louise Fredman. Tomorrow if I can. I've got a strong hunch she hasn't gone away at all."

He headed toward his room and got a cup of coffee on the way. He almost collided with Norén and remembered the photos he had asked to have taken of the crowd standing outside the cordon and watching the police work.

"I gave the film to Nyberg," said Norén. "But I don't think I'm much of a photographer."

"Who the hell is?" said Wallander, without sounding unkind. He went into his room and closed the door. He sat staring at his telephone and collecting his thoughts before he called the automobile inspection station and asked for a new appointment. When he heard that the slot they offered him was during the time he intended to spend at Skagen with Baiba he got mad. When he told the woman who answered about all the atrocities he was busy trying to solve, she gave him a reserved time that was suddenly free. He wondered silently who that slot had been assigned to. After he hung up he decided to do his laundry that evening. If there wasn't a free time in the laundry room, at least he could put his name on the waiting list.

The phone rang. It was Nyberg.

"You were right," he said. "The fingerprints on that bloody piece of paper you found behind the road maintenance hut matched the ones we found on the piece torn off the Phantom comic book. So we no longer have any doubt that the same person is involved. In a couple of hours we'll also know whether we can tie him to the blood-soaked van at Sturup. We're also going to try and get some prints off Björn Fredman's face."

"Will that work?"

"If someone poured acid in his eyes he must have used one hand to hold his eyelids open," said Nyberg. "It's unpleasant, but true. If we're lucky we'll find prints on the eyelids themselves."

"It's a good thing people can't hear the way we talk to each other," said Wallander. "How about that bulb? The light that didn't work above Wetterstedt's garden gate."

"I was just getting to that," said Nyberg. "You were right about that too. We found fingerprints."

Wallander sat up straight in his chair. His earlier bad mood was gone. Now he could feel his excitement rising. The investigation was showing signs of breaking wide open.

"Have we got him in the archives?" he asked.

"No, unfortunately," said Nyberg. "But I asked Central Records to check one more time."

"Let's assume for a moment that you're right," Wallander went on. "That means we're dealing with someone who has no record."

"Could be."

"Run the prints through Interpol too," said Wallander. "And Europol. Ask for highest priority. Tell them it concerns a serial killer."

Wallander hung up and grabbed the phone again. He asked the girl at the switchboard to find Mats Ekholm. In a few minutes she called back and said he'd gone out for lunch.

"Where?" asked Wallander.

"I think he said the Continental."

"Get hold of him there," said Wallander. "Tell him to get over here right away."

It was two-thirty when Ekholm knocked on the door. Wallander was talking on the phone to Per Åkeson. He pointed to a chair and asked Ekholm to have a seat. Wallander ended the conversation after he had convinced a skeptical Åkeson that nothing about the investigation could be done better in the short term with an expanded investigative team. Åkeson finally gave in, and they agreed to postpone the decision for a few more days.

Wallander leaned back in his chair and clasped his hands behind his head. He told Ekholm about the positive ID on the fingerprints.

"The prints we're going to find on Björn Fredman's body will be the same ones too," he said. "We don't have to assume or suspect any longer. Starting right now we know that we're dealing with the same killer. The only question is: who is he?"

"I've been thinking about the eyes," said Ekholm. "All available experience tells us that aside from the genitals, the eyes are the part of the body most often subjected to the final revenge."

"What does that mean?"

"Simply put, it means that killers seldom begin by putting out someone's eyes. They save that for last."

Wallander nodded for him to continue.

"We can approach it from two directions," said Ekholm. "We might ask why Björn Fredman was the one to have his eyes burned out with acid. We could also turn the whole thing around and ask why the eyes of the other two men weren't attacked."

"What's your answer?"

Ekholm raised his hands in a dismissive gesture.

"I don't have one," he said. "When we're talking about someone's psyche, especially that of a disturbed or sick person with a defective mental relationship to the world, we're getting into territory in which there are no absolute answers."

Ekholm looked as if he was waiting for a comment. But Wallander just shook his head.

"I have a hint of a pattern," Ekholm went on. "The person who did this selected his victims in advance. There's a fundamental reason why all this is happening. He has some kind of relationship with these men. It's not necessary for him to have known them personally. It might be a symbolic relationship. Except for Björn Fredman. I'm as certain as I can be that the mutilation of eyes reveals that the perpetrator knew his victim. And indications are that they knew each other well."

Wallander leaned forward and gave Ekholm a penetrating look.

"How well?" he asked.

"They might have been friends. Colleagues. Rivals."

"And something happened?"

"Something happened, yes. In reality or in the perpetrator's imagination."

Wallander tried to decide what Ekholm's words might mean for the case. At the same time he asked himself whether he believed what Ekholm had said.

"In other words, we ought to concentrate on Björn Fredman," he said after he had thought it out.

"That's one possibility."

Wallander was suddenly irritated at Ekholm's habit of running away from any firm opinion. It bothered him, even though he knew that Ekholm was right about leaving most of the doors wide open.

"Let's say you were in my place," said Wallander. "I promise not to quote you. Or blame you if you're wrong. But what would you do?"

"I would concentrate on retracing Fredman's life," he said. "But I'd keep my eyes open."

Wallander nodded. He understood.

"What kind of person are we actually looking for?" he asked.

Ekholm batted at a bee that had flown in through the window.

"The basic conclusions you can draw yourself," he said. "That it's a man. That he's apparently strong. That he's practical, meticulous, and not afraid of blood."

"And he's not in the criminal records either," Wallander added. "In other words, he's a first-timer."

"That reinforces my belief that he fundamentally leads a quite normal life," said Ekholm. "The psychotic ego, the mental breakdown, is well insulated from rational insight. He could sit down at the dinner table with the scalps in his pocket and eat dinner with a healthy appetite."

"In other words, there are only two ways we can get him," Wallander said. "Either we catch him in the act, or we gather a body of evidence that spells out his name in neon letters."

"That's about right. So it's no easy task we have ahead of us."

Just as Ekholm was about to leave, Wallander formulated his last question.

"Will he strike again?"

"It might be over," said Ekholm. "Björn Fredman and his eyes as the grand finale."

"Do you think so?"

"No. He'll strike again. What we've seen up to now is just the beginning of a very long series."

When Wallander was alone he shooed the bee out the window with his jacket. Then he sat quite still with his eyes closed, thinking over everything Ekholm had told him. At four o'clock he went to get some more coffee. Then he continued on to the conference room, where the rest of the investigative group was waiting for him.

He asked Ekholm to repeat everything he had said earlier. Afterwards it was quiet for a long time. Wallander waited out the silence because he knew that each of them was trying to grasp the significance of what they had just heard. Right now the individual adjustments are being made, he thought. Later we'll figure out what the collective opinion of the investigative team will actually be.

They agreed with Ekholm. They were going to concentrate on Björn Fredman's life. But at the same time they weren't going to forget to keep looking back over their shoulders.

They ended the meeting by planning the next steps in the investigation.

Just after six o'clock they broke up. Martinsson was the only one who left the police station. He had to go pick up his kids. The rest of them went back to work.

Wallander stood by his window looking out at the summer evening.

Something was bothering him.

The thought that they were still on the wrong track.

What was it he was missing?

He turned and looked around the room, as if an invisible visitor had entered.

So that's how things are, he thought. I'm chasing a ghost. When I ought to be searching for a living human being. And all this time he might have been in a totally different direction than where I happen to be looking.

He sat there pondering the case until midnight.

Not until he left the station did he remember the dirty laundry still heaped on his floor.

Chapter Twenty-four

Next morning at dawn Wallander walked half asleep downstairs to the laundry room and discovered to his dismay that someone had gotten there first. The washing machine was in use, and he had to settle for signing up for a slot that afternoon. The whole time he kept trying to recapture the dream he'd had during the night. It had been erotic, frenzied, and passionate, and Wallander had watched himself from a distance, participating in a drama he never would have come close to in his waking life. But the woman who had stepped into his dream wasn't Baiba. Not until he was on his way back up the stairs from the laundry room did he realize that the woman in the dream reminded him of the female pastor he had met at the Smedstorp parish pastor's office. At first it surprised him, and then he felt a little ashamed of his dream. Later, when he got back to his apartment, it dissolved into what it actually was: a dream that was created and obliterated according to its own special rules.

He sat down at the kitchen table and drank the coffee he had already brewed. He could feel the heat coming in through the half-open window. Maybe the prediction by Ann-Britt Höglund's grandmother was right: they were in for a truly beautiful summer. It was a few minutes past six. He drank his coffee and thought about his father. Often, especially in the morning, his thoughts would wander back in time, to the era of the Silk Knights, when they had gotten along well and he awoke each morning knowing he was a child beloved by his father. But now, more than forty years later, he had a hard time discerning what his father had really been like as a young man. His paintings were the same back then: he had painted that landscape with or without the grouse with the same unswerving determination not to change anything from one painting to the next. Wallander thought that in reality his father had only painted one single picture in his whole life. Right from the start he had been pleased with the result. He never tried to improve anything. The result had been perfect from the first completed attempt.

He drank the last of his coffee and tried to imagine a world in which his father was no longer alive. This was difficult. He wondered what he would do with the emptiness that would remain when his constant feelings of guilt were gone. The trip to Italy they were going to take in September would probably be their last chance ever to understand each other, maybe even to reconcile, and to merge the happy days of the Silk Knights with everything that came afterwards. He didn't want his memories to end after he carted out the last of the paintings and placed them in some buyer's huge American car and then stood by his father's side waving to the Silk Knight driving off in a cloud of dust, on his way to sell the paintings for three or four times what he had paid his father.

At six-thirty he became a cop again and swept the memories aside. He got dressed as he tried to decide how to go about all the tasks he had set himself for that day. At seven o'clock he walked through the door of the police station, after exchanging a few words with Norén, who arrived at the same time. Norén was actually supposed to be coming to his last day of work before vacation. But he had postponed it, just as many of his colleagues had done.

"No doubt it'll start raining as soon as you catch the killer," he said. "What does a weather god care about a simple policeman when there's a serial killer on the loose?"

Wallander muttered something unintelligible in reply. But he couldn't ignore the possibility that there might be some dark truth in what Norén had just said.

He went in to see Hansson, who seemed to spend all his time at the station, weighed down by anxiety about the difficult case and the burden he was forced to bear because he was acting chief. His face was as gray as the sidewalk. He was shaving with an ancient electric razor when Wallander came into his office. His shirt was wrinkled and his eyes bloodshot.

"You've got to try and get a few hours' sleep once in a while," said Wallander. "Your responsibility isn't any greater than anyone else's."

Hansson turned off the shaver and gloomily observed the result in a pocket mirror.

"I took a sleeping pill yesterday," he said. "But I still didn't get any sleep. All I got was a headache."

Wallander looked at Hansson in silence. He empathized with him. Being chief had never been one of Hansson's dreams. Wallander thought he knew him that well, at least.

"I'm going back to Malmö," he said. "I want to talk to the members of Fredman's family again. Especially the ones who weren't there yesterday."

Hansson gave him a quizzical look.

"Are you going to interrogate a fourteen-year-old boy? That's not legally permitted."

"I was thinking more of the daughter," said Wallander. "She's seventeen. And I don't intend to 'interrogate' anyone."

Hansson nodded and got up from his desk with an effort. He pointed to a book lying open on the desk.

"I got this from Ekholm," he said. "Behavioral science based on a number of case studies of infamous serial killers. It's unbelievable the things people will do if they're deranged enough."

"Is there anything about scalping in it?" asked Wallander.

"That's one of the milder forms of trophy collecting. If you only knew the things that have been found in people's homes, it would make you sick."

"I feel sick already," said Wallander. "I think I can imagine what's in that book."

"Ordinary human beings," said Hansson in dismay. "Completely normal on the surface. Underneath, mentally ill beasts of prey. A man in France, the foreman of a coal depot, used to cut open the stomachs of his victims and stick his head inside to try and suffocate himself. And that's just one example."

"I think that'll do," said Wallander, trying to discourage him.

"Ekholm wanted me to give you the book when I'm done reading it," said Hansson.

"I bet he did," said Wallander. "But I really don't think I have the time to read it. Or the inclination."

Wallander made himself a sandwich in the lunchroom and took it with him when he left the station. He ate it in the car while he wondered whether he dared call Linda. But he decided not to. It was still too early.

W allander arrived in Malmö at around eight-thirty. The summer calm had already started to descend on the countryside. The traffic on the roads that intersected the highway into Malmö was lighter than usual. He headed toward Rosengård and pulled up outside the house he had visited the day before. He turned off the engine and sat there trying to figure out for himself what it was that made him come back so soon. They had decided to direct the investigation at Björn Fredman's life. He could follow his motive that far. Besides, it was necessary that he meet the absent daughter. The four-year-old boy was less important.

He found a dirty gasoline charge slip in the glove compartment and took out a pen. To his great irritation he saw that it had leaked ink around the breast pocket where he kept it. The spot was half the size of his hand. On the white shirt it looked as if he'd been shot right through the heart. The shirt was almost new. Baiba had bought it for him at Christmas after she went through his wardrobe and cleaned out the old, worn-out clothes.

He immediate impulse was to return to Ystad in resignation and go back to bed. He didn't know how many shirts each year he had to throw away because he forgot to cap the pen properly before he stuck it in his breast pocket.

He thought about driving downtown and buying a new shirt. That would mean he'd have to wait at least an hour until the stores opened. He decided against it. He tossed the leaky pen out the window and then looked for another one among the junk in the glove compartment. He wrote down some key words on the back of the gas receipt. *B.F.'s friends. Then and now. Unexpected events.* He crumpled up the note and was just about to stuff it in his breast pocket when he caught himself. He got out of the car and took off his jacket. The ink from his shirt pocket hadn't reached the jacket lining. He tugged at his shirt and looked at it gloomily. Then he went into the building and pushed open the elevator door. The broken glass from the day before was still there. He got out on the fifth floor and rang the doorbell. There was no sound from inside the apartment. Maybe they were still asleep. He waited over a minute. Then he rang again. The door opened. It was the boy, Stefan. He seemed surprised to see Wallander. He smiled, but his eyes were wary.

"I hope I haven't come too early," said Wallander. "I should have called first, of course. But I was in Malmö anyway. I thought I'd drop by."

It was a flimsy lie, he thought. But it was the best he could come up with.

The boy let him into the entryway. He was dressed in a cut-off T-shirt and a pair of jeans. He was barefoot.

"I'm here by myself," he said. "My mother went out with my little brother. They were going to Copenhagen."

"It's a great day for a trip to Copenhagen," said Wallander ingratiatingly.

"Yes, she likes going there a lot. To get away from it all."

His words echoed disconsolately in the entryway. Wallander thought the boy had sounded strangely unmoved last time when he mentioned the death of his father. They went into the living room. Wallander laid his jacket on a chair and pointed at the ink spot.

"This happens all the time," he said.

"It never happens to me," said the boy, smiling. "I can fix some coffee if you want."

"No thanks."

They sat down at opposite ends of the table. A blanket and pillow on the sofa indicated that someone had slept there. Under a chair Wallander glimpsed the neck of an empty wine bottle. The boy noticed at once that he had seen it. His alertness didn't flag for an instant. Wallander hastily asked himself whether he actually had the right to subject a minor to a conversation dealing with his father's death without having a relative present. At the same time he didn't want to pass up this opportunity. Anyway, the boy was incredibly mature for fourteen. Wallander kept feeling that he was talking to someone his own age. Even Linda, who was several years older, might seem childish in comparison.

"What are you going to do this summer?" asked Wallander. "We've got fine weather."

The boy smiled.

"I've got plenty to do," he replied.

Wallander waited for more, but he didn't continue.

"What grade are you going to be in this fall?"

"Eighth grade."

"Is school going well?"

"Yes."

"What's your favorite subject?"

"None of them. But math is the easiest. We started a club to study numerology."

"I'm not sure I know what that is."

"The Holy Trinity. The seven lean years. Trying to predict your future by combining the numbers in your own life."

"That sounds interesting."

"It is."

Wallander could feel himself becoming more and more fascinated by the boy sitting across from him. His husky body contrasted sharply with his childish face. But there was obviously nothing wrong with his mind.

Wallander took the crumpled gas receipt out of his jacket. His house keys dropped out of the pocket. He put them back and sat down again.

"I have a few questions," he said. "But this is not an interrogation, by any means. If you want to wait until your mother comes home, just say so."

"That's not necessary. I'll answer if I can."

"Your sister," said Wallander. "When is she coming back?"

"I don't know."

The boy looked at him. The question didn't seem to bother him. He had answered without hesitation. Wallander began to wonder if he had been mistaken the day before.

"I assume that you're in contact with her? That you know where she is?"

"She just took off. It's not the first time. She'll come home when she feels like it."

"I hope you understand that I think that sounds a little unusual."

"Not for us."

The boy seemed imperturbable. Wallander was convinced that he knew where his sister was. But he wouldn't be able to force an answer out of him. Nor could he disregard the possibility that the girl was so upset that she really had run away from the whole situation.

"Isn't it true that she's in Copenhagen?" he asked cautiously. "And that your mother went there today to see her?"

"She went over to buy some shoes."

Wallander nodded.

"Well, let's talk about something else," he went on. "You've had time to think. Now do you have any idea who might have killed your father?"

"No."

"Do you agree with your mother, that a lot of people might have wanted to?"

"Yes."

"Why's that?"

For the first time it seemed as though the boy's unflappable politeness was about to crack. He replied with unexpected vehemence.

"My father was an evil man," he said. "He lost the right to live a long time ago."

Wallander was shaken by what he heard. How could a young person be so full of hatred?

"That's not something you ought to say," he replied. "That a person has lost his right to live. No matter what he did."

The boy was still unmoved.

"What did he do that was so bad?" Wallander continued. "Lots of people are thieves. Lots of them sell stolen goods. They don't have to be monsters because of that."

"He scared us."

"How'd he do that?"

"We were all afraid of him."

"Even you?"

"Yes. But not for the past year."

"Why not?"

"The fear went away."

"What about your mother?"

"She was scared."

"Your brother?"

"He'd run and hide when he thought Pappa was coming home."

"Your sister?"

"She was more afraid than any of us."

Wallander heard an almost imperceptible shift in the boy's voice. There had been an instant of hesitation, he was sure of it.

"Why?" he asked cautiously.

"She was the most sensitive."

Wallander quickly decided to take a chance.

"Did your pappa touch her?"

"What do you mean?"

"I think you know what I mean."

"Yes, I do. But he never touched her."

There it is, thought Wallander, and tried to avoid revealing his reaction. He may have abused his own daughter. Maybe the younger boy too. Maybe even the boy I'm talking to.

Wallander didn't want to go any further. The question of where the sister was and what may have happened to her in the past was something he didn't want to deal with alone. The thought of the possible abuse upset him.

"Did your pappa have any good friends?" he asked.

"He hung around with a lot of people. But whether any of them were friends, I don't know."

"If you were to name someone who knew your pappa well, who do you think I should talk to?"

The boy smiled involuntarily but then regained his composure at once.

"Peter Hjelm," he replied.

Wallander wrote down the name.

"Why did you smile?"

"I don't know."

"Do you know Peter Hjelm?"

"I've met him, sure."

"Where can I get hold of him?"

"He's in the phone book under 'Handyman.' He lives on Kungsgatan."

"How did they know each other?"

"They used to drink together. I know that. What else they did I can't say."

Wallander looked around the room.

"Did your pappa have any of his things here in the apartment?"

"No."

"Nothing at all?"

"Not a thing."

Wallander stuffed the paper into his pants pocket. He had no more questions.

"What's it like to be a policeman?" the boy asked all at once.

Wallander could tell that he was really interested. His alert eyes gleamed.

"It's a little of this, a little of that," said Wallander, suddenly unsure of what he actually thought about his profession at the moment.

"What's it like to catch a murderer?"

"Cold and gray and miserable," he replied, thinking with distaste of all the lying TV shows the boy must have seen.

"What are you going to do when you catch the person who killed my pappa?"

"I don't know," said Wallander. "That depends."

"He must be dangerous. Since he's already killed several other people."

Wallander found the boy's curiosity annoying.

"We'll catch him," he said firmly, to put an end to the conversation. "Sooner or later we'll catch him."

He got up from the chair and asked where the bathroom was. The boy pointed to a door in the hall leading to the bedroom. Wallander closed the door behind him. He looked at his face in the mirror. What he needed most was some sunshine. After he took a piss he cautiously opened the medicine cabinet. There were a few bottles of pills in it. One of them had Louise Fredman's name on it. He saw that she was born on November 9th. He memorized the name of the medicine and the doctor who had prescribed it. *Saroten.* He had never heard of this drug before. He would have to look it up in the police catalog of drugs and medications when he got back to Ystad.

When he went back to the living room the boy was still sitting in the same position as before. Wallander wondered briefly whether the boy was normal after all. His precociousness and self-control made a strange impression.

The boy turned toward him and smiled. For a moment the wariness in his eyes seemed to have vanished. Wallander pushed away the thought he had just had and picked up his jacket.

"I'll be calling you again," he said. "Don't forget to tell your mamma that I was here. It would be good if you told her what we talked about."

"Can I come and visit you some time?" asked the boy.

Wallander was surprised by the question. It was like having a ball tossed at you and not being able to catch it.

"You mean you want to come to the police station in Ystad?"

"Yes."

"Of course you could do that," said Wallander. "But call ahead of time. I'm often out. And sometimes it's not convenient."

Wallander went out to the landing and pressed the elevator button. They nodded to each other. The boy closed the door. Wallander rode down and walked out into the sunshine.

It was the hottest day yet this summer. He stood still for a moment, enjoying the heat. At the same time he tried to decide what to do. He made his decision quickly. He drove down to the Malmö police station. Forsfält was in his office. Wallander told him about his talk with the boy. He gave Forsfält the name of the doctor, Gunnar Bergdahl, and asked him to get hold of him as soon as possible. Then he told him about his suspicions that Fredman may have abused his daughter and possibly the two boys as well. Forsfält wasn't sure that any allegations of that type of assault had ever been directed at Fredman. But he promised to look into the matter as soon as he could.

Wallander changed the subject to Peter Hjelm. Forsfält told him that he was a man who resembled Björn Fredman in many ways. He'd been in and out of many prisons. On one occasion he was nabbed along with Fredman in a joint fencing operation. Forsfält was of the opinion that Hjelm was the one who supplied the stolen goods, and Fredman then resold them. Wallander wondered whether Forsfält would mind if he talked to Hjelm alone.

"I'm happy to get out of it," said Forsfält.

"I'd like to use you as a backup," said Wallander.

Wallander looked up Hjelm's address in Forsfält's phone book. He also gave Forsfält his mobile telephone number. They decided to have lunch together. Forsfält hoped that by then he would have a copy ready of all the material the Malmö police had gathered over the years about Björn Fredman.

Wallander left his car outside the police station and walked toward Kungsgatan. He went into a clothing store and bought a shirt, which he put on right away. He threw away the one that had been ruined by the ink, but he did so with some reluctance. It was a present from Baiba, after all. He went back out in the sunshine. For a few minutes he sat on a bench with his eyes closed, facing the sun. Then he walked over to the building where Hjelm lived. The door had an entry code. Wallander was lucky. After a few minutes an elderly man came out with his dog. Wallander gave him a friendly nod and stepped in the main door. He saw on the apartment directory that Hjelm lived on the fourth floor. Just as he was about to open the elevator door, his cell phone rang. It was Forsfält.

"Where are you?" he asked.

"I'm standing outside the elevator in Hjelm's building."

"I was hoping you hadn't gotten there yet."

"Has something happened?"

"I got hold of the doctor. It turned out we knew each other. I'd totally forgotten about it."

"What'd he say?"

"Something he probably shouldn't have. But I promised I wouldn't mention his name. In other words, you can't either."

"I promise."

"He thought that the person we're talking about—I won't mention the name since we're on cell phones—was admitted to a psychiatric clinic."

Wallander held his breath.

"That explains why she left," he said.

"No, it doesn't," said Forsfält. "She's been there for three years."

Wallander stood there in silence. Someone pressed the button for the elevator and it rumbled upstairs.

"We'll talk later," he said.

"Good luck with Hjelm."

He hung up.

Wallander thought for a long time about what he had just heard.

Then he started up the stairs to the fourth floor.

Chapter Twenty-five

Wallander knew he had heard the music coming out of Hjelm's apartment on some other occasion in his life. He listened with one ear pressed against the door. Then he remembered that Linda used to play it, and that the band was called the Grateful Dead. He rang the doorbell and took a step back. The music was on very loud. He rang again with no response. He had to bang sharply on the door before the music was turned down. He heard steps and then the door opened. For some reason Wallander had expected the door to be opened just a crack. When it was opened wide he had to take a step back so the door wouldn't hit him in the face. The man who opened it was completely naked. Wallander also saw that he was under the influence of something. There was an almost imperceptible swaying motion possessing his large body. Wallander introduced himself and showed his badge. The man didn't bother looking at it. He kept staring at Wallander.

"I've seen you," he said. "On the tube. And in the papers. I never actually read the papers. So I must have seen you on the front page. Or on a placard. The cop they were looking for. The one who shoots people without asking permission. What did you say your name was? Wahlgren?"

"Wallander. Are you Peter Hjelm?"

"Yep."

"I want to talk to you."

The naked man made a knowing gesture toward the inside of the apartment. Wallander assumed that meant he had female company.

"It can't be helped," said Wallander. "It probably won't take very long anyway."

Hjelm reluctantly let him into the entryway.

"Put some clothes on," said Wallander firmly.

Hjelm shrugged, pulled an overcoat from a hanger, and put it on. As if at Wallander's request, he also jammed an old hat down over his ears. Wallander followed him down a long hallway. Hjelm lived in an old-fashioned, spacious apartment. Wallander sometimes dreamed of finding one like it in Ystad. Once he inquired about one of the apartments in the bookstore's red building on the square. But he was shocked when he heard how much the rent was.

To his astonishment when they reached the living room, Wallander discovered a naked man wrapping a sheet around himself. Wallander was facing something he wasn't prepared for. In his pared-down and sometimes prejudiced view of reality, a naked man who opened a door and made a meaningful gesture meant that he had a naked woman in the apartment, not a naked man. To conceal his embarrassment, Wallander assumed a tone of determined authority. He sat down in a chair and waved Hjelm to a seat facing him.

"Who are you?" he then asked the other man, who was considerably younger than Hjelm.

"Geert doesn't understand Swedish," said Hjelm. "He's from Amsterdam. He's just visiting, you might say."

"Tell him I want to see some ID," said Wallander. "Now."

Hjelm spoke very poor English, much worse than Wallander. The man in the sheet disappeared and came back with a Dutch driver's license. As usual, Wallander had nothing to write with. He memorized the man's last name, van Loenen, and handed back the driver's license. Then he asked a few brief questions in English. Van Loenen claimed that he was a waiter in a café in Amsterdam and that he had met Peter Hjelm there. This was the third time he'd been to Malmö. He was going back on the train to Amsterdam in two days. Then Wallander asked him to leave the room. Hjelm had sat down on the floor, dressed in his overcoat with the hat pulled low over his forehead. Wallander got mad.

"Take off that damn hat!" he yelled. "And sit in a chair. Otherwise I'll call a patrol car and have you taken downtown."

Hjelm did as he was told. He tossed the hat in a wide arc so that it landed between two flowerpots on one of the window seats. Wallander was still angry when he began asking questions. His anger made him start to sweat.

"Björn Fredman is dead," he said brutally. "But I suppose you already know that."

Hjelm's smile disappeared. He didn't know, Wallander realized.

"He was murdered," Wallander continued. "Someone poured acid in his eyes. And cut off part of his scalp. This happened three days ago. Now we're looking for the person who did it. The perpetrator has already killed two other people. A former politician by the name of Wetterstedt and an art dealer named Arne Carlman. But maybe you knew all this."

Hjelm nodded slowly. Wallander tried to interpret his reactions but with no luck.

"Now I understand why Björn didn't answer his phone," he said after a while. "I tried to call him all day yesterday. And this morning I tried again."

"What did you want from him?"

"I was thinking of inviting him over for dinner."

Wallander saw at once that this was a lie. Since he was still mad about Hjelm's arrogant attitude, it was easy for him to tighten his grip. In all his years as a police officer Wallander had only lost control on two occasions and struck individuals he was interrogating. He could usually control his rage.

"Don't lie to me," he said. "The only way you're going to see me walk out that door any time soon is if you give me clear, truthful answers to my questions. Otherwise all hell will break loose here. We're dealing with an insane serial killer. Which means the police have special authority in this case."

The last part wasn't true, of course. But Wallander saw that it made an impression on Hjelm.

"I was calling him about a gig we had together."

"What sort of gig?"

"A little import and export. He owed me a little money."

"How little?"

"A little. A hundred thousand, maybe. No more than that."

Wallander thought that this "little" sum of money was equivalent to many months' wages for himself. This made him even angrier.

"We can get back to your business with Fredman later," he said. "That's something the Malmö police will have to deal with. What I want to know is whether you can tell me who might have killed Fredman."

"Not me, that's for sure."

"I wasn't suggesting you did. Anyone else?"

Wallander saw that Hjelm was really trying to concentrate.

"I don't know," he finally said.

"You seem hesitant."

"Björn was into a lot of things I didn't know about."

"Such as?"

"I don't know."

"Give me a straight answer!"

"Well, shit! I just don't know. We did some deals with each other. What Fredman did with the rest of his time I can't tell you. In this business you're not supposed to know too much. You can't know too little either. But that's something else again."

"Give me a for-instance. What do you think Fredman might have been into?"

"I think he was doing collections quite a bit."

"He was what you call an enforcer, you mean?"

"Something like that."

"Who was his boss?"

"Dunno."

"Don't lie to me."

"I'm not lying. I just don't know."

Wallander almost believed him.

"What else?"

"He was a pretty secretive type. He traveled a lot. And when he came back he was always tan. And he brought home souvenirs."

"Where did he go?"

"He never said. But after his trips he usually had plenty of money."

Björn Fredman's passport, thought Wallander. We haven't found it.

"Who else knew Fredman besides you?"

"There must have been lots of people."

"Who knew him as well as you do?"

"Nobody."

"Did he have a woman?"

"What a question! Of course he had women!"

"Was there anyone special?"

"He switched around a lot."

"Why did he switch?"

"Why does anyone switch? Why do I switch? Because I meet somebody from Amsterdam one day and somebody from Bjärred the next."

"Bjärred?"

"It's just an example, damn it! Halmstad, if that's any better!"

Wallander stopped asking questions. He looked at Hjelm with a furrowed brow. He felt an instinctive animosity toward him. Toward a thief who regarded a hundred thousand kronor as "a little money."

"Gustaf Wetterstedt," he said finally. "And Arne Carlman. I saw by your face that you knew they had been killed."

"I don't read the papers. But I watch TV."

"Do you remember if Fredman ever mentioned their names?"

"No."

"Do you think you may have forgotten? Is it possible he did know them after all?"

Hjelm sat in silence for more than a minute. Wallander waited.

"I'm positive," he said finally. "But he might have known them and I just didn't know about it."

"This man who's on the loose is dangerous," said Wallander. "He's ice-cold and calculating. And crazy. He poured acid in Fredman's eyes. It must have been incredibly painful. Do you get my point?"

"Yes, I do."

"I want you to do a little footwork for me. Spread it around that the police are looking for some connection between these three men. I assume you agree that we have to get this nut case off the streets. A man who pours acid in somebody's eyes."

Hjelm grimaced with distaste.

"Sure."

Wallander got up.

"Call Detective Forsfält," he said. "Or give me a call. In Ystad. Anything you can come up with is important."

"Björn had a girlfriend named Marianne," said Hjelm. "She lives over by the Triangle."

"What's her last name?"

"Eriksson, I think."

"What kind of work does she do?"

"I don't know."

"Have you got her phone number?"

"I can look it up."

"Go ahead."

Wallander waited while Hjelm left the room. He could hear whispering voices, at least one of which sounded annoyed. Hjelm came back and handed Wallander a piece of paper. Then he followed him out to the entryway.

Hjelm seemed to have sobered up from whatever it was he'd been taking. But he still seemed completely unfazed by what had happened to his friend. Wallander felt a great uneasiness at the coldness Hjelm exhibited. It was incomprehensible to him.

"That crazy man…" Hjelm began, without finishing his sentence. Wallander understood the intent of his unasked question.

"He's after specific individuals. If you can't see yourself in any connection with Wetterstedt, Carlman, and Fredman, you have nothing to worry about."

"Why haven't you brought him in?"

Wallander stared at Hjelm. He could feel his anger returning.

"One reason is that people like you have such a hard time answering questions," he said.

He left Hjelm and didn't feel like waiting for the elevator. When he got down to the street he stood there facing the sun and closed his eyes. He thought over the conversation with Hjelm, and the feeling that they were off the track returned. He opened his eyes and walked over to the side of the building, where there was some shade. He couldn't shake the feeling that he was about to steer the whole investigation into a blind alley. He was also reminded of the instinctive feeling he had had on several occasions, that something someone had said was significant. *There's something I'm missing in all this,* he thought. *There's a link between Wetterstedt and Carlman and Fredman that I'm tripping over without noticing it.* He could feel anxiety settling in his stomach. The man they were searching for could strike again, and Wallander knew that the truth about the case was very simple. They had no idea who he was. And they didn't even know where to look. He left the shadow of the wall and hailed an empty cab passing by.

It was past noon when he paid and got out in front of the Malmö police station. When he reached Forsfält's office he had a message to call Ystad. Again he had the feeling that something serious had happened. Ebba picked up the phone. She reassured him and then switched him over to Nyberg. They had found a fingerprint on Fredman's left eyelid. It was smudged, but it was still good enough for them to confirm a match with the prints they found at the previous two crime scenes. There was no longer any doubt they were after a single perpetrator. The forensic examination confirmed that Fredman was murdered less than twelve hours before the body was discovered. The medical examiner was also sure that the acid had been poured into his eyes while he was alive.

After the conversation with Nyberg, Ebba switched him over to Martinsson, who had received a positive confirmation from Interpol that Dolores María Santana's father recognized the medallion. It had definitely belonged to her. Martinsson also said that the Swedish embassy in the Dominican Republic had shown themselves to be extremely unwilling to foot the cost of transporting the coffin with her remains back to Santiago.

Wallander was listening with half an ear. When Martinsson finished complaining about the embassy's stonewalling, Wallander asked him what Svedberg and Höglund were working on. Martinsson said they were digging, but neither of them had come up with much. Wallander said he would be back in Ystad that afternoon and hung up. Forsfält stood out in the corridor sneezing the whole time.

"Allergies," he said, blowing his nose. "Summer is the worst."

They walked in the dazzling sunshine to a restaurant where Forsfält liked to eat spaghetti. After Wallander told him about his meeting with Hjelm, Forsfält started talking about his summer house, up near Älmhult. Wallander gathered that he didn't want to disturb their lunch by talking about the investigation in progress. Normally Wallander would have had a hard time remaining patient. But in Forsfält's company it was easy. Wallander listened with growing fascination as the old detective across the table lovingly described how he was restoring an old smithy. He wouldn't let them return to the topic of the investigation until they were having coffee. He promised that he would interview Marianne Eriksson that same day. But even more important was the revelation that Louise Fredman had been a patient in a psychiatric hospital for the past three years.

"I'm not sure," said Forsfält. "But I'd guess that she's in Lund. At St. Lars Hospital. That's where the more serious cases wind up, I think."

"It's hard to get through all the roadblocks you come across when you want to get patient records," said Wallander. "And that's a good thing, of course. But I think this situation with Louise Fredman is important. Especially since the family never told the truth."

"Maybe, maybe not," Forsfält countered. "Mental illness in the family isn't something people want to talk about. I had an aunt who was in and out of various institutions her whole life. I remember that we almost never talked about her when strangers were around. It was a disgrace."

"I'll ask one of the prosecutors in Ystad to get in touch with Malmö," said

Wallander. "There's probably going to be a lot of red tape."

"What reason are you going to give?" asked Forsfält.

Wallander thought for a moment.

"I don't know," he said. "I have a suspicion that Fredman may have abused her."

"That's not good enough," said Forsfält firmly.

"I know," said Wallander. "Somehow I have to show that it's crucial to the whole homicide investigation to obtain information on Louise Fredman. About her and from her."

"What do you think she could help you with?"

Wallander threw out his hands.

"I don't know," he said. "Maybe nothing will be cleared up by finding out what it is that's keeping her locked up in the hospital. Maybe she's incapable of holding a conversation with anyone."

Forsfält nodded pensively. Wallander knew that Forsfält's objections were wellfounded. But he couldn't ignore his own intuition, which told him that Louise Fredman was an important person in the case. But he wasn't about to discuss intuitive hunches with Forsfält.

Wallander bought lunch. When they got back to the police station Forsfält went to the reception desk and got a black plastic bag.

"Here's a few kilos of photocopies on Björn Fredman's troubled life," he said, smiling.

Suddenly he turned serious, as if his smile had been inappropriate.

"That poor devil," he said. "The pain must have been incredible. What could he possibly have done to deserve it?"

"That's just it," said Wallander. "What did he do? What did Wetterstedt do? Or Carlman? And to whom?"

"Scalping and acid in the eyes. Where the hell are we headed?"

"According to the National Police Board, toward a society where a police district like Ystad doesn't need to be manned at all on weekends," said Wallander.

Forsfält stood silent for a moment before he replied.

"I hardly think that's the correct reaction to these developments," he said.

"Tell it to the national commissioner," said Wallander.

"What can he do?" said Forsfält. "He's got a board of directors on his back. And above them are the politicians."

"He could always refuse," said Wallander. "Or he could resign if things get too out of hand."

"Could be," said Forsfält absently.

"Thanks for the help," said Wallander. "Especially the story about the smithy."

"You'll have to come up and visit sometime," said Forsfält. "I don't know whether Sweden is as fantastic as all the magazines say it is. But it's a great country all the same. And beautiful. And surprisingly untouched. If you just take the trouble to look."

"What about Marianne Eriksson?" asked Wallander.

"I'm going to see if I can track her down right now," replied Forsfält. "I'll call you later this afternoon."

Wallander unlocked his car and tossed in the plastic bag. Then he drove out of town and onto the E65. He rolled down the window and let the summer wind blow across his face. When he arrived in Ystad he turned off at the supermarket on the right side of the road and bought groceries. He was already at the checkout when he discovered he had to go back for laundry detergent. He drove home and carried the bags up to his apartment.

When he got to his door he discovered that he had dropped his house keys somewhere.

He went back downstairs and searched the car without finding them. He called Forsfält and was told that he had gone out. One of his colleagues went into his office and looked to see whether Wallander had left his keys on the desk. They weren't there either. He called Peter Hjelm, who picked up the phone almost at once. He came back a few minutes later and said he didn't see them anywhere.

Wallander fished out the piece of paper with the Fredmans' number in Rosengård. The son answered. Wallander waited while he looked for the keys, but he couldn't find them either. Wallander briefly considered whether he ought to tell him that he now knew his sister Louise had been in a hospital for several years. But he decided against it.

He thought for a while. He might have dropped his keys at the place where he ate lunch with Forsfält. Or in the store where he bought the new shirt. Annoyed, he went back to his car and drove to the police station. Ebba kept a couple of spare keys for him at the reception desk. He told her the name of the clothing store and the restaurant in Malmö. She promised to check whether they had found his keys. Wallander left the station and went home without talking to any of his colleagues. He felt a great need to think over all that had happened that day. In particular, he wanted to plan his conversation with Per Åkeson. He carried in the groceries and put them away in the cupboards and refrigerator. He had already missed the laundry slot he had signed up for. He took the box of detergent and gathered up the huge pile of laundry. When he got downstairs, the laundry room was still empty. He sorted the pile, guessing which types of clothes required the same water temperature. With some fumbling he managed to get the two machines started. Satisfied, he went back up to his apartment.

He had just closed the door when the phone rang. It was Forsfält, who told him that Marianne Eriksson was in Spain. He was going to keep trying to reach her at the hotel where the travel bureau said she was staying. Wallander unpacked the contents of the black plastic bag. The files covered his whole kitchen table. With a sudden feeling of repugnance he took a beer out of the refrigerator and sat down in the living room. He listened to Jussi Björling on the stereo. After a while he stretched out on the sofa with the can of beer next to him on the floor. Soon he was asleep.

He awoke with a start when the music ended. The can of beer was half empty. Lying on the sofa, he finished it off.

The phone rang. He went into the bedroom and picked it up. It was Linda. She wondered whether she could stay at his place for a few days. Her girlfriend's parents were coming home that day. Wallander suddenly felt energized. He gathered up all the papers spread out on the kitchen table and carried them to his bed. Then he made up the bed in the room where Linda usually slept. He opened all the windows and let the warm evening breeze blow through the apartment. She wouldn't arrive until nine o'clock. He had time to go downstairs and get his laundry out of the two machines. To his surprise none of his clothes or sheets had run. He hung the laundry in the drying room and returned to his apartment. Linda had told him that she wouldn't want any food when she came. He boiled some potatoes and broiled a piece of meat for himself. As he ate he wondered whether he should call Baiba.

He also thought about his lost keys. About Louise Fredman. About Peter Hjelm. And about the stack of papers waiting for him in his bedroom.

Above all he thought about the man who was out there somewhere in the summer night.

The man they would have to bring in soon. Before he struck again.

He stood by the open window and saw Linda coming down the street.

"I love you," he said aloud to himself.

Then he dropped his keys out the window and she caught them in her hand.

Chapter Twenty-six

Even though Wallander had sat up half the night talking with Linda, he forced himself to get out of bed at six o'clock. Groggy, he stood in the shower for a long time before managing to shake off the weariness in his body. He moved quietly through the apartment and thought that it was only when either Baiba or Linda was there that the apartment really felt like home. When he was alone the apartment felt like a hideout, merely a temporary roof over his head. He made coffee and went down to the laundry room to empty the drying cupboard. One of his neighbors who was putting laundry into a machine pointed out that he hadn't cleaned up after himself the day before. It was an elderly woman who lived alone, and he usually nodded to her when they ran into each other. He didn't even know her name. She showed him a spot on the floor where there was a little heap of spilled detergent. Wallander apologized and promised to do better in the future. What a nag, he thought as he headed up the stairs. At the same time he knew she was right. He had been too lazy to clean up.

He dumped his laundry on the bed and then carried the report folders Forsfält had given him out to the kitchen. He had a guilty conscience because he hadn't gotten around to reading them the night before. But the talk with Linda for hours had been important in so many ways. The night was very warm and they sat out on the balcony. Listening to her, he felt for the first time that she was an adult. Something had happened that he had never noticed before. She told him that Mona was talking about remarrying. That made Wallander unexpectedly depressed. He knew that Linda had been sent to inform him. The news, which made him feel bad although he didn't understand why, prompted him to talk to her seriously for the first time about his view on why the marriage had fallen apart. From her comments he could tell that Mona had described it quite differently. Then she asked him about Baiba, and he tried to answer her as honestly as he could, even though there was a lot that was still unclear even to him about their relationship. And yet when they finally called it quits and went to bed, he felt that he had been given confirmation of what was most important to him—that she didn't blame him for what had happened, and that now she could view her parents' divorce as something that had been necessary.

He sat down at the kitchen table and looked at the first page of the extensive material describing Björn Fredman's restless and complicated life. It took him two hours just to skim through it all. Once in a while he would jot down a note in one of his notebooks that he took from a kitchen drawer. By the time he pushed aside the last folder and stretched, it was eight o'clock. He poured another cup of coffee and stood by the open window. It was going to be another beautiful summer day. He couldn't remember the last time it had rained.

In his mind he tried to summarize what he had read. Björn Fredman had been a sorry character from the first day of his life. He had had a difficult and troubled home life as a child, and his first contact with the police occurred at the age of seven in connection with a stolen bicycle. Since then he had been in constant trouble. From the beginning, Björn Fredman had struck back at a life that had never given him any pleasure. Wallander thought that during his life as a cop he was always forced to read these gray, colorless sagas in which you could tell from the first sentence that the story would come to a bad end.

Sweden was a country that had pulled itself out of poverty, largely under its own power, aided by fortunate circumstances. Wallander could remember from his own childhood that there had still been desperately poor people back then, even though by that time they were few in number. But the other kind of poverty, he thought as he stood with his coffee cup by the kitchen window. We never dealt with that. It was hibernating behind all the façades. And now that progress seemed to have stopped for the time being, and the welfare state was being tugged at and depleted from all directions, the poverty and family misery that had been in hibernation were beginning to rise to the surface.

Björn Fredman was never alone. We never succeeded in creating a society where people like him could feel at home. When we blew up the old society, the one where families still stuck together, we forgot to replace them with something else. The great loneliness that resulted was a price we didn't know we were going to have to pay. Or maybe we chose to ignore it.

He put the folders back in the black plastic bag and then listened once again outside Linda's door. She was asleep. He couldn't resist the temptation to crack open the door and peek in at her. She was sleeping curled up, turned toward the wall. He left a note for her on the kitchen table and wondered what to do about his keys. He went into his bedroom and called the police station. Ebba was at home, the girl who answered told him. He looked up her home number. When she answered she didn't have any positive news for him. Neither the lunch restaurant nor the clothing store had found any keys. He added to the note in the kitchen that Linda should put the house keys under the doormat. Then he left the apartment and drove up to the police station.

He arrived just before eight-thirty. Hansson was sitting in his office and his face seemed grayer than ever. Wallander suddenly felt sorry for him. He wondered how long Hansson would last. Together they went to the lunch-room and had some coffee. Since it was a Saturday in July, there was little sign that the biggest manhunt in the history of the Ystad police was under way. Wallander wanted to tell Hansson that now he realized they needed rein-forcements. More precisely, Hansson needed a break. He still thought they had enough manpower to send out in the field. But Hansson needed relief on the home front. He tried to protest, but Wallander refused to back down. Hansson's gray face and harried eyes were argument enough. Finally Hansson gave in and promised to speak with the county chief of police on Monday. They would have to borrow a sergeant from somewhere.

The investigative team had a meeting set for ten o'clock. Wallander left Hansson, who already seemed relieved. He sat down in his office and called Forsfält, who couldn't be located. It took fifteen minutes before Forsfält called him back. Wallander brought up the matter of Björn Fredman's passport.

"It should be in his apartment, of course," said Forsfält. "Funny we haven't found it."

"I don't know if this means anything," said Wallander. "But I still want to find out more about those trips Peter Hjelm was talking about."

"European countries hardly ever use entry and exit stamps anymore," said Forsfält.

"I got a feeling that Hjelm was talking about longer trips," replied Wallander. "But of course I could be wrong."

Forsfält promised that they would start searching for Fredman's passport right away.

"I spoke with Marianne Eriksson last night," he went on. "I thought about calling you, but it was pretty late."

"Where did you find her?"

"In Málaga. She didn't even know that Fredman was dead."

"What did she have to say?"

"Not much, I must say. Obviously she was upset. I couldn't spare her any details, unfortunately. They had met occasionally over the past six months. I got a strong feeling that she actually liked Fredman."

"In that case, she's the first," said Wallander. "If you don't count Peter Hjelm."

"She thought he was a businessman," Forsfält continued. "She had no idea he had been involved in illegal activities his whole life. She also didn't know he was married and had three kids. I think she was quite upset. I smashed the image she had of Fredman to smithereens with that phone call, I'm afraid."

"How could you tell she liked him?"

"She was hurt that he had lied to her."

"Did anything else come out?"

"Not really. But she's on her way back to Sweden. She's coming home on Friday. I'm going to talk to her then."

"And then you're going on vacation?"

"I was thinking of it, anyway. Weren't you supposed to start yours soon too?"

"Right now I don't even want to think about it."

"Things can happen fast once they start moving."

Wallander didn't respond to Forsfält's last remark. They said goodbye. Wallander picked up the receiver again, dialed the switchboard, and asked the receptionist to look for Per Åkeson. After more than a minute she came back and told him Åkeson was at home. Wallander looked at the clock. Four minutes past nine. He made a quick decision and left his office. In the hall he ran into Svedberg, still wearing his strange cap.

"How's it going with the burn?" asked Wallander.

"Better. But I don't dare go out without the cap."

"Do you think any locksmiths are open on Saturday?" asked Wallander.

"I doubt it. But if you've locked yourself out, there are locksmiths on call."

"I need to get a couple of keys copied."

"Did you lock yourself out?"

"I lost my house keys."

"Were your name and address on them?"

"Of course not."

"Then at least you don't need to change your lock."

Wallander told Svedberg that he might be a little late for the meeting. He had to see Per Åkeson about something important first.

Åkeson lived in a residential neighborhood up the hill from the hospital. Wallander had been to his house before and knew the way. When he arrived and got out of the car, he saw Åkeson running a power mower in his yard. He turned it off when he saw Wallander coming.

"Has something happened?" he asked when they met at the gate.

"Yes and no," said Wallander. "Something is always happening. But nothing crucial. I need your help investigating someone."

They went into the back yard. Wallander thought gloomily that it looked like most of the other yards he had been in. He turned down an offer of coffee. They sat in the shade of a roofed patio with a brick barbecue pit.

"My wife might come out," said Åkeson. "I'd appreciate it if you didn't mention that I'm going to Africa this fall. It's still quite a sensitive topic."

Wallander promised not to. Then he told Åkeson briefly about Louise Fredman and his suspicion that she might have been abused by her father. He said candidly that it was probably just another blind alley and that it might not add anything to the investigation. He explained the new tack they were trying in the case, which included the confirmation that Fredman had been killed by the same perpetrator as Wetterstedt and Carlman. "Björn Fredman was the black sheep in the scalped 'family,'" he said, and felt at once the description was less than apt.

How did he fit into the picture? How didn't he fit? Maybe they could find the point of convergence by starting with Fredman at a place where the connection was by no means obvious. Åkeson listened intently. He didn't interrupt.

"I talked to Ekholm," he said when Wallander had finished. "A good man, I thought. Competent. Realistic. The impression I got from him was that the man we're looking for may strike again."

"I'm always thinking about that."

"How's it going with getting reinforcements?"

Wallander told him about his conversation with Hansson earlier that morning. Åkeson reacted dubiously.

"I think you're making a mistake," he said. "It's not enough for Hansson to have support. I think you have a tendency to overestimate the workload that you and your colleagues can handle. This case is big, in fact it's too big. I want to see more people working on it. More manpower means more things can be done at the same time. We're dealing with a man who could kill again. That means we have no time to waste."

"I know what you mean," said Wallander. "I keep worrying that we're already too late."

"Reinforcements," Per Åkeson said again. "What do you think?"

"For the time being I have to say no. That's not the problem."

An instant tension arose between them.

"Let's say that I, as the leader of the preliminary investigation, can't accept that," said Åkeson. "But you don't want more manpower. Where does that leave us?"

"In a difficult situation."

"Very difficult. And unpleasant. If I request more manpower against the will of the police, my only argument is that the present investigative team has not lived up to expectations. I'd have to declare your team incompetent, even though I'd phrase it in kinder terms. And I don't want to do that."

"I assume you'll do it if you have to," said Wallander. "And that's when I'll resign from the force."

"God damn it, Kurt!"

"You were the one who started this discussion, not me."

"You've got your regulations. I've got mine. So I regard it as a dereliction of my duty if I don't request that you have more personnel put at your disposal."

"And dogs," said Wallander sarcastically. "I want police dogs. And helicopters."

The discussion was at an end. Wallander regretted that he flew off the handle. He couldn't really figure out why he was so opposed to getting reinforcements. From experience he knew that problems in collaboration often arose that could damage and delay an investigation. But he couldn't argue with Åkeson's claim that more things could be investigated at the same time.

"Talk to Hansson," Wallander said. "He's the one who decides."

"Hansson doesn't do anything without asking you. And then he does whatever you say."

"I can refuse to tell him my opinion. I'll give you that much help."

Åkeson stood up and turned off a dripping water faucet with a green hose attached to it. Then he sat down again.

"Let's wait until Monday," he said.

"Let's do that," said Wallander. Then he returned to Louise Fredman. He emphasized several times that there was nothing to prove that Björn Fredman had abused his daughter. But Wallander couldn't rule out that it might be true; he couldn't rule out anything, and that's why he needed Åkeson's help now to open the doors to Louise Fredman's hospital room.

"It's possible I'm making a big mistake," Wallander concluded. "In which case it wouldn't be the first time. But I can't afford to ignore any leads. I want to know why Louise Fredman is in a psychiatric hospital. And when I find out, we'll decide whether there's any reason to take the next step."

"Which would be?"

"Talking to her."

Åkeson nodded. Wallander was sure he could count on his cooperation. They knew each other well. Åkeson respected Wallander's intuitive judgment calls, even when they lacked any basis in solid evidence.

"It can be a complicated process," said Åkeson. "But I'll try to do something this weekend."

"I'd appreciate it," said Wallander. "You can call me at the station or at home, whenever you like."

Åkeson went inside to make sure he had all of Wallander's phone numbers in his address book.

The tension between them seemed to have vanished. Åkeson followed him out to the gate.

"Summer is off to a good start," he said. "But I have a feeling you haven't had much time to think about that."

Wallander could hear that Åkeson was feeling slightly sympathetic.

"Not much," he replied. "But Ann-Britt's grandmother predicted that the good weather is going to last for a long time."

"Can't she predict where we should look for the perpetrator instead?" asked Åkeson.

Wallander shook his head in resignation.

"We're getting lots of tips all the time. Our usual prophets, and some of those who claim to be psychic have also started calling in. We have some police trainees sorting out all the stuff that comes in. Then Höglund and Svedberg go through it. But so far nothing has come of it. No one saw a thing, either outside Wetterstedt's house or at Carlman's farm. There aren't many tips yet about the pit outside the railroad station or the van at the airport. But they don't seem to have produced any leads either."

"The man you're hunting for is cautious," said Åkeson.

"Cautious, cunning, and totally without human emotions," said Wallander. "I can't imagine how his mind works. Even Ekholm seems dumbstruck. For the first time in my life I've got a feeling that a monster is on the loose."

For a moment Åkeson seemed to be pondering what Wallander had said.

"Ekholm told me he's inputting all the data into the computer. He's using the program developed by the FBI. It might come up with something."

"Let's hope so," said Wallander.

Wallander said no more. But Åkeson understood what was implied. Before he strikes again.

Wallander drove back to the police station. He entered the conference room a few minutes late. To cheer up his hard-working detectives, Hansson had driven down to Fridolf's bakery and bought pastries. Wallander sat down in his usual spot and looked around. Martinsson showed up wearing shorts for the first time that season. Höglund was showing the first signs of a tan. He wondered enviously how she managed to find time to sunbathe. The only one dressed appropriately was Ekholm, who had established his headquarters at the far end of the table.

"I saw that one of our evening papers had the good taste to provide its readers with historical background on the art of scalping," Svedberg said gloomily. "We can only hope that it won't be the next craze with all the nut cases running around."

Wallander tapped on the table with a pencil.

"Let's get started," he said. "We're searching for the worst perpetrator we've ever had to deal with. He has already committed three savage murders. We know it's the same man. But that's all we know. Except for the fact that there's a great risk he'll strike again—it's perfectly conceivable."

A hush fell around the table. Wallander hadn't intended to create an oppressive atmosphere. He knew from experience that complex investigations were made easier if the tone was light, even when the crimes being investigated were brutal and tragic. He knew that everyone in the room was just as depressed as he was. The feeling that they were chasing a human monster, whose emotional degeneracy was so great it was almost impossible to imagine, was shared by everyone on the investigative team.

It was one of the most depressing meetings Wallander had ever experienced during his years as a police officer. Outside the window the summer was almost unnaturally beautiful, Hansson's pastries were melting and sticky in the heat, and his own revulsion made him feel sick. Although he paid attention to everything being said around the table, he was also thinking about how he could stand to remain a cop. Hadn't he reached a point where he ought to realize he had done his share? There had to be more to life. But he also knew that what made him downhearted was the fact that they couldn't see a single chance of a break, a crack in the wall that they could widen and then squeeze through. They weren't stuck, because they still had a lot of leads. What they were lacking was the clear choice of a specific direction. In most cases there was almost always an invisible navigation point against which they could correct their course. But this time they were lacking that fixed point. It was no longer enough that they were looking for a common point of contact. They were starting to doubt their conviction that it even existed at all.

Three hours later, when the meeting was over, they only knew the thing to do was to keep going. Wallander looked at the exhausted faces all around him and told them to try and get some rest. He canceled all meetings for Sunday. On Monday morning they would meet again. He didn't have to mention the one exception: unless something serious happened. Unless the man who was out there somewhere in the summertime decided to strike again.

When Wallander got home that afternoon he found a note from Linda saying that she would be out that evening. Wallander was tired and fell asleep for a few hours. Then he called Baiba twice without reaching her. He talked to Gertrud, who said everything was fine with his father. The only difference was that he was talking a lot about the trip to Italy they were going to take in September. Wallander vacuumed the apartment and fixed a broken window latch. The whole time the thought of the unknown perpetrator churned in his head. At seven o'clock he fixed a simple dinner of frozen cod fillet and boiled potatoes. Then he sat on the balcony with a cup of coffee and absentmindedly paged through an old issue of *Ystad's Allehanda*. At nine-fifteen Linda arrived. They drank tea in the kitchen. The next day Wallander would be allowed to see a rehearsal of the revue she was working on with Kajsa. She was very secretive and didn't want to tell him what it was about. At eleven-thirty they both went to bed.

Wallander fell asleep almost at once. Linda lay awake in her room listening to the night birds. Then she fell asleep too, leaving the door to her room ajar.

Neither of them heard when the front door was opened cautiously at two in the morning. Hoover was barefoot. He stood motionless in the entryway, listening in the silence. He could hear a man snoring from a room to the left of the living room. He stepped carefully into the apartment. A door to another room stood ajar. He saw that someone was in there sleeping. A girl who might have been his sister's age. He couldn't resist the temptation to go in and stand right next to her. His power over the sleeper was absolute. Then he left the room and continued toward the room where the snoring was coming from. The policeman named Wallander lay on his back and had kicked off all but a small part of the sheet. He was sleeping heavily. His chest heaved with his deep breathing.

Hoover stood utterly motionless and watched him.

He thought about his sister, who would soon be freed from all this evil. Who would soon return to life.

He looked at the sleeping man and thought about the girl in the next room, who must be his daughter.

He made his decision.

In a few days he would return.

He left the apartment as soundlessly as he had come, locking the door with the keys he had taken from the policeman's jacket.

The silence was broken by a moped starting up.

Then all was quiet again, except for the night birds singing.

Chapter Twenty-seven

When Wallander awoke on Sunday morning he felt that he had gotten enough sleep for the first time in a long while. It was past eight o'clock. Through a gap in the curtains he could see a patch of blue sky. He stayed in bed and listened for Linda. Then he got up, put on his newly washed bathrobe, and peeked through the doorway to her room. She was still asleep. For a brief moment he felt himself transported back in time to her childhood. He smiled at the memory and went out to the kitchen to fix coffee. The thermometer outside the kitchen window showed that it was already 19 degrees Celsius. When the coffee was ready he prepared a breakfast tray for Linda. He remembered what she liked. One three-minute egg, toast, a few slices of cheese, and a cut-up tomato. Just water to drink.

He drank his coffee and waited until a quarter to nine. Then he went in and woke her up. She was startled out of her sleep when he called her name. When she caught sight of the tray he had in his hands she burst out laughing. He sat down at the foot of the bed and watched while she ate. He hadn't given a thought to the homicide case except during the first fleeting moments right after he woke up. He had experienced this before, like the time they were struggling with a difficult case looking for the killers of an elderly farming couple who lived on a lonely farm near Knickarp. Every morning the investigation would sweep through his head, condensed into a few brief seconds that contained all the details and unanswered questions.

Linda pushed aside the tray, leaned back in bed, and stretched.

"What were you doing up last night?" she asked. "Did you have trouble sleeping?"

"I slept like a rock," said Wallander. "I didn't even get up to go to the bathroom."

"Then I must have been dreaming," she said, yawning. "I thought you opened my door and came into my room."

"You probably were dreaming," he said. "For once I slept the whole night through without waking up."

An hour later Linda left the apartment. They agreed to meet at Österport Square at seven that evening. Linda asked him if he knew that Sweden would be playing in the quarter-finals against Saudi Arabia then. Wallander said he didn't give a damn. On the other hand, he had bet that Sweden would win it 3–1 and paid Martinsson another hundred kronor. The girls had managed to borrow an empty meeting hall where they could hold their rehearsals.

After she left, Wallander took out his ironing board and started ironing his newly washed shirts. After doing a passable job on two of them, he got bored and called Baiba in Riga. She answered almost at once, and he could hear that she was glad he had called. He told her that Linda was visiting and that he felt rested for the first time in several weeks. Baiba was busy finishing up her work at the university before the summer break. She talked about the trip to Skagen with an almost childlike anticipation. After they hung up, Wallander went into the living room and put on *Aïda* full blast.

He felt happy and full of energy. He sat out on the balcony and read carefully through the newspapers from the past few days. But he skipped over the account of the murder case. He had granted himself half a day off and total escape until noon. Then he was going to get busy again. But it didn't work out exactly the way he planned, because Per Åkeson called him at eleven-fifteen. He had been in touch with the chief prosecutor in Malmö and they had discussed Wallander's request. Åkeson figured it should be possible for Wallander to obtain answers to some of his questions about Louise Fredman within the next few days. But he had one reservation, which he shared with Wallander.

"Wouldn't it be simpler to get the girl's mother to answer these questions?" he asked.

"I don't know," said Wallander. "I'm not sure I'd get the truth I'm looking for out of her."

"Which is what? If there's more than one truth, that is."

"The mother is protecting her daughter," said Wallander. "It's only natural. I would too. No matter what she told me, it would be colored by the fact that she's protecting her. Medical journals and physicians' reports speak another language."

"You know best," said Åkeson, promising that he'd be in touch again on Monday, as soon as he had something more to tell him.

The talk with Åkeson got Wallander thinking about the case again. He decided to take a notebook and sit outside to go over the investigative plan for the coming week. He was starting to get hungry, though, and figured he could permit himself to eat out this Sunday. Just before noon he left the apartment, dressed all in white like a tennis player, wearing sandals. He drove east out of town along Österleden, thinking that he could drop in on his father later that day. If he didn't have the investigation hanging over his head, he could have taken Gertrud and his father to lunch somewhere. But right now he felt he needed time to himself. The past few weeks he had been constantly surrounded by people, involved in individual conversations and the meetings of the investigative team. Now he wanted to be alone. Without noticing it he drove all the way to Simrishamn. He stopped down by the marina and took a walk. Then he went to eat at the Harbor Inn. He found a corner table to himself and sat watching all the vacationers who filled the restaurant. One of the people sitting here could be the man I'm looking for, he thought. If Ekholm's theories are right—that the perpetrator lives a completely normal life, with no outward signs that he has a warped soul which allows him to subject other people to the worst violence imaginable—he could be one of the people sitting right here eating lunch.

At that instant the summer day slipped out of his hands. He started going over everything that had happened one more time. For some reason he didn't understand, his thoughts started with the girl who burned herself to death in Salomonsson's rapeseed field. She had nothing to do with the other events; it had been a suicide, caused by some as yet unknown reason. Still, that's where Wallander began. It happened each time he started one of his reviews of the case.

But on this particular Sunday, as he sat in the Harbor Inn in Simrishamn, something started churning in his subconscious. He vaguely recalled that someone had said something in conjunction with the dead girl in the rapeseed field. He sat there with his fork in his hand and tried to coax the thought to the surface. Who had said it? What had been said? Why was it important? After a while he gave up. He knew that sooner or later he'd remember what it was. His subconscious always demanded patience. As if to prove that he actually possessed that patience, he decided to order dessert. With satisfaction he noticed that the shorts he was wearing for the first time that year weren't quite as tight around the waist as they had been the year before. He ate some apple pie and then ordered coffee.

For the next hour he went through the entire case one more time. He tried to read his thoughts the way a discerning actor reads through his part for the first time. Where were the gaps? Where were the faults in his thought process? Where did he combine fact and circumstance too sloppily and draw a wrong conclusion? In his mind he went through Wetterstedt's house again, through the garden, out onto the beach; he imagined Wetterstedt in front of him, and Wallander himself became the perpetrator stalking him like a silent shadow. He climbed up on the garage roof and read a torn Phantom comic book while he waited for Wetterstedt to sit down at his desk and maybe leaf through his collection of antique pornographic photographs.

Then he did the same thing with Carlman; he put a motorcycle behind the road maintenance hut and followed the tractor path up toward the hill where he had a view over Carlman's farm. Now and then he made a note on his pad. *The garage roof. What did he hope to see? Carlman's hill. Binoculars?* Methodically he went over everything that had happened, deaf and blind to all the noise around him. He paid another visit to Hugo Sandin, he talked once more with Sara Björklund, and he made a note that he ought to get in touch with her again. Maybe the same questions would provoke different, more extensive answers. And what would the difference be? He thought for a long time about Carlman's daughter, who had slapped him in the face, and he thought about Louise Fredman. And her brother, who was so well brought up. All at once he felt that his re-examination was starting to flow again. He was rested, his fatigue was gone, and his thoughts rose easily and soared on the updrafts inside him.

By the time he called over his waiter and paid the bill, more than an hour had passed. The time lay buried in the traces of his re-examination. He glanced at what he had scribbled on his pad, as if it were magic, automatic writing, and left the Harbor Inn. He sat down on one of the benches in the park outside the Hotel Svea and looked out over the sea. There was a warm, gentle breeze blowing. The crew on a sailboat with a Danish flag was struggling hopelessly with an unruly spinnaker. Wallander read over his hasty notes, then shoved the pad under his thigh.

The point of contact was always shifting, from parents to children. He thought about Carlman's daughter and Louise Fredman. Was it really a coincidence that one of them tried to commit suicide when her father was dead and the other had been in a psychiatric clinic for a long time? Suddenly he wasn't convinced.

Wetterstedt was the exception. He had only two grown children. Wallander remembered something Rydberg said once. *What happens first is not necessarily the beginning.* Could that be true in this case? He tried to imagine that the perpetrator they were looking for was a woman. But the thought was impossible. The physical strength they had seen signs of, the scalps, the axe blows, the acid in Fredman's eyes. It had to be a man, he decided. A man who kills men. While women commit suicide or become mentally ill.

He got up and moved to another bench, as if to mark the fact that there were other conceivable explanations. Gustaf Wetterstedt had been mixed up in shady deals, no matter how good a justice minister he was. There was a vague but still unexplained connection between him and Carlman. It had to do with art, theft, maybe forgery. Above all it had to do with money. It wasn't inconceivable that Björn Fredman could also be roped into the same area, if they dug deep enough. In the material he had received from Forsfält he hadn't found a thing. But he couldn't write it off yet. Nothing could be written off yet; that presented both a problem and an opportunity at the same time.

Wallander watched the Danish sailboat pensively. The crew had begun packing up the spinnaker. Then he took out his pad and looked at the last word he had written. *Mystery.* There was a tinge of ritual to the murders. He had thought so himself, and Ekholm too had pointed it out at the last meeting of the investigative team. The scalps were a ritual, as trophy collecting always was. The significance of the scalp was the same as that of a moose head on a hunter's wall. It was the proof. The proof of what? For whom? For the perpetrator alone, or for someone else as well? For a god or a demon conjured up in the mind of a sick human being? For someone else, whose undramatic demeanor was just as ordinary and inconspicuous as the perpetrator's?

Wallander thought about what Ekholm had said about invocations and initiation rites. A sacrifice was made so that some other person could obtain grace. Become rich, make a fortune, get well? There were many possibilities. There were motorcycle gangs with rules about how new members had to prove themselves worthy. In the States it wasn't unusual to have to kill someone, picked at random or specially chosen, to be deemed worthy of membership in a particular group. This macabre rite had already started spreading, even to Sweden. Wallander suddenly thought about the motorcycle gangs that existed in Skåne, and he remembered the road maintenance hut at the bottom of Carlman's hill. The thought was dizzying, that the tracks, or rather the lack of tracks, might lead them to motorcycle gangs. Wallander put aside the idea, although he knew that nothing could be ruled out.

He got up and walked back to the bench where he had sat before. He was back to the starting point. Where had this re-examination taken him? He realized that he couldn't go any farther without discussing it with someone. He thought of Ann-Britt Höglund. Could he possibly permit himself to bother her on a Sunday? He got up and went over to his car to call her. She was home. He was welcome to drop by. With a guilty conscience he quickly postponed his visit to his father. Now was the time to have someone else confront his ideas. If he waited, there was a good chance he would get lost among multiple trains of thought. He drove back toward Ystad, keeping just above the speed limit. He hadn't heard about any speed traps planned for this Sunday.

It was three o'clock when he pulled up in front of Höglund's house. She met him in a light summer dress. Her two children were playing in a neighbor's yard. She offered Wallander the porch swing while she sat in a wicker chair.

"I really didn't mean to bother you," he said. "You could have said no."

"Yesterday I was tired," she replied. "As we all were. *Are*, I mean. But today I feel better."

"Last night was definitely the night of the sleeping cops," said Wallander. "It reaches a point where you can't push yourself any farther. All you get is empty, gray fatigue. We reached that point yesterday."

He told her about his trip driving along Österleden, about how he went back and forth between the benches in the park down by the harbor.

"I went over everything again," he said. "Sometimes it's possible to make unexpected discoveries. But you already know that."

"I'm hoping for something to come of Ekholm's work," she said. "Computers that are correctly programmed can cross-reference the investigative material and come up with unexpected relationships. They don't *think*. But sometimes they *combine* better than we can."

"My distrust of computers is partly because I'm getting old," said Wallander. "But it doesn't mean I don't want Ekholm to succeed with his behavioral method of hunting murderers. For me, of course, it's of no importance who sets the snare that catches the killer. Just as long as it happens. And soon."

She gave him a somber look.

"Will he strike again?"

"I think so. Without being able to get a handle on it, I think there's something *unfinished* about this murder scenario. If you'll pardon the expression. There's something missing. It scares me. It makes me think he'll strike again."

"How are we going to find where Fredman was killed?" she asked.

"We won't," said Wallander, "unless we're lucky. Or unless somebody heard something."

"I've been checking up on whether there have been any tips coming in from anyone who heard screams," she said. "But I haven't found anything."

The silent scream hung over their heads. Wallander swung slowly back and forth on the plastic-covered sofa.

"It's rare that a solution comes entirely unexpectedly," he said when the silence lasted too long. "When I was walking back and forth between the benches in the park, I wondered whether I had already had the idea that would give me the solution. I might have thought things through correctly without being aware of it."

She pondered his words silently. Now and then she glanced over at the neighbor's yard where her children were playing.

"We didn't learn anything at the police academy about a man who takes scalps and pours acid in the eyes of his victims," she said. "Reality has proven to be just as unpredictable as I imagined."

Wallander nodded without replying. Then he started in, unsure whether he could pull it off, and went over what he had been thinking about in Simrishamn. He knew from experience that telling someone else would shed a different light on it. But even though Ann-Britt listened intently, almost like a student at her master's feet, she never stopped him to say that he had made a mistake or drawn a wrong conclusion. All she said when he finished was that she felt overwhelmed by his ability to dissect and then wrap up the whole complicated investigation, which, at least for her, seemed so overwhelming. But she had nothing to add or subtract. Even if Wallander's equations were correctly stated, they lacked the crucial components. Höglund couldn't help him, no more than anyone else could.

She went inside and got some cups and a thermos of coffee. Her youngest girl came and crept into the porch swing next to Wallander. She didn't resemble her mother, so he assumed she took after her father, who was in Saudi Arabia. Wallander realized he still hadn't met him.

"Your husband is a living riddle," he said. "I'm starting to wonder if he really exists. Or if he's just someone you dreamed up."

"I sometimes ask myself the same question," she answered, laughing.

The girl went inside the house.

"What about Carlman's daughter?" asked Wallander, watching the girl go. "How's she doing?"

"Svedberg called the hospital yesterday," she said. "The crisis wasn't over yet. But I had a feeling that the doctors were a little more hopeful."

"She didn't leave a note?"

"Not a thing."

"The most important thing, of course, is that she's a human being," said Wallander. "But I can't help thinking of her as a witness."

"To what?"

"To something that might have a bearing on her father's death. I have a hard time believing that the timing of the suicide attempt was coincidental."

"What makes me think you aren't too convinced about what you're saying?"

"I'm not convinced," said Wallander. "I'm groping and fumbling my way along. There's only one fact that is incontrovertible in this investigation. We have no concrete clues to go on."

"So we have no idea if we're on the right track?"

"Or if we're going in circles. Or trampling down the same spot."

She hesitated before she asked the next question.

"Do you think maybe there aren't enough of us?"

"Up to now I've dug in my heels on that issue," said Wallander. "But I'm starting to have my doubts. The question will come up tomorrow full force."

"Per Åkeson?"

Wallander nodded.

"What have we got to lose?"

"Small units move more easily than large ones. To that you could argue that more heads do better thinking. And then there's Åkeson's argument: that we can work better on a broader front. The infantry is spread out and covers a larger area."

"As if we were all sweeping the area."

Wallander nodded. Her image was telling. What was missing was that the sweep they were doing was happening in a terrain where they were only barely able to take their bearings. And they had no idea whom they were looking for.

"There's something we're all missing," said Wallander after a moment of silence. "But I'm still searching for something someone said right after Wetterstedt was murdered. I can't remember who said it. All I know is that it was important. But it was too early for me to understand then."

"You like to say that police work is most often a question of patience."

"And it is. But patience has its limits. Something can always happen at that very moment. Someone can get killed. We can never escape the fact that our investigation is not just a matter of solving crimes that have already been committed. Right now it feels like we have to prevent more murders."

"We can't do any more than we're doing already."

"How do we know that?" asked Wallander. "How do we really know we're putting forth our best effort?"

She had no answer to that. Wallander couldn't answer his own question either.

He sat there for a while longer. At four-thirty he turned down an invitation to have dinner with them.

"Thanks for coming," she said as she followed him to the gate. "Are you going to watch the game?"

"No. I have to meet my daughter. But I think we're going to win, 3–1."

She gave him a quizzical look.

"That's what I bet, too."

"Then we'll both win or we'll both lose," said Wallander.

"Thanks for coming," she said again.

"Thanks for what?" he asked in surprise. "For disturbing your Sunday?"

"For thinking I might have something worthwhile to say."

"I've said it before and I'll say it again, I think you're a talented cop. Besides, you believe in the ability of computers not only to make our work easier, but to improve it. I don't. But maybe you can change my mind."

Wallander got into his car and drove toward town. He stopped at a store that was open on Sundays and bought groceries. Then he lay down on the deck chair on his balcony and waited for seven o'clock. His need for sleep was enormous, and he dozed off. But at five to seven he was standing on the square at Österport. Linda came to get him and took him to the empty storefront nearby. They had rigged some photo lamps and put out a chair for him. At once he felt embarrassed and self-conscious that he might not understand or maybe laugh in the wrong place. The girls vanished into an adjoining room. Wallander waited. More than fifteen minutes passed. When they finally returned they had changed clothes and now looked exactly alike. After arranging the lamps and the simple set, they finally got started. The hour-long performance was about a pair of twins. Wallander was nervous about being the only one in the audience. He was used to sitting anonymously in the darkness when he went to an opera in Malmö or Copenhagen. Most of all he was worried that Linda might not be very good. But it wasn't long before he realized that the two girls had written a witty script that presented a critical view of Sweden with dark humor. Sometimes they lost the thread, sometimes he noticed their acting wasn't quite convincing. But they believed in what they were doing, and that made him happy. When it was all over and they asked him what he thought, he told them that he was surprised, that it was funny, that it was thought-provoking. He could see that Linda paid close attention to whether he was telling the truth or not. When she realized he meant what he said, she was very happy. She accompanied him to the street when it was time for him to leave.

"I didn't know you could do stuff like this," he said. "I thought you wanted to be a furniture upholsterer."

"It's never too late," she said. "Let me give it a try."

"Of course you have to do that," he said. "When you're young you have plenty of time. Not when you're an old cop like me."

They were going to rehearse for a few more hours. He would wait for her at home.

The summer evening was beautiful. He walked slowly toward Mariagatan, thinking about what he had just seen. Absentmindedly he noticed that honking cars were driving past. Then he realized that Sweden must have won. He asked a man he met on the sidewalk what the score was. Sweden had won, 3–1. He broke out laughing. Then his thoughts returned to his daughter. He wondered what he really knew about her. He still hadn't asked her if she had a boyfriend these days.

It was nine-thirty when he entered his apartment. He had just closed the door when the phone rang. At once he felt a pang in his stomach. When he picked it up and heard Gertrud's voice, he calmed down.

But he had reacted too soon. Gertrud was upset. At first he had a hard time understanding what she was saying. He asked her to calm down.

"You've got to come over," she said. "Right away."

"What happened?"

"I don't know. But your father has started burning his paintings. He's burning everything in his studio. And he locked the door. You've got to come now."

She hung up so he couldn't ask any questions but would have to get in his car right away.

He stared at the telephone.

Then he wrote a quick note to Linda and put it on the doormat.

A few minutes later he was on his way to Löderup.

Chapter Twenty-eight

That night Wallander stayed with his father in Löderup.
When he reached the little farmhouse after a stressful trip in his car, Gertrud met him in the courtyard. He could see that she'd been crying, although she was in control and answered his questions with restraint. His father's breakdown, if that's really what it was, had come on quite unexpectedly. They had eaten dinner that evening and everything seemed normal. They hadn't had anything to drink. After the meal his father had gone out to the remodeled barn to continue painting, as usual. Suddenly she heard a great racket. When she went out on the front steps she saw his father tossing a bunch of empty paint cans into the yard. At first she thought he was busy cleaning out his chaotic studio. But when he started to throw out unused frames she took action. When she went over to him and asked what he was doing, he didn't reply. He gave the impression of not being there at all and not hearing that she was speaking to him. When she grabbed his arm he yanked it away and then locked himself inside. Through the window she could see him starting a fire in the stove, and when he started ripping up his canvases and stuffing them in the stove she decided to call Wallander.

They hurried across the courtyard as she talked. Wallander saw gray smoke billowing from the chimney. He went up to the window and peered into the studio. His father looked wild and demented. His hair was standing on end, he had lost his glasses, and the whole studio was demolished. His father was squishing around barefoot among tipped-over pots of paint, and trampled canvases were strewn all over. Wallander thought he saw one of his shoes burning in the stove. His father was tearing up a canvas and stuffing the pieces into the fire. Wallander knocked on the windowpane. But his father didn't react. He tried the door, which was definitely locked. He banged on it and yelled that he had come to visit. There was no answer from inside, but the racket continued. Wallander looked around for something to use to break down the door. But he knew that his father kept all his tools and implements in the room he was now locked inside.

Wallander gave the door, which he had helped build, a stern look. He took off his jacket and handed it to Gertrud. Then he backed up and slammed his shoulder against the door as hard as he could. The whole doorjamb came off, and Wallander tumbled into the room and hit his head on a wheelbarrow. His father just glanced at him vacantly. Then he went on ripping up his canvases.

Gertrud wanted to come in, but Wallander raised his hand to stop her. He had seen his father this way once before, this strange combination of remoteness and manic confusion. On that occasion he had been walking in his pajamas across a muddy field with a suitcase in his hand. Now he went up to him, took him by the shoulders, and began talking soothingly to him. He asked if there was something wrong. He said the paintings were fine, they were the best he'd ever done, and the grouses were painted beautifully. Everything was all right. Anyone could have a bad day once in a while. But he had to stop burning things for no reason. Why should they have a fire in the middle of summer, anyway? Then they could get cleaned up and talk about the trip to Italy. Wallander talked nonstop and kept a strong grip on his father's shoulders—not as though he was going to arrest him, but to keep him in touch with reality.

His father had fallen silent and was squinting at him myopically. While Wallander kept up his reassuring chatter he discovered his father's glasses trampled to bits on the floor. He quickly asked Gertrud, who was standing in the background, whether his father had a spare pair. He did, and she ran to the house to get them. She handed them to Wallander, who wiped them on his sleeve and then set them on his father's nose. The whole time he spoke in a soothing voice, repeating his words as if he were reading the verses of the only prayer he could remember. His father looked at him uncertainly and in bewilderment at first, then astonishment, and finally it seemed as though he had come to his senses again. Wallander then released his grip. His father looked around cautiously at the destruction.

"What happened here?" he asked. Wallander could tell he had forgotten everything. Gertrud started to cry. Wallander sternly told her to go in the kitchen and make some coffee. They'd be there in a minute. Finally his father seemed to realize that he had actually been involved in the destruction.

"Did I do all this?" he asked, looking at Wallander with restless eyes, as if he feared the answer that would come.

"Who doesn't get sick and tired of things?" Wallander replied tentatively. "But it's all over now. We'll get this mess cleaned up soon."

His father looked at the smashed door.

"Who needs a door in the middle of summer?" said Wallander. "There aren't any closed doors in Rome in the summer. You have to start getting used to that now."

His father walked slowly through the debris from the frenzy that neither he nor anyone else could explain. Wallander realized that his father had absolutely no clue what had happened. He couldn't grasp the fact that he had done all this himself. Wallander felt a lump in his throat. There was something helpless and forsaken about his father, and he couldn't figure out how to deal with it. Wallander lifted the broken door and leaned it against the wall of the stable. Then he started cleaning up the room, discovering that many of his father's canvases had survived after all. His father sat down on the stool at his workbench and followed his movements. Gertrud came in and told them that coffee was ready. Wallander nodded to her to take his father by the arm and escort him back to the house. Then he cleaned up the worst of the mess.

Before he went into the kitchen he called home from his car phone. Linda had arrived. She wanted to know what had happened; she could barely decipher his quickly scribbled note. Wallander didn't want to worry her, so he said that her grandfather had just been feeling bad, but now everything was fine. To be on the safe side he'd decided to stay overnight in Löderup. Then he went in the kitchen. His father was feeling tired and had gone to lie down right away. Wallander stayed up with Gertrud for a couple of hours, sitting at the kitchen table. There was no way to explain what had happened except that it was a symptom of his father's insidious illness. But when Gertrud said this incident ruled out the trip to Italy in the fall, Wallander protested. He wasn't afraid of taking responsibility for his own father. He wasn't afraid of taking the long trip with him. It was going to happen, if his father still wanted to go and was still able to stand on his own two feet.

That night he slept on a fold-out bed in the living room. For a long time he lay staring out into the light summer night before he fell asleep.

In the morning when they were drinking coffee, his father seemed to have forgotten all about the episode. He couldn't understand what had happened to the door. Wallander told him the truth, that he was the one who had broken it down. The studio needed a new door, and he would make it himself.

"When are you going to have time to do that?" asked his father. "You don't even have time to call ahead of time and tell me you're coming to visit."

Wallander knew then that everything was back to normal. Just after seven he left Löderup and drove to Ystad. He knew it wasn't the last time something like this might happen. With a shiver he thought about what might have occurred if Gertrud wasn't around.

At seven-fifteen Wallander walked through the doors of the police station. The good weather was still holding. Everyone was talking about soccer. He was surrounded by cops in summer clothes. Only the ones who had to wear uniforms looked anything like cops. Wallander thought that in his white clothes he could have stepped out of the cast of one of the Italian operas he had seen in Copenhagen. When he passed the reception desk Ebba waved to him that he had a call. It was Forsfält; despite the early hour he reported that they had found Björn Fredman's passport, well hidden in his apartment, along with a large sum of cash in foreign currencies. Wallander asked about the stamps in the passport.

"I'm afraid I have to disappoint you," said Forsfält. "He had the passport for four years. During that time he got stamps in Turkey, Morocco, and Brazil. That's all."

Wallander was disappointed, but he wasn't sure what he had expected. Forsfält promised to fax over all the details on the passport and the stamps; he said he had something else to tell him with no direct bearing on the investigation, but which still gave Wallander some ideas.

"We found some keys to an attic when we were looking for the passport," said Forsfält. "Among all the junk up there we found a box containing some antique icons. We were able to determine pretty quickly that they were loot from a burglary. Guess where."

Wallander thought for a moment but couldn't come up with anything. "I give up."

"A break-in at a house outside Ystad," said Forsfält. "About a year ago. A house that was under the administration of an executor. For an attorney named Gustaf Torstensson."

Wallander remembered him. One of the two lawyers murdered the year before. Wallander himself had seen the collection of icons in the basement belonging to the older of the two lawyers. He even had one of them hanging on the wall of his bedroom. A present he received from the dead lawyer's secretary. Now he also recalled the break-in; Svedberg had been in charge of the investigation.

"So now we know," said Wallander. "I assume that case was never solved?"

"You'll be getting the follow-up report," Forsfält told him.

"Not me," said Wallander. "Svedberg."

Forsfält asked how it was going with Louise Fredman. Wallander told him about his last phone conversation with Per Åkeson.

"With a little luck we'll know something later today," said Wallander.

"I hope you'll keep me informed."

Wallander promised he would. After they hung up he checked his list of unanswered questions. He could cross out some of them, while others he would have to bring up at the investigative team meeting. But before that he had to pay a visit to the two trainees who were keeping track of the tips coming in from the public. He asked whether anything had come in that might indicate exactly where Fredman was murdered. Wallander knew it could be highly significant for the investigation if they could pin down where the murder took place.

One of the trainees had close-cropped hair and was named Tyrén. He had intelligent eyes and was said to be competent. Wallander didn't know any more about him. He quickly explained what he was looking for.

"Someone who heard screams?" asked Tyrén. "And saw a Ford van? On Monday, June 27th?"

"That's right."

Tyrén shook his head.

"I would have remembered that," he said. "A woman screamed in an apartment in Rydsgård. But that was on Tuesday. And she was drunk."

"I want to be informed immediately if anything comes in," said Wallander.

He left Tyrén and went down to the meeting room. Hansson stood talking to a reporter in the reception area. Wallander remembered seeing him before. He was a stringer for one of the big national evening papers, but he couldn't remember which one. They waited a few minutes until Hansson got rid of the reporter, and then closed the door. Hansson sat down and gave Wallander the floor at once. Just as he was about to start, Per Åkeson came in and sat at the far end of the table, next to Ekholm. Wallander raised his eyebrows and gave him an inquiring look. Åkeson nodded. Wallander knew that meant there was news about Louise Fredman. Even though he had a hard time containing his curiosity, he called first on Ann-Britt Höglund, who reported the latest news from the hospital, where Carlman's daughter was being treated. The doctors now said she was in stable condition. It would be possible to talk to her within twenty-four hours. No one had any objections to Höglund and Wallander visiting the hospital together and talking to her.

Then Wallander went quickly down the list of unanswered questions. Nyberg was well prepared, as usual, able to fill in many of the gaps with the lab results now available. But nothing was startling enough to provoke a long discussion. It was mostly confirmations of conclusions they had already drawn. The only thing that got the attention of the group were the faint traces of kelp that were found on Björn Fredman's clothes. This could be interpreted as an indication that Fredman had been near the sea on the last day of his life. Wallander thought for a moment.

"Where are the traces of kelp?" he asked.

Nyberg checked his notes.

"On the back of his sport coat."

"He could have been killed somewhere near the sea," said Wallander. "As far as I can recall, there was a slight breeze blowing that night. If the surf was loud enough, it might explain why no one heard any screams."

"If it happened on the beach we would have found traces of sand," said Nyberg.

"Maybe it was on a boat," Svedberg suggested.

"Or a dock," said Höglund.

The question hung in the air. It would be impossible to check thousands of pleasure boats and docks. Wallander noted only that they should be extra observant for any tips that came in from people who lived near the sea.

Then he gave the floor to Åkeson.

"I succeeded in gathering some information about Louise Fredman," he said. "I hardly need to point out that this is highly confidential and cannot be mentioned in any connection outside the investigative team."

"We'll be as quiet as mice," said Wallander.

"Louise Fredman is at Saint Lars Hospital in Lund," Åkeson continued. "She has been there for over three years. The diagnosis is severe psychosis. She has stopped talking, sometimes has to be force-fed, and shows no sign of improvement. She's seventeen years old. According to a photograph I saw she's quite pretty."

The whole group was silent.

"Psychosis is usually caused by something," said Ekholm.

"She was admitted on Friday, January 9th, 1991," said Åkeson, after looking through his papers. "If I have understood the case correctly, her illness struck like the proverbial lightning bolt from a clear blue sky. She had been missing from home for a week. It appears that she was having serious problems at school and usually didn't show up at all. There were signs of drug abuse. But she didn't use any heavy narcotics. Mostly amphetamines. Maybe cocaine. They found her in Pildamm Park. She was completely irrational."

"Did she show any signs of external injuries?" asked Wallander, who was listening attentively.

"Not according to the material I've received to date."

Wallander thought about this.

"Well, we can't talk to her," he finally said. "But I want to know whether she had any injuries. And I want to talk to whoever found her."

"That was three years ago," said Åkeson. "But I assume the people involved could be traced."

"I'll talk to Forsfält at the criminal division in Malmö," said Wallander. "A uniformed patrol must have been involved if they found her in a confused state in Pildamm Park. There must be a report on it somewhere."

"Why do you wonder if she had any injuries?" asked Hansson.

"I just want to fill in the picture as completely as possible," Wallander replied.

They left Louise Fredman and went on to other topics. Since Ekholm was still waiting for the computers to finish cross-referencing all the investigative material and possibly discover some unexpected correlation in the combinations, Wallander turned the discussion to the matter of reinforcements. Hansson had already received a positive response from the county chief of police about the loan of a sergeant from Malmö. He would arrive in Ystad at lunchtime.

"Who is it?" asked Martinsson, who had so far been silent.

"His name is Sture Holmström," said Hansson.

"We don't know who that is," said Martinsson.

No one knew him. Wallander promised to call Forsfält to check on the gossip about him.

Then Wallander turned to Åkeson.

"The question now is whether we should ask for additional reinforcements," Wallander began. "What's the general view? I want everyone to state an opinion. I also promise to bow to the will of the majority. Even though I'm still doubtful that additional personnel will improve the quality of our work. I'm afraid we might lose the pace of our investigation. At least in the short run. But I want to hear your views."

Martinsson and Svedberg were in favor of requesting additional personnel for the case. Höglund, on the other hand, sided with Wallander, while Hansson and Ekholm had no opinion at all. Wallander saw that another invisible but burdensome mantle of responsibility had been draped around his shoulders. Åkeson opted to postpone the matter for a few more days.

"If we have another murder, it'll be unavoidable," he said. "But for the time being let's keep going the way we have been."

The meeting broke up just before ten o'clock. Wallander went to his room. The draining weariness that had overcome him on Saturday was gone. It had been a good meeting, even though they hadn't made any progress. They had shown one another that their energy and will were still strong.

Wallander was just about to call Forsfält when Martinsson appeared in his doorway.

"There's one more thing I happened to think of," he said, leaning against the doorjamb.

Wallander waited for him to continue.

"Louise Fredman was found wandering around on a path in the park," said Martinsson. "I just thought there was a similarity with the girl who was running around in the rapeseed field."

Martinsson was right. There was a similarity, even though it was remote.

"I agree," he said. "It's a shame that they have nothing to do with each other."

"Still, it's weird," said Martinsson.

He kept standing in the doorway.

"You bet right this time."

Wallander nodded.

"I know," he said. "Ann-Britt did too."

"You'll have to split a thousand."

"When's the next match?"

"I'll let you know," said Martinsson and left.

Wallander called Malmö.

While he waited he looked out the open window. The weather was still beautiful.

Then he heard Forsfält's voice on the other end of the line and pushed all thought of summer aside.

Hoover left the basement just after nine in the evening. He took a long time selecting the right axe from the ones lying polished on the black silk cloth. Finally he decided on the smallest one, the one he hadn't used yet. He stuck it in his wide leather belt and pulled the helmet over his head.

As before, he was barefoot when he left the room and locked the door.

It was a very warm evening. He rode along side roads that he had carefully selected on the map. It would take him almost two hours. He figured he'd get there just before eleven.

The day before he'd had to change his plans. The man who had left the country had suddenly returned. He immediately decided not to risk the chance that he might take off again. He had listened to Geronimo's heart. The rhythmic thumping of the drums inside his chest had delivered their message to him. He must not wait. He had to seize the opportunity.

The summer landscape took on a bluish tinge from inside his helmet. He could see the sea to his left, the blinking lights of ships, and the coast of Denmark. He felt elated and happy. It wouldn't be long now before he could bring his sister the last sacrifice that would help her escape the fog surrounding her. She would return to life in the most beautiful part of the summer.

He got to the city just after eleven. Fifteen minutes later he stopped on a street next to the large villa hidden away in an old garden full of tall, sheltering trees. He leaned his moped against a streetlight and locked it with a chain. On the opposite sidewalk an elderly couple was walking their dog. He waited until they disappeared before he pulled off his helmet and stuffed it into his backpack. Under cover of shadow he ran to the back of the large yard, which faced a gravel soccer field. He hid his backpack in the grass and then crept through the hedge, where he had prepared an opening a long time ago. The hedge scratched and pricked his bare arms and feet. But he steeled himself against all pain. Geronimo would not stand for him showing the slightest sign of weakness. He had a sacred mission, as it was written in the book he had received from his sister. The mission required all his strength, which he was prepared to sacrifice with devotion.

He was inside the garden now, closer to the beast than he had ever been before. There was a light on upstairs, while the entire ground floor was dark. He thought angrily that his sister had been here before him. She had described the house, and he thought that one day he would burn it to the ground. But not yet. Cautiously he ran up to the wall of the house and carefully pried open the basement window from which he had earlier removed the latches. It was easy to crawl inside. He knew that he was in an apple cellar, surrounded by the faint odor of sour apples. He listened. Everything was quiet. He cautiously slunk up the cellar stairs. He entered the big kitchen. Still quiet. The only thing he heard was the faint sound of some water pipes running. He turned on the stove and opened the oven door. Then he continued up the stairs leading to the top floor. He had taken the axe out of his belt. He was completely calm.

The door to the bathroom was ajar. In the darkness of the corridor he caught a glimpse of the man he was going to kill. He was standing in front of the bathroom mirror rubbing cream on his face. Hoover slipped in behind the bathroom door. Waiting. When the man turned off the light in the bathroom he raised the axe. He struck only once. The man fell to the bathmat without a sound. With his axe he sliced off a piece of the man's hair on top of his head. He stuffed the scalp in his pocket. Then he dragged the man down the stairs. He was dressed in pajamas. The pants slipped off the body and were dragged along by one foot. He avoided looking at him.

After he dragged the man into the kitchen he leaned the body over the oven door. Then he shoved the man's head into the oven. Almost at once he smelled the face cream starting to melt. He left the house the same way he had come.

In the dawn light he buried the scalp beneath his sister's window. Now all that was left was the extra sacrifice he would offer her. He would bury one last scalp. Then it would all be over.

He thought about what awaited him. The man whose chest had risen and fallen in deep undulations. The man who had sat across from him on the sofa and understood nothing of the sacred mission he had to perform.

He still hadn't decided whether he should also take the girl sleeping in the next room.

Now he had to rest. It was close to dawn.

The next day he would make his final decision.

Skåne 5–8 July 1994

Chapter Twenty-nine

Waldemar Sjösten was a middle-aged criminal detective in Helsingborg who devoted all his free time during the summer months to an old mahogany boat from the 1930s he had found by accident. It wasn't his intention to interrupt his routine on this Tuesday morning, the 5th of July, when he let the shade on his bedroom window roll up with a snap just before six in the morning. He lived in a newly renovated rental building downtown. One street, the railroad tracks, and the harbor area were all that separated him from the Sound. The weather was as beautiful as the newspapers had promised the day before. His vacation wouldn't start until the end of July. In anticipation of his last day at work he spent a few early-morning hours on his boat, docked at the pleasure boat marina a short bike ride away. Waldemar Sjösten was going to celebrate his fiftieth birthday this fall. He had been married three times and had six children. Now he was planning his fourth marriage. The woman he had met shared his interest in the old mahogany boat, which bore the imposing name *Sea King II*. He had taken the name from the beautiful double-ender in which he had spent his childhood summers with his parents, the *Sea King I*. To his great sorrow, when he was ten years old, his father had sold it to a man from Norway. He had never forgotten it. He often wondered whether the boat still existed, or whether it had sunk or rotted away.

He quickly drank a cup of coffee and prepared to leave. Just then the telephone rang. He was surprised to hear it ring at such an early hour. He picked up the receiver from the phone hanging on the kitchen wall.

"Waldemar?" asked a voice he recognized as that of detective sergeant Birgersson.

"Yes, speaking."

"I hope I didn't wake you."

"I was just on my way out."

"Lucky I caught you, then. You'd better get down here right away."

Waldemar Sjösten knew Birgersson never would have called unless something serious had happened.

"I'll be right there," he said. "What is it?"

"There was smoke coming out of one of those old villas up on Tågaborg. When the fire department went inside they found a man in the kitchen."

"Dead?"

"Murdered. You'll understand why I called you when you see him."

Waldemar Sjösten saw his morning hours with his boat about to disappear. Since he was a dutiful policeman, he had no trouble changing his plans. Instead of the key to his bike lock he grabbed his car keys and left the apartment. It took him only a few minutes to drive to the police station. Birgersson was standing on the stairs waiting. He got in the car and gave him directions.

"Who died?" asked Sjösten.

"Åke Liljegren."

Sjösten whistled. Åke Liljegren was well known, not just in the city but all over Sweden. He called himself "the Auditor" and had gained his notoriety as the gray eminence behind a number of famous dummy corporation deals during the eighties. Apart from a suspended sentence of six months, the police and the courts hadn't had any success winning convictions against the obviously illegal operation he was running. Åke Liljegren had become a symbol for the worst type of financial crime, while the fact that he always got off scot-free exhibited how ill-prepared the justice system was to handle criminals like him. He was originally from Båstad, but in recent years he resided in Helsingborg whenever he was home in Sweden. Sjösten recalled a newspaper article attempting to uncover how many houses Liljegren actually owned, spread over the entire globe.

"Can you give me a timetable?" asked Sjösten.

"A jogger out running early this morning discovered smoke coming out of the house vents. He called in an alarm. The fire department got there at quarter past five. When they went inside they found him in the kitchen."

"Where was the fire?"

"Nowhere."

Sjösten gave Birgersson a quizzical look.

"Liljegren was leaned over the open oven door," Birgersson continued. "His head was stuck in the oven, which was on full blast. He was literally being roasted."

Sjösten grimaced. He was beginning to get an idea what he was going to have to look at.

"Did he commit suicide?"

"No. Someone planted an axe in his head."

Sjösten stomped involuntarily on the brake. He looked at Birgersson, who nodded.

"His face and hair were almost completely burnt off. But the doctor thought he could still see that someone had sliced off part of his scalp."

Sjösten said nothing. He was thinking about what had happened in Ystad. That was the big news this summer. An insane killer who axed people to death and then took their scalps.

They arrived at Liljegren's villa on Aschebergsgatan. A fire engine stood outside the gates along with a few police cars and an ambulance. The huge estate was cordoned off with crime scene tape and signs. Sjösten got out of the car and waved off a reporter. He ducked under the cordon with Birgersson and walked up toward the villa. When they entered the house Sjösten noticed a funny smell. Then he realized that it came from Liljegren's corpse. He got a handkerchief from Birgersson and held it in front of his nose and mouth. Birgersson nodded toward the kitchen. A very pale uniformed officer stood guard outside the door. Sjösten peered into the kitchen. The sight that greeted him was grotesque. The half-naked man was on his knees. His body was bent over the oven door. His head and neck were out of sight inside the oven. With disgust Sjösten suddenly recalled the story of Hänsel and Gretel and the witch. The doctor was kneeling down next to the body, shining a flashlight into the oven. Sjösten tried to breathe without holding the handkerchief in front of his face. He breathed through his mouth. The doctor nodded at him. Sjösten leaned forward and looked in the oven. He thought of a blackened steak.

"Jesus," he said. "That's not a pretty sight."

"He took a blow to the back of the head," said the doctor.

"Here in the kitchen?"

"No, upstairs," said Birgersson, standing behind him.

Sjösten straightened up.

"Take him out of the oven," he said. "Is the photographer done?"

Birgersson nodded. Sjösten followed him upstairs. They walked carefully since the stairs were covered with traces of blood. Birgersson stopped outside the bathroom door.

"As you saw, he was wearing pajamas," said Birgersson. "Here's how it probably happened: Liljegren was in the bathroom. When he tried to leave, the killer was waiting for him. He struck Liljegren with an axe in the back of the head and then dragged the body down to the kitchen. That could explain why the pajama pants were hanging from one leg. Then he arranged the body in front of the oven, turned it on full blast, and left. We don't know yet how he got into the house and out again. I thought you might be able to take care of that."

Sjösten said nothing. He was thinking. Then he went back down to the kitchen. The body was now lying on a plastic sheet on the kitchen floor.

"Is it him?" asked Sjösten.

"It's Liljegren, all right," said the doctor. "Even though he doesn't have much face left."

"That's not what I meant. Is it the man who takes scalps?"

The doctor pulled back a corner of the plastic sheet covering the blackened face.

"I'm convinced that he cut or tore off the hair at the front of his head," said the doctor.

Sjösten nodded. Then he turned to Birgersson.

"I want you to call the Ystad police. Get hold of Kurt Wallander. I want to talk to him. Now."

For once Wallander had fixed a proper breakfast on this Tuesday morning. He had fried some eggs and was just sitting down at the table with his newspaper when the telephone rang. A detective sergeant introduced himself as Sture Birgersson from the Helsingborg police.

He realized at once that what he had feared had finally happened. The unknown man had struck again. He swore silently to himself, an oath that contained equal parts rage and horror.

Waldemar Sjösten came to the phone. They had met before. In the early eighties they had collaborated on an investigation of a narcotics ring extending all over Skåne. Despite their great differences in personality they had had an easy time working together and developed the beginnings of a friendship.

"Kurt?"

"Yes, it's me."

"It's been a long time since we talked last."

"So what's happened? Is what I hear true?"

"Unfortunately it is. The perpetrator you're looking for has turned up here in Helsingborg."

"Is it confirmed?"

"There's nothing to indicate otherwise. An axe blow to the head. Then he cuts off the victim's scalp."

"Who was it?"

"Åke Liljegren. Does that name ring a bell?"

Wallander thought for a moment.

"Don't they call him the Auditor?"

"Precisely. A former justice minister, an art dealer, and now a white-collar crook."

"And a fence too," said Wallander. "Don't forget that."

"I'm calling because I think you should come up here. We have chiefs who can work out the red tape for crossing into each other's jurisdictions."

"I'll come right away," said Wallander. "I wonder whether it wouldn't be a good idea to bring Sven Nyberg, our head forensic technician."

"Bring whoever you want. I won't stand in your way. I just don't like it that the perp has shown up here."

"I'll be in Helsingborg in two hours," said Wallander. "If you can tell me whether there's some connection between Liljegren and the others who were killed, we'll be ahead of the game. Did he leave any clues?"

"Not directly. But we know how it happened. Except this time he didn't pour acid in his eyes. He roasted him. His head and half his neck, at least."

"Roasted?"

"In an oven. Be glad you don't have to look at it."

"What else do you know?"

"I just got here. I don't really know anything else."

After Wallander hung up he looked at his watch. Ten past six. He looked up Nyberg's number and called him. Nyberg answered at once. Wallander told him briefly what had happened. Nyberg promised to be outside Wallander's building on Mariagatan within fifteen minutes. Then Wallander dialed Hansson's number. But he changed his mind, put down the receiver, lifted it again, and called Martinsson. As always, Martinsson's wife answered. It took a couple of minutes before her husband came to the phone.

"He's struck again," said Wallander. "In Helsingborg this time. A crook named Åke Liljegren. They call him the Auditor."

"The corporate raider?" asked Martinsson.

"That's the one."

"The murderer has taste."

"That's bullshit," said Wallander. "I'm driving up there with Nyberg. They called and asked us to come. I want you to tell Hansson. I'll give you a call as soon as I know anything."

"This means that the NCB is going to be called in," said Martinsson. "Maybe it's just as well."

"The best thing would be if we could bring this maniac in soon," said Wallander. "I'm leaving now. I'll call you later."

He stood waiting outside when Nyberg turned onto Mariagatan in his old Amazon. Wallander got in next to him. They drove out of Ystad. The morning was quite beautiful. Nyberg drove fast. At Sturup they turned off toward Lund and reached the freeway to Helsingborg. Wallander told him what few details he knew. After they passed Lund, Hansson called on the mobile phone. Wallander could hear that he was out of breath. Hansson has been even more afraid this would happen than I have, he thought.

"It's terrible that it's happened again," said Hansson. "This changes every-thing."

"For the time being it doesn't change a thing," replied Wallander. "It depends entirely on what actually happened."

"It's time for the NCB to take over," said Hansson. Wallander could tell from Hansson's voice that this is what he wanted most of all, to be relieved of his responsibility. Wallander felt annoyed. He couldn't ignore the hint of disparagement toward the work of the investigative team in what Hansson had said.

"Whatever happens is your responsibility—yours and Per Åkeson's," said Wallander. "What occurred in Helsingborg is their problem. But they asked me to come up there. We'll talk when the time comes about what we're going to do later."

Wallander hung up. Nyberg didn't say a word. But Wallander knew he had been listening.

They were met by a patrol car at the exit to Helsingborg. Wallander thought that it must have been somewhere near here that Sven Andersson from Lunnarp had stopped to give Dolores María Santana a lift on what was to be her last journey. They followed the police car up toward Tågaborg and stopped outside Liljegren's large estate. Wallander and Nyberg passed through the police cordon and were met by Sjösten, who stood at the bottom of the steps to the large villa. Wallander guessed it had been built around the turn of the century. They said hello and exchanged a few words about the last time they had seen each other. Then Sjösten introduced Nyberg to the forensic technician from Helsingborg who was in charge of the crime scene examination. The two of them went into the house.

Sjösten put out his cigarette on the ground and buried the butt in the gravel with his heel.

"It's your man who did this," he said. "There's no reason to think otherwise."

"What do you know about the dead man?"

"Åke Liljegren was famous."

"Infamous, I'd call him."

Sjösten nodded.

"There are probably plenty of people who have killed him in their dreams," he said. "With a criminal justice system that worked better, with fewer loopholes in the laws that are supposed to control financial crime, this wouldn't have happened. He would have been locked up. And so far, Swedish prison cells haven't been equipped with either bathrooms or barbecues."

Sjösten took Wallander into the house. The stench of burnt flesh was still noticeable. Sjösten gave Wallander a mask, which he put on reluctantly. They went into the kitchen, where the body lay under a plastic sheet. Wallander nodded to Sjösten to let him see the body. He might as well get the unpleasant part over with right away. He didn't know what he had expected to see. But he still flinched when he saw Liljegren's face. It was gone. The skin was burned away and large sections of the skull were clearly visible. There were just two holes where the eyes had been. The hair and ears were also burned off. Wallander nodded to Sjösten to put back the plastic sheet. Sjösten quickly described how Liljegren had been found leaning over the oven door. Wallander got some Polaroids from the photographer, who was just about to leave the kitchen to start working upstairs. It was almost worse to see the whole thing in pictures. Wallander shook his head with a grimace and handed back the photos. Sjösten took him to the second floor, pointing out the blood on the stairs and describing how the whole thing had apparently happened. Wallander occasionally asked a question about some detail. But from the start Sjösten's description seemed convincing.

"Were there any witnesses?" asked Wallander. "Traces left by the murderer? How did he get into the house?"

"Through a basement window."

They returned to the kitchen and went down to the large basement extending under the whole house. In a room where Wallander could smell the residual aroma of stored winter apples from previous years, a little window stood ajar.

"We think he got in this way," said Sjösten. "And left the same way. Even though he could have walked straight out the front door. Liljegren lived alone."

"Did he leave anything behind?" Wallander wondered. "Each time he has been very careful not to leave us any clues. On the other hand, he hasn't been excessively meticulous. We have a whole set of fingerprints. According to Nyberg, we're missing only the left little finger."

"Fingerprints he knows the police don't have on file," said Sjösten.

Wallander nodded. Sjösten's comment was quite right. He just hadn't formulated that thought the same way before.

"We found a footprint in the kitchen next to the stove," said Sjösten.

"So he was barefoot again," said Wallander.

"Barefoot?"

Wallander told him about the footprint they had found in Björn Fredman's bloody van. He knew that one of the first things they had to do was share with Sjösten and his colleagues all the investigative material they had gathered in their work on the first three murders.

Wallander inspected the basement window. He thought he could see faint scrape marks near one of the latches, which had been broken off. When he bent down he found it, although it was hard to see against the dark floor. He didn't touch it.

"It seems that it might have been loosened in advance," he said.

"You think he prepared for his visit?"

"It's conceivable. It fits with his habit of making preparations. He puts his victims under surveillance. He stakes them out. Why, and for how long, we have no idea. Our behavioral specialist, Mats Ekholm, claims this is often characteristic of people with psychotic tendencies."

They went into an adjoining room in which the windows were of the same type. The latches were intact.

"We should probably search for footprints in the grass outside the second window," said Wallander.

He regretted it immediately. He had no cause to tell an experienced criminal investigator like Waldemar Sjösten what ought to be done.

They returned to the kitchen. Liljegren's body was being removed.

"What I've been looking for the whole time is the point of contact," said Wallander. "First I looked for one between Gustaf Wetterstedt and Arne Carlman. I finally found it. Then I looked for one between Björn Fredman and the two others. We haven't been able to find a link yet. But I'm convinced there is one. And now I'm thinking this is one of the first things we should do here. Is it possible to find some connection between Åke Liljegren and the other three? Preferably to all of them, but at least to one of them."

"In a way we already have a very clear link," said Sjösten quietly.

Wallander gave him a questioning glance.

"What I mean is, the perpetrator is an identifiable link," Sjösten went on. "Even if we don't know who he is."

Sjösten nodded toward the door to the outside. Wallander realized that Sjösten wanted to speak with him in private. When they were outside in the garden they both squinted at the sun. It was going to be another hot, dry summer day. Wallander couldn't recall the last time it had rained. Sjösten lit a cigarette and led Wallander over to some garden furniture a little way from the house. They moved the chairs into the shade.

"There are plenty of rumors about Åke Liljegren," said Sjösten. "His dummy corporations are only a part of his operations. Here in Helsingborg we've heard about a lot of other things. Low-flying Cessnas dropping cocaine bundles. Heroin, marijuana. Just as hard to prove as to deny. Personally I have a hard time associating this type of activity with Liljegren. It might just be my limited imagination, of course. You keep thinking that it's still possible to sort criminals into various categories. Certain types of crime can be divided into groups. Then the criminals are supposed to stay within their respective boundaries and not encroach on other people's territory, which messes up our classifications."

"I've sometimes thought along those same lines," Wallander admitted. "But those days are probably gone. The world we live in is becoming more comprehensible and more chaotic at the same time."

Sjösten waved his cigarette at the huge villa.

"There have been other rumors too," he said. "More concrete. About wild parties in this house. Women, prostitution."

"Wild?" asked Wallander. "Have you had to come out here?"

"Never," said Sjösten. "I actually don't know why I called the parties wild. But people used to come here a lot. And disappeared just as quickly as they came."

Wallander said nothing. He was thinking about what Sjösten had just said. A dizzying thought flitted through his head. He saw Dolores María Santana standing at the southern freeway entrance from Helsingborg. Could there be some connection with what Sjösten was talking about? Prostitution? He pushed away the thought. It was not only unjustified, it was a sign that he was mixing up two different investigations in his head.

"We're going to have to work together," said Sjösten. "You and your colleagues have a jump of several weeks on us. Now we add Liljegren to the picture. How does it look now? What's changed? What seems clearer?"

"I think it's out of the question that the NCB won't get involved," said Wallander. "That's good, of course. But I'm always afraid that we'll have problems working together and that information won't get to the person who needs it."

"I have the same concern," said Sjösten. "That's why I want to suggest something. That you and I become an informal unit, so we can step aside for private discussion when we need to."

"Fine," said Wallander.

"We both remember the way it was in the days of the old National Homicide Commission," said Sjösten. "Something that was working very efficiently was dismantled. And things have never really been as good since."

"Times were different," said Wallander. "Violence had a different face, and there were fewer homicides. There were patterns to the way the really nasty criminals operated that were recognizable in a different way than they are today. I agree with you that the National Homicide Commission was a good thing. But I'm not sure it would have been as effective today."

Sjösten stood up.

"But we're in agreement?" he said.

"Of course," replied Wallander. "Whenever we think it's necessary, we'll talk."

"You can sleep at my place," said Sjösten, "if you ever have to stay overnight. It's nice not to have to stay at a hotel."

"I'd like that," Wallander thanked him. But deep inside he didn't mind staying at a hotel if it was necessary. He had a great need to have at least a few hours to himself every day.

They walked back toward the house. To the left was a large garage with two doors. While Sjösten went into the house, Wallander decided to take a look in the garage. With difficulty he lifted one of the doors. Inside was a black Mercedes. Wallander went in and looked at the car from the side. Then he discovered that the windows were tinted to make it impossible to look inside. He stood there thinking.

Then he went into the house and borrowed Nyberg's cell phone.

He called Ystad and asked to speak with Höglund. He told her briefly what had happened. Then he got to the real reason for his call.

"I want you to contact Sara Björklund," he said. "Do you remember her?"

"Wetterstedt's housekeeper?"

"Precisely. I want you to call her and bring her up here to Helsingborg. Without delay."

"Why?"

"I want her to take a look at a car. And I'll be standing next to her hoping that she recognizes it."

Höglund asked no more questions.

Chapter Thirty

S ara Björklund stood for a long time looking at the black car. Wallander stayed close to her, but in the background. He wanted his presence to give her confidence. But he didn't want to stand so close to her that he would be a disturbing factor in the task he had assigned her. He knew that she was making her best effort to be absolutely sure. Had she seen this car before, on the Friday morning she had come to Wetterstedt's house because she thought it was Thursday? Had it looked the same, could it even be the very same car she had seen pull out from the house where the old minister of justice lived?

Sjösten agreed with Wallander when he explained his idea. Even if Sara Björklund, the "charwoman" held in such contempt by Wetterstedt, agreed that it could have been a car of the same make she had seen, that wouldn't prove a thing. All they would get was an indication, a possibility. Even so, it was important; they both realized that.

Sara Björklund hesitated. Since there were keys in the ignition, Wallander asked Sjösten to drive it once around the block. If she closed her eyes and listened, could she recognize the sound of the engine? Cars had different sounds. She did as he said, she listened.

"Maybe," she said afterwards. "It looks like the car I saw that morning. But whether it was the same one I can't say. I didn't see the license plates."

Wallander nodded.

"I didn't expect you to," he said. "I'm sorry I had to ask you to come all the way up here."

Höglund had planned ahead and brought Norén with her, who was now assigned to drive Sara Björklund back to Ystad. Höglund wanted to stay.

It was still early in the morning. Yet the whole country already seemed to know what had happened. Sjösten improvised a press conference out on the street, while Wallander and Höglund drove down to the ferry terminal and had lunch.

He gave her a detailed account of what had happened.

"Åke Liljegren appeared in our investigative material on Alfred Harderberg," she said afterwards. "Do you remember that?"

Wallander let his mind wander back to the year before. With distaste he remembered the notorious businessman and art patron who lived behind the walls of Farnholm Castle. The man they had finally prevented from leaving the country in some dramatic moments at Sturup Airport. Åke Liljegren's name had come up in the investigation. But it had been on the periphery. They had never considered bringing him in for questioning.

Wallander sat with his third cup of coffee and gazed out over the Sound, which on this summer morning was filled with sailboats and ferries.

"We didn't want this, but we got it anyway," he said. "Another dead, scalped man. According to Ekholm we have now reached the magic boundary where our opportunities for identifying the perpetrator will increase dramatically. All according to the FBI's models. Which might be of great importance. Now we'll be able to delineate even more clearly what the similarities and differences are."

"I think I feel that somehow the level of violence has increased," she said hesitantly. "If you can assign a grade to axe murders and scalps."

Wallander waited with interest for her to go on. He had learned that her hesitation often revealed that she was on the trail of something important.

"Wetterstedt lay underneath a rowboat," she went on. "He had been cut down from behind. His scalp was sliced off. As if the perpetrator had taken the time to do it carefully. Or maybe there was some uncertainty. The first scalp. Carlman was killed from the front. He must have seen the man who did it. His hair was torn off, not sliced. It seems to indicate a frenzy or a contempt, or maybe a rage, almost uncontrolled. Then comes Björn Fredman. He apparently lay on his back. Probably tied up. Otherwise he would have resisted. He had acid poured in his eyes. The perpetrator forced open his eyelids. The blow to the head was done with tremendous power. And now Liljegren. Who gets his head stuck in an oven. Something is getting worse. Is it hatred? Or a sick person's enjoyment of demonstrating his power?"

"Repeat what you just said to Ekholm," said Wallander. "Let him put it into his computer. I agree with you. Certain changes in his behavior are evident. Something is shifting. But what does it tell us? Sometimes it seems as though we're supposed to interpret footprints that are millions of years old. The footprints of extinct animals that were petrified in volcanic ash. What I worry about most is the chronology. Which is based on the fact that we found the victims in a certain order. Since they were killed in a certain order. So for us a natural chronology is created. But the question is whether there's some other order among them that we can't interpret. Are some of them perhaps more important than others?"

She thought for a moment.

"Were any of them closer to the person who did it than the others?"

"Precisely," said Wallander. "Was Liljegren closer to the center than Carlman, for example? And which of them is farthest away? Or do all of them have the same relationship to the perpetrator?"

"A relationship which may only exist in his confused mind?"

Wallander pushed aside his empty coffee cup.

"The only thing we can be sure of is that these men were not chosen at random," he said.

"Björn Fredman is different," she said when they got up.

"Yes, he is," said Wallander. "But if you turn it around you could say that it's the other three who are different from him."

They returned to Tågaborg, where they were given the message that Hansson was on his way to Helsingborg to meet with the chief.

"Tomorrow the NCB will be here," said Sjösten.

"Has anyone talked to Ekholm?" asked Wallander. "He should come up here as soon as possible."

Höglund went to look into the matter. Meanwhile Wallander went through the house again with Sjösten. Nyberg was on his knees in the kitchen with the other techs. When they were heading up the stairs to the top floor, Höglund caught up with them and said that Ekholm was on his way in the same car with Hansson. They all continued their inspection of the house. None of them spoke. They were all hunting along their own invisible trails.

Wallander was trying to feel the killer's presence, the same way he had searched for him in the dark at Wetterstedt's house, or in the bright arbor in Carlman's garden. Less than twelve hours ago the murderer had climbed these same stairs. The invisible impression of his presence was still in the house. Wallander moved more slowly than the others. He stopped often and stared into space. Or he would sit down on a chair and look at a wall or a rug or a door, as if he were in an art museum, deeply engrossed in the objects on display. Occasionally he would go back and retrace his steps.

Watching him, Höglund got the impression that Wallander was acting as though he were walking on an extremely fragile layer of thin ice. If Wallander had known what she was thinking, he would probably have agreed with her. Each step involved a risk, a new way of looking at things, a renegotiation with himself about a thought he had just had. He moved as much in his mind as in the crime scene where he happened to be. Gustaf Wetterstedt's house had been strangely empty. Wallander had never sensed the presence of the man he was looking for. It finally convinced him that the man who killed Wetterstedt had never been inside the house. He had never come closer than the garage roof where he had waited, reading a Phantom comic book and then ripping it to pieces. But here, in Liljegren's house, it was different.

Wallander went back to the stairs and looked down the hall toward the bathroom. From here he could see the man he was about to kill. If the bathroom door was open, that is. And why would it have been closed if Liljegren was alone in the house? He walked toward the bathroom door and stood by the wall. Then he went into the bathroom and assumed for a moment the role of Liljegren in the lonely play he was performing. He walked out the door, imagining the axe blow which came without hesitation and with full force from behind him at an angle. He saw himself fall to the carpet in the hallway. Then he switched to the other role, the man holding an axe in his right hand. Not in his left; they had determined that in Wetterstedt's death. The man was right-handed. Wallander walked slowly down the stairs, dragging the invisible corpse behind him. Into the kitchen, over to the stove. He continued down into the basement and stopped at the window, which was too narrow for him to squeeze through. Only a man with no excess kilos could use the window as an entrance to Liljegren's house. The man they were looking for must be thin.

He went back up to the kitchen and then continued out to the garden. Near the basement window at the back of the house the techs were busy trying to find footprints. Wallander could have told them in advance that they wouldn't find anything. The man had been barefoot, as in the previous cases. He looked toward the hedge, the shortest distance between the basement window and the street. He pondered why the killer had been barefoot. He had asked Ekholm about it several times, but didn't think he got a satisfactory answer. Going barefoot meant taking a risk of injury. Of slipping, puncturing his foot, getting cut. And yet he still did it. Why did he go barefoot? Why did he choose to remove his shoes? This was another of the inexplicable details he had to keep in mind. He took scalps. He used an axe. He was barefoot. Wallander stopped in his tracks. The thought came to him in a flash. His subconscious had drawn a conclusion and relayed the message. Now he had received it.

An Indian, he thought. A warrior.

Suddenly he knew he was right. The man they were looking for was a lone warrior moving along an invisible path he had chosen. He was an impersonator. Used an axe to kill, cut off scalps, went barefoot. Why would an Indian go around in the Swedish summertime killing people? Who was really committing these murders? An Indian or someone playing the role?

Wallander held on tight to the thought so he wouldn't lose it before he had followed it to the end. He traveled over great distances, he thought. He must have a horse. A motorcycle. Which had stood behind the road maintenance hut. You drive in a car, but you ride on a motorcycle.

He walked back to the house. For the first time in this case he thought he glimpsed an image of the man he was looking for. The excitement of the discovery was instantaneous. His alertness sharpened. For the time being, however, he would keep his thoughts to himself.

A window on the top floor was opened. Sjösten leaned out.

"Come up here," he shouted.

Wallander went back in the house, wondering what they had found. Sjösten and Höglund were standing in front of a bookcase in a room that must have been Liljegren's office. Sjösten had a plastic bag in his hand.

"I'm guessing cocaine," he said. "Could be heroin, of course."

"Where was it?" asked Wallander.

Sjösten pointed at an open drawer.

"There may be more," said Wallander.

"I'll see about getting a narcotics dog in here," said Sjösten.

"I also think you ought to send out a few people to talk to the neighbors," said Wallander. "Ask if they noticed a man on a motorcycle. Not just last night, but earlier too. Over the last few weeks."

"Did he come on a motorcycle?"

"I think so. That would fit with his earlier means of getting around. You'll find it in the investigative material."

Sjösten left the room.

"There's nothing about a motorcycle in the investigative material," said Höglund, surprised.

"There should be," said Wallander, sounding distracted. "Didn't we confirm that it was a motorcycle that stood by the road outside Carlman's house?"

At the same moment he saw out the window that Ekholm and Hansson were on their way up the gravel path lined with rosebushes. They had another man with them, who Wallander assumed was the Helsingborg chief of police. Sergeant Birgersson met them halfway.

"We'd probably better go down there," he said. "Did you find anything?"

"The house reminds me of Wetterstedt's," she said. "The same gloomy bourgeois respectability. But at least here there are some family photos. Whether they make it more cheerful I don't know. Liljegren seems to have had cavalry officers in his family. Scanian Dragoons. If you can believe the photographs."

"I haven't looked at them," Wallander apologized. "But I believe you. His dummy company scams undoubtedly had much in common with primitive warfare."

"There's a photo of an old couple outside a cottage," she said. "If I understood what was written on the back, the picture was of his maternal grandparents on the island of Öland."

They continued down to the ground floor. Half of the stairs were cordoned off to protect the blood traces.

"Old bachelors," said Wallander. "Their houses resemble each other because maybe they were alike. How old was Åke Liljegren, anyway? Was he over seventy?"

Höglund didn't know.

A conference room was improvised in Liljegren's dining room. Ekholm, who didn't have to attend, was assigned an officer to fill him in on the recent developments. When they had all introduced themselves and sat down, Hansson surprised Wallander by being quite determined about what should happen.

During the trip up from Ystad he had also managed to confer by phone with both Per Åkeson and the NCB in Stockholm.

"It would be a mistake to claim that our situation has changed significantly because of what happened in this house," Hansson began. "The situation has been dramatic enough ever since we understood that we were dealing with a serial killer. Now we might say that we have crossed a sort of boundary. There's nothing to indicate that we will actually crack this series of murders. But we have to hope. As far as the National Criminal Bureau is concerned, they are prepared to give us all the help we request. The formalities involved in setting up an investigative group that not only crosses the boundaries of various police districts but also includes personnel from Stockholm shouldn't present any serious difficulties either. I assume no one has anything against Kurt being assigned leader of the new investigative team?"

No one had any objections. Sjösten nodded approval from his side of the table.

"Kurt has a certain notoriety," said Hansson, without the slightest indication that his words held any hidden meaning. "The chief of the NCB regarded it as obvious that Kurt should continue to lead the investigation."

"I agree," said the chief of the Helsingborg police. That was also the only thing he said during the whole meeting.

"Guidelines have been drawn up for how a collaboration such as this can be implemented in the shortest possible time," Hansson continued. "The prosecutors have their own preparation procedures to follow. The most important thing right now is to pin down what type of assistance we actually need from Stockholm."

Wallander had been listening to what Hansson was saying with a mixture of pride and anxiety. At the same time he was self-assured enough to realize that no one else could be more suitable to lead the investigation.

"Has anything resembling this series of homicides ever happened in Sweden?" asked Sjösten.

"Not according to Ekholm," said Wallander.

"It would be good to have some colleagues who have experience with this type of crime, of course," Sjösten continued.

"In that case we'll have to get them from the continent, or the States," said Wallander. "And I don't think that's such a good idea. Not yet, at any rate. What we need, obviously, is experienced homicide investigators. Who can add to our overall expertise."

It took them less than twenty minutes to make the necessary decisions. Afterwards Wallander hastily left the room in search of Ekholm. He ran into him upstairs outside the bathroom. Wallander took him into a guest room that didn't seem to have been used in a long time. Wallander opened the window to air out the stuffy room. Then he sat down on the edge of the bed and told Ekholm about his thoughts earlier that morning.

"You could be right," Ekholm said afterwards. "A person with serious psychosis who has taken on the role of a lone warrior. The history of crime has many examples of that. But not in Sweden. They are usually people who metamorphose into someone else before they go out to exact their revenge, which is the most common motive. The disguise frees them from guilt. The actor doesn't feel the pangs of conscience for actions performed by his character. But don't forget that there's a type of psychopath who kills with no motive other than his own intense enjoyment."

"That's hardly conceivable in this case," said Wallander.

"The difficulty lies in the fact that the role the killer has taken on, if we take for example the Indian warrior, doesn't necessarily tell us anything about the motive for the murder. There doesn't have to be any external correspondence. If we assume that you're right—a barefoot warrior who has chosen his disguise for reasons unknown to us—then he could just as well have chosen to turn himself into a Japanese samurai or a *tonton macoute* from Haiti. There's only one person who knows the reasons for the choice. The killer himself."

Wallander recalled one of the earliest conversations he had had with Ekholm.

"That would mean that the scalps are a red herring," he said. "That he's just taking them as a ritual act in the performance of the role he's selected for himself. Not that he's collecting trophies to reach some goal that serves as the basis for all the murders he has committed."

"That's possible."

"Which means that we're back to square one."

"The combinations have to be tested over and over," said Ekholm. "We never return to the starting point once we have left it. We have to move the same way the perpetrator does. He doesn't stand still. What happened last night confirms what I'm saying."

"Have you formed any opinion?"

"The oven is interesting."

Wallander reacted to Ekholm's choice of words. But he didn't say anything.

"In what way?"

"The difference between the acid and the oven is striking. In one case he uses a chemical agent to torture a man who's still alive. It's part of the killing itself. In the second case it serves more as a greeting to us."

Wallander looked at Ekholm intently. He tried to interpret the words he just heard.

"A greeting to the police?"

"It doesn't really surprise me. The murderer is not unaffected by his own actions. His image of himself is growing. It often reaches a point where he has to start looking for a contact outside himself. He's about to burst from self-congratulation. He has to seek confirmation of his greatness from outside. The victim can't rise up from the dead and applaud him. Sometimes he then turns to the police. The ones who are hunting him. The ones who want to prevent him from continuing. This can take various forms. Anonymous telephone calls or letters. Or why not a dead man arranged in a grotesque position?"

"He's taunting us?"

"I don't think he sees it that way. To himself he's invulnerable. If it's true that he selected the role of a barefoot warrior, the invulnerability might be one of the reasons. It's not uncommon for warrior peoples to smear themselves with salves to make themselves invulnerable to swords and arrows. In our day and age the police might symbolize those swords."

Wallander sat silently for a while.

"What's our next move?" he asked. "He's challenging us by stuffing Liljegren's head in the oven. What about next time? If there is one."

"There are many conceivable possibilities. One that isn't altogether unknown to the rest of the world is for psychopathic killers to seek contact with individual police officers."

"Why is that?"

Ekholm couldn't hide the fact that he hesitated before he replied.

"Police have been killed, you know."

"You mean this madman has his eye on us?"

"It's not impossible. Without our knowing it, he might amuse himself by popping up very close to us. And then vanishing again. One day this may not be enough."

Wallander thought back to the experience he had had outside the cordon at Carlman's farm. He thought he recognized one of the faces among the curious onlookers watching the police work. Someone who had also been on the beach outside the tape when they turned over the boat and pulled out the dead justice minister.

Ekholm looked at him gravely.

"I think you above all ought to be aware of this," he said. "Even if we hadn't had this conversation, I was thinking of talking to you about it."

"Why me?"

"You're the most visible one of us. The search for the man who committed these four murders involves a lot of people. But the only name and the only face that are seen regularly are yours."

Wallander grimaced.

"Do you really expect me to take what you're saying seriously?"

"That's for you to decide."

When they finished talking and Ekholm had left the room, Wallander stayed behind. He tried to figure out for himself what his real reaction was to Ekholm's words.

It was like a cold wind blowing through the room, he thought.

But nothing more.

Just after three that afternoon Wallander drove back to Ystad with the others. They had decided that the manhunt would continue to be directed from Ystad. Wallander sat in silence for the whole trip, giving only terse replies when Hansson asked him something. When they arrived they held a short briefing with Svedberg, Martinsson, and Åkeson. Svedberg told them that it was now possible to speak with Carlman's daughter, who had recovered sufficiently from her suicide attempt. They decided that Wallander and Höglund would pay a visit to the hospital the next morning. At six o'clock Wallander called his father. Gertrud picked up the phone. She said his father was completely back to normal. He already seemed to have forgotten what had happened a few days before.

Wallander also called home. No one answered. Linda wasn't there. On his way out of the police station he asked Ebba whether there was any news about his keys. Nothing. He drove down to the harbor and took a walk along the pier. Then he sat down in the harbor café and had a beer. He sat and watched the people passing by. Depressed, he got up and went out on the pier to the bench next to the red Sea Rescue shack.

The summer evening was warm, and there was no wind. Someone was playing a concertina on a boat. On the other side of the pier he saw one of the ferries from Poland coming into the terminal. Without actually being conscious of it, he suddenly started to see the connection in his mind. He sat perfectly still and let his thoughts work. He was beginning to discern the contours of a drama that was worse than he could have ever imagined. There were still a lot of holes, but now he thought he could see where they should concentrate their investigation.

He didn't think that the investigative plan they had been working from so far was to blame.

The problem was with the thoughts and conclusions he had come up with.

He drove home and wrote down a summary at his kitchen table.

Just before midnight Linda arrived. She had seen what had happened in the newspaper.

"Who is doing this?" she asked. "What is someone like this made of?"

Wallander thought for a moment before he replied.

"He's like you and me," he said at last. "By and large, just like you and me."

Chapter Thirty-one

Wallander woke up with a jolt.

His eyes flew open and he lay completely still. The light of the summer night was still gray. Someone was moving around in the apartment. He glanced quickly at the clock on the nightstand. It was quarter past two. His terror was instantaneous. He knew that it wasn't Linda. Once she fell asleep she never got out of bed until morning. He held his breath and listened. The sound was very faint.

The person moving around was barefoot.

Wallander crept carefully out of bed. He looked around for something to defend himself with. He had locked his service revolver in his desk at the police station. The only thing in the bedroom he could use was the broken arm of a wooden chair. He removed it cautiously and listened again. The footsteps seemed to be coming from the kitchen. He left his robe behind, since it would hinder his freedom of movement. He came out of the bedroom and looked toward the living room. He passed the door to Linda's room. It was closed. She was asleep. Now he was very scared. The sound was coming from the kitchen. He stood in the doorway of the living room and listened. So Ekholm was right after all. He prepared himself to meet someone who was very strong. The wooden chair arm he had in his hand wouldn't be much help. He remembered that he had a replica of a pair of old-fashioned brass knuckles in one of the drawers in the bookshelf. They had been the idiotic prize in some police lottery once. He decided that his fists were better protection than the chair arm. He could still hear the sounds in the kitchen. He moved cautiously across the parquet floor and opened the drawer. The brass knuckles were underneath a copy of his latest tax return. He put them on his right hand. At the same instant he realized that the sounds in the kitchen had stopped. He spun around and raised his arms.

Linda stood in the doorway looking at him with a mixture of astonishment and fear. He stared back at her.

"What are you doing?" she asked. "What's that on your hand?"

"I thought it was somebody breaking in," he said, taking off the brass knuckles.

She could see that he was shaken.

"It was just me. I had trouble sleeping."

"The door to your room wasn't open."

"I must have closed it. I had to get a drink of water. I guess I was afraid it might slam shut in the draft."

"But you never wake up at night."

"Those days are long gone. Sometimes I don't sleep well. When I've got a lot on my mind."

Wallander thought that he ought to feel foolish. But his relief was too great. His reaction had now confirmed something. He had taken Ekholm's words much more seriously than he thought. He sat down on the sofa. She was still standing there looking at him.

"I've often wondered how you can sleep as well as you do," she said. "When I think about all the things you have to look at, all the things you're forced to do."

"You get used to it," said Wallander, knowing that his answer wasn't true at all.

She sat down next to him on the sofa.

"I was looking through an evening paper while Kajsa was buying cigarettes," she went on. "There was quite a bit about what happened in Helsingborg. I don't know how you stand it."

"The papers exaggerate."

"How do you exaggerate somebody getting their head stuffed in an oven?"

Wallander tried to avoid her questions. He didn't know whether it was for his own sake or for hers.

"That's a matter for the medical examiner," he said. "I do an examination of the crime scene and try to figure out what happened."

She shook her head, resigned.

"You never could lie to me. To Mama, maybe, but never to me."

"I never lied to Mona, did I?"

"You never told her how much you loved her. What you don't say can be a false affirmation."

He looked at her in surprise. Her choice of words was unexpected.

"When I was little I used to sneak looks at all the papers you brought home at night. I invited my friends too, sometimes, when you were working on something we thought was exciting. We would sit in my room and read through the transcripts of witnesses' testimony."

"I had no idea."

"You weren't supposed to, either. So tell me who you thought was in the apartment."

She changed the subject very abruptly. He decided just as fast to tell her at least part of the truth. He told her that sometimes, but very seldom, policemen in his position, especially those who had their pictures in the paper a lot or were on TV, might catch the attention of criminals who then became fixated on them. Or perhaps "fascinated" was a better term. Normally there was nothing to worry about. But nobody could predict anymore what was normal or not. It was a good idea to acknowledge the phenomenon, to be aware of what might fascinate or fixate somebody. But from that point it was a big leap before you had to start worrying.

She didn't believe him for a second.

"That wasn't somebody standing there with brass knuckles on, showing how aware he was," she said at last. "What I saw was my pappa who's a cop. And he was scared."

"Maybe I had a nightmare," he said dubiously. "Tell me why you can't sleep."

"I'm worried about what to do with my life," she said.

"You and Kajsa were good in the piece you showed me."

"But not as good as we ought to be."

"You've got time to feel your way."

"But what if I want to do something else entirely?"

"Like what?"

"That's what I think about when I wake up in the middle of the night. I open my eyes and think that I still don't know."

"You can always wake me up," he said. "As a cop at least I've learned how to listen. Unfortunately, you can probably get better answers from someone else."

She leaned her head on his shoulder.

"I know," she said. "You're a good listener. A lot better than Mama. But the answers are probably things I have to figure out for myself."

They sat on the sofa for a long time. Not until it was four o'clock and already bright sunshine outside did they go back to bed. Something Linda said made Wallander feel good: That he listened better than Mona did.

In some future life he wouldn't mind doing everything better than Mona. But not now, when there was Baiba.

Wallander got up a little before seven. Linda was still asleep. He had a quick cup of coffee before he left. The weather was still beautiful. But the wind had started to blow. When he got to the police station he met an agitated Martinsson, who told him that the whole vacation schedule had been thrown into chaos. So many vacations had been postponed indefinitely because of the difficult investigation hanging over them.

"Now I probably won't be able to get time off until September," he said angrily. "Who the hell wants a vacation at that time of year?"

"Me," said Wallander. "Then I can go to Italy with my father."

When Wallander entered his office he suddenly realized that it was already

Wednesday, the 6th of July. On Saturday morning, in barely three days, he was supposed to be waiting at Kastrup Airport to meet Baiba. This was the first time he seriously realized that their vacation would have to be canceled, or at least postponed indefinitely. He had avoided thinking about it over these last few hectic weeks. Now he understood that he couldn't continue like this. He would have to cancel the tickets and hotel reservations. He dreaded Baiba's reaction. He sat in his chair and noticed that the whole topic was giving him a stomach ache. There must be some alternative, he thought. Baiba can come here. Maybe we could still manage to catch this damned perp soon—this man who kills people and then cuts off their scalps.

He was afraid of her disappointment. Even though she had once been married to a cop, Wallander thought she probably imagined that everything was different in a country like Sweden. But he couldn't wait any longer to tell her that they wouldn't be going to Skagen as they had planned. He ought to pick up the phone and call Riga right now. But he put off the unpleasant conversation. He wasn't ready yet. He grabbed a notebook and wrote down all the cancellations he would have to call in.

Then he turned into a cop again.

He mulled over what he thought had been revealed to him the night before, when he was sitting out on the Sea Rescue bench. Before he left home he had torn out the pages from his notebook with the summary he had written down. He put them on the desk in front of him and read what he had written. He still thought they made sense. He picked up the phone and asked Ebba to get hold of Waldemar Sjösten in Helsingborg. A few minutes later she called back.

"He seems to be spending his mornings scraping barnacles off a boat," she said. "But he was on his way in. He'll probably call you in the next ten minutes."

It was almost fifteen minutes before Sjösten called back. Wallander listened briefly to what he had to say about the ongoing crime investigation. They had located some witnesses, an elderly couple, who claimed to have seen a motorcycle on Aschebergsgatan the same evening Liljegren was murdered.

"Check it out carefully," said Wallander. "It could be very important."

"I thought I'd do it myself."

Wallander leaned forward over his desk, as if he had to brace himself before tackling the next question.

"I'd like to ask you to do one more thing," he said. "Something that should take the highest conceivable priority. I want you to find some of those women who worked at the parties that were held at Liljegren's villa."

"Why?"

"I think it's important. We have to find out who was at those parties. I need to be a guest after the fact. You'll understand when you go through the investigative material."

Wallander knew very well that his question wouldn't be answered in the material they had assembled for the other three murders. But right now he didn't want to delve too deeply. He needed to hunt alone for a while longer.

"So you want me to pick out a whore," said Sjösten.

"Yes, I do. If there were any at those parties."

"It's rumored there were."

"I want you to get back in touch with me ASAP. Then I'll come up to Helsingborg."

"If I find one, should I bring her in?"

"Bring her in for what?"

"No idea."

"I just want to talk to her, that's all. You should make it clear to her that she has nothing to worry about. Someone who's afraid and says what she thinks I want to hear won't do me a bit of good."

"I'll try," said Sjösten. "Interesting assignment in the middle of summer."

They hung up. Wallander returned to his notes from the night before. Just after eight o'clock Höglund called him and asked if he was ready. He got up, took his jacket, and met her in the reception area. At his suggestion they walked down to the hospital so they would have time to plan their conversation with Carlman's daughter. Wallander didn't even know the name of the young woman who had slapped his face.

"Erika," said Höglund. "A name that doesn't suit her."

"Why not?" asked Wallander, surprised.

"I get the impression of a robust kind of woman when I hear the name Erika," she said. "The manager of a hotel smörgåsbord or an overhead crane operator."

"Is it okay that my name is Kurt?" he asked.

She nodded cheerfully.

"Of course it's nonsense that you can match a personality to a name," she said. "But it amuses me, like a puzzle with no deeper meaning. On the other hand, you could hardly imagine a cat named Fido. Or a dog named Kitty."

"There probably are some," said Wallander. "So what do we know about Erika Carlman?"

They had the wind at their backs and the sun on their left side as they walked toward the hospital. Höglund told him that Erika Carlman was twenty-seven years old. That for a short time she had been a flight attendant for a small domestic British charter carrier. That she had dabbled in lots of different things without ever being able to stick with them for long or show any deeper involvement. She had traveled all over the world, no doubt supported financially by her father. A marriage with a Peruvian soccer player had dissolved after a short time.

"Sounds to me like a normal upper-class girl," said Wallander. "Who got everything on a silver platter right from the start."

"According to her mother she was already exhibiting hysterical tendencies as a teenager. That's the word she used, hysterical. It's probably more correct to speak of neurotic predispositions."

"Has she ever attempted suicide before?"

"Never. Not that anyone knows of, at least. I didn't get the feeling the mother was lying."

Wallander thought for a moment.

"She must have been serious about it," he said. "She really wanted to die."

"That's my impression too."

They kept walking. Wallander knew that he could no longer keep from telling Ann-Britt that Erika had slapped him. It was very possible that she might mention the incident. Then there wouldn't be any explanation for why he hadn't told her about it, other than masculine vanity, perhaps.

Not far from the hospital Wallander stopped and told her about it. He could see that what he said surprised her.

"I don't think it was anything more than a manifestation of the hysterical tendencies her mother was talking about," he concluded.

They continued walking. Then she stopped again.

"This might cause a problem," she said. "She's probably in pretty bad shape. She probably realizes that she was at death's door for several critical days. We don't even know if she feels regret or curses the fact that she didn't manage to kill herself. If you walk into the room, her fragile ego might collapse—she's already feeling guilty. Or it might make her aggressive, scared, unreceptive."

Wallander knew at once that she was right.

"Then the best thing would be for you to speak to her alone. I'll sit in the cafeteria and wait."

"First we'll have to go over what we actually want to learn from her."

Wallander pointed to a bench by the hospital's taxi stand. They sat down.

"In an investigation like this we always hope that the answers will be more interesting than the questions," he began. "What did her almost successful suicide attempt have to do with her father's death? That'll have to be the basis for your questioning. How you get there is up to you. You'll have to draw your own map. Her answers will prompt more questions you need to ask."

"Let's assume that she says she was so crushed by grief that she didn't want to go on living."

"Then we'll know that much."

"But what else do we actually know?"

"That's where you have to ask the follow-up questions, which we can't predict yet. Was it a normal loving relationship between father and daughter? Or was it something else?"

"And if she denies it was something else?"

"Then you have to start by not believing her. Without telling her so. But I refuse to accept that she has any other reason for going to such lengths to attempt to arrange a double funeral."

"In other words, a denial would mean that I should be interested in the reasons she might have for not telling the truth?"

"More or less. But there's a third possibility, of course. That she tried to commit suicide because she knew something about her father's death that she couldn't deal with in any other way except by taking the information with her to the grave."

"Could she have seen the killer?"

"That's possible."

"And she doesn't want him to be caught?"

"Also conceivable."

"Why doesn't she?"

"Once again, there are at least two possibilities. She wants to protect him. Or she wants to protect her father's memory."

She sighed hopelessly.

"I don't know if I can handle this."

"Of course you can. I'll wait for you in the cafeteria. Or out here. Take all the time you need."

Wallander accompanied her inside to the front desk. He recalled the time a few weeks earlier when he had been at the same hospital and found out that Salomonsson had died. Little did he know back then what was in store for him. Höglund asked directions at the information counter and disappeared down the corridor. Wallander went to the cafeteria, but then changed his mind and went back outside to the taxi stand bench. Once again he went over his thoughts from the night before. He was interrupted by the cell phone ringing in his jacket pocket. It was Hansson, and his voice sounded harried.

"Two investigators from the NCB are arriving at Sturup Airport this afternoon. Ludwigsson and Hamrén. Do you know them?"

"Just by name. They're supposed to be good. Hamrén was involved in solving that case with the laser man, wasn't he?"

"Could you possibly pick them up?"

"No, I can't," said Wallander after thinking for a moment. "I'll probably have to go back up to Helsingborg."

"Birgersson didn't mention that. I spoke to him a little while ago."

"They probably have the same internal communications problems we do," Wallander said patiently. "I think it would be a good sign if you went out there yourself to pick them up."

"Sign of what?"

"Respect. When I was in Riga a few years back I was picked up in a limousine. An old Russian one. But even so. It's important for people to feel that they're being welcomed and taken care of."

"All right," said Hansson. "I'll do it. Where are you now?"

"At the hospital."

"Are you sick?"

"Carlman's daughter. Did you forget about her?"

"To tell you the truth, I did."

"We should be glad we don't all forget the same things," said Wallander.

He never figured out whether Hansson had understood his attempt to be ironic. He put the phone down next to him on the bench and watched a sparrow balancing on the edge of a city garbage can. Ann-Britt had already been gone for almost half an hour. He closed his eyes and raised his face to the sun. Tried to figure out what he would tell Baiba. A man with his leg in a cast sat down with a thud next to him. He kept looking toward the sun. After five minutes a taxi arrived. The man with the cast left. Wallander paced back and forth in front of the hospital entrance. Then he sat down again. An hour had passed.

She came out of the hospital after an hour and five minutes and sat down next to him on the bench. He couldn't tell from the expression on her face how it had gone.

"I think we missed one reason why a person would want to commit suicide," she said. "Being tired of life."

"Was that her answer?"

"I didn't even have to ask. She was sitting on a chair in a white room, dressed in one of the hospital's bathrobes. Her hair uncombed, pale, out of it. No doubt still deeply immersed in a mixture of her own crisis and the medications. 'Why go on living?' That was her greeting. To be honest, I think she'll try to kill herself again. Out of sheer loathing."

Wallander recognized his mistake. He had overlooked the most common motive for committing suicide. Simply not wanting to live any longer.

"I assume you managed to talk about her father, though."

"She despised him. But I'm quite sure that she was never abused by him."

"Did she say that?"

"Some things don't have to be said out loud."

"What about the murder?"

"She was oddly uninterested in it."

"And she seemed to be telling the truth?"

"I think she said exactly what she felt. She wondered why I had come. I told her the truth. We're searching for a perpetrator. She said there were probably plenty of people who wanted her father dead. Because of his ruthlessness in business dealings. Because of the way he was."

"She didn't mention anything about the possibility that he might have had another woman?"

"Not a thing."

Wallander despondently watched the sparrow, which had returned to the garbage can.

"So, at least we know that much," he said. "We know that we don't know anything else."

They walked back to the station. It was a quarter to eleven. The wind, which they now had in their faces, had died down a bit. When they were halfway there, Wallander's phone rang. He turned away from the wind to answer it. It was Svedberg.

"We think we found the place where Björn Fredman was killed," he said. "A dock just west of town."

Wallander felt his despondency following the fruitless visit to the hospital vanish at once.

"Great," he said.

"A tip," Svedberg continued. "The person who called mentioned blood stains. It could have been somebody cleaning fish, of course. But I don't think so. The man who called was a lab technician. He's worked with blood samples for thirty-five years. Besides, he claimed that there were tire tracks right near-by. Where there aren't usually any. A vehicle had been parked there. Why not a '67 Ford van?"

"In five minutes we can drive over there and start figuring it out," said Wallander.

They continued up the hill, much more quickly now. Wallander told Höglund the news.

Neither of them was thinking about Erika Carlman anymore.

H oover got off the train in Ystad at 11:03 A.M. He had decided to leave his moped at home today. When he walked out the back of the train station and saw that the police crime scene tape around the pit where he had dumped his father was gone, he felt a twinge of disappointment and anger. The cops who were pursuing him were much too weak. They would never have passed the simplest entrance exam to the FBI's academy. He felt Geronimo's heart start to drum inside him. He understood the message, simple and clear. He was going to fulfill the mission he had already been chosen for. Before his sister returned to life he would bring her his two final sacrifices. Two scalps beneath her window. And the girl's heart. As a gift. Then he would walk into the hospital to get her and they would leave together. Life would be completely different. One day they might even read her diary together, remembering the events that had led her back, out of the darkness.

He strolled to the center of town. He had put on shoes so he wouldn't attract attention. His feet didn't like it. When he got to the square he turned right and went to the house where the policeman lived with the girl who must be his daughter. He had come into town today to take a closer look. He was planning the action itself for the next evening. Or at the latest, after one more day. No more. His sister shouldn't have to stay at that hospital any longer. He sat down on the steps of one of the neighboring buildings. He practiced forgetting time. Just sitting, empty of thought, until he again took hold of his mission. He still had a lot to learn before he mastered the art of perfection. But he had no doubt that one day he would succeed.

His waiting ended after two hours. That's when she came out the front door. She was obviously in a hurry and walked off toward town.

He followed her and never let her out of his sight.

Chapter Thirty-two

When they reached the dock Wallander was immediately convinced that they had come to the right place. It was just as he had imagined it. The reality of the place, as it looked here by the sea about ten kilometers west of Ystad, matched his earlier suppositions. They had driven along the coast highway and stopped where a man in shorts and a T-shirt advertising the golf course in Malmberget stood waving by the side of the road. He directed them down an almost invisible dirt road, and they saw the dock, hidden from the highway, at once. They stopped so they wouldn't disturb the tire tracks.

The lab technician, Erik Wiberg, about fifty, told them that in the summertime he lived in a cabin on the north side of the highway. He often came down to this dock to read his morning paper, as he had on the morning of June 29th. At that time, he had noticed the tire tracks and the dark spots on the brown wood. But he thought nothing more about it. The same day he left on a trip to Germany with his family, and it wasn't until he came back and saw in the newspaper that the police were looking for a murder scene, probably near the sea, that he again remembered those dark spots. Since he worked in a laboratory where they often did analyses of blood from cattle, he thought he could confirm that what was on the dock at least looked like blood. Nyberg, who had arrived by car just after Wallander and the others, was on his knees by the tire tracks. He had a toothache and was more irritable than ever. Wallander was the only one he could stand to talk to.

"It could be Fredman's Ford van," he said. "But we'll have to do a proper examination."

They walked out on the dock together. Wallander knew they had been lucky. The dry summer helped. If it had rained they wouldn't have been able to secure any traces. He looked for confirmation from Martinsson, who had the best memory of the weather.

"Has it rained since June 28th?" he asked.

Martinsson answered at once.

"It drizzled on the morning of Midsummer Eve," he said. "Ever since then it's been dry."

"Then we'll cordon off the whole place," said Wallander, nodding to Höglund, who went to phone for personnel to seal off the area around the dock.

"Be careful where you put your feet," said Wallander.

He stood near the land end of the dock and looked at the patches of blood. They were concentrated in the middle of the dock, which was four meters long. He turned around and looked up toward the highway. He could hear the traffic noise, but he couldn't see the cars, just part of the roof of a tall semi-trailer flashing by. He had an idea. Höglund was still talking on the phone to Ystad.

"Tell them to bring me a map," he said. "One that includes Ystad, Malmö, and Helsingborg." Then he walked all the way to the end of the dock and looked down into the water. The bottom was rocky. Erik Wiberg was standing on the beach a few meters away.

"Where's the nearest house?" asked Wallander.

"A couple of hundred meters from here," replied Wiberg. "Across the highway. To the west."

Nyberg had come out onto the dock.

"Should we call in divers?" he asked.

"Yes," said Wallander. "We'll start with a radius of twenty-five meters around the dock."

Then he pointed at the rings set into the wood.

"Fingerprints," he said. "If Björn Fredman was killed here he must have been tied down. Our perpetrator goes barefoot and doesn't wear gloves."

"What are the divers looking for?"

Wallander thought about it.

"I don't know," he said. "Let's see if they come up with anything. But I think you're going to find traces of kelp on the slope, from the place where the tire tracks stop all the way down to the dock."

"The van didn't turn around," said Nyberg. "He backed it all the way up to the highway. He couldn't have seen whether any cars were coming. So there are only two possibilities. Unless he's totally crazy."

Wallander raised his eyebrows.

"He *is* crazy," he said.

"Not in that way," said Nyberg.

Wallander understood what he meant. He wouldn't have been able to back up onto the highway unless he had an accomplice who signaled him when there wasn't any traffic coming. Or else it happened at night. When the headlights would tell him that it was safe to back out onto the highway.

"He doesn't have an accomplice," said Wallander. "And we know that it must have happened at night. The only question is why he drove Fredman's body to the pit outside the train station in Ystad."

"He's crazy," said Nyberg. "You said so yourself."

A few minutes later a car arrived with the map. Wallander asked Martinsson for a pen and then sat down on a rock next to the dock. He drew circles around Ystad, Bjäresjö, and Helsingborg. Then he marked the dock, which lay just next to the side road toward Charlottenlund. He wrote numbers next to his marks. Then he waved over Höglund, Martinsson, and Svedberg, who had arrived last, wearing a dirty sun hat instead of his cap for a change. He pointed at the map on his knee.

"Here we have his movements," he said. "And the murder sites. Like everything else they form a pattern."

"A road," said Svedberg. "With Ystad and Helsingborg as the end points. The scalp murderer on the southern plain."

"That wasn't funny," said Martinsson.

"I'm not trying to be funny," Svedberg protested. "I'm just telling it like it is."

"Looking at the big picture, you're probably right," said Wallander. "The area is limited. One murder takes place in Ystad. One murder occurs here, perhaps, we aren't sure yet, and the body is taken to Ystad. One murder happens just outside Ystad, in Bjäresjö, where the body is also discovered. And then we have Helsingborg."

"Most of them are concentrated around Ystad," said Höglund. "Does that mean that the man we're looking for lives here?"

"With the exception of Björn Fredman the victims were found close to or inside their homes," said Wallander. "This is the map of the victims, not the murderer."

"Then Malmö should be marked too," said Svedberg. "That's where Björn Fredman lived."

Wallander also circled Malmö. The wind tore at the map.

"Now the picture is different," said Höglund. "We get an angle, not a straight line. Malmö is in the middle."

"It's always Fredman who's different," said Wallander.

"Maybe we should draw another circle," said Martinsson. "Around the airport. What do we get then?"

"An area of movement," said Wallander. "Revolving around Fredman's murder."

He knew that now they were on their way toward a crucial conclusion.

"Correct me if I'm wrong," he continued. "Björn Fredman lives in Malmö. Together with the man who kills him, either held captive or not, he is driven east in the Ford. They come here, where Björn Fredman dies. The trip continues toward Ystad. The body is dumped in a hole under a tarp in Ystad. Later the van returns westward. It's parked at the airport, about halfway between Malmö and Ystad. There all the tracks vanish."

"From Sturup there are plenty of ways to get transportation," said Svedberg. "Taxicabs, airport buses, rental cars. Another vehicle parked there earlier."

"In other words, it means that the murderer probably doesn't live in Ystad," said Wallander. "Malmö's a good possibility. But it could just as well be Lund. Or Helsingborg. Or why not Copenhagen?"

"Unless he's leading us on a wild-goose chase," said Höglund. "And he really does live in Ystad. But doesn't want us to figure it out."

"That's possible, of course," said Wallander dubiously. "But I have a hard time believing it."

"In other words, we ought to concentrate on Sturup more than we have so far," said Martinsson.

Wallander nodded.

"I think the man we're looking for uses a motorcycle," he said. "We talked about this before. A motorcycle may also have been seen outside the house in Helsingborg where Liljegren died. There are witnesses who may have seen something. Sjösten is working on that right now. Since we're getting reinforcements this afternoon, I think we can afford to do a careful examination of the transportation options from Sturup. We're searching for a man who parked the Ford there the night of June 28th. And somehow he got out of there. Unless he works at the airport."

"There's one question we can't answer at all," said Svedberg. "What does this monster look like?"

"We don't know anything about his face," said Wallander. "But we know this much: he's strong. In addition, a basement window in Helsingborg shows that he's thin. We're dealing with someone in good shape. Who also goes barefoot."

"You mentioned Copenhagen just now," said Martinsson. "Does that mean he might be a foreigner?"

"Hardly," replied Wallander. "I think we're dealing with a genuine Swedish serial killer."

"That's not much to go on," said Svedberg. "Haven't we found a single hair? Does he have light or dark hair?"

"We don't know," said Wallander. "According to Ekholm he probably doesn't try to attract attention. And we can't say anything about the way he's dressed when he commits the murders."

"Does this person have an age?" asked Höglund.

"No," said Wallander. "His victims have been elderly men. Except for Björn Fredman. The fact that he's in good shape, goes barefoot, and may ride a motorcycle doesn't imply an older man. We just can't guess."

"Over eighteen," said Svedberg. "If he rides a motorcycle."

"Or sixteen," said Martinsson. "If it's a motorbike."

"Can't we start with Björn Fredman?" asked Höglund. "He differs from the other men, who are considerably older. Maybe we can assume an age correspondence between Björn Fredman and the one who killed him. Then we're talking about a man who's under fifty. And there are quite a few of them who are in good shape."

Wallander gave his colleagues a gloomy look. They were all under fifty; Martinsson, the youngest, was barely thirty. But none of them was in particularly good shape.

"Ekholm is working on his sketches for this man's psychological profile," said Wallander, getting to his feet. "It's important that we all read through it every day. It might give us some ideas."

Norén came toward Wallander with a telephone in his hand. Wallander squatted down out of the wind. It was Sjösten.

"I think I've got someone for you," he said. "A woman who was at three different parties at Liljegren's villa."

"Good," said Wallander. "When can I meet her?"

"Any time."

Wallander looked at his watch. It was twenty past twelve.

"I'll be up there no later than three," he said. "By the way, we think we've found the place where Björn Fredman died."

"I heard about it," said Sjösten. "I also heard that Ludwigsson and Hamrén are on their way from Stockholm. They're good men, both of them."

"How's it going with the witnesses who saw a man on a motorcycle?"

"They didn't see a man," said Sjösten. "But they did see a motorcycle. We're trying to figure out what kind it was. But it's difficult. Both the witnesses are old. They're also both passionate health nuts who despise all gasoline-powered vehicles. In the long run it may turn out to be a wheelbarrow they saw."

A scratchy noise came from the phone. The conversation sputtered out in the wind. Nyberg was standing next to the dock rubbing his swollen cheek.

"How's it going?" asked Wallander cheerfully.

"I'm waiting for the divers," said Nyberg.

"Are you in a lot of pain?"

"It's a wisdom tooth."

"Get it pulled."

"I will. But first I want those divers to get here."

"Is it blood on the dock?"

"Almost certainly. Tonight you'll also find out whether it ever ran around inside Fredman's body."

Wallander left Nyberg and told the others he was going to Helsingborg. On his way to the car he remembered something he had almost forgotten. He went back.

"Louise Fredman," he said to Svedberg. "Did Per Åkeson come up with anything else on her?"

Svedberg didn't know. But he promised to talk to Åkeson.

Wallander turned off at Charlottenlund, thinking about the care the man had taken in selecting the spot where Fredman was murdered. The closest house was far enough away that Fredman's screams wouldn't be heard. He drove up to highway E65 and headed toward Malmö. The wind was buffeting the car. But the sky was still totally clear. He thought about the conversation they had had over the map. There were a lot of reasons to think the killer lived in Malmö. He didn't live in Ystad, at least. But why did he take the trouble to dump Fredman's body in a pit outside the railroad station? Was Ekholm's idea correct, that now he was taunting the police? Wallander took the road to Sturup and briefly considered stopping at the airport. But he changed his mind. What good would that do? The interview in Helsingborg was more important. He headed for Lund, wondering what sort of woman Sjösten had found for him.

Her name was Elisabeth Carlén. She was sitting across from Wallander at the Helsingborg police station in the office normally used by detective inspector Waldemar Sjösten. It was four o'clock, and the woman, about thirty years old, had just entered the room. Wallander shook hands with her and thought she reminded him of the female pastor he had met the week before in Smedstorp. Maybe it was because she was dressed in black and wore heavy makeup. He asked her to take a seat, thinking that Sjösten's description of her was quite apt. Sjösten had said that she was attractive precisely because she always looked at the world with a cold, disparaging expression. To Wallander it seemed as if she had decided to challenge any man who came near her. He didn't think he'd ever seen eyes like hers before. They exuded contempt and interest at the same time. He quickly went over her story in his mind as she lit a cigarette. Sjösten's account had been a model of brevity and conciseness.

"Elisabeth Carlén is a whore," he had said. "The question is whether she has ever been anything else since the age of twenty. She left middle school and then worked as a waitress on one of the ferries crossing the Sound. Got tired of that and tried opening a boutique with a girlfriend. That was a total flop. She had invested borrowed money that her parents had co-signed for. After that she did nothing but fight with them, and she drifted around a lot. Copenhagen for a while, then Amsterdam. When she was seventeen she went there as a courier with a load of amphetamines. She probably used it herself too, but seemed to be able to control it. That was also the first time I met her. Then she was away for a few years, a black hole I don't know anything about. But suddenly she popped up in Malmö in a very cleverly disguised ring of brothels."

At that point in Sjösten's story Wallander had to interrupt.

"Are there still brothels?" he asked in surprise.

"Whorehouses, then," said Sjösten. "Call them what you like. But there sure are plenty of them. Don't you have them in Ystad? Just wait, they'll show up."

Wallander didn't interrupt again. Sjösten took up where he left off.

"She never walked the streets, of course. She set herself up at home. Built up a circle of exclusive clients. She evidently had something that was attractive and could raise her market value to the skies. She didn't even put those classified ads in the porno magazines. You can ask her what it is that makes her so special. It might be interesting to find out. It's during the last few years that she's shown up in certain circles that have contact with Åke Liljegren occasionally. She's been seen with a number of his directors at restaurants. Stockholm notes that she has turned up on a number of not altogether appropriate occasions, when the police had reason to be interested in the man or men who happened to be escorting her. That's Elisabeth Carlén in a nutshell. Quite a successful Swedish prostitute, on the whole."

"Why did you choose her?"

"She's a lot of fun. I've spoken with her many times. She isn't timid. If I tell her she isn't suspected of anything, she believes me. I also imagine that she has a whore's sense of self-preservation. In other words, she notices things. She doesn't like cops. A good way to get rid of us is to stay on good terms with people like you and me."

Wallander had hung up his jacket and moved a pile of papers on the table. Elisabeth Carlén was smoking. She followed all his movements with her eyes. Wallander was reminded of a wary bird.

"You already know that you aren't suspected of anything," he began.

"Åke Liljegren was roasted in his kitchen," she said. "I saw his stove. Quite fancy. But I wasn't the one who turned it on."

"Nor do we think you did," said Wallander. "What I'm looking for is information. I'm trying to create a picture. I've got an empty frame. I'd like to put a photo in it. Taken at a party at Liljegren's villa. I want you to point out his guests."

"No," she said, "that's not what you want. You want me to tell you who killed him. And I can't."

"What did you think when you heard Liljegren was dead?"

"I didn't think anything. I burst out laughing."

"Why? A person's death shouldn't be laughable."

"You obviously don't know that he had other plans than winding up in his own oven. The mausoleum in the cemetery outside Madrid? That's where he was going to be buried. A virtual fortress built according to his own blueprints. Out of Italian marble. But he wound up dying in his own oven. I think he would have laughed himself."

"His parties," said Wallander. "Let's get back to them. I've heard they were wild."

"They sure were."

"In what way?"

"In every way."

"Can you be a little more specific?"

She took a couple of deep drags on her cigarette while she thought about this. The whole time she looked Wallander straight in the eye.

"Åke Liljegren liked to bring people together who had the ability to live life to the fullest," she said. "Let's say they were insatiable. Insatiable with regard to power, wealth, and sex. And Liljegren had a reputation for being discreet. He created a safety zone around his guests. No hidden cameras, no spies. Nothing ever leaked out about his parties. He also knew which women he could invite."

"Women like you?"

"Yes, women like me."

"And who else?"

She didn't seem to understand his question at first.

"What other women were there?"

"That depended on their desires."

"Whose desires?"

"The desires of the guests. The men."

"And what might they be?"

"Some wanted *me* to be there."

"I understood that. Who else?"

"You won't get any names."

"Who were they?"

"Young girls, some very young, blond, brown, black. Older ones sometimes, some of them very hefty. It varied."

"You knew them?"

"Not always. Not often."

"How did he get hold of them?"

She put out her cigarette and lit a new one before she answered. She didn't release his gaze even when she was stubbing it out.

"How does a person like Åke Liljegren get whatever he wants? He had unlimited money. He had helpers. He had contacts. He could fly in a girl from Florida to attend his party. She probably had no idea she was going all the way to Sweden. Not to mention Helsingborg."

"You say he had helpers. Who were they?"

"His chauffeurs. His assistant. He often had a hired butler with him. English, of course. But they varied."

"What was his name?"

"No names."

"We'll find out about them anyway."

"You probably will. But that doesn't mean the names are going to come from me."

"What would happen if you gave me some names?"

She seemed utterly unmoved when she replied.

"Then I might be killed. Maybe not with my head in an oven, but in an equally unpleasant manner, I'm sure."

Wallander thought for a moment before he continued. He knew that he'd never get any names out of Elisabeth Carlén.

"How many of his guests were public figures?"

"A lot of them."

"Politicians?"

"Yes."

"Former justice minister Gustaf Wetterstedt?"

"I said you wouldn't get any names."

Suddenly he realized that she was sending him a message. Her words had a subtext. She knew who Gustaf Wetterstedt was. But he had never been at any of the parties.

"Businessmen?"

"Yes."

"Arne Carlman, the art dealer?"

"Did he have almost the same name as me?"

"Yes."

"You won't get any names. I'll say it one last time. Or I'll get up and leave."

Not him either, thought Wallander. Her signals were very clear.

"Artists? Celebrities?"

"Once in a while. But seldom. I don't think Åke trusted them. Probably with good reason."

"You talked about young girls. Brown girls. Did you mean brunettes, or girls with brown skin?"

"Brown skin."

"Do you remember ever meeting a girl named Dolores María?" ▪

"No."

"A girl from the Dominican Republic?"

"I don't even know where that is."

"Do you remember a girl named Louise Fredman? Seventeen, maybe younger. Blonde."

"No."

Wallander shifted the conversation in another direction. So far she still seemed willing to continue.

"So the parties were wild."

"Yes, they were."

"Tell me about it."

"Do you want details?"

"Please."

"Descriptions of naked bodies?"

"Not necessarily."

"They were orgies. You can imagine the rest."

"Can I?" said Wallander. "I'm not so sure."

"If I undressed and lay down on your desk it would be completely unexpected," she said. "Something like that."

"Unexpected events?"

"That's what happens when insatiable people get together, isn't it?"

"Insatiable men?"

"Exactly."

Wallander made a hasty outline in his head. He was still just scraping the surface.

"I've got a proposal," he said. "And another question."

"I'm still sitting here."

"My proposal is that you give me the opportunity to meet you one more time. Soon, within a few days."

She nodded her assent. Wallander got an unpleasant feeling that he was entering into some sort of agreement.

"My question is simple," he said. "You were speaking of Liljegren's chauffeurs. And his ever-changing personal butlers. But you said that he had an assistant. Not plural. Is that correct?"

He saw a faint change in her face. She knew she had said too much without mentioning any names.

"This conversation will only be in my memoirs," said Wallander. "Did I hear correctly or not?"

"You heard wrong," she said. "Of course he had more than one assistant."

So, I was right, thought Wallander.

"That'll be all for this time, then," he said, getting up.

"I'll leave when I finish my cigarette," she said. For the first time in the whole conversation she released him from her gaze.

Wallander opened the door to the corridor. Sjösten was sitting on a chair reading a boating magazine. Wallander nodded. She put out her cigarette, stood up, and shook his hand. When Sjösten had shown her out and returned, Wallander was standing by the window, watching the woman get into her car.

"Did it go well?" asked Sjösten.

"Maybe," said Wallander. "She agreed to meet me again."

"What did she say?"

"Nothing, actually."

"And you think that was good?"

"It was what she didn't know that interested me," said Wallander. "I want 24-hour surveillance of Liljegren's house. I also want you to put a tail on Elisabeth Carlén. Sooner or later somebody will show up who we'll have to talk to."

"That sounds like quite an inadequate reason for surveillance," said Sjösten.

"I'll make that decision," said Wallander kindly. "I was unanimously chosen to be leader of this investigation."

"I'm glad it wasn't me," replied Sjösten. "Are you staying overnight?"

"No, I'll drive home."

They went down the steps to the ground floor.

"Did you read about the girl who burned herself to death in a rapeseed field?" asked Wallander just before they said goodbye.

"I read about it. Terrible story."

"She hitchhiked from Helsingborg," Wallander went on. "And she was scared.

I'm just wondering whether she might have had something to do with this. Although it seems highly improbable."

"There were rumors about Liljegren and the trade in girls," said Sjösten. "Among a thousand other rumors."

Wallander looked at him intently.

"Trade in girls?"

"There were rumors that Sweden was being used as a transit country for poor girls from South America, on their way to brothels in southern Europe, and to the former Eastern bloc countries. We've actually found a couple of girls who have managed to escape. But we never got hold of the ones running this business. And we haven't been able to prove anything either. But we know what we know."

Wallander stared at Sjösten.

"And you waited until now to tell me this?"

Sjösten shook his head, baffled.

"You never asked me before now."

Wallander stood motionless. The girl who burned to death had started running through his head again.

"I changed my mind," he said. "I'm spending the night."

It was five o'clock on Wednesday, the 6th of July.

They took the elevator back up to Sjösten's office.

Chapter Thirty-three

J ust after seven on that lovely summer evening Wallander and Sjösten took the ferry over to Helsingør on the Danish side and ate dinner at a restaurant Sjösten knew. As if by tacit agreement, he entertained Wallander during dinner with stories about the boat he was restoring, about his numerous marriages and his even more numerous children. Not until they were having coffee did they begin talking about the investigation again. Wallander listened gratefully to Sjösten, who was a charming storyteller. He was very tired. After the excellent dinner he was feeling drowsy. But his mind was rested. Sjösten had drunk a few shots of aquavit with beer, while Wallander had stuck with mineral water.

When the coffee came they exchanged roles. Sjösten listened while Wallander talked. He went over everything that had happened. For the first time he let the girl who burned herself to death in the rapeseed field serve as the prelude to the series of murders. He talked to Sjösten in a way that forced him to clarify things to himself as well. It had seemed quite improbable to him before that Dolores María Santana's death might be connected to what happened afterwards. But now he admitted that it was a faulty conclusion, or presumably no conclusion at all, just a sign of irresponsible and sloppy thinking. Sjösten was an attentive listener who instantly pounced on him when he was being vague.

Afterwards he would recall that evening in Helsingør as the point when the entire investigation sloughed off its skin. The pattern he thought he had discovered as he sat on the Sea Rescue bench was confirmed. Gaps were filled in, holes were sealed up; questions found their answers, or at least were formulated more clearly and arranged in a pattern. He marched back and forth through the landscape of the case and thought for the first time that he had an overall view. But the whole time he also had a nagging feeling of guilt that he should have seen everything he now saw much sooner, that he had been wandering doggedly down sidetracks instead of realizing that he ought to go in an altogether different direction. Although he avoided mentioning it to

Sjösten, there was one question always on his mind. Could any of the murders have been prevented? Or at least the last one—if it *was* the last one—the murder of Liljegren. He couldn't answer that question, he could only ask it. And he knew that it would haunt him for a very long time; maybe he would never get an answer that made sense, that he could live with.

The only problem that really remained was that they had no perpetrator. Nor were there any solid clues that led in a specific direction. They had no suspect, not even a group of people among whom they could cast their net and hope to bring in the one they were looking for.

Earlier in the day, when Elisabeth Carlén had left them and Sjösten stood on the steps of the police station and mentioned in passing that Sweden, and especially Helsingborg, was suspected of serving as a transit point for the trade in girls from South America who were destined for southern European brothels, Wallander's reaction had been instantaneous. They returned to Sjösten's office, where the smell of Elisabeth Carlén's cigarettes still lingered even though the window was open. Sjösten was surprised at Wallander's sudden burst of energy. Without thinking, Wallander had sat down in Sjösten's chair, so he had to take the visitor's chair in his own office. After Wallander told him all he knew about Dolores María Santana, and that she was apparently fleeing when she hitchhiked from Helsingborg, Sjösten had begun to understand Wallander's interest.

"A black car came once a week to Gustaf Wetterstedt's house," said Wallander. "By chance the housekeeper noticed it. She was here and, as you already know, thought she almost recognized the car in Liljegren's garage. What conceivable conclusion do you draw from that?"

"None at all," said Sjösten. "There are plenty of black Mercedes with tinted windows."

"Put it together with the rumors surrounding Liljegren. The rumor of trading in girls. Is there anything that would prevent him from having parties somewhere else besides his house? Why couldn't he also run a home delivery service?"

"Nothing at all to prevent that," said Sjösten. "But there doesn't seem to be any basis for it."

"I want to know whether that car left Liljegren's house on Thursdays," said Wallander. "And came back on Fridays."

"How can we find that out?"

"There are neighbors who may have seen something. Who drove the car? There seems to be such a vacuum around Liljegren. He had personal employees. He had an assistant. Where are all these people?"

"We're working on that," said Sjösten.

"Let's set our priorities," said Wallander. "The motorcycle is important. Liljegren's assistant is too. And the car on Thursdays. Start with that. Assign all the personnel you have to check this out."

Sjösten left the room to organize the investigative work. When he came back he told Wallander that the surveillance of Elisabeth Carlén had already begun.

"What's she doing?" asked Wallander.

"She's in her apartment," said Sjösten. "Alone."

Wallander called Ystad and talked to Per Åkeson.

"I don't think I can avoid having a talk with Louise Fredman," he said.

"You'll have to present some pretty strong investigative reasons," said Åkeson. "Or I can't help you."

"I know it might be important."

"It has to be something concrete, Kurt."

"There's always a way around all this bureaucratic crap."

"What is it you think she can tell you?"

"Whether she ever had the soles of her feet cut with a knife, for instance."

"Good Lord. Why would that have happened to her?"

Wallander didn't feel like telling him.

"Can't her mother give me permission?" he asked. "Fredman's widow?"

"That's just what I was wondering," said Åkeson. "That's the way we'll have to proceed."

"Then I'll drive to Malmö tomorrow," said Wallander. "Do I need any kind of papers from you?"

"Not if she gives you her permission," said Åkeson. "But you can't pressure her."

"Am I in the habit of threatening people?" asked Wallander, surprised. "I didn't know that."

"I'm just telling you how you have to proceed. That's all."

It was after the conversation with Åkeson that Sjösten had suggested they take a ferry across to Denmark and have dinner, so they would have time to talk in peace and quiet. Wallander had nothing against the idea. It was still too early to call Baiba. Or maybe not too early to call, but it was certainly too early for him. It occurred to him that Sjösten, with all his marital experience, might be able to give him some advice on how to explain to Baiba, who was looking forward to their trip, that they would have to postpone it indefinitely. They had taken the ferry across the Sound, with Wallander wishing the journey was longer. Then they ate dinner, which Sjösten insisted on buying. It was about nine-thirty when they strolled through Helsingør to take the ferry back. Sjösten stopped at a flight of stairs leading up to a building entrance.

"In here lives a man who appreciates Swedes," he said, smiling.

Wallander read on a brass plate that a doctor had his practice here.

"He writes prescriptions for diet drugs that are banned in Sweden," said Sjösten. "There's a long line of overweight Swedes here every day."

"Where do the Danes go?" asked Wallander as they walked toward the ferry terminal.

Sjösten didn't know.

They were on their way up the stairs to the departure hall when Sjösten's cell phone rang. Sjösten kept walking as he listened.

"One of my colleagues named Larsson has found what seems to be a real gold mine," said Sjösten when he put away his phone. "A man who lives near Liljegren's house saw a number of things."

"What did he see?"

"Black cars, motorcycles. We'll talk to him tomorrow."

"We'll talk to him tonight," said Wallander. "It'll only be ten by the time we get back to Helsingborg."

Sjösten nodded without replying. Then he called the police station back and asked Larsson to meet them at the terminal.

The young police officer waiting for them on the other side reminded Wallander of Martinsson. They got into his car and drove up to Tågaborg. On the way he told them what to expect. Wallander noticed an HIF banner from the local soccer team hanging from his rearview mirror.

"His name is Lennart Heineman, and he's a retired embassy counselor," said Larsson in a Skåne accent so thick that Wallander had to strain to understand him. "He's almost eighty years old. But quite sharp. His wife is still alive, but she seems to be away. Heineman's yard is just across from the main entrance to Liljegren's grounds. He observed and remembered a number of things."

"Does he know we're coming?" asked Sjösten.

"I called," said Larsson. "He said it was fine, since he seldom goes to bed before three in the morning. He claimed that he was writing a critical examination of the Swedish foreign ministry's administration. Whatever that may involve."

Wallander remembered with distaste an officious woman from the foreign ministry who had visited them in Ystad several years before, in conjunction with the investigation that led him to go to Latvia and meet Baiba. He tried to remember her name without success. It had something to do with roses. He pushed the thought aside as they pulled up outside Heineman's house. Across the street a police car was parked outside Liljegren's villa. A tall man with short white hair came walking toward them on the other side of the gate. He had a powerful handshake, and Wallander trusted him instantly. The large villa he ushered them into was built in the same period as Liljegren's, yet the differences were great. The house had an air of vitality about it, a reflection of the energetic old man who lived there. He asked them to have a seat and whether he might offer them something to drink. They all declined. Wallander got the feeling he was used to playing host and receiving people he had never met before.

"Terrible things going on," said Heineman after he sat down.

Sjösten gave Wallander an almost imperceptible nod to lead the interview.

"That's why we couldn't postpone this conversation until tomorrow," said Wallander.

"Why postpone it?" said Heineman. "I've never understood why Swedes go to bed so early at night. The continental habit of taking a siesta is much healthier. If I'd gone to bed early I would have been dead long ago."

Wallander pondered for a moment Heineman's strong criticism of Swedish bedtime hours.

"We're interested in any observations you may have made," he said, "about the traffic going in and out of Liljegren's villa. But there are some questions that interest us more than others. Let's start by talking about Liljegren's black Mercedes."

"He must have had at least two," said Heineman.

Wallander was surprised at the answer. He hadn't imagined more than one car, even though Liljegren's big garage could have held two or three.

"What makes you think he had more than one car?"

"I don't just think so," said Heineman, "I know it. Two cars sometimes left the house at the same time. Or came back at the same time. When Liljegren was away the cars remained here. From my upper floor I can see part of his grounds. There were two cars over there."

That means that one is missing, thought Wallander. Where is it now?

Sjösten had pulled out a notebook. Wallander saw that he was taking notes.

"I'd like to ask about Thursdays," Wallander went on. "Can you recall whether one or perhaps both cars regularly left Liljegren's villa late in the afternoon or evening on Thursdays? And whether they returned during the night or in the morning the next day?"

"I'm not much for remembering dates," said Heineman. "But it's true that one of the cars used to leave the villa in the evening. And return the next morning."

"It's very important we ascertain it was Thursdays," said Wallander.

"My wife and I have never held to the idiotic Swedish dining tradition of eating pea soup on Thursdays," said Heineman.

Wallander waited while Heineman tried to remember. Larsson sat looking at the ceiling, and Sjösten was tapping his note pad lightly on one knee.

"It's possible," said Heineman all of a sudden. "Perhaps I can piece together an answer. I recall definitely that my wife's sister was here on one occasion last year when the car left on one of its regular trips. Why I'm so certain of this I can't tell you. But I'm quite positive. She lives in Bonn and doesn't visit very often. That's why I noticed it."

"Why do you think it was a Thursday?" asked Wallander. "Did you write it down on the calendar?"

"I've never had much use for calendars," said Heineman with distaste. "During all my years at the foreign ministry I never wrote down a single meeting. But during forty years of service I never missed one either, unlike the people who did nothing but write notes in their calendars."

"Why Thursday?" Wallander repeated.

"I don't know whether it was a Thursday," said Heineman. "But it was my wife's sister's name day. I know that for sure. Her name is Frida."

"What month?" asked Wallander.

"February or March."

Wallander patted his jacket pocket. His pocket calendar didn't have the previous year in it. Sjösten also shook his head. Larsson had no pocket almanac at all.

"Might there be an old calendar somewhere in the house?" asked Wallander.

"It's possible that one of the grandchildren's Christmas calendars is still up in the attic," said Heineman. "My wife has the bad habit of saving a lot of old junk. I'm always throwing things out. Also a trait I picked up at the FM. The first day of the month I ruthlessly threw out everything that didn't need to be saved from the month before. My rule was, better to throw out too much than too little. I never missed a thing I had discarded."

Wallander nodded to Larsson.

"Call and find out what day is the name day for Frida," he said. "And what day of the week it was in 1993."

"Who would know that?" asked Larsson.

"Damn it," said Sjösten. "Call the station. You have precisely five minutes to come back with the answer."

"There's a telephone in the entryway," said Heineman.

Larsson vanished.

"I must say that I appreciate when clear orders are given," said Heineman contentedly. "That ability also seems to have been lost in recent years."

Wallander had a hard time proceeding while they waited for the answer. To kill time, Sjösten asked where Heineman had been stationed abroad. It turned out that he had been posted to a large number of missions.

"It got better toward the end," he said. "But back when I started my career, the people who were sent out to represent our country on faraway continents were often of a deplorably low caliber."

When Larsson returned, almost ten minutes had passed. He had made a note on a piece of paper he was holding.

"Frida has her name day on February 17th," he said. "In 1993 it fell on a Thursday."

"Just as I thought," said Wallander.

Police work was basically all a matter of refusing to give up until a crucial detail was confirmed on a piece of paper, he thought.

After this, it seemed better to wait with most of the other questions he had planned to ask Heineman. For appearances' sake he asked a few more questions: whether Heineman had observed anything related to what Wallander vaguely termed "possible traffic in girls."

"There were parties," Heineman said stiffly. "From the top floor of our house, seeing into some of the rooms was unavoidable. Of course there were women involved."

"Did you ever meet Åke Liljegren?"

"Yes," replied Heineman, "I met him once in Madrid. It was during one of my last years as an active member of the FM. He had requested help with certain introductions to some large Spanish construction companies. We knew quite well who Liljegren was, of course. His dummy corporation scam was in full swing. We treated him as politely as we could. But he was not a pleasant man to deal with."

"Why not?"

Heineman thought for a moment before he answered.

"To put it bluntly, he was disagreeable. He regarded the world around him with open and unqualified contempt."

Wallander indicated that he had no intention of prolonging the interview.

"My colleagues will be contacting you again," he said, getting to his feet.

Heineman followed them out to the gate. The police car outside Liljegren's villa was still there. The house was dark. Wallander went across the street after he said goodbye to Heineman. One of the officers in the car got out and saluted. Wallander raised his hand and gave a slight wave in response to the exaggerated greeting.

"Anything going on?" he asked.

"It's calm here. A few rubberneckers stopped by. That's about it."

They drove back to the police station and Larsson dropped them off before continuing home to get some sleep. While Wallander made a few phone calls, Sjösten went back to his boating magazine. Wallander started by calling Hansson, who told him that Ludwigsson and Hamrén from the NCB had arrived. He had put them up at the Hotel Sekelgården.

"They seem to be good men," said Hansson. "Not at all as stuck-up as I feared."

"Why would they have been stuck-up?"

"Stockholmers," said Hansson. "You know how they are. Don't you remember that prosecutor who filled in for Per Åkeson? What was her name? Bodin?"

"Brolin," said Wallander. "But I don't remember her."

Wallander remembered quite well. He could feel the embarrassment creeping over his body when he thought about the time he totally lost control and threw himself on her when he was drunk. It was one of the things he was most ashamed of in his whole life. And it didn't help that Anette Brolin had later spent a night with him in Copenhagen under considerably more pleasant circumstances.

"They're going to start working on Sturup Airport tomorrow," said Hansson.

Wallander gave him a brief rundown of what had happened at Heineman's house.

"In other words, it means we've got a break," said Hansson. "So you think that Liljegren sent a prostitute once a week to Wetterstedt in Ystad?"

"I do."

"Could it have been going on with Carlman too?"

"Maybe not in the same way. But I should think that Carlman's and Liljegren's circles must have overlapped. As yet we don't know where."

"And Björn Fredman?"

"He's still the big exception. He doesn't fit in anywhere. Least of all in Liljegren's circles. Unless he was one of his enforcers. I think I'll go back to Malmö tomorrow and talk to his family again. And I especially want to meet his daughter, who's in the hospital."

"Åkeson told me about your conversation. You realize that the encounter might turn out as badly as your meeting with Erika Carlman, don't you?"

"Of course I do."

"I'll get hold of Höglund and Svedberg tonight," said Hansson. "You've finally turned up some good news, anyway."

"Don't forget Ludwigsson and Hamrén," said Wallander. "They're also part of the team, starting now."

Wallander hung up. Sjösten had gone to get some coffee. Wallander dialed his own number in Ystad. To his surprise Linda answered at once.

"I just got home," she said. "Where are you?"

"In Helsingborg. I'm staying here overnight."

"Has something happened?"

"We went over to Helsingør and had dinner."

"That's not what I meant."

"We're working."

"We are too," said Linda. "We rehearsed the whole thing again tonight. We had an audience too."

"Who?"

"A boy who asked if he could watch. He was standing outside on the street and said he had heard we were working on a play. We let him watch. I think the people at the hot dog stand told him about it."

"So it wasn't anyone you know?"

"He was just a tourist here in town. He walked home with me afterwards."

Wallander felt a pang of jealousy.

"Is he in the apartment now?"

"He walked me home to Mariagatan. It takes about five minutes, if you walk slow. Then he went home."

"I was just wondering."

"He had a funny name. He said it was Hoover. But he was very nice. I think he liked what we were doing. He said he'd come back tomorrow if he had time."

"I'm sure he will," said Wallander.

Sjösten came in with two plastic coffee cups. Wallander asked him for his home number, which he gave to Linda.

"My daughter," he said after he hung up. "Unlike you, I only have one child.

She's going to Visby tomorrow to take a theater course."

"Kids tend to give life a glimmer of meaning," said Sjösten, handing the coffee cup to Wallander.

They went over the conversation with Lennart Heineman one more time. Wallander could tell that Sjösten was quite dubious that Wetterstedt's access to prostitutes through Liljegren might mean they had come a small step closer to closing in on the killer.

"Tomorrow I want you to find all the material about this traffic in girls that mentions Helsingborg being used as a way station. Why here, anyway? How did they get here? There must be an explanation. Besides, this vacuum surrounding Liljegren is unbelievable. I don't get it."

"That stuff about the girls is mostly speculation," said Sjösten. "We've never done an investigation of it. We simply haven't had reason to. One time Birgersson brought it up with one of the prosecutors, but he instantly rejected an investigation and said we had more important things to do. He was right, of course."

"I still want you to check it out," said Wallander. "Do a summary for me tomorrow. Fax it to me in Ystad as soon as you can."

It was almost eleven-thirty by the time they drove out to Sjösten's apartment. Wallander knew he had to call Baiba. There was no escaping it. Soon it would be Thursday, and she was already packing. He could no longer postpone telling her the news.

"I have to make a phone call to Latvia," he said. "Just a couple of minutes."

Sjösten showed him where the phone was. Wallander waited until Sjösten had gone into the bathroom before he picked it up. He dialed the number. When it rang the first time he hung up. He had no idea what to say. He didn't dare tell her. He thought he should wait until tomorrow night and then make up a story: that the whole thing had come up suddenly and now he wanted her to come to Ystad instead.

He figured this was the best solution. At least for himself.

They talked for another half hour over a glass of whisky. Sjösten made a phone call to check that Elisabeth Carlén was still under surveillance.

"She's asleep," he said. "Maybe we ought to go to bed too."

With the sheets Sjösten gave him Wallander made up a bed for himself in a room with children's drawings on the walls. He turned off the light and fell asleep almost instantly.

When he woke up he was soaked with sweat. He must have had a nightmare, although he couldn't remember a thing. He saw by his watch that it was two-thirty. He had only slept for two hours. He wondered why he woke up, and turned over on his side to go back to sleep. But suddenly he was wide awake. Where the feeling came from he had no idea. There was no reason for it. But he was gripped with panic.

He had left Linda alone in Ystad. She shouldn't be staying there alone. He had to go home.

Without another thought he got up, put on his clothes, and quickly scribbled a note to Sjösten. At quarter to three he was in his car and on the way out of town. He thought he ought to call her. But what would he say? She'd just be frightened. He drove through the light summer night. He didn't understand where the panic had come from. But it was definitely there, and it wouldn't let him go.

Just before four o'clock he parked on Mariagatan. When he got to his apartment he carefully unlocked the door. The terror of something unknown had not abated. Not until he carefully pushed open her door, which was ajar, saw her head on the pillow and heard her breathing, did he calm down again.

He sat down on the sofa. The fear had been replaced by embarrassment. He shook his head at himself, then wrote a note to her, which he put on the coffee table, saying that his plans changed and that he had come home during the night. Before he got into bed he set the alarm clock for five. He knew that Sjösten got up quite early to spend some morning hours working on his boat. He didn't know how he was going to explain his sudden departure in the middle of the night.

He lay in bed and wondered why that feeling of panic had seized him. But he couldn't find an answer.

It took a long time before he fell asleep.

Chapter Thirty-four

When the doorbell rang he knew at once that it couldn't be anyone but Baiba. Strangely enough, it didn't make him nervous at all, even though he was going to have a hard time explaining to her why he hadn't told her that their trip had to be postponed. But when he gave a start and sat up in bed, of course she wasn't there. It was only the alarm clock ringing, with the hands positioned like a gaping maw at three minutes past five. After the first brief confusion passed, he put his hand over the alarm button and then sat motionless in the silence. Reality slowly came back to him. The town was still quiet. Few sounds other than the trilling of birds penetrated his room and his consciousness. He couldn't even remember whether he had dreamed about Baiba or not. The sudden flight from the child's room in Sjösten's apartment now seemed like an inconceivably embarrassing departure from his normal ability to behave rationally.

With a loud yawn he got up and went into the kitchen. Linda was asleep. On the kitchen table he discovered a note from her. I communicate with my daughter through an endless series of notes, he thought. Whenever she makes one of her occasional stops in Ystad. He read over what she had written and realized that the dream about Baiba, waking up and believing that she was standing outside his door, had contained a warning. When he came home the night before he hadn't seen Linda's note. Now he saw that Baiba had called and asked Linda to tell her father to call right away. He sensed her annoyance in Linda's account. It was hardly noticeable, but it was there.

He couldn't call her, not now. He'd call her late tonight, or maybe tomorrow. Or should he have Martinsson do it? He could give her the unfortunate news that the man she was intending to go to Skagen with, the man she assumed would be standing at Kastrup Airport in two days to meet her, was at the moment embroiled in a manhunt for a maniac who smashed axes through the skulls of his fellow human beings and then cut off their scalps. What he might tell Martinsson to say was true, and yet not true. It was a lie with a couple of phony wings pasted on; it looked like the truth, and it made sense. But it could never explain or defend the fact that he was too chicken to do the right thing and call Baiba himself.

At five-thirty he picked up the phone, not to call Baiba, but Sjösten in Helsingborg, to explain why he had left during the night. What could he possibly say? The truth was one option. His sudden concern for his daughter, a concern all parents feel without being able to explain where the sudden panic comes from. But when Sjösten answered he said something totally different, that he had forgotten about a meeting he had planned with his father for early that morning. It was something Sjösten could never check up on should he feel so inclined. And something that could never be revealed by accident, since Sjösten and his father would never cross paths. They agreed to talk later in the day, after Wallander had been to Malmö.

Afterwards everything seemed much easier. It wasn't the first time in his life he had started his day with a bunch of white lies, evasions, and self-deceptions. He took a shower, had some coffee, wrote a new note to Linda, and left the apartment just after six-thirty. Everything was quiet at the police station when he arrived. It was during this early, lonely hour, when the weary graveyard shift was on its way home and it was still too early for the daytime staff, that Wallander liked to walk down the corridor to his office. Life took on quite a special meaning in this early morning solitude. He never understood why this was so. But he could remember the feeling from deep down in his own personal past, maybe as far back as twenty years.

Rydberg, his old friend and mentor, had been the same way. *Everyone has small but extremely personal sacred moments,* Rydberg had told him once, on one of the few occasions when they had sat in either his or Wallander's office and split a small bottle of whisky behind locked doors. No alcohol was permitted in the police station. But sometimes they had occasion to celebrate something. Or grieve over something, for that matter. Wallander couldn't remember the reason. But he sorely missed those brief and strangely philosophical times with Rydberg. They had been moments of friendship, of utterly irreplaceable intimacy.

Wallander sat down at his desk and leafed quickly through a stack of messages. In a memo from somewhere he saw that Dolores María Santana's body had been released for burial and now rested in a grave in the same cemetery as Rydberg. This brought him back to the investigation; he rolled up his sleeves as though going out in the world to fight, and then skimmed as fast as he could through the copies of investigative material his colleagues had prepared. There were papers from Nyberg, various lab reports on which Nyberg had scrawled question marks and comments, and charts of the tips from the public that had come in. Tyrén must be an extraordinarily zealous young man, Wallander thought, without being able to decide whether that meant Tyrén would be a good cop out in the field in the future, or whether he was already showing signs that he belonged somewhere in the hunting grounds of the bureaucracy. Wallander read quickly but attentively. Nothing of value escaped him. The most important thing seemed to be that they had quickly established that Björn Fredman had indeed been murdered on the dock below the side road to Charlottenlund.

He shoved the stacks of papers aside and leaned back pensively in his chair. What do these men have in common? he thought. Fredman doesn't fit in the picture. But he belongs to this group just the same. A former justice minister, an art dealer, an auditor, and a petty thief. They're all murdered by the same perpetrator, who also takes their scalps. Wetterstedt, the first, is barely hidden, just pushed out of sight. Carlman, the second, is killed in the midst of a summertime party in his own arbor. Björn Fredman is kidnapped, taken to a lonely dock and then dumped in the middle of Ystad, as if being put on display. He lies in a drainage pit with a tarp over his head, like a statue waiting to be unveiled. Finally, the perpetrator moves to Helsingborg and kills Åke Liljegren. Almost immediately we pin down a connection between Wetterstedt and Liljegren. Now we have to find the links between the others. After we know exactly what connected them, we might also ask: Who might have had reason to kill them? And why the scalps? Who is the lone warrior?

Wallander sat for a long time thinking about Björn Fredman and Åke Liljegren. There was a similarity there. The kidnapping and acid in the eyes in Fredman's case, and Liljegren's head in the oven. That was something extra. For the perpetrator it hadn't been enough to kill them and take their scalps. Why? He took another step. The water got deeper around him. The bottom was slippery. Easy to lose his footing. There was a difference between Fredman and Liljegren, a very clear one. Björn Fredman had hydrochloric acid poured into his eyes while he was alive. Liljegren was dead before he was stuck in the oven. Wallander tried to imagine the perpetrator again. Thin, in good condition, barefoot, insane. If he hunts evil men, Fredman must have been the worst. Then Liljegren. Carlman and Wetterstedt in about the same category.

Wallander got up and went to the window. There was something about the sequence that bothered him. Fredman was the third. Why not the first? Or the last—at least so far? The root of evil, the first or the last to be hauled up, by a perpetrator who was insane but cautious and well-organized. The dock must have been chosen because it was handy. *How many docks did he look at before he chose that one?* Is this a man who is always near the sea? A well-behaved man; a fisherman, or someone in the Coast Guard? Or why not a member of the Sea Rescue Service, which has the best bench in town if you want to sit and think in peace? And someone who also managed to drive Fredman away, in his own van. Why did he go to all that trouble? Because it was his only way to get to him? They met somewhere. They knew each other. Peter Hjelm had been quite clear. Fredman traveled a lot and always had plenty of money afterwards. It was rumored that he was an enforcer. But Wallander only knew about parts of

Fredman's life. The rest was unknown, and it was up to the police to try and bring it to light.

Wallander sat down in his chair again. The sequence didn't make sense. What could the explanation be? He went to get some coffee. Svedberg and Höglund had arrived. Svedberg had changed to a new cap. His cheeks were a blotchy red. Höglund was tanner, and Wallander was paler. Just then Hansson arrived with Mats Ekholm right behind him. Even Ekholm had managed to get a tan. Hansson's eyes were bloodshot with fatigue. He looked at Wallander with astonishment, and at the same time he seemed to be searching for some misunderstanding. Hadn't Wallander said he'd be in Helsingborg? It wasn't even seven-thirty yet. Had something happened to make him come back to Ystad early? Wallander knew what Hansson was thinking, and shook his head almost imperceptibly. Everything was all right, no one had misunderstood anything—at the same time no one could have fully understood either. They hadn't planned to have a meeting of the investigative team. Ludwigsson and Hamrén had already driven out to Sturup, Höglund was planning to join them, while Svedberg and Hansson were busy with follow-up work on Wetterstedt and Carlman. Someone stuck in his head and said that Wallander had a phone call from Helsingborg. Wallander took the call on the phone next to the coffee machine. It was Sjösten, who told him that Elisabeth Carlén was still sleeping. No one had visited her, and no one except some curiousity-seekers had been seen near Liljegren's villa.

"Did Åke Liljegren have any family?" asked Martinsson, almost angrily, as if Liljegren had behaved highly inappropriately by not marrying.

"He left behind only a few grieving, plundered corporations," said Svedberg.

"They're working on Liljegren in Helsingborg," said Wallander. "We'll just have to wait."

Wallander knew that Hansson had been meticulous about passing on the information. All of them agreed that Liljegren must have been supplying women to Wetterstedt at regular intervals.

"In other words, he's living up to the old rumor about him," said Svedberg.

"We have to find a similar link to Carlman," Wallander went on. "It's there, I know it is. Forget about Wetterstedt for the time being. It's more important to concentrate on Carlman."

Everyone was in a hurry. The link that had been established was like a shot in the arm for the investigative team. Wallander took Ekholm to his office. He told him about the ideas he had had earlier that morning. Ekholm was an attentive listener, as always.

"The hydrochloric acid and the oven," said Wallander. "I'm trying to interpret the killer's language. He talks to himself and he talks to his victims. What is he actually saying?"

"Your idea about the sequence is interesting," said Ekholm. "Psychopathic killers often have an element of pedantry in their bloody handiwork. Something may have happened to upset his plans."

"Like what?"

"He's the only one who can answer that."

"Still, we have to try."

Ekholm didn't answer. Wallander got the feeling that he didn't have a lot to say at the moment.

"Let's number them," said Wallander. "Wetterstedt is number one. What do we see if we rearrange them?"

"Fredman first or last," said Ekholm. "Liljegren just before or after, depending on which variant is correct. Wetterstedt and Carlman in positions which tie them to the others."

"Can we assume that he's finished?" asked Wallander.

"I have no idea," said Ekholm. "He's following his own agenda."

"What do your computers say? What combinations have they managed to come up with?"

"Not a thing, actually." Ekholm seemed surprised by his own answer.

"How do you interpret that?" asked Wallander.

"We're dealing with a serial killer who differs from his predecessors in crucial ways."

"And what does that mean?"

"That he'll provide us with totally new data. If we catch him."

"We've got to," said Wallander, noticing how unconvincing he sounded.

He got up and they both left the room.

"Behavioral scientists at both the FBI and Scotland Yard have been in touch with us," said Ekholm. "They're following our work with great interest."

"Have they got any suggestions? We'll take all the help we can get."

"I'm supposed to let them know if anything comes in."

They parted at the reception desk. Wallander took a moment to exchange a few words with Ebba, who no longer had the cast on her wrist. Then he drove straight to Sturup. He found Ludwigsson and Hamrén in the office of the airport police. With great distaste, Wallander caught sight of a young policeman who had fainted right in front of him the year before when they were arresting a man trying to flee the country. But he shook his hand and tried to pretend that he was sorry about what had happened.

Wallander realized he had met Ludwigsson before, during a visit to Stockholm. He was a large, powerful man who no doubt suffered from high blood pressure. His face was red, but not from the sun. Hamrén was his diametrical opposite, small and wiry, with thick glasses. Wallander greeted them a little brusquely and asked how it was going.

"There seems to be a lot of rivalry between the different taxi companies out here," Ludwigsson began. "Just like at Arlanda. So far we haven't managed to pin down all the options he may have had for leaving the airport during the hours in question. And nobody noticed a motorcycle. But we've just gotten started."

Wallander had a cup of coffee and answered a number of questions the two NCB men had. Then he left them and drove on to Malmö. It was ten o'clock when he parked outside the building in Rosengård. It was very hot. Still no wind. He took the elevator up to the fifth floor and rang the doorbell. This time it wasn't the son but Björn Fredman's widow who opened the door. Wallander noticed at once that she smelled of wine. At her feet cowering close by was a little boy three or four years old. He seemed extremely shy. Or afraid, rather. When Wallander bent down toward him he acted terrified. At the same moment a fleeting memory whirled through Wallander's mind. He couldn't catch it, but filed the thought in his memory. It was something that had happened before, or something someone had said—something important had again been imprinted on his subconscious.

She asked him to come in. The boy clung to her legs. Her hair wasn't combed and she wore no makeup. The blanket on the sofa told him she had spent the night there. They sat down, Wallander in the same chair for the third time. Then Stefan, the older son, came in. His eyes were just as wary as the last time Wallander had been there. He came forward and shook hands and said good day with the same grown-up manners. He sat down next to his mother on the sofa. Everything was repeating itself. The only difference was the presence of the younger brother, who sat curled up on his mother's lap. Something didn't seem quite right about him. His eyes never left Wallander.

"I came about Louise," said Wallander. "I know it's hard to talk about a family member who's in a psychiatric hospital. But it's necessary."

"Why can't she be left in peace?" asked the woman. Her voice sounded tormented and unsure, as if from the start she doubted her ability to defend her daughter.

Instantly Wallander felt depressed. He would have liked to avoid this conversation more than anything. He was also unsure of where he was going with it.

"Of course she'll be left in peace," he said. "But it's part of the sad duty of the police to gather all conceivable information so that we can solve a brutal crime."

"She hadn't seen her father in many years," she said. "There's nothing important she can tell you."

Suddenly an idea occurred to him.

"Does Louise know that her father is dead?"

"Why should she?"

"It's not altogether unreasonable, is it?"

Wallander saw that the woman on the sofa was about to break down. The distaste inside him increased with each question and each answer. Without wanting to, he had put her under a pressure she could hardly endure. The boy next to her said nothing.

"First of all, you have to understand that Louise no longer has any relationship to reality," the woman said in a voice that was so faint that Wallander had to lean forward to hear her. "Louise has left everything behind. She's living in her own world. She doesn't speak, she doesn't listen. She's pretending that she doesn't exist."

Wallander thought carefully before he continued.

"Even so, it could be important for the police to know why she became ill. I actually came here to ask for your permission to meet with her. Speak to her. Now I realize that it may not be appropriate. But then you'll have to answer my questions instead."

"I don't know what to tell you," she said. "She got sick. It came out of nowhere."

"She was found in Pildamm Park," said Wallander.

Both the son and the mother stiffened. Even the little boy on her lap seemed to react, affected by the others.

"How do you know that?" she asked.

"There's a report on how and when she was taken to the hospital," said Wallander. "But that's all I know. Everything concerning her illness is confidential between her and her doctor. And you. I understand that she was having some difficulty in school before she got sick."

"She never had any trouble. But she was always very sensitive."

"I'm sure she was. Still, it's usually true that there are certain specific events that trigger acute cases of mental illness."

"How do you know that? Are you a doctor?"

"I'm a police officer. But I know what I'm talking about."

"Nothing happened."

"But you must have wondered about it. Night and day."

"I've hardly done anything else."

Wallander felt the atmosphere becoming so intolerable that he wished he could break off the conversation and leave. The answers he was getting were leading him nowhere, even though he believed they were mostly the truth, or at least part of the truth.

"Do you have a photograph of her I could look at?"

"Is it necessary?"

"Please."

Wallander noticed that the boy sitting next to her made a move to say something. He checked it instantly. Wallander wondered why. Didn't the boy want him to see his sister? Why not?

The mother got up with the little boy hanging on to her body. She pulled open a drawer and returned with some photographs. Louise was blonde, smiling, and resembled the older of the two boys. But in her eyes there was nothing of that wariness he now felt surrounding him. She smiled openly and trustingly at the camera. She was quite pretty.

"A nice-looking girl," he said. "Let's hope she gets better some day."

"I've stopped hoping," the mother said. "Why should I hope anymore?"

"Doctors can work wonders these days," said Wallander.

"One day Louise is going to leave that hospital," the boy said suddenly. His voice was quite determined. He smiled at Wallander.

"And one of the most important things is that she has a family to support her," said Wallander, annoyed that he expressed himself so stiffly.

"We support her in every way," the boy went on. "The police have to search for the person who killed our pappa. Not go bothering her."

"If I visit her at the hospital it's not to bother her," said Wallander. "It's part of the investigation."

"We'd prefer it if you left her in peace," he said firmly.

Wallander nodded. The boy was quite determined.

"If the prosecutor, the leader of the preliminary investigation, makes the decision, then I'll have to visit her," said Wallander. "And I presume that will happen. Very soon. Either today or tomorrow. But I promise that I won't even mention that her father is dead."

"Then why are you going there at all?"

"To see her," said Wallander. "A photograph is still just a photograph. But I'll have to take it with me."

"Why?"

The boy's response was instantaneous. Wallander was surprised by the animosity in his voice.

"I have to show the photograph to some people," he said. "To see whether they recognize her. That's all."

"You're going to give it to the newspapers," said the boy. "Her face will be plastered all over the country."

"Why would I do that?" asked Wallander.

The boy jumped up from the sofa, leaned over the table, and grabbed the two pictures. It happened so fast that Wallander didn't have time to react. Then he regained his composure, but he was angry.

"Now I'm going to be forced to come back here with a warrant to make you hand over those pictures," he said, although this wasn't true. "Then there's a risk that some reporters will hear about it and follow me here. I can't stop them. If I can borrow a picture now and copy it, this won't have to happen."

The boy stared at Wallander. His previous wariness had now evolved into something else. Without a word he handed back one of the photos.

"I have only one more question," said Wallander. "Do you know if Louise ever met a man named Gustaf Wetterstedt?"

The mother gave him a baffled look. The boy had gotten up from the sofa and stood looking out the open balcony door with his back turned to them.

"No," she said.

"Does the name Arne Carlman mean anything to you?"

She shook her head.

"Åke Liljegren?"

"No."

She doesn't read the papers, thought Wallander. Under that blanket there's probably a bottle of wine. And in that bottle is her life.

He got up from his chair. The boy by the balcony door turned around.

"Are you going to visit Louise?" he asked again.

"It's a possibility," said Wallander.

Wallander said goodbye and left the apartment. When he got to the street he felt relieved. The boy was standing in the fifth-floor window looking down at him. Wallander got into his car and decided to put off visiting Louise Fredman for the time being. On the other hand, he wanted to find out right away whether Elisabeth Carlén recognized her from the photo. He rolled down his window and called Sjösten from his car phone. The boy in the window was gone. While the phone rang, he searched for an explanation for the uneasiness he felt at the sight of the frightened little boy. But he still couldn't figure out what it was. Sjösten answered. Wallander told him he was on his way to Helsingborg. He had a photograph he wanted Elisabeth Carlén to see.

"According to the latest report she's lying on her balcony sunbathing," said Sjösten.

"How's it going with Liljegren's employees?"

"We're working on locating the one who was supposed to be his right-hand man. A man by the name of Hans Logård."

"Did Liljegren have any family?" asked Wallander.

"Apparently not. We spoke with his attorney. Strangely enough, he left no will. There was no information about any direct heirs. Åke Liljegren seems to have lived in his own universe."

"That's good," said Wallander. "I'll be in Helsingborg within the hour."

"Should I bring Elisabeth Carlén downtown?"

"Do that. But treat her nicely. Bring her in a patrol car. I've got a feeling we're going to be needing her for a while. She might stop cooperating if it doesn't suit her anymore."

"I'll pick her up myself," said Sjösten. "How's your father?"

"My father?"

"Weren't you going to meet him this morning?"

Wallander had forgotten the excuse he had given for leaving Sjösten's apartment during the night.

"Oh, he's fine," he said. "But it was very important for me to see him."

Wallander hung up the phone. He glanced up at the window on the fifth floor. No one was there.

He started the engine and drove off, glancing at the clock in the car. He had to be in Helsingborg before noon.

Hoover went into his basement just after one o'clock. He locked the door and took off his shoes. The coolness from the stone floor permeated his whole body. The sunlight shone weakly through some cracks in the paint he had put on the basement window. He sat down on his chair and looked at his face in the mirrors.

He couldn't allow the policeman to visit his sister. They were so close to their goal now, the sacred moment, when the evil spirits in her head would be driven out for good. He couldn't let anyone get close to her.

He knew his thought had been correct. The policeman's visit had been a reminder that he couldn't wait any longer. For safety's sake his sister couldn't stay where she was any longer than necessary.

Now was the time to act.

He thought about the girl it had been so easy to meet. In some way she had reminded him of his sister. That was a good sign, too. His sister would need all the strength he could give her.

He took off his jacket and looked around the room. Everything he needed was there. The axes and knives gleamed, laid out on the black silk cloth.

Then he took one of the wide brushes and drew a single line across his forehead.

Time was running out.

Chapter Thirty-five

Wallander placed the photograph of Louise Fredman face down. Elisabeth Carlén followed his movements with her eyes. She was dressed in a white summer dress, which Wallander guessed was very expensive. They were in Sjösten's office, Wallander at the desk, Sjösten in the background, leaning against the door jamb, Elisabeth Carlén in the visitor's chair. It was ten minutes past twelve. The summer heat swept in through the open window. Wallander felt himself sweating.

"I'm going to show you a photograph," he said. "And I simply want you to tell me whether you recognize the person in it."

"Why do cops have to be so dramatic?" she asked.

Her haughty imperturbability annoyed Wallander, but he controlled himself.

"We're trying to catch a man who has killed four people," said Wallander. "And he scalps them too. Pours hydrochloric acid in their eyes. And stuffs their heads into ovens."

"You can't let a maniac like that run around loose, of course," she replied calmly. "Shall we look at that photograph?"

Wallander slid it over and watched Elisabeth Carlén's face. She picked up the photo and seemed to be thinking. Almost thirty seconds passed, then she shook her head.

"No," she said. "I've never seen her before. At least not that I can remember."

"It's very important," said Wallander.

"I have a good memory for faces," she said. "I'm sure. I've never met her. Who is she?"

"That doesn't matter for the time being," said Wallander. "Think carefully."

"Where do you want me to have seen her? At Åke Liljegren's house?"

"Yes."

"She may have stopped by sometime when I wasn't there."

"Did that happen a lot?"

"Not in the past few years."

"How many years are we talking about?"

"About four."

"But she could have been there?"

"Young girls are popular with some men. The real creeps."

"What creeps?"

"The ones with a single fantasy. To go to bed with their own daughters."

Wallander started to get mad. What she said was true, of course. But her indifference bothered him. She was part of this whole market that sucked in more and more innocent children and ruined their lives.

"If you can't tell me whether she was ever at any of Wetterstedt's parties, who could?"

"Somebody else."

"Give me a straight answer. Who? I want a name and address."

"It was always completely anonymous," said Elisabeth Carlén patiently. "That was one of the prerequisites for these parties. You recognized a face now and then. But nobody exchanged business cards."

"Where did the girls come from?"

"All over. Denmark, Stockholm, Belgium, Russia."

"They came and then they disappeared?"

"That's about it."

"But you live here in Helsingborg?"

"I was the only one who did."

Wallander looked at Sjösten, as if wanting confirmation that the conversation hadn't completely gotten off the track before continuing.

"The girl in the picture is named Louise Fredman," he said. "Does that name mean anything to you?"

She gave him a puzzled look.

"Wasn't that *his* name? The one who was murdered? Fredman?"

Wallander nodded. She looked at the picture again. For a moment she seemed moved by the connection.

"Is this his daughter?"

"Yes."

She shook her head again.

"I've never seen her before."

Wallander knew she was telling the truth, if only because she had nothing to gain by lying. He retrieved the photograph and turned it over again, as if to spare Louise Fredman from further participation.

"Were you ever at the house of a man named Gustaf Wetterstedt?" he asked. "In Ystad?"

"What would I be doing there?"

"The same thing you normally do to make your living. Was he your client?"

"No."

"Are you sure?"

"Yes."

"Completely sure?"

"Yes."

"Were you ever at the house of an art dealer named Arne Carlman?"

"No."

Wallander had an idea. Maybe names weren't used in those cases either.

"I'm going to show you some other photographs," he said, getting to his feet. He took Sjösten with him outside.

"What do you think?" Wallander asked.

Sjösten shrugged his shoulders.

"She's not lying," he said.

"We need photos of Wetterstedt and Carlman," said Wallander. "Fredman too. They're in the investigative material."

"Birgersson has the folder," said Sjösten. "I'll go get it."

Wallander went back in the room and asked whether she wanted any coffee.

"I'd rather have a gin and tonic," she said.

"The bar isn't open yet," said Wallander.

She laughed. His reply appealed to her. Wallander went back out in the corridor. Elisabeth Carlén was very beautiful. Her body was perfectly visible through her thin dress. He thought Baiba must be furious that he hadn't called. Sjösten came of out Birgersson's office with a plastic folder in his hand. They went back in the room. Elisabeth Carlén was sitting there smoking. Wallander placed a picture of Wetterstedt in front of her.

"I recognize him," she said. "From TV. Wasn't he the one who ran around with whores in Stockholm?"

"He may have continued doing so later on."

"Not with me," she replied, still equally unperturbed.

"And you've never been to his house in Ystad?"

"Never."

"Do you know anyone else who's been there?"

"No."

Wallander replaced the picture with one of Carlman. He was standing beside an abstract painting. Wetterstedt had been somber in his picture, but Carlman was smiling broadly at the camera. This time she didn't shake her head.

"This one I've seen," she said firmly.

"At Liljegren's?"

"Yes."

"When was that?"

Wallander saw that Sjösten had taken a note pad out of his pocket. Elisabeth Carlén thought for a moment. Wallander sat surreptitiously looking at her body.

"About a year ago," she said.

"Are you sure about that?"

"Yes."

Wallander nodded. Something flared up inside him. Another one, he thought. Now all we have to do is find the right box to put Fredman in.

He showed her Björn Fredman. It was a prison photo. Fredman was playing guitar. The picture must have been old. Fredman had long hair and was wearing bell-bottoms; the colors were faded.

She shook her head once again. She had never seen him.

Wallander let his hands drop with a smack on the desk.

"That's all I wanted to know for now," he said. "Now I'll trade places with Sjösten."

Wallander took up the position by the door. He also took over Sjösten's note pad.

"How the hell can you live a life like yours?" Sjösten began, surprisingly. He asked the question with a big smile. He sounded quite friendly. Elisabeth Carlén didn't let down her façade for a moment.

"What business is that of yours?"

"None. Just curious, that's all. How can you stand looking at yourself in the mirror every morning?"

"What do you think when *you* look in the mirror?"

"That at least I'm not making a living by lying on my back for anyone who happens to have a certain number of kronor. Do you take credit cards?"

"Go to hell."

She made a move to get up and leave. Wallander was already getting annoyed at the way he was needling her. She might still be useful to them.

"Please pardon me," said Sjösten, still just as sincere and friendly. "Let's forget about your private life. Hans Logård? Does that name sound familiar?"

She looked at him without replying. Then she turned and looked at Wallander.

"I asked you a question," said Sjösten.

Wallander understood her glance. She only wanted to give Wallander the answer to that question. He went out in the corridor and signaled to Sjösten to follow him. There he explained that Sjösten had blown any trust Elisabeth Carlén may have had in him.

"Then we'll arrest her," said Sjösten. "I'll be damned if I'll let a whore give me the runaround."

"Arrest her for what?" asked Wallander. "Wait here, I'll go in and get the answer. Calm down, damn it!"

Sjösten shrugged his shoulders. Wallander went back in and sat down behind the desk.

"Hans Logård used to hang out with Liljegren," she said.

"Do you know where he lives?"

"Out in the country somewhere."

"What do you mean?"

"He doesn't live in town."

"But you don't know where?"

"Right."

"What does he do?"

"I don't know that either."

"But he was at the parties?"

"Yes."

"As guest or host?"

"As the host. And a guest."

"You don't know where I can get hold of him?"

"No."

Wallander still believed she was telling the truth. They probably wouldn't be able to track down Logård through her.

"How did they get along? Liljegren and Logård."

"Hans Logård always had plenty of money. Whatever he did for Liljegren, he was well paid."

She stubbed out her cigarette. Wallander felt as if he had been granted a private audience with her.

"I'm going," she said, getting to her feet.

"I'll see you out," said Wallander.

Sjösten came sauntering down the corridor. When they passed she looked straight through him. Wallander watched as she walked to her car, a Nissan with a sunroof. When she drove off, Wallander waited on the steps until he saw someone follow her, then went back up to the office. She was still under surveillance.

"Why were you needling her?" he asked.

"She stands for something I despise," said Sjösten. "Don't you?"

"We need her," said Wallander evasively. "We can despise her later."

They got coffee and sat down to go over what they knew. Sjösten brought in Birgersson to help out.

"The problem is Björn Fredman," said Wallander. "He just doesn't fit. Otherwise we now have a number of links that seem to hang together. A number of fragile points of contact."

"Or maybe it just looks that way," said Sjösten thoughtfully.

Wallander's instincts were alerted. He could tell that Sjösten was worried about something. He waited for him to continue, but he didn't.

"You're thinking about something," he said.

Sjösten kept staring out the window.

"Why couldn't that be possible?" he asked. "That Fredman doesn't fit in the picture? We can assume he was killed by the same man as the others. But maybe for a completely different reason."

"That doesn't make sense," said Birgersson.

"What does make sense in this case?" Sjösten went on. "Nothing."

"In other words, we should be looking for two different motives," said Wallander. "Is that what you mean?"

"That's about it. But I could be wrong. It was just an idea, that's all."

Wallander nodded.

"You may be right," he said. "We shouldn't disregard that possibility."

"It's a sidetrack," said Birgersson. "A blind alley, a dead end. It just doesn't sound believable."

"We can't rule it out," said Wallander. "The same way we can't rule out anything else. But right now we have to find Hans Logård. That's the most important thing."

"Liljegren's villa is a very strange place," said Sjösten. "There wasn't one piece of paper there. No address books. Nothing. Because he was found so early in the morning and the villa has been under surveillance ever since, no one could have gone in and cleaned up."

"Which means that we're the ones who haven't searched hard enough," said Wallander. "Without Hans Logård we're not going to get anywhere."

Sjösten and Wallander ate a quick lunch at a restaurant next to the police station. Just after two o'clock they pulled up outside Liljegren's villa. The cordons were still up. An officer opened the gates and let them in. Sunlight filtered through the trees. Wallander thought it all suddenly seemed surreal. Monsters belonged in the cold and darkness. Not to a summer like the one they were having this year. He recalled something Rydberg once said, as an ironic joke. *It's best to chase insane killers in the fall. In the summer we prefer a good old-fashioned mad bomber.* He laughed at the thought. Sjösten gave him a funny look, but he didn't explain.

They walked inside the huge villa. The police techs had finished their work. With distaste Wallander took a look in the kitchen. The oven door was closed. He thought about Sjösten's idea from earlier in the day. About Björn Fredman, who didn't fit in, and thus assumed his proper place in the investigation. A perpetrator with two motives? Did such birds exist? He looked at the telephone on a nearby table. He picked up the receiver. It hadn't been disconnected yet. He called Ystad. Ebba got hold of Ekholm for him. It took almost five minutes before he came to the phone. In the meantime Wallander watched Sjösten wandering through the rooms on the ground floor, drawing back the curtains from the windows. The sunlight was suddenly very bright. Wallander could smell the residual odor of the chemicals used by the forensic techs.

Ekholm picked up the phone. Wallander asked his question at once. It was actually intended for Ekholm's computers. What was the history of serial killers who combined different types of motives? Did the collective behavioral criminologists of the world have anything to say about this? As always, Ekholm thought that what Wallander said was interesting. Wallander started wondering whether Ekholm was being honest or whether he was really so naïvely charmed by everything they told him. It was starting to remind him of all the satirical songs sung about the absurd incompetence of the Swedish Security Police. In recent years they had relied more and more on various specialists. And no one could explain why.

At the same time, Wallander didn't want to be unfair to Ekholm. During his time in Ystad he had proven to be a good listener. In that sense he had learned something basic about police work. Cops had to be able to listen, and do it at least as well as they had supposedly mastered the difficult art of questioning. Cops always had to listen for hidden meanings and motives that might not be obvious. They had to be able to listen for the invisible impressions left by perpetrators. Just like in this house. Something is always left behind after a crime is committed, something that was not seen and could not be detected by the brushes of the technicians. An experienced detective should be able to listen his way to what it was. The perpetrator may not have forgotten his shoes, but maybe he did leave his thoughts behind. Wallander hung up and went to join Sjösten, who had sat down behind a desk. Wallander didn't say a thing. Neither did Sjösten. The villa invited silence. Liljegren's spirit, if he had one, hovered restlessly around their heads.

Wallander went upstairs and opened the doors to room after room. There were no papers anywhere. Liljegren had lived in a house in which emptiness was the most noticeable characteristic. Wallander thought back to what Liljegren had been famous or infamous for. The dummy corporation scams, the looting of company finances. He had made his way in the world by hiding his money. Did he do the same thing in his private life? He had houses in several different countries. The villa was one of his many hideouts. Wallander stopped by a door that seemed to lead up to the attic. When he was a kid he had built a hideout for himself in the attic of his childhood home. He opened the door. The stairs were narrow and steep. He twisted the old-fashioned light switch. The main room of the attic with its prominent beams was almost empty. There were just some skis and a few pieces of furniture. Wallander smelled the same odor as in the rest of the house. The forensic techs had been here too. He looked around.

No secret doors leading to equally secret rooms. It was hot underneath the roofing tiles. He went back down the stairs and started to do a more systematic search. He pulled back the clothes in Liljegren's large wardrobes. Still nothing. Wallander sat down on the edge of the bed and tried to think. It didn't make sense that Liljegren had kept everything in his head. At the very least there had to be an address book somewhere. But there wasn't. Something else was missing too. At first he couldn't figure out what it was. He went over things in his mind and asked the fundamental question again: Who was Åke Liljegren, "the Auditor"? Åke Liljegren was a traveling man, but there were no suitcases in the house. Not even a briefcase. Wallander went downstairs to see Sjösten.

"Liljegren must have had another house," said Wallander. "Or at least an office."

"He has houses all over the world," said Sjösten distractedly.

"I mean here in Helsingborg. This place is too empty."

"I don't think he did," said Sjösten. "We would have known about it."

Wallander nodded without saying any more. He was still sure his hunch was right. He continued his tour through the house. But now he was more persistent. He went down to the basement. In one room there was an exercise machine and some barbells. There was a wardrobe down there, too, which contained some exercise clothes and rain gear. Wallander thoughtfully regarded the clothes. Then he went back upstairs to Sjösten.

"Did Liljegren have a boat?".

"I'm sure he did. But not here. I would have known about it."

Wallander nodded mutely. He was just about to leave Sjösten when an idea struck him.

"Maybe it was in someone else's name."

"What?"

"A boat. Maybe it was registered under another name. Why not in Hans Logård's name?"

Sjösten could tell that Wallander was serious.

"Why do you think Liljegren had access to a boat?"

"There are clothes in the basement that look to me like they're for sailing."

Sjösten followed Wallander to the basement.

"You may be right," he said when they stood in front of the open wardrobe.

"At any rate, it could be worth looking into," said Wallander. "This house is too empty to be normal."

They left the basement. Sjösten sat down by the telephone. Wallander opened the balcony doors and stepped out in the sunshine. He thought of Baiba again and got an instant knot in his stomach. Why didn't he call her? Did he still think it would be possible for him to meet her at Kastrup Airport on Saturday morning? In less than two days? He was also worrying about asking Martinsson to lie to her on his behalf. Now it was his only way out. Everything else was too late. With a feeling of utter self-loathing he went back inside the villa, into the shadows. Sjösten was talking to someone on the phone. Wallander wondered when the perpetrator would strike next. Sjösten hung up and dialed another number. Wallander went into the kitchen and drank some water. He tried to avoid looking at the stove. As he came back, Sjösten slammed the phone down.

"You were right," he said. "There's a sailboat in Logård's name down at the boat club. The same one I belong to."

"Let's go," said Wallander, feeling the tension rise.

When they reached the harbor they were met by a dock watchman who showed them where Logård's boat was berthed. Wallander could see that it was a beautiful, well-maintained boat. The hull was plastic but it had a teak deck.

"A Komfortina," said Sjösten. "Very nice. They handle well, too."

He hopped on board like a sailor and discovered that the entrance to the cabin was locked.

"Do you know Hans Logård?" Wallander asked the watchman standing beside him on the dock. He had a weatherbeaten face and wore a T-shirt advertising canned Norwegian fish-balls.

"He's not that talkative. But we do say hello to each other when he comes down here."

"When was he here last?"

The man thought for a moment.

"Last week, I think. But it's high summer, you know, our busiest time, so I might be mistaken."

Sjösten had managed to pick the cabin lock. From inside he opened the two half-doors. Wallander clambered clumsily aboard. Boat decks were like walking on newly polished ice. He crept down into the cockpit and then into the cabin. Sjösten had had the foresight to bring along a flashlight. They quickly searched through the cabin without finding anything.

"I don't get it," said Wallander when they were back on the dock. "Liljegren must have been running his affairs from somewhere."

"We're checking his cell phones," said Sjösten. "Maybe that will produce something."

They headed back to shore. The man with the fish-ball shirt went with them.

"I guess you'll want to take a look at his other boat too," he said as they stepped off the long dock. Wallander and Sjösten reacted at the same time.

"Logård has another boat?" asked Wallander.

The man pointed toward the farthest pier.

"The white one, all the way at the end. A Storö class. It's called the *Rosmarin*."

"Of course we want to look at it," said Wallander.

They ended up standing in front of a long, powerful, sleek motor cruiser.

"These cost money," said Sjösten. "Lots and lots of money."

They went aboard. The cabin door was locked. The man on the dock was watching them.

"He knows I'm a cop," said Sjösten.

"We don't have time to wait," said Wallander. "Break the lock. But do it the cheapest way."

Sjösten managed to do it without breaking off more than a piece of the doorjamb. They entered the cabin. Wallander saw at once that they had hit pay dirt. Along one wall was a shelf with a number of folders and plastic binders.

"The most important thing is to find an address for Hans Logård," said Wallander. "We can go through the rest later."

It took them ten minutes to find a membership card to a golf club outside Ängelholm with Hans Logård's name and address on it.

"He lives in Bjuv," said Sjösten. "That's not far from here."

They were just about to leave the boat when Wallander, driven by instinct, opened a cupboard. To his surprise there was women's clothing inside.

"Maybe they had parties on board too," said Sjösten.

"Maybe," said Wallander pensively. "But I'm not so sure."

They left the boat and went back down to the dock.

"I want you to call me if Hans Logård shows up," Sjösten told the dock watchman.

He gave him a card with his phone number on it.

"But I shouldn't let on that you're looking for him, right?" said the man expectantly.

Sjösten smiled.

"Quite right," he replied. "Pretend that everything's normal. And then call me. No matter what time it is."

"There's nobody here at night," said the man.

"Then we'll have to hope he shows up in the daytime."

"May I ask what he did?"

"You can ask," said Sjösten, "but you won't get an answer."

They left the boat club. It was three o'clock.

"Should we take more men along?" asked Sjösten.

"Not yet," replied Wallander. "First we have to locate his house and see if he's home."

They left Helsingborg and drove out toward Bjuv. They were in a part of Skåne that Wallander didn't know. The weather had turned muggy. Wallander sensed that there would be a thunderstorm that evening.

"When's the last time it rained?" he asked.

"In June, around Midsummer," said Sjösten after thinking it over. "And it didn't rain much."

They had just reached the exit to Bjuv when Sjösten's cell phone rang. He slowed down and answered it.

"It's for you," he said, handing it to Wallander.

It was Ann-Britt Höglund calling from Ystad. She got straight to the point.

"Louise Fredman has escaped from the hospital."

It took a moment before Wallander grasped what she said.

"Could you repeat that?"

"Louise Fredman has escaped from the hospital."

"When did it happen?"

"About an hour ago."

"How did you find out?"

"Someone contacted Per Åkeson. He called me."

Wallander thought for a moment.

"How did it happen?"

"Someone came and picked her up."

"Who?"

"I don't know. No one saw it happen. Suddenly she was just gone."

"God damn it to hell!"

Sjösten hit the brakes when he realized something serious had happened.

"I'll call you back in a while," Wallander said. "In the meantime, try to find out absolutely everything you can about what happened. Above all, who it was that picked her up."

Höglund promised to do as he said. Wallander hung up.

"Louise Fredman has escaped from the hospital," he told Sjösten.

"How?"

Wallander gave it some thought before he replied.

"I don't know," he said. "But this has something to do with our perpetrator. I'm sure of it."

"Should I turn around?"

"No. Let's keep going. Now it's more important than ever to get hold of Logård."

They drove into the village and stopped. Sjösten rolled down the window and asked the way to the street where Hans Logård supposedly lived.

They asked three people and got the same answer.

Nobody had ever heard of the address they were looking for.

Chapter Thirty-six

They were just about to give up and call in extra manpower when they finally picked up the trail to Hans Logård and his address. Some scattered rain showers had started falling over Bjuv by that time. But the main thunderstorm passed by farther to the west. The dry weather was going to continue.

The address they had been looking for was "Hördestigen." It had a Bjuv postal code. But they couldn't find it. Wallander went into the post office himself to check it out. Hans Logård didn't have a post office box either, at least not in Bjuv. Finally there was nothing to do but think Logård's address was phony. At that point, Wallander walked determinedly into the bakery in the middle of Bjuv and struck up a conversation with the two ladies behind the counter while he bought a bag of cinnamon rolls. One of them knew the answer. Hördestigen wasn't a road. It was the name of a farm, north of the village, a place that was hard to find if you didn't know the way.

"There's a man living there named Hans Logård," Wallander told them. "Do you know him?"

The two women looked at each other as if searching their collective memory and then shook their heads in unison.

"I had a distant relative who lived at Hördestigen when I was a girl," said one of the women, the thinner of the two. "When he died it was sold to a stranger. But Hördestigen is the name of the farm, I know that. I'm sure it must have a different mailing address, though."

Wallander asked her to draw him a map. She tore up a bread bag and drew the route on it for him. Sjösten was waiting in the car. It was almost six o'clock. They drove out of town, following the road to Höganäs. Wallander navigated according to the bread bag. They got to an area where the farms started thinning out. That's where they took the first wrong turn. They wound up in an enchantingly beautiful beech forest, but they were in the wrong place.

Wallander told Sjösten to turn around, and when they got back to the main road they started over.

They took the next side road to the left, then to the right, and then left. The road ended in the middle of a field. Wallander swore to himself, got out of the car, and looked around. He was searching for a church tower the ladies at the bakery had told him about. Out there in the field he felt like someone floating on the ocean, searching for a lighthouse to navigate by. He found the church spire and then understood, after a conference with the bread bag, why they had gotten lost. Sjösten was directed back; they started over, and this time they found it.

Hördestigen was an old farm, not much different from Arne Carlman's, and it lay in an isolated spot with no neighbors, surrounded by a beech wood on two sides and gently sloping fields on the others. The road ended at the farmhouse. Wallander noticed there was no mailbox. No country mailman ever visited Logård at this address. His mail must go somewhere else. Sjösten was just getting out of the car when Wallander stopped him.

"What can we expect?" he asked. "Hans Logård—who is he?"

"You mean is he dangerous?"

"We don't really know whether he might be the one who killed Liljegren," said Wallander. "Or the others. We don't know a thing about him."

Sjösten's reply surprised Wallander.

"There's a shotgun in the trunk. And ammunition. You take that. I've got my service revolver."

Sjösten reached for it, where it was stuck under the seat.

"Against regulations," he said, smiling. "But if you had to follow all the regulations that exist, police work would have been forbidden long ago by the occupational-safety watchdogs."

"Forget the shotgun," said Wallander. "Have you got a license for the revolver?"

"Of course I have a license," said Sjösten. "What did you think?"

They got out of the car. Sjösten stuffed his pistol in his jacket pocket. They stood still and listened. There was thunder in the distance. Around them it was silent and extremely muggy. No sign of a car or a living soul. The whole farm seemed abandoned. They walked up to the house, shaped like an elongated L.

"The third wing must have burned down," said Sjösten. "Or else it was torn down. But it's a nice house. Well preserved. Just like the sailboat."

Wallander went up and knocked on the door. No answer. Then he banged on it hard. Nothing. He peered in through a window. Sjösten stood in the background with one hand in his jacket pocket. Wallander didn't like being this close to a weapon. They walked around the house. Still no sign of life. Wallander stopped, lost in thought.

"There are stickers all over saying that the windows and doors have alarms on them," said Sjösten. "But it would take a hell of a long time for anyone to get out here if it was set off. We'll have time to go inside and get out of here before then."

"There's something that doesn't fit here," said Wallander, as if he hadn't even heard Sjösten's comments.

"What's that?"

"I don't know."

They went over toward the wing that served as a toolshed. The door was locked with a big padlock. Through the windows they could see all kinds of junk inside.

"There's nobody here," said Sjösten flatly. "We'll have to put the farm under surveillance."

Wallander looked around. There was something wrong, he was sure of it. But he couldn't tell what it was. He walked around the house again and looked in several of the windows, listening. Sjösten followed. When they had gone around the house for the second time, Wallander stopped by some black trash bags next to the house. They were sloppily fastened and tied with ropes. Flies buzzed around them. He opened one of the sacks. Food remains, paper plates. He picked up a plastic wrapper from the Scan Deli between his thumb and forefinger. Sjösten stood next to him, watching. He looked at the various expiration dates that were legible. He could still smell the fresh meat from the plastic wrap. They hadn't been here very many hours. Not in this heat. He opened the other sack. It was filled with processed food wrappers too. It was a lot of food to eat in a few days.

Sjösten stood next to Wallander looking at the sacks.

"He must have had a party."

Wallander tried to think. The muggy heat was making the pressure build in his head. Soon he would have a headache, he could feel it.

"We're going in," he said. "I want to look around inside the house. Isn't there any way to get around the alarm?"

"Maybe down the chimney," said Sjösten.

"Then I guess we'll have to take our chances," said Wallander.

"I've got a crowbar in the car," said Sjösten.

He went and got it. Wallander examined the front door of the house. He thought about the door he had recently had to break down at his father's studio in Löderup. He went to the back of the house with Sjösten. The door there seemed less solid. Wallander decided to pry it open. He shoved in the crowbar between the two door hinges. Then he looked at Sjösten, who glanced at his watch.

"Go," he said.

Wallander braced himself and shoved on the crowbar with all his might. The hinges broke off along with some chunks of wall plaster and old tile. He jumped to one side so the door wouldn't fall on him.

The house looked even more like Carlman's house on the inside, if that was possible. Walls had been torn down, the space opened up. Modern furniture, newly laid hardwood floor. They listened again. Everything was quiet. Too quiet, Wallander thought. As if the entire house were holding its breath. Sjösten pointed to a telephone that was also a fax machine on a table. The light on the answering machine was blinking. Wallander nodded. Sjösten pushed the play-back button. It crackled and clicked. Then there was a voice. Wallander saw Sjösten jump. A man's voice asked Hans Logård to call him as soon as possible. Then it was silent again. The tape stopped.

"That was Liljegren," said Sjösten, obviously shaken. "God damn."

"Then we know that message has been here for quite a while," said Wallander.

"Even Logård hasn't been here since then," said Sjösten.

"Not necessarily," Wallander countered. "He might have listened to the message but not erased it. If the power goes off later, the light will start blinking again. They may have had a thunderstorm here. We don't know."

They went through the house. A narrow hallway led to the part of the house at the angle of the L. The door there was closed. Wallander suddenly raised his hand. Sjösten stopped short behind him. Wallander heard a sound. At first he couldn't tell what it was. It sounded like a growling animal, then like a cautious muttering. He looked at Sjösten. Then he tried the door. It was locked. The muttering had stopped. By now Sjösten had heard it too.

"What the hell is going on?" he whispered.

"I don't know," said Wallander. "I can't break this door open with the crowbar."

"I'm guessing we're going to have a car from the security company here in about fifteen minutes."

Wallander thought hard. He didn't know what was on the other side, except that it was at least one person, maybe more. He was feeling sick. He knew that he had to get the door open.

"Give me your pistol," he said.

Sjösten took it out of his pocket.

"Get back from the door," Wallander shouted as loud as he could. "I'm going to shoot it open."

He looked at the lock. Took a step back, cocked the gun, and shot. The blast was deafening. He shot again, then once more. The ricochets whined out to the far wall in the hallway. He handed the pistol back to Sjösten and kicked open the door. His ears were ringing from the shots.

The room was large. It had no windows. There were a number of beds and a partition enclosing a toilet. A refrigerator, glasses, cups, some thermoses. Huddled together in a corner of the room, frightened by the shots, sat four young girls holding on to each other. At least two of them reminded Wallander of the girl he had seen from twenty meters away in Salomonsson's rapeseed field before she burned herself to death. For a brief moment, with his ears ringing from the shots, Wallander thought he could see it all before him, one event after another, how it all fit together and how everything suddenly made sense. But in reality he saw nothing at all. There was just a feeling rushing straight through him, like a train going through a tunnel at high speed, leaving behind only a light shaking of the ground.

"What the hell is going on?" Sjösten asked.

"We have to get some backup here from Helsingborg," said Wallander. "As fast as we can."

He knelt down, and Sjösten did the same. Wallander tried to talk to the frightened girls in English. But they didn't seem to understand the language, or at least not the way he spoke it. Some of them couldn't be much older than Dolores María Santana.

"Do you know any Spanish?" he asked Sjösten. "I don't know a word."

"What do you want me to say?"

"Do you know Spanish or not?"

"I can't speak Spanish! Shit! I know a few words. What do you want me to say?"

"Anything! Just tell them to be calm."

"Should I say I'm a cop?"

"No! Whatever you do, don't say that!"

"*Buenos días,*" said Sjösten hesitantly.

"Smile," said Wallander. "Can't you see how scared they are?"

"I'm doing the best I can," complained Sjösten.

"Say it again," said Wallander. "Friendly this time."

"*Buenos días,*" Sjösten repeated.

One of the girls answered. Her voice was very unsteady. Wallander felt as if he was now getting the answer he'd been waiting for ever since that day when the girl stood in the rapeseed field and stared at him with her terrified eyes.

At the same moment something else happened. Somewhere behind them in the house they heard a sound, maybe a door opening. The girls heard it too, and huddled together again.

"It must be the security guards," said Sjösten. "We'd better go meet them. Otherwise they'll wonder what's going on here and start making noise."

Wallander gestured to the girls to stay. Then the two of them went back down the narrow hallway, this time with Sjösten in the lead.

It almost cost him his life. When they stepped out into the open room where the walls had been torn down, several shots rang out. They came in such rapid succession that they must have been fired from a semiautomatic weapon. The first bullet slammed into Sjösten's left shoulder and broke his collarbone. He was thrown backwards by the impact and rammed into Wallander like a human wall. The second, third, and maybe fourth shots landed somewhere above their heads.

"Don't shoot! Police!" Wallander shouted.

Whoever was shooting fired off another burst. Sjösten was hit again, this time in the right ear.

Wallander threw himself behind one of the walls. He pulled Sjösten with him, who screamed and passed out.

Wallander found Sjösten's pistol and fired into the room. He thought there must be two or three shots left in the clip.

There was no answer. He waited with his heart pounding, pistol raised and ready to shoot. Then he heard the sound of a car starting. He let Sjösten go and, crouching low, ran over to a window. He saw the back end of a black Mercedes disappearing down the narrow road, vanishing into the beech woods. He went back to Sjösten, who was bleeding and unconscious. He found a pulse on his bloody neck. It was fast, and Wallander thought that was good. Better than too slow. Still holding the pistol in his hand, he picked up the phone and dialed 90-000.

"Officer down," he shouted when they answered. Then he managed to calm down, tell them who he was, what had happened, and where they were located. He went back to Sjösten, who had now regained consciousness.

"It'll be all right," said Wallander, over and over again. "Help is on the way."

"What happened?" asked Sjösten.

"Don't talk," said Wallander. "Everything will be fine."

He searched feverishly for entrance wounds. He thought Sjösten had been hit by at least three bullets. But finally he realized that it was only two. He made two simple pressure bandages, wondering what happened to the security company and why it was taking so long for help to arrive. He also thought about the Mercedes and knew he wouldn't rest until he caught the man who had shot Sjösten.

Finally he heard the sirens. He got up and went outside to meet the cars from Helsingborg. First came the ambulance, then Birgersson and two other patrol cars, and last the fire department. All of them were shocked when they saw Wallander. He hadn't noticed how bloody he was. And he still had Sjösten's pistol in his hand.

"How's he doing?" asked Birgersson.

"He's inside. I think he'll be fine."

"What the hell happened?"

"There are four girls locked up here," said Wallander. "They're probably some of the ones being taken through Helsingborg to brothels in southern Europe."

"Who shot at you?"

"I never saw him. But I assume it was Hans Logård. This house belongs to him."

"There was a Mercedes that crashed into a car from the security company down by the main road," said Birgersson. "No injuries, but the driver of the Mercedes stole the security guards' car."

"Then they saw him," said Wallander. "It must be him. The guards were on their way here. The alarm must have gone off when we broke in."

"You broke in?"

"Never mind that now. Put out the word on that security company car. And get the techs out here right away. I want them to lift a lot of prints. They'll have to be compared to the ones we found at all the other homicide scenes. Wetterstedt, Carlman, all of them."

Birgersson suddenly turned pale. The connection seemed to dawn on him for the first time.

"You mean it was him?"

"It could have been. But we don't know. Now get going. And don't forget the girls. Take them all in. Treat them nicely. And get hold of some Spanish interpreters."

"It's amazing how much you know already," said Birgersson.

Wallander stared at him.

"I don't know a thing," he said. "Now get moving."

Sjösten was carried out. Wallander rode into town with him in the ambulance. One of the ambulance drivers gave him a towel. He wiped himself off with it as best he could. Then he used the ambulance phone to check in with Ystad. It was just after seven. He got hold of Svedberg and explained what had happened.

"Who is this Logård?" asked Svedberg.

"That's what we have to find out. Is Louise Fredman still missing?"

"Yes, she is."

Wallander felt the need to think. What had seemed so clear in his mind a while before was no longer making sense.

"I'll be in touch later," he said. "But you'll have to let the investigative team know about this."

"Ludwigsson and Hamrén have found an interesting witness out at Sturup," said Svedberg. "A night watchman. He saw a man on a moped. The timetable fits."

"A moped?"

"Yep."

"You don't think our perp is riding around on a moped, do you? Those are for kids, for God's sake."

Wallander felt himself starting to get mad. He didn't want to, least of all at Svedberg. He said goodbye quickly and hung up.

Sjösten looked up at him from the stretcher.

Wallander smiled. "It's going to be fine," he said.

"It was like getting kicked by a horse," moaned Sjösten. "Twice."

"Don't talk," said Wallander. "We'll be at the hospital soon."

The night of July 7th was one of the most chaotic Wallander had ever experienced. There was an air of unreality about everything that happened.

He would never forget that night, but he would never really be sure if he remembered it all correctly. Sjösten was admitted to the hospital, and the doctors reassured Wallander that his life was not in danger. Wallander was driven to the police station in a patrol car.

Sergeant Birgersson had proven to be a good organizer, and he also seemed to have understood everything Wallander said out at the farmhouse where Sjösten was shot. He had the presence of mind to establish an outer perimeter where they herded all the reporters who had immediately started gathering. Inside, where the actual manhunt was being directed, no reporters were permitted.

It was ten o'clock when Wallander arrived from the hospital. A colleague loaned him a clean shirt and pair of pants. They were so tight around the waist that he couldn't zip the fly. Birgersson, noticing the problem, called the owners of Helsingborg's most elegant haberdashery and put Wallander on the line. It was a strange experience to stand in the middle of all the tumult and try to remember his waist size. But finally several pairs of pants were delivered by messenger to the police station, and one of them fit.

By the time Wallander got back from the hospital, Höglund, Svedberg, Ludwigsson, and Hamrén had already arrived in Helsingborg and had been briefed on the work that was under way. The alarm about the security company car had gone out, but the vehicle hadn't been located yet. Interviews were being conducted in different rooms. The Spanish-speaking girls had each been supplied with an interpreter. Höglund was talking to one of them, while three female officers from Helsingborg took care of the others. The two security guards whose car had collided with the fleeing man's Mercedes had also been interviewed, while forensic technicians were already busy cross-checking fingerprints. Finally, several officers were leaning over a number of computers, busy inputting all the material they could find about Hans Logård.

The activity was intense. Birgersson went around and around keeping order so that their work didn't get off the track. When Wallander had been briefed on the status of the investigation, he took his colleagues from Ystad into a room and closed the door. He had spoken with Birgersson and obtained his approval. Wallander knew that Birgersson was an exceptional cop who performed his job impeccably. In him there was almost none of the jealous cliquishness that so often haunted and degraded the quality of police work. Birgersson seemed to be interested in what he should be interested in: catching the man who shot Sjösten, figuring out exactly what had happened and who the perpetrator was.

Wallander told his version of what had happened. But what he wanted to resolve above all else was the reason for his own unrest. There were too many things he couldn't get to add up. The man who had shot Sjösten, Liljegren's associate, who kept the girls hidden—was he really the same man who had taken on the role of the lone warrior? He had a hard time believing it. But there hadn't been enough time for him to think, when everything around him was in chaos. He would have to do his thinking now, out loud with all of them gathered together and one thin door separating them from the world where the manhunt was going on, and where time for reflection didn't exist. Wallander had taken his colleagues aside, and Sjösten would have been among them if he weren't in the hospital, so that they could serve as a kind of counterweight at the bottom of the investigative work now being pushed ahead. Wallander looked around and wondered why Ekholm wasn't there.

"He left for Stockholm this morning," said Svedberg.

"Now is when we need him most," said Wallander, dismayed.

"He's supposed to come back tomorrow morning," said Höglund. "I think one of his kids was hit by a car. Nothing serious. But even so…"

Wallander nodded. Just as he was about to continue, the phone rang. It was Hansson for Wallander.

"Baiba Liepa has called a number of times from Riga," he said. "She wants you to call her right away."

"I can't right now," said Wallander. "Explain to her if she calls again."

"If I understood her correctly, you're supposed to meet her at Kastrup on Saturday. To go on a vacation together. How were you planning to pull that off?"

"Not now," said Wallander. "I'll call you later."

No one but Höglund seemed to notice that the conversation with Hansson had dealt with a private matter. Wallander caught her eye. She smiled. But she didn't say a word.

"Let's continue," he said. "We're searching for a man who assaulted both Sjösten and me with a deadly weapon. We find some girls locked up inside a farmhouse in the countryside near Bjuv. We can assume that Dolores María Santana once came from such a group, passing through Sweden on the way to brothels and the devil knows what else in other parts of the world. Girls who are lured here by people associated with Liljegren. In particular, a man named Hans Logård, if that's his real name. We think he was the one who shot at us. But we aren't sure about anything. We don't even have a picture of the man. Maybe the guards he stole the car from can give us a usable description. But they seem to be pretty shaken up. They may have seen nothing but his gun. Now we're hunting for him. But are we actually tracking our perpetrator? The one who killed Wetterstedt, Carlman, Fredman, and Liljegren? We don't know. I'm doubtful. All we can hope is that this man running around in the guards' car will be caught as soon as possible. In the meantime, I think we have to keep working as if this were simply one event on the periphery of the major investigation. I'm just as interested in what has happened to Louise Fredman. And what was discovered at Sturup. But first, of course, I'd like to hear if you have any reactions to my view of the case right now."

The room was silent, then Hamrén spoke up. "For me, coming from outside and not needing to be afraid of stepping on anyone's toes, since I certainly step on everyone's toes all the time anyway, the whole thing seems like a real attitude problem. The police sometimes have a tendency to think about only one thing at a time—while the perps they're chasing are thinking about ten."

Wallander listened approvingly even though he wasn't sure Hamrén meant what he was saying.

"Louise Fredman disappeared without a trace," said Höglund. "She had a visitor. Then she followed the visitor out. The rest of the staff never saw who came. The name written in the guest book was completely illegible. Because there were only summer temps working, the normal system of controls had almost completely fallen apart."

"Someone must have seen the person who came to get her," said Wallander.

"Someone did," said Höglund. "An assistant nurse named Sara Pettersson."

"Did anyone talk to her?"

"She's left town."

"Where is she?"

"She's got an Interrail card. She could be anywhere."

"Damn it!"

"We can trace her through Interpol," said Ludwigsson. "That'll probably work."

"All right," said Wallander. "I think we should do that. And this time we won't wait. I want someone to contact Per Åkeson about it tonight."

"This is Malmö's jurisdiction," Svedberg pointed out.

"I don't give a shit whose jurisdiction we're in," said Wallander. "Do it. It'll have to be Åkeson's headache."

Höglund said she would get hold of him. Wallander turned to Ludwigsson and Hamrén.

"I heard rumors about a moped," he said. "A witness who saw something interesting at the airport."

"That's right," said Ludwigsson. "The timetable fits. A moped drove off toward highway E65 on the night in question."

"Why is that of interest?"

"Because the night watchman is quite sure that the moped left at just about the same time the van arrived. Björn Fredman's Ford."

Wallander knew that this could be extremely significant.

"We're talking about a time of night when the airport is closed," Ludwigsson went on. "Nothing's happening. No taxicabs, no traffic. Everything is quiet. A van comes up and stops in the parking lot. Then a moped drives off."

The room grew still.

For the first time, they were close to the perpetrator. If there were magic moments in a complex criminal investigation, this was definitely one of them.

"A man on a moped," said Svedberg. "Can this really be true?"

"Is there a description?" asked Höglund.

"According to the watchman, the guy on the moped was wearing a helmet that covered his whole head. He never saw his face. He's worked at Sturup for many years. That was the first time a moped left there at night."

"How can he be sure the guy headed toward Malmö?"

"He wasn't. And I didn't say that either."

Wallander stopped breathing. The voices of the others were far away, like the distant, unintelligible white noise of the universe.

He knew that now they were very, very close.

Chapter Thirty-seven

S omewhere in the distance Hoover could hear thunder.
Silently, so he wouldn't wake his sleeping sister, he counted the
seconds between the lightning flashes and the delayed thunderclaps. The
thunderstorm was passing by far away. It wouldn't come in over Malmö. He
watched her sleeping on the mattress. He had wanted to offer her something
better, but everything happened so fast. The policeman whom he now hated,
the cavalry colonel with the blue trousers, whom he had decided to name
"Perkins" because he thought it fit, and "the Man with the Great Curiosity"
when he drummed his message in silence to Geronimo, had demanded
pictures of Louise. He had also threatened to visit her.

At that moment Hoover realized that he had to change his plans right away.
He would pick up Louise even before the row of scalps and the last gift, the
girl's heart, were all buried outside her window. Suddenly everything had to
be done fast. That's why he had only managed to take a mattress and a blanket down to the basement. He had imagined doing something quite different
for her. There was a big vacant building in Limhamn. The woman who lived
there alone went to Canada every summer to see her relatives. Once she had
been his teacher. Afterwards he had visited her sometimes and run errands
for her. That's how he knew she was away. He had copied a key to her front
door long ago. They could have lived in her building while they planned
their future. But now the nosy policeman had gotten in the way. Until he was
dead, and that would happen very soon, they would have to settle for the
mattress in the basement.

She was asleep. He had taken medicines from a cabinet when he went to
get her at the hospital. He had gone there without painting his face. But he
had both an axe and some knives with him, in case anyone had tried to prevent him from taking her. It had been strangely quiet at the hospital, with almost
no nurses around. Everything went much smoother than he could have imagined. Louise hadn't recognized him at first, but when she heard his voice she

put up no resistance. He had brought along some clothes for her. They walked across the hospital grounds and then took a taxi, without any problems. She didn't say a word, never questioning why she had to sleep on a bare mattress, and she lay down and fell asleep almost at once. He was getting tired himself. He had lain down beside her and slept. They were closer to the future than ever before, he had thought just before he fell asleep. The power from the scalps he had buried had already started working. She was on her way back to life again. Soon everything would be changed.

He looked at her. It was evening, past ten o'clock. He had decided. At dawn the next morning he would return to Ystad for the last time.

In Helsingborg it was getting close to midnight. A great crowd of reporters besieged the outer perimeter that Sergeant Birgersson had set up. The chief of police was there, and a nationwide alarm had been sent out on the security company car, but so far it had not yet been tracked down. At Wallander's stubborn and repeated insistence, Interpol was trying to trace Sara Pettersson, who was traveling by train on an Interrail pass with a friend. They contacted the girls' parents and tried to put together a possible itinerary. It was a hectic night at the police station.

In Ystad, Hansson sat with Martinsson, handling incoming calls. They sent over parts of the investigative material Wallander suddenly discovered he needed. Per Åkeson was at home but could be reached at any time. Although it was late, Wallander sent Höglund to Malmö to visit the Fredman family. He wanted to make sure they weren't the ones who had taken Louise from the hospital. He would have preferred going there himself. But he couldn't be in two places at once. She had left home at ten-thirty, after Wallander had phoned Fredman's widow. He estimated she'd be back by one.

"Who's going to take care of your kids while you're away?" he asked when she was getting ready to leave for Malmö.

"I've got a neighbor who has kids of her own," she said. "Otherwise it'd never work."

Right after she left, Wallander called home.

Linda was there. He explained as best he could what had happened. He didn't know when he'd be home, maybe sometime that night, maybe not until dawn.

"Will you get here before I leave?" she asked.

"Leave?"

"Did you forget I'm going to Gotland? Kajsa and I are leaving tomorrow. And you're going to Skagen."

"Of course I didn't forget," he said evasively. "I'll be home in plenty of time."

"Did you talk to Baiba?"

"Yes," said Wallander, hoping she couldn't hear that he was lying.

He gave her the phone number in Helsingborg. Then he wondered whether he ought to call his father, but it was late. They were probably already in bed.

He went to the command center where Birgersson was directing the manhunt. Five hours had passed, and no one had seen the stolen security company car. Birgersson agreed with Wallander that it could only mean that Logård, if it really was him, wasn't out on the roads in the car.

"He had two boats at his disposal," said Wallander. "And a house outside Bjuv that we could barely locate. I'm sure he has more hideouts."

"We've got a man going over the boats," said Birgersson. "And Hördestigen. I told them to look for addresses of other hideouts."

"Who is this damned Hans Logård, anyway?" asked Wallander.

"They've already started checking the prints," said Birgersson. "If he's ever had a run-in with the police, we'll find him in no time."

Wallander went over to the room where the four girls were being interviewed. It was a laborious process, since everything had to go through interpreters. Besides, the girls were scared. Wallander had told the officers to explain first to the girls that they weren't accused of any crime. But he wondered how deep their fear really went. He thought about Dolores María Santana's fear, which was the worst he had ever seen. But now, at midnight, a picture had finally started taking shape.

All the girls were from the Dominican Republic. Without knowing each other, they had all moved from their villages into some of the largest cities to look for work as domestic help or factory workers. They had been contacted by various men, all very friendly, and they had been offered work as domestic help in Europe. They had been shown pictures of big, beautiful houses by the Mediterranean, and their wages were going to be ten times what they could hope to earn at home, if they found any jobs at all. Some of them had been hesitant, but in the end they all said yes.

They were supplied with passports but were never allowed to keep them. First they were flown to Amsterdam—at least that's what two of the girls thought the city they landed in was called. Then they were driven in a little bus to Denmark. About a week ago they had been taken across to Sweden by boat on a dark night. The whole time there were different men involved, and their friendliness decreased the farther from home the girls traveled. The fear had begun in earnest when they were locked up at the lonely farm. They had been given food, and a man had explained in poor Spanish that they would soon be traveling on, the last stretch of the way. But by now they had begun to understand that nothing would happen as promised. Their fear had begun to turn to terror.

Wallander asked the officers doing the interviews to be thorough when they asked about the men the girls met during the days they were locked up. Were there more than one? Could they give a description of the boat that took them to Sweden? What did the captain look like? Was there any crew? He told them to take one of the girls down to the boat club to see whether she recognized the cabin of Logård's motor cruiser. A lot of questions remained. But a pattern was starting to emerge. Wallander went around trying to find an empty room where he could lock himself in and think his own thoughts.

He waited impatiently for Höglund to return. Above all, he was waiting for them to get some information on Hans Logård. He tried to connect a moped at Sturup Airport, a man who took scalps and killed with an axe, and another man who shot people with a semiautomatic weapon. The whole investigation swam back and forth in his head. The headache he had predicted earlier had arrived, and he tried unsuccessfully to fight it off with painkillers. The air was very muggy. There were thunderstorms over Denmark. In less than forty-eight hours he was supposed to be at Kastrup Airport.

At twelve twenty-five in the morning Wallander was standing by a window, looking out at the light summer night and thinking that the world had dissolved into unimaginable chaos. Birgersson came stomping down the corridor, triumphantly waving a piece of paper.

"You know who Erik Sturesson is?" he asked.

"No, who?"

"Then do you know who Sture Eriksson is?"

"No."

"They're one and the same. And later he changed his name again. This time he didn't settle for switching his first and last names. Now he's invented a name that carries an aura of more aristocratic lineage. Hans Logård."

"Great," he said. "What have we got?"

"The prints we found at Hördestigen and in the boats are in the registry. Under Erik Sturesson and Sture Eriksson. But not for anyone named Hans Logård. Erik Sturesson, if we start with him, since that was Hans Logård's real name, is forty-seven years old. Born in Skövde, father a career soldier, mother a housewife. The father was also an alcoholic. Both died in the late sixties. Erik soon wound up in bad company. First arrested at fourteen. Downhill from there. To sum it up, he's done time in Österåker, Kumla, and Hall prisons. And a short stretch at Norrköping. By the way, he changed his name for the first time when he got out of Österåker."

"What type of crimes?"

"From simple odd jobs to specialization, you might say. Burglaries and con games at first. An occasional assault. Then more serious crimes. Narcotics, of course. The hard stuff. He seems to have been a field worker for Turkish and Pakistani gangs. Keep in mind this is just an overview. We'll have more coming in tonight. We're checking on everything we can find."

"We need a picture of him," said Wallander. "And the fingerprints have to be cross-checked against the ones we found at Wetterstedt's and Carlman's. And the ones on Fredman too. Don't forget the prints we got from the left eyelid."

"Nyberg in Ystad is on top of it," said Birgersson. "But he seems so pissed off all the time."

"That's just the way he is," said Wallander. "But he's good at his job."

They sat down at a table overflowing with used plastic coffee cups. Telephones rang constantly all around them. They erected an invisible wall around themselves, admitting only Svedberg.

"The interesting thing is that Hans Logård suddenly stopped paying visits to our prisons," said Birgersson. "The last time he was in was 1989. Since then he's been clean. As if he found salvation or something."

"If I remember correctly, that corresponds pretty well with when Liljegren got himself a house here in Helsingborg."

Birgersson nodded. "We're not too clear on that yet. But it seems that Logård acquired title to Hördestigen in 1991. That's a gap of a couple of years. But there's nothing to prevent him from living somewhere else in the meantime."

"We'll need an answer to that one right away," said Wallander, grabbing a telephone. "What's Elisabeth Carlén's number? It's on Sjösten's desk. Have we still got her under surveillance, by the way?"

Birgersson nodded again. Wallander made a quick decision.

"Pull them off," he said.

Someone placed a piece of paper in front of Wallander. He dialed the number and waited. She answered almost immediately.

"This is Kurt Wallander," he said.

"I don't come downtown at this time of night," she said.

"I don't want you to. I just have one question: Was Hans Logård hanging out with Liljegren as early as 1989? Or 1990?"

He could hear her lighting a cigarette and blowing smoke straight into the mouthpiece.

"Yes," she said, "I think he was there then. In 1990, at least."

"Good," said Wallander.

"Why are you tailing me, anyway?" she asked.

"I was wondering myself," said Wallander. "We don't want anything to happen to you, of course. But we're lifting the surveillance now. Just don't leave town without telling us. I might get mad."

"Right," she said, "I bet you can get mad."

She hung up.

"Logård was there," said Wallander. "It seems he appeared at Liljegren's as soon as he moved here to Helsingborg. A couple of years later he acquired Hördestigen. Apparently Åke Liljegren took care of Logård's salvation."

Wallander tried to fit the different pieces together.

"That's about when the rumors of the trade in girls started. Isn't that right?"

Birgersson nodded.

"Does Logård have a violent history?" asked Wallander.

"A few charges of aggravated assault," replied Birgersson. "But he's never shot anyone. Not that we know of, at any rate."

"No axes?"

"No, nothing like that."

"In any case, we've got to find him," said Wallander, getting up. "Where the hell is he hiding?"

"We'll find him," said Birgersson. "Sooner or later he'll crawl out of his hole."

"Why did he shoot at us?" asked Wallander.

"You'll have to ask him that yourself," said Birgersson and left the room.

Svedberg had taken off his cap. "Is this really the same man we're looking for?" he asked doubtfully.

"I don't know," said Wallander. "I doubt it. Although I could be wrong. Let's hope I am."

Svedberg left the room. Wallander was alone again. More than ever he missed Rydberg. *There's always another question you can ask.* Rydberg's words, repeated often. So what was the question he hadn't asked yet? He searched for it and found nothing. All the questions had been asked. Only the answers were missing.

That's why it was a relief when Höglund stepped into the room. It was three minutes to one. Once again he was jealous of her tan. They sat down together.

"Louise wasn't there," she said. "Her mother was drunk. But her concern about her daughter seemed genuine. She couldn't understand what had happened. I think she was telling the truth. I felt really sorry for her."

"You mean she actually had no idea?"

"Not a clue. And she'd been worrying about it."

"Had it ever happened before?"

"Never."

"And her son?"

"The older or the younger one?"

"The older one. Stefan."

"He wasn't home."

"Was he out looking for his sister?"

"If I understood the mother correctly, he stays away occasionally. But there was one thing I did notice. I asked to have a look around. Just in case Louise was there. I went into Stefan's room. The mattress of his bed was gone. There was just a bedspread. The mattress was gone, and there wasn't any pillow or blanket either."

"Did you ask her where he was?"

"Unfortunately, no. But I suspect she wouldn't have been able to tell me."

"Did she say how long he'd been gone?"

She thought about it and looked at her notes.

"Since late yesterday afternoon."

"The same day and time that Louise disappeared."

She looked at him in surprise.

"You think he was the one who went and got her? Then where are they now?"

"Two questions, two answers. I don't know. I don't know."

Wallander felt a sense of uneasiness creep over his body. He couldn't figure out what it meant.

"Did you happen to ask the mother whether Stefan has a moped?"

He saw that she immediately understood where he was heading.

"No."

Wallander nodded toward the telephone on the table.

"Call her up," he said. "Ask her. She drinks at night. You won't wake her up."

She did as he said. It took a long time before she got an answer. The conversation was very brief. She hung up again. He saw that she was relieved.

"He doesn't have a moped," she said. "At least not that she knows of. Besides, Stefan isn't fifteen yet, is he?"

"It was just a thought," said Wallander. "We have to know. Anyway, I doubt that young people today always care whether something is permitted or not."

"The little boy woke up when I was about to leave," she said. "He was sleeping on the sofa next to his mother. That's what probably bothered me the most."

"That he woke up?"

"When he saw me. I've never seen such frightened eyes in a child before."

Wallander slammed his fist on the table. She jumped.

"Now I've got it," he said. "What it was I've been forgetting all this time. Damn it!"

"What?"

"Wait a minute. Wait a minute…"

Wallander rubbed his temples to squeeze out the image that had been bothering him for so long. Finally he captured it.

"Do you remember that doctor who did the autopsy of Dolores María Santana in Malmö?"

She tried to remember.

"Wasn't it a woman?"

"Yes, it was. A woman. What was her name? Malm something?"

"Svedberg's got a good memory," she said. "I'll go get him."

"That's not necessary," said Wallander. "Now I remember. Her name was Malmström. We've got to get hold of her. And we need to get hold of her right away. I'd like you to take care of it. As fast as you can!"

"Why?"

"I'll explain later."

She got up and left the room. Could Stefan Fredman really be mixed up in what had happened? Wallander picked up the phone and called Per Åkeson. He answered at once.

"I want you to do me a favor," he said. "Now. In the middle of the night. Call the hospital where Louise was a patient. Tell them to copy the page with the signature of the person who picked her up. And tell them to fax it here to Helsingborg."

"How the hell do you think they can do that?"

"I have no idea," said Wallander. "But it could be important. They can cross out all the other names on the page. I just want to see that one signature."

"Which was illegible?"

"Precisely. I want to see the illegible signature."

Wallander stressed his final words. Åkeson understood that he was after something that might be important.

"Give me the fax number," said Åkeson. "I'll try."

Wallander gave him the number and hung up. The clock on the wall said five past two. It was still muggy. Wallander was sweating in his new shirt. He vaguely wondered whether it was the state that had paid for the shirt and his new pants. At twenty past two Höglund returned and said that Agneta Malmström was on a sailing vacation with her family somewhere between Landsort and Oxelösund.

"What's the name of the boat?"

"It's supposed to be some kind of Maxi class. The name is *Sanborombon*. It also has a number."

"Call Stockholm Radio," Wallander continued. "They must have a two-way radio on board. Ask them to call the boat. Tell them it's a police emergency. Talk to Birgersson. I want to get in touch with her right away."

Wallander could feel he had gotten his second wind. Höglund left to go talk to Birgersson. Svedberg almost collided with her in the doorway as he came in with some papers describing the security guards' account of when they had their car stolen.

"You're right," he said. "Basically all they saw was the gun. Besides, it all happened very fast. But he had blond hair, blue eyes, and was dressed in some kind of jogging suit. Normal height, spoke with a Stockholm accent. Gave the impression of being high on something."

"What did they mean by that?"

"His eyes."

"I assume the description is on its way out?"

"I'll check on it."

Svedberg left the room as fast as he came in. Excited voices came from the corridor. Wallander guessed that a reporter had tried to cross the boundary that Birgersson had drawn. He found a note pad and quickly wrote a few notes. They lacked any internal structure and were just jotted down in the sequence he remembered them. He was sweating profusely, constantly watching the wall clock, and in his mind Baiba was sitting by the phone in her spartan apartment in Riga waiting for the call he should have made long ago.

It was getting close to three in the morning. The security company car was still missing. Hans Logård was hiding somewhere. The Dominican girl who had been taken to the harbor couldn't make a positive ID of the boat. Maybe it was the same one, maybe not. A man who had always kept in the shadows had been at the wheel. She couldn't remember any crew. Wallander told Birgersson that the girls had to get some sleep now. Hotel rooms were arranged. One of the girls smiled shyly at Wallander when they met in the corridor. Her smile made him feel good, for a brief moment almost exhilarated. At regular intervals Birgersson would come into whatever room Wallander happened to be in and turn over supplementary information on Hans Logård. At three-fifteen Wallander found out that Logård had been married twice and had two children under eighteen. One of them, a girl, lived with her mother in Hagfors, the other in Stockholm, a boy of nine. Seven minutes later Birgersson came back and reported that Logård apparently had one other child, but that they hadn't managed to confirm it.

At three-thirty an exhausted patrolman came into the room where Wallander was sitting with a coffee cup in his hand and his feet on the desk and told him that Stockholm Radio had managed to contact the Maxi sailboat occupied by the Malmström family, heading for Arkösund. Wallander jumped up and followed him to the command center, where Birgersson stood yelling into a phone. Then he handed it to Wallander.

"They're somewhere between two lightships named the *Hävringe* and the *Gustaf Dalén,*" he said. "I've got a Karl Malmström on the line."

Wallander quickly handed the phone back to Birgersson.

"I've got to talk to his wife. I don't give a damn about him."

"I hope you realize that there are hundreds of pleasure boats out there listening to the conversation going out over the coastal radio."

Wallander had forgotten about that in his haste.

"A cell phone is better," he said. "Ask if they have one on board."

"I've already done that," said Birgersson. "These are people who think you should leave cell phones at home when you're on vacation."

"Then they'll have to put into shore," said Wallander. "And call me from there."

"How long do you think that will take?" said Birgersson. "Do you have any idea where the *Hävringe* is? It's the middle of the night. Are they supposed to set sail now?"

"I don't give a shit where the *Hävringe* is," said Wallander. "Besides, they might be sailing at night and not lying at anchor. Maybe there's some other boat nearby with a cell phone. Just tell them that I have to get in touch with her within an hour. With her. Not him."

Birgersson shook his head. Then he started yelling into the phone again.

Precisely thirty minutes later Agneta Malmström called from a cell phone they had borrowed from a boat they met out in the channel. Wallander got right to the point.

"Do you remember the girl who burned herself to death?" he asked. "In a rapeseed field a few weeks ago?"

"Of course I remember."

"Do you also recall a phone conversation we had at that time? I asked you how a young person could do such a thing to herself. I don't remember my exact words."

"I have a vague memory of it," she replied.

"You answered by giving an example of something you had recently experienced. You told me about a boy, a little boy, who was so afraid of his father that he tried to put out his own eyes."

Her memory was good.

"Yes," she said. "I remember that. But it wasn't something I had experienced myself. One of my colleagues told me about it."

"Who was that?"

"My husband. He's a doctor too."

"Then I'll have to talk to him. Please get him for me."

"It'll take a while. I'll have to row over and get him in the dinghy. We put down a drift anchor a ways from here."

Now Wallander apologized for bothering her.

"Unfortunately, it's necessary," he said.

"It'll take a while," she said.

"Where the hell is the *Hävringe?*" asked Wallander.

"Way out in the Baltic," she said. "It's quite lovely out here. But just now we're making a night sail to the south. Even though the wind is poor."

It took twenty minutes before the phone rang again. Karl Malmström came to the phone. In the meantime Wallander had found out that he was a pediatrician in Malmö. Wallander returned to the conversation he had had with his wife.

"I remember the case," he said.

"Can you remember the name of the boy off the top of your head?"

"Yes, I can. But I can't stand here yelling it into a cell phone."

Wallander understood his point. He thought feverishly.

"Let's do this, then," he said. "I'll ask you a question. You can answer yes or no. Without naming any names."

"We can try," said Malmström.

"Does it have anything to do with Bellman?" asked Wallander.

Malmström instantly understood the reference to *Fredman's Epistles* by the famous Swedish poet.

"Yes, it certainly does."

"Then I thank you for your help," said Wallander. "I hope I won't have to bother you again. Have a nice summer."

Karl Malmström didn't seem annoyed.

"It's nice to know we have police who work hard," was all he said.

He hung up. Wallander handed the phone to Birgersson.

"Let's have a meeting in a while," he said. "I need a few minutes to think."

"Take my office," said Birgersson. "It's empty right now."

Wallander suddenly felt very tired. His sense of revulsion felt like a dull ache in his body. He still didn't want to believe that what he was thinking could be true. He had fought against this conclusion for a long time. But he couldn't do that any longer. The pattern that appeared was intolerable. The little boy's fear of his father. A big brother nearby. Who pours hydrochloric acid in his father's eyes as revenge. Who acts out an insane retribution for his sister, who had been abused in some way. It was all suddenly very clear. The whole thing made sense and the result was appalling. He also thought that his subconscious had seen it long ago. But he had pushed the knowledge aside. Instead he chose to follow sidetracks, leading him away from his goal.

A police officer knocked on his door.

"We just got a fax from Lund," he said. "From a hospital."

Wallander took it. Per Åkeson had acted fast. It was a copy of a visitors' list for the psychiatric ward where Louise Fredman was a patient. All the names but one were crossed out. The signature really was illegible. He took a magnifying glass from Birgersson's desk drawer and tried to make it out. Still illegible. He put the paper on the table. The officer was still standing in the doorway.

"Get Birgersson over here," said Wallander. "And my colleagues from Ystad. How's Sjösten, by the way?"

"He's sleeping," said the officer. "They removed the bullet from his shoulder."

A few minutes later they were all gathered in the room. It was almost four-thirty. Everyone was exhausted. Hans Logård was still missing. Still no trace of the security guards' car. Wallander nodded to them to sit down.

The moment of truth, he thought. This is it.

"We're searching for a person named Hans Logård," he began. "We have to keep doing so, of course. He shot Sjösten in the shoulder. He's mixed up in the smuggling of young girls. But he's not the one who killed the others. It wasn't Logård who took the scalps. It was somebody else entirely."

He paused.

"Stefan Fredman is the person who did all this," he said. "In other words, we're looking for a fourteen-year-old boy. Who killed his father, along with the others."

There was complete silence in the room. No one moved. They were all staring at him.

It took Wallander half an hour to explain. Afterwards there was no doubt in anyone's mind. They decided to return to Ystad. The greatest secrecy would have to be attached to what they had just discussed. Afterwards Wallander couldn't tell which feeling was stronger among his colleagues, shock or relief.

They got ready to drive to Ystad.

Svedberg stood looking at the fax that had come from Lund as Wallander called Åkeson and talked to him.

"Strange," he said.

Wallander turned to him.

"What's strange?"

"This signature," said Svedberg. "It looks almost as if he signed the name Geronimo."

Wallander grabbed the fax out of Svedberg's hand.

It was ten minutes to five.

Svedberg was right.

Chapter Thirty-eight

They said goodbye in the dawn outside the police station in Helsingborg. Everyone looked tired and haggard, but more than anything they were shaken by what they now realized had to be the truth about the perpetrator they had been hunting for so long. They agreed to meet at eight o'clock at the Ystad police station. That meant they all had time to get home and shower, but not much more. Then they had to keep on working. Wallander had been quite blunt about the whole case. He believed that everything had happened because of the sick sister. But they couldn't be sure. It was also possible that she might be in great danger. There was only one approach to take: fear the worst.

Svedberg rode in Wallander's car. It was going to be a beautiful day. Neither of them could remember the last time a real rainstorm had passed over Skåne. They spoke very little during the trip. On the way into Ystad Svedberg discovered that he must have left his keys somewhere. It reminded Wallander that his own keys had never shown up either. He told Svedberg to come home with him. They reached Mariagatan just before seven. Linda was asleep. After they had each taken a shower and Wallander loaned Svedberg a shirt, they sat in the living room and had coffee.

Neither of them noticed that the door to the closet next to Linda's room, which had been closed when they arrived, was now ajar.

Hoover had arrived at the apartment at ten to seven. He was just on his way into Wallander's bedroom with the axe in his hand when he heard a key turn in the front door lock. He quickly hid in the closet. He heard two voices. When he could tell that they were in the living room, he cautiously opened the door a crack. He heard Wallander call the other man Svedberg. Hoover assumed that he was a policeman too. He gripped the axe in his hand the whole time, listening to their conversation. At first he didn't understand what they were talking about. The name Hans Logård came up over and over. Wallander was clearly trying to explain something to Svedberg. He listened more attentively and finally understood that it was holy providence, the power of Geronimo, that had started working again. The man named Hans Logård had been Åke Liljegren's right-hand man. He had smuggled girls in from the Dominican Republic, and maybe from other parts of the Caribbean too. And he was also the one who probably brought girls to Wetterstedt and maybe even Carlman. He also heard Wallander predict that Hans Logård was on the death list that must exist in Stefan Fredman's mind.

Then the conversation stopped. A few minutes later Wallander and Svedberg left the apartment.

Hoover came out of the closet and stood utterly still.

Then he left, as soundlessly as he had come.

He had gone to the empty storefront where Linda and Kajsa had held their rehearsals. He knew they wouldn't be using it again, so he left Louise there while he went to the apartment on Mariagatan to kill cavalry colonel Perkins and his daughter. But when he stood in the closet, the axe ready in his hand, and heard the conversation he started to have doubts. There was one more person he had to kill. A man he had overlooked. A man named Hans Logård.

When they described him he understood that he must have been the one who once brutally raped and abused his sister. That was before she had been drugged and taken to both Gustaf Wetterstedt and Arne Carlman—events that finally forced her into the darkness from which he was now trying to rescue her. All of it was written down in the book he had taken from her. The book containing the words that controlled his actions. He had assumed that Hans Logård was someone who didn't live in Sweden. A foreign visitor, an evil man. Now he realized that he had made a mistake.

It was easy to get into the empty storefront. Earlier he had seen Kajsa hide the key on top of the door frame. Since he was now moving around in broad daylight, he hadn't painted his face. He didn't want to scare Louise, either. When he came back she was sitting on a chair staring blankly into space. He had already decided to move her. And he knew where. Before he went to Mariagatan he took the moped and checked to see that the situation was as he had thought. The house was empty. But they weren't going to move there until evening. He sat down on the floor at her side and tried to figure out how to find Hans Logård before the police did. He turned inward and asked Geronimo for advice. But his heart was strangely still this morning. The drums were so faint that he couldn't hear their message.

At eight o'clock they gathered in the conference room. Per Åkeson was there, as was a representative from Malmö. Sergeant Birgersson in Helsingborg was hooked up via speaker phone. Everybody was pale but focused. Wallander looked around the table and said they'd start by bringing everyone up to date. The detective from Malmö was discreetly looking for a hiding place they assumed Stefan Fredman had access to. They still hadn't found it. But one of the neighbors in the building told them that he had seen Stefan Fredman on a moped several times, even though his mother never knew about it. The building where the family lived was under surveillance. From Helsingborg, Birgersson told them on the speaker phone that Sjösten was doing fine. Unfortunately his ear would be badly deformed.

"Plastic surgeons can work wonders these days," Wallander shouted encouragingly. "Say hello to him from all of us."

Birgersson went on to say that the ongoing cross-check showed that it wasn't Hans Logård's fingerprints on the torn Phantom comic book, the bloody paper bag behind the road maintenance hut, Liljegren's stove, or Björn Fredman's left eyelid. This confirmation was crucial. The Malmö police were busy trying to get Stefan Fredman's prints from objects taken from his room in the Rosengård apartment. Nobody doubted any longer that they would match, now that Logård's didn't.

They talked about Hans Logård. The security company car still hadn't been found. Since he had fired a weapon and both Sjösten and Wallander could have been killed, the hunt had to continue. They had to assume he was dangerous, even though they still couldn't explain why. Wallander realized that he ought to point out another possibility.

"Even though Stefan Fredman is just fourteen years old, he's dangerous," he said. "He may be crazy, but he's not stupid. He's very strong and reacts quickly and decisively. In other words, we have to be careful."

"This is all so damned disgusting!" Hansson broke out. "I still can't believe it's true."

"Nor can any of us," said Åkeson. "But what Kurt says is absolutely right. And we need to act accordingly."

"Stefan Fredman got his sister Louise out of the hospital," Wallander went on. "We're looking for the nurse on the train, who will be able to identify him. Let's assume it'll be a positive ID. We don't know whether he intends to hurt Louise. The only thing that's important now is to find them. He has a moped and rides around with her on the back. They can't get very far. Besides, the girl is sick."

"A nut case on a moped with a mentally ill girl on the back," said Svedberg. "It's so macabre."

"He knows how to drive a car," Ludwigsson pointed out. "He used his father's Ford van. So he may have stolen a car by now."

Wallander turned to the detective from Malmö.

"Stolen cars," he said. "Within the past few days. Above all in Rosengård. Or near the hospital."

The policeman from Malmö got up and picked up a phone.

"Stefan Fredman carries out his actions after careful planning," continued Wallander. "Naturally we have no way of knowing whether the abduction of his sister was also planned in advance. But now we have to try and get into his mind to figure out what he plans to do. Where are they headed? It's a shame Ekholm isn't here when we need him most."

"He'll be here in about an hour," said Hansson, glancing at the clock. "Someone's picking him up at the airport."

"How'd it go with his daughter?" asked Höglund.

Wallander felt ashamed at having forgotten the reason for Ekholm's absence.

"Good," said Svedberg. "A broken foot, that's all. But she was very lucky."

"This fall we're going to have a big traffic safety campaign in all the schools," said Hansson. "Far too many children are being killed in traffic accidents."

The detective from Malmö hung up the phone and returned to the table.

"I presume you've also looked for Stefan in his father's apartment," said Wallander.

"We've already searched there and everywhere else his father usually hung out. And we've picked up a man named Peter Hjelm and asked him to try and think of other hideouts Fredman may have had access to that his son might have known about. Forsfält is taking care of it."

The meeting continued. But Wallander knew that they were really just waiting for something to happen. Stefan Fredman was somewhere with his sister Louise. Hans Logård was out there too. A large contingent of police officers was looking for all of them. They went in and out of the conference room, getting coffee, sending out for sandwiches, dozing in their chairs, drinking more coffee. The German police discovered Sara Pettersson at the Hamburg Hauptbahnhof. She had been able to identify Stefan Fredman at once. At a quarter to ten, Mats Ekholm arrived from the airport, still shaken and pale.

Wallander asked Höglund to come with him to the peace and quiet of his office and give him the details he still was missing. Just before eleven they got the confirmation they were waiting for. Stefan Fredman's fingerprints had been identified on his father's eyelid, on the Phantom comic book, the bloody scrap of paper behind the road maintenance hut, and Liljegren's stove. There was silence in the conference room. The only sound was the faint hiss of the speaker phone linked to Birgersson, who was listening in Helsingborg. There was no turning back. All the sidetracks and phony leads, especially those they had thought up themselves, had now ceased to exist. All that was left was the realization of the truth, and that truth was appalling. They were searching for a fourteen-year-old boy who had committed four cold-blooded, premeditated murders.

Finally Wallander broke the silence and turned to Ekholm.

"What's he doing? What's he thinking?"

"I know this could be a dangerous statement," said Ekholm. "But I don't think he intends to hurt his sister. There's a pattern, call it logic if you will, to his behavior. Revenge for his little brother and his sister is the actual goal. If he diverges from that goal, then everything he so laboriously built up will collapse."

"Why did he take her from the hospital?" Wallander asked.

"Maybe he was afraid that you would influence her somehow."

"How?" asked Wallander in surprise.

"We picture a confused boy who has taken on the role of a lone warrior. We assume that many men must have done his sister irreparable harm. That's what drives him. Assuming this theory is correct. That means he'll want to keep all men away from her. He's the only exception. And you can't rule out the fact that he may have suspected you were on his trail. I'm sure he knows that you're in charge of the investigation."

Wallander suddenly remembered something that had slipped his mind.

"The pictures that Norén took," he said. "Of the spectators outside the cordons? Where are they?"

Sven Nyberg, who most of the time had sat quiet and meditative at the meeting table, went to get the photos. Wallander spread them out on the table. Someone got a magnifying glass. They gathered around the pictures. It was Höglund who found him.

"There he is," she said, pointing.

He was almost hidden behind some other onlookers. But part of his moped was visible, along with his head.

"I'll be damned," said Hamrén.

"It should be possible to identify the moped," said Nyberg. "If we blow up the details."

"Do that," said Wallander. "Every detail is important."

Wallander thought it was obvious now that there had been a good reason for the other feeling gnawing at his subconscious. With a grimace he thought that at least he could close the case on his own anxiety.

Except on one account. Baiba. It was twelve o'clock. Svedberg was asleep in his chair, and Åkeson was on the phone with so many different people that no one could keep track of them. Wallander gestured to Höglund to follow him out into the corridor. They sat down in his office and closed the door. Without beating around the bush, he told her about the situation he had gotten himself into. It required great effort on his part, and later he would never really understand how he could have broken his firm principle never to confide personal problems to any of his colleagues. He had stopped doing that when Rydberg died. Now he was doing it again. He was still unsure whether he could develop the same trusting relationship with Ann-Britt Höglund that he had enjoyed with Rydberg, especially since she was a woman. She listened attentively.

"What the hell am I going to do?"

"Nothing," she said. "You're right. It's already too late. But I could talk to her if you like. I assume she speaks English. Give me her phone number."

Wallander wrote it down on a Post-It note. But when she reached for his telephone he asked her to wait.

"A couple more hours," he said.

"Miracles don't happen very often," she said.

At that moment they were interrupted by Hansson, who tore open the door.

"They found his hideout," said Hansson. "A basement in a condemned schoolhouse. It's right near the building where he lives."

"Are they there?" Wallander asked, getting up from his chair.

"No. But they've been there."

They went back to the meeting room. Another speaker phone was hooked up. Wallander heard Forsfält's friendly voice. He described what they had found. Mirrors, brushes, makeup. A cassette player with drums on it. He played a few seconds of the tape. It echoed spookily in the meeting room. *War paint*, thought Wallander. *How had he signed in at the hospital? Geronimo?* There were several axes on a piece of cloth, and knives too. Despite the impersonal speaker phone they could hear that Forsfält was upset.

"But we didn't find any scalps," he said. "Although we're still looking."

"Where the hell are they?" said Wallander.

"The scalps," said Ekholm. "Either he has them with him, or else he's left them as a sacrifice somewhere."

"Where? Does he have his own sacrificial grove?"

"Could be."

The waiting continued. Wallander lay down on the floor of his office and managed to sleep for half an hour. When he woke up he felt more tired than before. His body ached all over. Now and then Höglund would give him a questioning look. But he shook his head and felt his self-loathing grow.

It was six o'clock in the evening, and there was still no trace of Hans Logård, Stefan Fredman, or his sister. They had had a long discussion about whether to put out a nationwide alarm for Stefan and Louise Fredman. Almost everyone was reluctant to do so. The risk that something would happen to Louise was considered too great. Åkeson agreed. They kept waiting.

J ust after six o'clock Hoover took his sister to the deserted house he had chosen. He parked the moped on the beach side. He quickly picked the lock on the gate to the back yard. Gustaf Wetterstedt's villa was deserted. They walked up along the gravel path to the main door. Suddenly he stopped and held Louise back. There was a car parked in the garage. It hadn't been there this morning when he checked that the house was empty. He carefully pushed Louise down to sit on a rock behind the garage wall. He took out an axe and listened. All was quiet. He walked forward and looked at the car. It belonged to a security company. One of the front windows was open. He peered into the car. There were some papers lying on the seat. He picked them up and saw that there was a receipt among them, made out to Hans Logård. He put it back and stood completely still, holding his breath. The drums started to pound. He remembered the conversation he had heard that morning. Hans Logård was on the run too.

So he'd had the same idea about the empty house. He was somewhere inside. Geronimo had not failed him. He had helped him track the monster to his lair. He didn't have to search anymore. The cold darkness that had penetrated his sister's soul would soon be gone. He went back to her and told her to stay there for a while, and keep as quiet as she could. He would be back very soon.

He went into the garage. There were some cans of paint, and he opened two of them carefully. With his fingertip he drew two lines across his forehead. One red line, then a black one. He already had the axe in his hand. He took off his shoes. Just as he was about to leave he had an idea. He held his breath again, which he had learned from Geronimo. Compressed air in the lungs made thoughts clearer. He knew that his idea was a good one. It would make everything easier. Tonight he would bury the last of the scalps outside the hospital window alongside the others. There would be two of them. And he would also bury a heart. Then it would be all over. In the last hole he would bury his weapons. He gripped the axe handle hard and started walking toward the house and the man he was now going to kill.

A t six-thirty Wallander suggested to Hansson, who was formally in charge along with Per Åkeson, that they could start sending people home. Everyone was exhausted. They might as well wait in their own homes. They would all remain on call throughout the night.

"So who should stay here?" asked Hansson.

"Ekholm and Höglund," said Wallander. "And one more. Whoever's the least tired."

Ludwigsson and Hamrén both stayed.

They all moved down to one end of the table instead of spreading out as usual.

"The hideout," said Wallander. "What would be the requirements for a secret and preferably impregnable fortress? What would be the requirements of an insane boy who transforms himself into a lone warrior?"

"In this case I think his plans must have fallen apart," said Ekholm. "Otherwise they would have stayed in the basement room."

"Smart animals dig extra exits," said Ludwigsson thoughtfully.

"You mean that he might have another hideout in reserve?"

"Maybe. In all likelihood it's also somewhere in Malmö."

The discussion petered out. No one said anything. Hamrén yawned. A telephone rang down the hall. Soon after, someone stood in the doorway and said there was a call for Wallander. He got up, much too tired even to ask who it was. It didn't occur to him that it might be Baiba, not until he had picked up the phone in his own office. By then it was too late. But it wasn't Baiba. It was a man who spoke with a thick Skåne accent.

"Who is this?" asked Wallander angrily.

"Hans Logård."

Wallander almost dropped the receiver.

"I need to meet with you. Now."

Logård's voice was oddly strained, as if he was having a lot of trouble forming his words. Wallander wondered whether he was on drugs.

"Where are you?"

"First I want a guarantee that you'll come. Alone."

"You won't get it. You tried to kill me and Sjösten."

"God damn it! You have to come!"

The last words sounded almost like a shriek. Wallander grew cautious.

"What do you want?"

"I can tell you where Stefan Fredman is. And his sister."

"How can I be sure of that?"

"You can't. But you should believe me."

"I'll come. You tell me what you know. And then we'll bring you in."

"All right."

"Where are you?"

"Are you coming?"

"Yes."

"Gustaf Wetterstedt's house."

A feeling that he should have thought of that possibility raced through Wallander's mind.

"Do you have a weapon?" he said.

"The car is in the garage. The pistol is in the glove compartment. I'll leave the door to the house open. You'll see me when you come in the door. I'll keep my hands in plain sight."

"All right, I'm coming."

"Alone?"

"Yes, alone."

Wallander hung up, thinking feverishly. He had no intention of going alone. But he didn't want Hansson to start organizing a big strike force. Ann-Britt and Svedberg, he thought. But Svedberg was at home. He called him and told him to meet him outside the hospital in five minutes. With his service revolver. Did he have it at home? He did. Wallander told him briefly that they were going to arrest Hans Logård. When Svedberg tried to ask questions, Wallander cut him off. Meet me in five minutes, he said, outside the hospital. Until then, don't use the phone.

He unlocked a desk drawer and took out his pistol. He detested holding it in his hand. He loaded it and stuffed it in his jacket pocket, then went to the conference room and waved Höglund aside. He took her into his office and explained. They would meet outside the police station right away. Wallander told her to bring along her service revolver. They would take Wallander's car. He told Hansson he just wanted to run home and take a shower. Hansson nodded and yawned. Svedberg was waiting outside the hospital. He got in the back seat.

"What's going on?" he asked.

Wallander told them about the phone call. If the pistol wasn't in the car they'd call it off. Same thing if the door wasn't open. Or if Wallander suspected something was wrong. The two of them were supposed to stay out of sight but ready.

"Of course you realize that the guy might have another gun," said Svedberg. "He might try to take you hostage. I don't like this. How does he know where Stefan Fredman is? What does he want from you?"

"Maybe he's dumb enough to try and make a deal. People think Sweden is just like the States. But we haven't gone that far yet."

Wallander thought about Logård's voice. Something told him he really did know where Stefan Fredman was.

They parked the car out of sight of the house. Svedberg was supposed to watch the beach side. When he got there he was alone on the beach, except for a girl sitting on the rowboat under which they had found Wetterstedt's dead body. She seemed to be completely entranced by the sea and the black rain cloud bearing down on them. Höglund took up a position outside the garage. Wallander saw that the front door was open. He moved very slowly. The security company car was in the garage. The pistol was in the glove compartment. He took out his own pistol, took off the safety, and moved carefully toward the open front door. Everything was very still.

He stepped up to the door. Hans Logård stood inside in the darkness. He had his hands on his head. Wallander suddenly got a bad feeling. He didn't know where it came from. Instinctively he sensed danger. But he went inside. Logård looked at him. Then everything happened very fast. One of Logård's hands slipped down from his head. Wallander saw a gaping hole from an axe blow. Logård's body fell to the floor. Behind him stood the person who had been holding him upright. Stefan Fredman. He had lines painted on his face. He threw himself furiously at Wallander, with an axe lifted high. Wallander raised his pistol to shoot, but too late. Instinctively he ducked and slipped on a rug. The axe missed his head but grazed his shoulder with the side of the blade. He fired a shot and hit an oil painting on one of the walls. At the same instant Höglund appeared in the doorway. She stood crouched and ready to fire. Fredman saw her just as he was getting ready to slam the axe into Wallander's head. He jumped to the side. Wallander was in the line of fire.

Fredman vanished toward the open terrace door. Wallander thought of Svedberg. Slow Svedberg. He yelled to Höglund to shoot Stefan Fredman.

But he was already gone. Svedberg, who had heard the first shot, didn't know what to do. He yelled at the girl sitting on the rowboat to take cover, but she didn't move. He ran up toward the garden gate. It hit him in the head as it flew open. He saw a face he would never forget as long as he lived. He dropped his pistol. The man had an axe in his hand. Svedberg did the only thing he could do. He ran off, yelling for help. Fredman got his sister, sitting motionless on the rowboat. He started his moped. They rode off just as Wallander and Höglund came running out.

"Call for backup!" Wallander shouted. "And where the hell is Svedberg? I'll try and follow them in the car."

At that moment it started to rain hard. Wallander ran to his car, trying to figure out which way they would have headed. Visibility was poor even with the windshield wipers on full speed. He thought he had lost them but suddenly caught sight of them again. They were riding down the road toward the Saltsjöbad Hotel. Wallander kept a safe distance behind. He didn't want to frighten them. The moped was going very fast. Wallander frantically tried to figure out how to put an end to the whole thing. He was just about to call in his location when the moped wobbled. He hit the brake. The moped was heading straight for a tree. The girl sitting in back was thrown off, right into the tree. Stefan Fredman landed somewhere off to the side.

"Damn!" said Wallander. He stopped the car in the middle of the road and started running toward the moped.

He could see at once that Louise Fredman was dead. Her white dress seemed strangely bright next to all the blood running from her face. Stefan Fredman had escaped almost without injury. What was paint and what was blood on his face, Wallander couldn't tell. He watched the fourteen-year-old boy in front of him. Stefan fell to his knees beside his sister. The rain poured down. The boy started to cry. It sounded like he was howling. Wallander knelt next to the boy.

"She's dead," he said. "There's nothing we can do about it."

Stefan looked at him, his face distorted. Wallander quickly got up, afraid that the boy would jump on him. But nothing happened. The boy kept howling.

Somewhere behind him in the rain he heard the emergency vehicles. It wasn't until Hansson was standing next to him that he realized he had started to cry himself.

Wallander left all the work to the others. He told Höglund briefly what had happened. When he saw Per Åkeson, he took him to his car. The rain was drumming on the roof.

"It's over," said Wallander.

"Yes," said Åkeson, "it's over."

"I'm going on vacation tomorrow," said Wallander. "I realize there's a pile of reports that have to be written. But I thought I'd go anyway."

Åkeson's reply came without hesitation.

"Do that," he said. "Go."

Åkeson got out of the car. Wallander thought he should ask him about his trip to the Sudan. Or was it Uganda?

He drove home. Linda wasn't there. He took a bath and was drying himself off when he heard her close the front door.

That evening he told her what had really happened. And how he felt.

Then he called Baiba.

"I thought you were never going to call," she said, hiding her annoyance.

"Please forgive me," said Wallander. "I've had so much to do lately."

"I think that's a pretty poor excuse."

"I know. But it's the only one I've got."

Neither of them said anything else. The silence traveled back and forth between Ystad and Riga.

"See you tomorrow," Wallander finally said.

"All right," she said. "I guess so."

They hung up. Wallander felt a knot in his stomach. Maybe she wouldn't come.

Afterwards he and Linda both packed their bags.

The rain stopped just after midnight.

It smelled fresh as they stood out on the balcony.

"The summer is so beautiful," she said.

"Yes," said Wallander. "It *is* beautiful."

The next day they took the train together to Malmö.

Then Wallander took the hydrofoil to Copenhagen.

He watched the water racing past the sides of the boat. Distracted, he ordered coffee and cognac.

In two hours Baiba's plane would be landing.

Something resembling panic gripped him.

He suddenly wished that the crossing to Copenhagen would take much longer.

But when she arrived he was waiting for her.

Not until then did the image of Louise Fredman finally disappear from his mind.

Skåne 16–17 September 1994

Epilogue

On Friday, the 16th of September, fall suddenly rolled in to southern Skåne.

Kurt Wallander woke up quite early that morning. His eyes flew open in the dark, as if he had been cast violently out of a dream. He lay completely still and tried to remember. But there was only the hissing echo of something that was already gone and would never return. He turned his head and looked at the clock next to the bed. The hands glowed in the dark. Quarter to five. He turned over on his side to go back to sleep. But the realization of what day it was kept him awake. He got up and went out in the kitchen. The streetlight hanging over the street swayed forlornly in the wind. He saw by the thermometer that the temperature had dropped. It was 7 degrees Celsius. He smiled at the thought that in less than two days he would be in Rome. It was still warm there. He sat down at the kitchen table and had some coffee. In his mind he went over all the preparations for the trip. A few days earlier he had been out at his father's house and finally fixed the door he had to break down to his father's studio. He had also taken a look at his father's new passport. He had exchanged some money for Italian lire at the savings bank and had a booklet full of traveler's checks. He was going to leave work early to pick up the plane ticket.

Now he had to go to work for the last day before his vacation. At quarter past seven, he left the apartment and went down to his car. The air felt cool. He zipped up his jacket and shivered when he got into the driver's seat. On the way to the police station he thought about the meeting he was going to have this morning.

It was exactly eight o'clock when he knocked on the door of Lisa Holgersson's office. When he heard her voice he opened the door. She nodded and asked him to have a seat. She had only been serving as their new chief for three weeks, ever since Björk's career had taken a different path. Even so, Wallander thought she had already managed to set her stamp on much of the work and atmosphere of the department.

Many had been skeptical about the woman, who came from a police district in Småland. Besides, Wallander was surrounded by colleagues who lived under the old misconception that women weren't even suited to be active-duty police officers. How could a woman be their chief? But Lisa Holgersson soon demonstrated her ability. Wallander was impressed by her great integrity, her fearlessness, and her ability to make amazingly clear presentations, no matter what the topic.

The day before she had asked him to meet with her. Now that Wallander was sitting in her visitor's chair he still didn't know what she wanted.

"You're going on vacation next week," she said. "I heard you were going to Italy with your father."

"It's a dream of his," said Wallander. "It may be the last chance we get. He's almost eighty."

"My father is eighty-five," she said. "Sometimes his mind is crystal clear. Sometimes he doesn't even recognize me. But I've come to terms with the fact that you never escape your parents. Suddenly the roles are reversed. You become your parents' parent."

"That's about what I was thinking," said Wallander.

She moved some papers on her desk.

"I don't have a specific reason for this meeting," she said. "But I suddenly realized that I've never had a proper chance to thank you for your work this summer. It was model detective work."

Wallander gave her a surprised look. Was she serious?

"That's putting it a little strongly," he said. "I made a lot of mistakes. I led the whole investigation off on a sidetrack. It could have failed miserably."

"The ability to lead an investigation often means knowing when to shift tactics," she said. "To look in a direction you may have just ruled out. The investigation was a model in many ways, especially because of your tenacity and your ability to think unexpected thoughts. I want you to know this. I've heard rumors that the chief of the National Police has expressed his satisfaction in various connections. Presumably you will be receiving an invitation to hold a number of lectures about this investigation at the police academy."

Wallander reacted immediately.

"I can't do that," he said. "Ask someone else. I can't speak to people I don't know."

"We can take this up again after you get back," she said, smiling. "Right now the most important thing is that I had a chance to tell you what I thought."

She got up as a sign that the brief meeting was over.

As Wallander walked down the hall he thought she actually meant what she said. Even though he tried to dismiss it, the appreciation made him feel good. It would be easy to work with her in the future.

He got some coffee in the lunchroom and exchanged a few words with

Martinsson about one of his daughters who had tonsillitis. When he got to his office he called the barber shop and made an appointment. He had made a list the day before, which lay in front of him on his desk. He thought about leaving the police station as early as noon so he could run all his errands. But it was quarter past four by the time he went to the travel agency. He also stopped at the state liquor store and bought a small bottle of whisky. When he got home he called Linda. He promised to send her a postcard from Rome. She was in a hurry, and he didn't ask why. The conversation was over much sooner than he would have wished.

At six o'clock he called Löderup and asked Gertrud if everything was all right. She told him that his father had such travel fever that he could hardly sit still. Wallander walked into the center of town and ate dinner at one of the pizzerias. When he got back to Mariagatan he poured himself a glass of whisky and spread out a map of Rome. He had never been there and didn't know a word of Italian. But there are two of us, he thought. My father has never been there either, except in his dreams. And he doesn't speak Italian either. We're heading into this dream together and will have to guide each other.

On a sudden impulse he called the tower at Sturup and asked one of the air-traffic controllers if he happened to know what the weather was like in Rome. They knew each other from a previous case.

"It's warm in Rome," said the controller. "Right now, at ten past eight, it's 21 degrees Celsius. Light wind from the southeast. Light fog too. The forecast for the next twenty-four hours is for more of the same."

Wallander thanked him for his help.

"Are you taking a trip?" asked the controller.

"I'm going on vacation with my father," said Wallander.

"That sounds like a good idea," said the controller. "Are you taking Alitalia?"

"Yes, the 10:45."

"I'll be thinking of you. Have a nice trip."

Wallander went over his packing one more time, checking his money and travel documents. At eleven o'clock he tried to call Baiba, then remembered that she was visiting relatives without a telephone.

He sat down with a glass of whisky and listened to *La Traviata*. He thought about the trip he had taken with Baiba to Skagen. Tired and disheveled, he had waited for her in Copenhagen. He stood there at Kastrup Airport like an unshaven, worn-out ghost. He knew she was disappointed, even though she didn't say anything. Not until they had reached Skagen and he had caught up on his sleep for a few nights did he tell her about everything that had happened. After that their vacation had started in earnest.

On one of the last days he asked her if she would marry him.

She had said no. Not yet, at any rate, not now. The past was still too close. Her husband, police captain Karlis, whom Wallander had also met, was still alive in her memory. His violent death still followed her like a shadow. Above all she doubted she could ever consider marrying another policeman. He understood. But he didn't feel that he could get along anymore without some kind of assurance. How long would she need to think about it?

He knew she liked him. He could tell.

But was that enough? What about him? Did he really want to live with someone else? He didn't know. Through Baiba he had escaped the loneliness that haunted him after his divorce from Mona. It was a big step, a great relief. Maybe he should settle for that. At least for the time being.

It was past one o'clock when he went to sleep, questions swirling in his head.

Gertrud picked him up at seven o'clock the next morning. It was still raining. His father was sitting in the front seat of the car, dressed in his best suit. Gertrud had given him a haircut.

"Now we're off to Rome," said his father happily. "To think we're actually going after all."

Gertrud dropped them off in Malmö at the train station, where they took the airport bus via Limhamn and Dragor. On the ferry his father insisted on tottering around the windy deck. He pointed to the Swedish mainland, to a spot south of Malmö.

"That's where you grew up. Do you remember?"

"How could I forget?" said Wallander.

"You had a very happy childhood."

"I know."

"You had everything."

"Everything."

Wallander thought about Stefan Fredman. About Louise. About the brother who had tried to put out his own eyes. About all they lacked or had been deprived of. But he pushed the thoughts away. They would still be there, lurking in the back of his mind; they would return. Right now he was on vacation with his father. That was the most important thing. Everything else would have to wait.

The plane took off at exactly 10:45. His father had a window seat, and Wallander sat on the aisle.

It was the first time his father had ever been on an airplane.

Wallander watched him as the plane picked up speed and slowly lifted off the ground. He pressed his face to the window so he could see.

Wallander could see him smiling, the smile of an old man, who had been granted, one last time in his life, the chance to feel the joy of a child.

Afterword

T his is a novel. None of the characters appearing in it exist in reality. All similarities, however, are not always possible or even necessary to avoid. I am grateful to everyone who helped me with the work on this book.

HENNING MANKELL, Paderne, July 1995